THE DISAPPEARANCE OF DERIK HARRISON

THE DISAPPEARANCE OF DERIK HARRISON

RONALD SAVAGE JR.

Acknowledgments

Thank you to God who helped me see this book to completion.
Thank you to my family and friends for your support.
Thank you to the readers who continue to trust me to tell them a good story.

\-

Geneology

This is the genealogy of the Harrison family.

Abraham Creeke, founder of Creeke and its church, took for a wife a woman by the name of Angelica; and begat a son, Nathaniel, and a daughter, Laverne. Nathaniel died at the age of sixteen. Laverne married Franklin Harrison, who had no prior familial roots in Creeke. Thus, the line of Creeke became the line of Harrison through Laverne's marriage to Franklin.

Franklin begat a son, Lionel. And Lionel took for a wife, Judith Morris. Lionel begat Derrick Jermaine Harrison. And Derrick took for a wife, Kiana Danette Barnett, whose father was Barry Barnett, whose father was Bartholomew Barnett.

Barry begat three daughters with his wife, Kimberly. The eldest was Kiana, named for her mother and her paternal grandmother, Ana. Paulette Jean Barnett was the second eldest, and Nancy Mae Barnett the youngest. Nancy married Joseph Keaton. Joseph begat a son, Joe Keaton. And Joe begat two sons – James Edmond Keaton and Jordan Elias Keaton – with his wife. Thus, the line of Barnett became the line of Keaton through Nancy's marriage and became the line of Harrison through Kiana's marriage to Derrick.

Derrick begat two sons, Marlin Trevor Harrison and Malcolm Drew Harrison. Malcolm begat a son, Derek Drumaine Harrison.

Marlin married Soleya Naima Perry, whose father was Bernard Perry. Bernard begat two daughters – Soriah Noelle and Soleya – with his wife Sophia Estelle, whose mother was Estelle. Soriah was married to Quincy Marcellus Campbell. And Quincy begat a son, Marcellus Bernard Campbell. Thus, the line of Perry became the line of Campbell through Soriah's marriage and the line of Harrison through Soleya's marriage to Marlin.

Marlin begat three sons, Matthias Jamal Harrison, Deidrick Aaron Harrison, Derik Tremaine Harrison, and one daughter, Allison Queen Harrison.

This is the genealogy of the Harrison family, the founding family of Creeke.

Chapter One: Allison

Allison Harrison did not know the time her sixteen-year-old brother, Derik, had vanished from Creeke, but she knew the day. It was the third Friday in December. Winter break had begun that afternoon, and the eighteen-year-old young lady had returned home from school to find a note informing her of her parent's weekend getaway. They would not return until that Sunday, and her mother had directed her to keep the house tidy and cook for herself and her brothers.

"So, now I'm a maid?" Allison had griped. "Why do I always have to do everything? The boys are just as capable of doing this as I am!"

Despite her complaints, Allison had resigned herself to her fate and did as her mother asked. After washing the dishes and sweeping the floor, she had told herself that her brothers would have to accept a frozen pizza for dinner or not eat at all. Satisfied with her efforts, Allison had started for her room when a peculiar sight halted her.

Sitting on the kitchen table was an opened envelope addressed to her mother, Mrs. Soleya Harrison, from Mrs. Harrison's mother, Lady Sophia Perry. Allison was not one to snoop through other's personal belongings, but she had a suspicion of the envelope's contents and had taken it upon herself to confirm it. Upon investigating the perfumed letter, Allison had discovered her suspicion correct–

To Mr. and Mrs. Marlin Harrison,

Mayor Bernard and Lady Sophia Perry cordially invite Mr. and Mrs. Marlin Harrison, Mister Deidrick, Miss Harrison, and

Mister Derik to the Perry's annual winter ball on the first Friday evening of the new year. This is a formal, all-white event, and reservation is necessary.

Allison knew her family would attend the ball because her mother would not want to disappoint her own parents by not showing up. She also knew that her mother's hair salon would see an increase in clients leading up to the ball and thus an increase in Mrs. Harrison's, and Allison's, irritability. Therefore, Allison had decided to cherish her last few moments of peace by retiring for a much-needed after-school nap. And it was from this very nap that someone tried to rouse her by rudely shaking her, to which Allison refused to oblige them, wishing instead they would leave her alone.

"Allison, wake up!" pleaded the youthfully male-sounding agitator, desperation tinging his every word. "Don't die!"

"Bro, why are you crying?" said another male. He too sounded young, but older than the other.

"My cousin almost died in a fire and you're asking me why I'm crying, Deidrick?!"

The mention of dying in a fire startled Allison. She forced her eyes open and let out a cough.

"She's alive!" cried her eighteen-year-old cousin Derek Harrison, throwing his arms around her. Tears stained his dark-brown face. Allison's twenty-one-year-old brother Deidrick Harrison stood a few feet away, covered in sweat and soot.

"What do you mean 'almost died in a fire'?" asked Allison. "What fire?"

"The house," said Deidrick. "It caught on fire."

"What?!" cried Allison. "Is everyone alright?!"

"Yeah."

Allison took in her surroundings and realized she was on the Green family's porch. Across the street, her house was a lively pyre of orange and red flames. They danced gleefully through the two-story giant, blanketing the night sky with black smoke that obscured whatever celestial view lay beyond it.

"Allison!" cried a high-pitched voice. Allison's neighbor and close friend, sixteen-year-old Althea Green, exited her house with three glasses of water. Derek grabbed the one tucked under her arm while Althea handed the other two to Allison and Deidrick. "I'm glad you're okay! I was so scared something was wrong when you wouldn't wake up."

"I'm fine," said Allison. "Does anyone know how the fire started?"

"No," said Derek. "I was at home when I heard the sirens, then Dad and I rushed over here when we saw the direction the smoke was coming from. When we arrived, Cornbread was running out the house with you slung over his shoulder."

Allison looked at her brother in amazement.

"I barely got you out of there," said Deidrick, acknowledging her gaze. "Dee-Three's room was completely covered in flames, so I couldn't even get in there."

"Dee-Three," uttered Allison. Realizing her younger brother was not present among them, she became panicky. "Where's Dee-Three?!"

"We don't know," said Derek. "We've been calling his phone, but he hasn't answered. Dad, Granddad, and Nanna are out looking for him."

"Could he still be...?" said Allison, glancing at the burning house.

"No," answered Althea. "Diana said she saw him leaving the house on her way to work."

"Good," said Allison. "That means no one was in there."

No one was inside the burning house. Allison watched as the firefighters extinguished the fire, leaving only half of the house intact. Eventually, public interest waned, and a paramedic determined she was alright enough to avoid a trip to the hospital. Then she went to wait at her grandparent's house, her new temporary home. She waited hours for any news on her brother or an idea of what would happen next until she could wait no longer, and exhaustion lulled her back to sleep.

That Saturday was an eventful one. The fire had left her with only her car and what was in it: her school backpack and her phone which she had forgotten to take inside the house. Everything else was gone. Her family's efforts to find her brother had been fruitless. Derik was missing, and Allison began her day by explaining what she knew about his disappearance. She sat at the kitchen table, watching as Police Chief Terrence Parker wrote in his notepad.

"When's the last time you saw Derik?" questioned Chief Parker as he pushed his glasses back into place. His curly black hair was gray at the roots, and a small paunch bulged at his waistline, contrasting with the broad shoulders that framed his light-brown head.

"The last time I saw him was at school," said Allison.

"Was he acting differently than he usually did?"

"No sir."

"And you didn't see him at home?"

"No sir."

"Did he tell you about any after school plans? Maybe going to hang out with friends?"

"No sir. But Althea told me her sister had seen him leaving the house around six in the evening."

"Yes, I have that information," said Chief Parker. "Do you believe he had any reason to want to run away from home?"

"Run away?"

"We're considering all possibilities," explained Chief Parker.

"Um...," said Allison. "I don't think so."

"Okay," said Chief Parker. "Do you know if anyone else was in the house before the fire started?"

"I'm not sure," answered Allison. "Deidrick doesn't usually get home till around seven at night, and my parents are out of town."

"Thank you, Allison," said Chief Parker.

After the interview, Allison attempted to locate her younger brother. She started at the creek near her grandparent's house, where she found other townsfolk employed in the same quest. Amongst them were sixteen-year-olds Danielle Lee and Priscella Payne, two girls that Allison absolutely abhorred.

"Derik!" called Priscella, her hands cupped in front of her light-brown face. "Come out, come out wherever you are!"

"That's not going to work," said Danielle, a frown etched into her medium-brown face.

"It works in hide-and-seek."

"He's not hiding, idiot!" griped Danielle, rolling her oval-shaped eyes. "He's missing!"

"You don't have to call me an idiot!"

"I wouldn't call you one if you'd use your brain for once!"

"You know what, forget it!" said Priscella, stomping away. "I'll look for Derik by myself!"

Despite her feelings toward them, it impressed Allison that even a group of self-centered mean girls treated her brother's disappearance as a serious issue. It seemed everyone in Creeke was searching for him. Nevertheless, no one succeeded in locating the youngest member of the Harrison family. Allison returned home feeling dejected and shed quickly-wiped-away tears. She hated crying, but she could not help it. Her brother was missing, and it seemed like there was nothing she could do to find him. Choosing not to dwell on her shortcomings any longer, Allison occupied herself with the Friday edition of the Creeke Courier. Ralph Brewer, Creeke's ace newspaper reporter, had published an unfortunately ill-timed front-page story on her grandfather's triumphant return to preaching.

Local pastor talks fresh start following church revival
by Ralph Brewer, Creeke Courier

Derrick Harrison always knew he would be a preacher. He came from a long line of preachers, and it made sense that he would follow in their footsteps. What he did not account for was how unpredictable his journey would be.

Harrison began preaching at 14 with once-a-month Sunday school sermonettes at Creeke Church. By age 16, he was the regular Sunday school teacher and held the position until becoming Creeke Church's head pastor at 36. His tenure as head pastor lasted 13 years, ending with termination for misconduct.

"I was trying so hard to be a manly man about it because I didn't want the elders to get the last laugh about getting rid of me," Harrison said, recalling the meeting where he learned of his firing. "But since they're all dead now, I can officially say that I was heartbroken."

Harrison was replaced by his father, Bishop Lionel Harrison, as head pastor. Although he was no longer in a pastoral position, Harrison says he never stopped preaching. He talked to anyone willing to listen.

"When I was first fired nobody would give me so much as a glance," Harrison said. "But over time, people started to come back around. First, they wanted me to announce at the games, then they wanted me to do speaking engagements at the school."

Despite the many opportunities he received to speak publicly, Harrison was never asked to return as head pastor. Following the death of Bishop Harrison, then-Youth Pastor Forrest Hall was promoted to head the church. Harrison was not surprised.

"It's one thing to trust someone to tell you so-and-so scored a touchdown at Friday night's game or tell your child to act like they have some sense," Harrison said. "But it's another thing to trust someone to lead you spiritually especially when they've already failed at it once before."

Harrison would not preach again at Creeke Church until the church revival last October. He said the idea was initially presented to him by his grandson. Harrison told his grandson he'd pray about the decision, and after doing so had a dream that night that confirmed his decision to preach.

"I was on the pulpit preaching and everyone in the congregation was dying," Harrison said, explaining his dream. "And as I began to speak to them, I saw them start to return to life, as if they were being revived by the message itself."

Community response to Harrison's return to preaching was overwhelmingly positive. Since then, he has returned to pastoring at the church as the new youth pastor. Harrison found it ironic that his return to pastoring was in the same position where it all started.

"It's like The Lord has given me a second chance to try again, but this time with more wisdom than I had before," Harrison said. "But I also have no desire to replace Forrest or even head a church again. All I want is for this second go-around to go a lot better than the first one did."

As Allison finished reading the article, someone knocked on the front door. Her grandmother, Nanna Kiana Harrison, went to answer it.

"Who is it?" asked Nanna Kiana.

"It's us," said a familiarly warm and loud voice. Nanna Kiana opened it and discovered her younger sisters, Aunt Paulette Barnett and Aunt Nancy Keaton, standing on the porch, huddled together with Aunt Nancy's twenty-year-old grandson James Keaton trying to keep warm.

"What are you two doing here?" asked Nanna Kiana as she ushered them inside.

"My nephew is missing, and I intend to do everything I can to find him!" said Aunt Nancy, who was the youngest sister. She bustled through the door and snatched her cap off her head, revealing her low-cut gray afro. "I'm not leaving until he's found!"

"She means it too," said James. He set Aunt Nancy's heavy brown suitcase on the ground and exhaled. "She brought every piece of clothing she owns with her."

"Oh, hush James!" chastised Aunt Nancy. She embraced Nanna Kiana and cried, "Oh Danette! How terrible this whole thing must be for you! I can't even imagine what you're going through!"

"I'm okay, Cece," reassured Nanna Kiana. "Really, I am."

"You don't have to be strong for me, Danette."

"Nancy, if she says she's okay, then she's okay," said Aunt Paulette, who was the middle sister.

"Just because you're emotionless doesn't mean Danette should be too," argued Aunt Nancy. She placed a hand over her bosom in response to Aunt Paulette's silence. "The distress I feel over my nephew being out there all alone comes straight from here, and I want Danette to know I feel the same way she does."

"And you don't think I feel the same way?" answered Aunt Paulette. "But it doesn't do any good to worry Danette any more than she probably already is. It's better to keep our emotions in check and instead think of a solution to find our nephew."

"Oh, honestly Lettie! Everything that's going on and you want to argue at a time like this!"

"The only one arguing is you, Cece! All I'm saying is you don't have to worry Danette up to comfort her!"

"Why am I the point of contention between sense and sensibility?" sighed Nanna Kiana, sitting on the couch next to her husband, Grand-dad Derrick Harrison.

"Because you're the stability that keeps them balanced," said Grand-dad Derrick, kissing Nanna Kiana's forehead. He cleared his throat and asked, "How long are you all staying?"

"Nanna is determined to stay until Dee-Three is found, and Aunty will stay with her," explained James. "But I'm going back to the city tomorrow because I've got work."

"And it's just the three of you?"

"Jordan came too," answered James, referring to his eighteen-year-old brother. "He was supposed to help bring the suitcases in, but I don't know what he's doing."

"I'll go see," volunteered Allison. She exited the house and spotted her cousin leaning against the car.

"My grandma dragged me down to this little hick town that my aunt and her family live in," complained Jordan to the person on the phone.

He swatted at something buzzing around his head. "And it's too many bugs out here. The first chance I get I'm going back to the city."

"Is that so?" interrupted Allison. Jordan turned to scowl at her but brightened up upon noticing who it was.

"I'll call you back," he said, ending his call. "Well, if it isn't little cousin Queenie?"

"You're only four months older than me, Jordan," said Allison, rolling her eyes.

"Those were the best four months of my life too," joked Jordan. He spread his arms and said, "Why don't you give your big cousin some love?"

"I don't think I will after the way you dissed my 'little hick town'."

"Aw, come on," whined Jordan. "You know there's nothing to do out here."

"So? What you said was still rude and shows a lack of decorum."

"There you go using those big words like always."

"And I'll keep using them as long as I live," declared Allison. She went to the car's trunk and began removing the remaining suitcases. "Help me get these in the house."

"You got it," said Jordan dismissively.

"No, I don't 'got it'," said Allison. "You're supposed to be doing this anyways."

"Well, I don't feel like it," said Jordan. He walked into the house, leaving Allison all alone with the suitcases.

"What a jerk," grumbled Allison. She picked up two of the suitcases and carried them into the house.

"Oh, Allison honey, you don't have to do that," said Aunt Nancy when she saw Allison carrying the suitcases. "James and Jordan will get those."

"Maybe James will, but Jordan certainly won't," uttered Allison. "He up and walked away when I asked him to help."

"He what?!" cried Aunt Nancy.

"Nancy," said Nanna Kiana, giving her a warning look. It was no secret to the Harrisons that Jordan could sometimes be troublesome.

"He won't be a problem," promised Aunt Nancy.

"He'd better not be," said Granddad Derrick. "My patience is already thin, and I don't have time to worry about your grandson while trying to find mine."

By evening time, most of the family, excluding Allison's parents and her eldest brother Matthias who usually forwent family gatherings, had convened at the house for dinner. Allison stood in a corner of the living room with Derek, filling him in on the day's earlier events.

"He just left you to fend for yourself with the luggage?" questioned Derek as Allison completed her recount.

"He sure did," confirmed Allison. "James had to pick up his slack as usual."

"I ought to chop him in his neck for that!" huffed Derek. "Causing more drama when there's already enough as it is!"

"You get his neck and I'll get upside his head," said Allison.

"Deal."

Allison looked around the room, observing the members of her family. Her paternal uncle Malcolm Harrison leaned in the kitchen doorway, talking to Granddad Derrick and Nanna Kiana as they finished preparing dinner. Uncle Malcolm was nine years younger than Allison's father, Marlin Harrison, and he was everything her father was not. He was Derek's warm and friendly father, though the pair acted more as brothers, which Allison attributed to their fourteen-year age difference.

"Falcon, when do you think you're going to return to attending church?" asked Nanna Kiana.

"I'll go anytime Dad preaches," said Uncle Malcolm. "But everything I can do at church I can do at home without having to deal with all the hypocrites there."

"There are hypocrites everywhere, son," said Granddad Derrick.

"Yeah, but church hypocrites are a whole other breed," said Uncle Malcolm. "They like to hold stuff against people *forever*, but then get mad when you point out there stuff too. You of all people should understand how that makes me feel Dad."

"All too well," sighed Granddad Derrick. "But that's no excuse for refusing to go."

"Here, help me set the table since you're already up," directed Nanna Kiana.

"Alright," said Uncle Malcolm, moving to do as he was told.

Seated on the big couch were Aunt Nancy, Aunt Paulette, and James. Aunt Nancy had put her favorite blonde wig on, while Aunt Paulette had opted to put a stylish green headscarf on. Deidrick and Jordan sat on the smaller couch watching football. They were similar in appearance, both being dark-brown, plump, and having their hair styled into a waved pattern on their heads.

"This food is taking too long," complained Jordan. "I'm starving."

"You're not that hungry, Jordan," chastised James.

"How do you know how hungry I am?" argued Jordan. "They need to hurry up!"

"Bro, who is 'they'?" questioned Deidrick.

"Jordan, just sit still and be quiet," said Aunt Nancy. "The food will be done in a minute."

"Ugh," grumbled Jordan.

"Forget chopping him," whispered Derek. "I'm just going to straight-up punch him."

"Either way, I still got upside his head," said Allison.

"Food's ready!" said Nanna Kiana, appearing in the kitchen doorway.

"Finally!" said Jordan, shooting up from his seat. Allison and Derek glared at him as he passed, causing Jordan to say, "What?"

"You've been annoying all day," griped Allison.

"And if you keep it up, it's going to be a problem," said Derek.

"Whatever," said Jordan, shooting them a dirty look before continuing to the kitchen. Everyone took their places at the table and waited for Granddad Derrick to say grace.

"Alright, let's dig in!" declared Jordan, grabbing his fork.

"Jordan!" chastised Aunt Nancy. "Can't you act like you have some home training and wait until after we say grace?"

"Oh, alright," grumbled Jordan.

"Go ahead, Derrick," said Aunt Nancy.

"Dear Heavenly Father," began Granddad Derrick. "I pray over this food, and I pray that it be nourishing to our bodies and the hands that prepared it be blessed in the name of Jesus. And I pray, Father that wherever Dee-Three is, You watch over him, Lord. Cover him and protect him from all harm and danger and return him to us, Lord, safe and sound. And I pray during these troubling times that you keep and cover our family, Father, from any feelings of distress, worry, or anxiety, Lord. Because you said in Your word that Your peace which passeth all understanding will keep our hearts and minds if we cast our cares upon You, Lord. These things we pray in Jesus's name, amen."

"Amen," repeated Allison with the rest of the family.

They began to eat in silence. The absence of Derik hung like a gloomy shadow over the family. Allison hoped her brother would be found soon so the missing joy of the family could return.

Chapter Two: Matthias

Matthias Harrison learned on Sunday that Derik had not perished in the house fire. But his younger brother was nowhere to be found in the town either. He had disappeared. Everyone was scouring to find Derik, some for their own selfish motives rather than for the sake of doing right. The worst offender was Mayor Bernard Perry.

Matthias had unfortunately been born half Perry in June twenty-two years prior. Even worse, he had been exiled from the proverbial royal Harrison line of Creeke at fourteen. But even banishment had perks, for he no longer had to uphold the façade of a picture-perfect family. At the time, he had taken advantage of his newfound freedom and explored it in every possible way. But in growing older, he had slowed on his wild ways and was trying to change for the better. However, his old self still sometimes appeared, especially when he was losing money like he was that Sunday afternoon.

"You suck," said one of his teammates on the video game he was playing.

"Not as much as you do," said Matthias. "I'm the best player on this team."

"Guys, please don't argue," said Matthias's friend, twenty-year-old Andrew Stone. "We're all on the same team."

"Tell him that," said Matthias. "I'm cool."

"Yeah, keep talking," said the teammate.

"I will keep talking because that's what your mama likes," said Matthias. "That's why she's going to make me your stepdaddy."

"Oh boy," sighed his best friend, twenty-two-year-old Alexander Brown, who sat beside him watching him play.

"Why don't you get off the game and get a life?" argued the teammate.

"I have a life, courtesy of your mama," said Matthias. "She takes real good care of me."

"Go take care of your kids, deadbeat!"

"Why, when you're doing such a great job?" laughed Matthias. "Ask your girl whose baby that really is, because it isn't yours."

"Matt!" cried Alexander.

"What did you say?!"

"Oh, that hit a nerve," said Matthias. "That's right. I'm the pappy and I'm fixing to be your pappy too."

"I'm going to catch you one of these days."

"I hope you do," said Matthias. "I haven't beat the brakes off someone in a while, so I could use the opportunity to get the rust off."

"Shut up!" yelled the teammate, logging off from the videogame.

"He left," remarked Matthias. "Guess he couldn't handle it."

"Why did you provoke him like that?" asked Andrew when the match ended. "We needed him to win."

"Andrew, a toddler would've done a better job at this game than he did," said Matthias. "Besides, he provoked me first."

"Dude, you have to be a team player if you're going to play with me," said Andrew. "That's my only rule and you know that."

"We can't all be peacemakers, Andrew."

"Yeah, well this peacemaker is peace-ing out for the day," said Andrew, logging out.

"Matt," said Alexander. "It's just a game. It's not that serious to be bringing people's family members into it."

"It is that serious," argued Matthias. "Andrew gets paid to play videogames, and he gets paid more when he wins. And since I'm on his team, if he wins, I win because he gives me a cut of what he gets. So, if he loses, I lose out too, and you know I don't play about my money."

"Well Matt, if you get a consistent job, you won't have to worry about that," chided Alexander.

"I work for myself," said Matthias. "Besides I don't hear you telling Andrew to get a job."

"Andrew is in college trying to become a doctor," said Alexander. "You're just floating between jobs and have fifty-eleven side hustles."

"We can't all be a music producer and songwriter like you, Alex," said Matthias. "Some of us are normal."

"Okay, but I have a regular job too," said Alexander. "And you need one too. Especially if you have a son like you say you do."

"Alex," laughed Matthias. "Be serious. Do you really think I'd have a son out here without you knowing?"

"You shouldn't joke about things like that, man," scolded Alexander.

"Why not?" said Matthias. "I don't ever want kids and I don't plan on having any. Besides, we're both good, wholesome, inactive men, right?"

"You, wholesome?" snorted Alexander. "Maybe in an alternate reality. And with the way you act there's no telling how long you'll remain inactive."

"We made a pact, Alexander," reminded Matthias. "I hold you accountable and vice versa. I'm a man of my word and you know that."

"Oh really?"

"Yeah really."

"Then why do you have these?" asked Alexander, holding up a pack of cigarettes.

"How did you find those?"

"I sat on them," said Alexander annoyedly. "Why do you have them?"

Matthias looked down at the Creeke Courier on the table.

16-year-old missing after house fire

by Ralph Brewer, Creeke Courier

Creeke police are searching for a missing 16-year-old who was last seen on Friday.

Derik Harrison was last seen by his family at his house two hours before it caught fire. Firefighters are still investigating the cause of the fire.

Derik is 5 feet 6 inches tall, is dark-brown, and has black shoulder-length curly hair. He was last seen leaving his house around 6:30pm wearing a black coat, red polo, black jeans, and black and red sneakers. Anyone with information regarding Derik's location is urged to contact Creeke Police Department immediately.

"They're for Cell," said Matthias, referring to his twenty-five-year-old cousin, Marcellus Campbell.

"For Marcellus," said Alexander, unconvinced. "Right."

"They are."

"Look, I know your brother going missing has you on edge, but this is not the way to deal with it," said Alexander. "You said you were quitting and I'm holding you to it."

"I wasn't going to use them," said Matthias, lifting his sleeve to show Alexander the patch on his arm. "Otherwise, this thing would be useless."

"Of course," said Alexander, sliding the pack into his coat pocket. "But I'll make sure you don't use these by taking them off your hands."

"Fine by me but Cell won't be too happy to know you stole his cigarettes," said Matthias, standing up.

"He doesn't need them either."

"Alright Dad," said Matthias. "You ready to go?"

"Yeah," said Alexander. As they exited the house to head to his truck, Alexander said, "Remind me why I'm driving you around again."

"I let Cell borrow my baby for work since his is in the shop, and therefore I need you to be my chauffeur."

"And where am I chauffeuring you today, sir?"

"The barbershop," said Matthias, getting in the passenger seat. "Mayor Perry is holding a town hall meeting tomorrow at the community center and he wants us all there to stand behind him like we're all one big happy family."

"I thought you didn't like him."

"I don't," said Matthias. "But Granddad is supposed to be speaking too, and I'm going to support him. I don't want to be up there looking rough, so Deidrick is going to edge me up for the occasion."

"Deidrick?"

"He's the only barber available on such short notice," explained Matthias. "But if he tries anything today, I'll–!"

"Stop," interrupted Alexander. "You shouldn't be plotting evil against your brother."

"The only brother I care about is missing."

"I know your grandfather is embarrassed."

"Not as embarrassed as you are of yours."

"Who?" grumbled Alexander. His face darkened at the mention of his abusive paternal grandfather, Leonard Brown.

"Exactly."

"Has anyone ever told you that you can be a real jerk sometimes?"

"Several people," said Matthias. "Swing by my grandparents. My cousin is coming with me."

Matthias turned the radio up loud enough to vibrate the car and leaned back in his seat. A lady belted riffs and runs over the end of what sounded like a gospel track. He pictured the lady dressed in her Sunday best, singing as a sea of choir members stood behind her. The song painted an image of church in Matthias's mind, and he recalled the last time he had been in church.

It was the revival when his grandfather preached. He had sat with Alexander and as far away from his parents as possible. Alexander had cried when he saw his father on stage, enjoying once again singing with his siblings for The Big Guy they all loved. The message that his grandfather had preached that night was powerful. So powerful that it made Matthias question how he lived his life. And months later, it still resonated with him, pushing him to make better choices.

"Good afternoon, everyone!" spoke a familiar voice. "You are tuned into the Hallelujah Hour on the best gospel radio station in the area! This is Drake the Intern here and..."

"Speaking of cousins, I'm glad to hear yours is doing well for himself out there in the city," said Matthias. "He's probably out there wilding out now since he turned twenty-one last week."

"I hope not," sighed Alexander. "You know, I still want to know how you had planned on paying for his little project back in the fall if it had worked out."

"Haven't I told you before not to ask a man how he gets his money?"

"Matthias," said Alexander, glaring at his best friend.

"Look, the man needed money and I knew a way to get it for him," said Matthias, shrugging his shoulders. "If that meant I had to place a few bets and play a few card games then so be it."

"I can't deal with you," muttered Alexander. "You were going to fund a gospel project with gambling money?!"

"Money is money."

"You know what, now I'm glad that project fell through. Because you would've had my baby cousin in some mess that had nothing to do with him fooling with you."

"And this is why you don't ask a man how he gets his money," grumbled Matthias. "Because then people start trying to preach at you when they don't like the method."

The pair arrived at the home of the Harrison grandparents. James stood in the driveway, putting bags in the trunk of his car.

"You coming in?" asked Matthias, exiting the vehicle.

"I think I'll wait out here," answered Alexander.

"Suit yourself," said Matthias. He approached James, who upon seeing him, broke into a grin. They embraced, and Matthias asked him, "What's going on?"

"I'm about to head back home," said James. "You?"

"Aunty Lettie asked me to get Jordan away from the house for a few hours," said Matthias. "What's up with him?"

"He's got too much freedom and doesn't know how to use it," complained James. "Nanna's hoping Uncle Derrick can straighten him out while they're here."

"She sure picked a fine time to do it."

"You going inside?"

"Who all is in there?"

"Jordan, your grandparents, and your sister."

"I guess I can stop in for a second then."

"Alright," said James. "I'm heading out, so I'll see you when I see you."

"See you when I see you," said Matthias, hugging his cousin. He entered the house and found his grandmother sitting on the couch with her eyes closed. "Hey Nanna. Where's everybody at?"

"I sent your aunts on an errand and your sister's getting ready for work," said Nanna Kiana, remaining seated with her eyes shut.

"What about Granddad?"

"In his study. I'm sure he won't mind the interruption though."

"I'll go see him in a minute," said Matthias. "How are you?"

"Right now, I'm doing okay," said Nanna Kiana, her eyes fluttering open. "We'll see how long that lasts when your aunts come back."

"They're that bad?"

"Your Aunt Lettie is fine," said Nanna Kiana. Her face contorted into one of annoyance, and through gritted teeth, she uttered, "But your Aunt Nancy is working my last nerve! She talks too much, she talks too loud, and she's just plain nosy! Just like when we were girls! And don't even get me started on that grandson of hers!"

"What's he doing?"

"I don't even want to talk about it," said Nanna Kiana, rubbing her temples. "I just want to enjoy my peace while I have it."

"I'll let you do that," said Matthias, excusing himself. He headed for his grandfather's study, located on the opposite end of the house. It was one of the many rooms his grandfather had annexed onto the original house after retiring from his construction job. As he walked, he observed all the family photos on the wall.

One photo made him stop. In it, a ten-year-old version of himself sat with all his younger siblings smiling together on a log. Allison sat on the left end next to Deidrick, showing off her missing front teeth. Matthias sat on the other side of Deidrick with his arm slung around his brother's shoulder. Derik sat on the right end, resting his head on Matthias's shoulder. Looking at his younger, happier self with his siblings made Matthias feel unsettled, and he resumed walking to the study.

"Granddad," said Matthias, knocking on the door.

"Matty," said Granddad Derrick. "What's going on?"

"I came to get Jordan," said Matthias, examining the football his grandfather prominently displayed on one of his bookshelves. The ball had been gifted to his grandfather upon graduating college and had 'To Samson. Hit 'em hard! –Coach Tucker' written on it in black ink. Matthias grabbed it and gently tossed it to its owner.

"No wonder you're frowning," said Granddad Derrick, receiving the football. "Still, I appreciate you taking him away for a bit. I need peace and quiet to work on what I'm saying tomorrow."

"I've got you covered," said Matthias.

"I know you do," said Granddad Derrick. "Hey, Rick wanted to know if you could help him work on his car sometime. He said he'll pay you for your trouble. I meant to tell you before everything happened."

"Sure," said Matthias. "Tell him to let me know when and I'll be out there."

"Thanks, Matty."

"I'll let you get back to work."

"Don't be a stranger."

"Alright."

Matthias returned to the living room to find Nanna Kiana tying on an apron. Matthias deduced she was about to start cleaning by the way she eyed a nearby broom.

"I let Jordan know you're here," said Nanna Kiana. "Can you do me a favor?"

"Anything you want."

"Would you come by after the town hall tomorrow? I need to talk to you about something."

"Why can't we talk now?"

"You're about to go," said Nanna Kiana. "Our conversation might take a minute to get through."

Heavy footfall coming up the hallway cut off their conversation. Jordan rounded the corner and his face lit up upon seeing his cousin.

"Hey cuz!" said Jordan. "You ready?"

"Yeah," said Matthias. "Let's go."

"Remember what I said, Matty," said Nanna Kiana.

"I'll think about it," answered Matthias. He led Jordan out to Alexander's car.

"Hello," said Alexander as they entered the vehicle.

Jordan did not respond.

"You don't hear Alex speaking to you?" said Matthias.

"What's up?" said Jordan.

"That's what I thought," mumbled Matthias.

"Where are we going?" asked Jordan.

"To the barbershop."

"The barbershop?" cried Jordan. "Man, I thought we were going somewhere fun!"

"Jordan," said Matthias, looking at his cousin. "Do you even care that your cousin is missing right now?"

"What kind of question is that?"

"A real one," said Matthias. "My brother is missing, and you think I'm trying to go somewhere fun?"

"Well, I figured since you were taking me out that you had something planned."

"I'm bringing you with me because you're getting on everybody's nerves," ranted Matthias. "At least pretend like you care about what's happening around you."

"Matt," said Alexander. "Calm down."

Matthias obeyed Alexander and settled into his seat. The rest of the car ride was silent, and upon arriving at the barbershop, Jordan exited the vehicle without saying anything.

"You've really got to start maintaining better control of your temper," lectured Alexander.

"I'm trying," complained Matthias.

"Well, try harder because I know you can do it," said Alexander. "Let me know when you're done, and I'll come get you."

"Alright," said Matthias, getting out of the car. The sign on the barbershop read '*Miss Leya's Beauty and Barbershop*'. Although his mother's name was on the shop, the business was actually owned by both of his parents. They would be returning to town soon, but Matthias did not care. To him, they were not parents; they were the people who threw him out at fourteen behind something Deidrick had started and could not finish. Matthias did not care about anything that had to do with them. All he wanted back was his missing brother.

-

Chapter Three: Deidrick

Deidrick Harrison let his mind wander as he pulled his pants on. His thoughts mostly anchored on Derik, as nothing else distracted Deidrick long enough to avoid thinking about him. The only thing that nearly occupied his mind as much was the loss of his shoe collection in the fire. Years of collecting various sneakers, dress shoes, and designer shoes were lost, and had he known it would happen, he would have chosen a fresher pair of kicks that day than plain white sneakers. Those and the sneakers that Derik had apparently borrowed that day were the only survivors of his collection. But even that paled in comparison to not knowing where his brother was. Footsteps leaving the bathroom caught his attention as he pulled his hoodie over his head.

"So, what are you about to go do?" asked twenty-one-year-old Sharon Pierce, holding a cheetah-print robe together to cover her body. Not even she could take Deidrick's mind off things.

"Go to work," said Deidrick, licking his lips as he eyed the golden anklet adorning her light-brown ankle before working his way up the rest of her body. She had become thicker since their first tryst in September. "I would say bye, but I know we'll be seeing each other again."

"What makes you think I would want to see you again?" said Sharon.

"Why wouldn't you?"

"I don't think Malik would like you saying that," said Sharon with a smirk as she motioned to the picture of her and her boyfriend on the nightstand. Malik was a chubby, medium-brown man of twenty-four with wavy black hair and a scraggly beard that he was trying to grow.

"Yeah, well obviously Malik isn't doing something right because I'm here with his girl and he's not," said Deidrick proudly. His phone rang, and Deidrick regretted accepting the call almost immediately after he said, "Hello?"

"Cornbread!" shouted Allison. "Where are you?!"

"Where I'm at!" griped Deidrick, annoyed at his sister's intrusiveness. "Can't a man have some time to himself?"

"Do you realize what time it is?!"

"It's a quarter to two," said Deidrick, looking at the clock on the nightstand. "What's so special about that?"

"How about the fact that you're supposed to be taking me to work at two!"

"Why can't you just drive yourself there?"

"The whole point of you taking me was because we were going to the same place!"

"I'm on my way."

"Don't bother! I'll drive myself!"

"What was the point of calling me then?"

"Because you always do this!" complained Allison. "You always say you'll do something and then you don't!"

"The time got away from me."

"Whatever Cornbread," huffed Allison before hanging up the phone.

"Trouble in paradise?" asked Sharon.

"Nah, just Allison," chuckled Deidrick. "I've got to go."

"Well, don't let me hold you up," said Sharon. "We're done here anyways."

It was a quarter past three when Deidrick arrived at the hair salon. Allison sat at the front desk doing her job as a part-time receptionist. Her face soured when she spotted him walking through the door.

"Oh, look who it is, Nisha," she yelled to one of the stylists. Her voice got more accusatory with each word as she yelled, "It's the idiot who can't be ON TIME FOR ANYTHING TO SAVE HIS LIFE!"

"Whatever Queenie," said Deidrick, rolling his eyes at his sister's insult. "You still made it to work on time."

"No thanks to you!"

"You *are* late, Deidrick," affirmed twenty-year-old Nisha Gardner. "Your brother and your cousin have been waiting on you in the barbershop."

"See?" added Allison. "Can't be on time for nothing!"

"Why don't you shut up?" huffed Deidrick.

"Why don't you go do your job?" retorted Allison.

"I will."

"Bye!"

"Bye!"

Deidrick passed through the door that connected the barbershop to the hair salon. Matthias sat in his barber chair while Jordan looked at a poster showcasing the different haircuts offered.

"What's up, Jordan?" said Deidrick.

"What's up," muttered Jordan.

"What's the matter with you?"

"Nothing," answered Jordan, glancing at Matthias, who glared back at him.

"Alright then," said Deidrick. "You getting a cut too?"

"Might as well," grumbled Jordan. "There's nothing else to do around here."

Deidrick went to his station and started on Matthias's head. It was not unusual for them to ignore each other, given they were not on good terms. But regardless of their personal relationship, Deidrick still had a job to do, and he did it well. He made sure Matthias and Jordan looked good when they left the barbershop and, after finishing his other clients, found himself in need of after-work entertainment. So, he went home with Nisha, the girl he had been dealing with since his senior year of high school.

Deidrick liked Nisha because she was smart, sweet, and caring. Nisha had things she wanted to accomplish in her life, and Deidrick respected that. He never worried about her leaving him behind. As he lay on her lap, he looked at her pudgy light-brown face and smiled, knowing that she would never desert him no matter what.

"What is it?" asked Nisha, returning his smile as she traced the name tattoo on his arm.

"Baby I'm hungry," moaned Deidrick as he held his stomach. "Make me a sandwich."

"Do I look like a maid to you?" said Nisha, raising her eyebrow.

"You sound like my Nanna."

"Do you speak to her like that?"

"Make me a sandwich *please*?" begged Deidrick.

"You are so stupid," grumbled Nisha as she pushed Deidrick's head off her lap. He watched as she sashayed her plump body into the kitchen.

"With extra mayo!"

"You'll get what I give you!"

"All I know is whatever you give me better have extra mayo on it!" declared Deidrick, followed by a triumphant grunt as he sat back on the couch.

He felt like the man then, sitting on that couch. His girl was in the kitchen making him food while he enjoyed the game after working hard all day. It was a life Deidrick could get used to when the time was right. But despite his current feeling, Deidrick knew he was not ready to settle down yet. There were still many things in life he wanted to enjoy. Deidrick wanted to take full advantage of his youth while he still had it, and he could not do that if he tied himself down to someone.

"Hey babe, what time do your roommates get home?" called Deidrick. Although he had pluralized the question, the only roommate of Nisha's Deidrick wanted to know about was the luscious Beverly Boyd. Deidrick always got excited seeing her honey-colored legs walk through the door and hoped he would see them that evening.

Nisha did not answer him. She placed his sandwich before him and quietly sat beside him.

"You didn't hear what I said?" asked Deidrick as he bit into the sandwich, pretending not to notice the change in her attitude.

"Deidrick?" said Nisha. "Can I ask you something?"

"What's up?"

"We've been working toward a relationship for three years now," said Nisha. "When are we going to make it official?"

"Nisha," said Deidrick, pausing to swallow his bite of food. "I've already told you I'm not ready for a relationship yet."

"Is that what you told Sharon?" asked Nisha, tilting her head to the side.

"Why are you asking me about Sharon?"

"She called," said Nisha, producing his phone from behind her back.

"And?"

"Why is she calling you?"

"Because she has my number. What's the issue?"

"What could you two possibly have to talk about?" asked Nisha. "She doesn't work at the shop anymore. She doesn't live in Creeke anymore since she moved to the city to live with her boyfriend. So, why is she still calling you?"

"Bro, why is that your business?" grunted Deidrick, growing irritated with Nisha questioning him. "I don't question you about your phone calls."

"The only women that should be calling your phone are your family members," said Nisha, pausing to level her face with Deidrick's. "And me."

"I can't control who calls me."

"Deidrick!" snapped Nisha. "If you don't want to be with me, just tell me now!"

"Why are you being like this?"

"Because I'm tired of waiting. I want commitment from you!"

"I'm not ready yet!"

"Ugh!" exclaimed Nisha. She tossed Deidrick's phone at him and stormed out of the room. "See your big-head self out!"

Deidrick picked up his phone and went through it. Nisha had deleted Sharon's number and blocked it. The argument only ruined his good mood and reinforced why he did not want a relationship yet. He liked being able to do what he wanted, and he did not need his girl trying to control him like a dog on a leash. His girl needed to allow him his own space, especially during troubling times such as the one he was facing with his brother's disappearance. If Nisha could not do that, then she was not the girl for him.

-

Chapter Four: Derek

Derek Harrison wholeheartedly believed his father had lost his mind. He truly did as he helped him straighten up the living room. It was the only reasonable explanation for his father's decision to let Uncle Marlin stay with them.

"Why are you letting him stay here?" asked Derek.

"Why do you keep asking me that?" replied Malcolm.

"Because I don't understand why you're doing this."

"Because he needs a place to stay since, you know, his house is burnt," said Malcolm sarcastically.

"Why can't he stay with Granddad and Nanna like everyone else?"

"He doesn't want to."

"But–!"

"Derek, Marlin is my brother," said Malcolm. "He's made sure I was good on several occasions and now I'm going to do the same for him."

"But he's so mysterious."

"He really isn't," said Malcolm. "All you have to do is get to know him. But just know if you ask him anything, he won't hold back with his answers."

"Sounds like you," said Derek. "I'm still scarred from those puberty talks."

"You made it to eighteen without any kids, didn't you?" said Malcolm. "I'd say it was successful."

"Yeah, successful at scarring your kid for life."

Someone knocked on the door. Standing on the other side of the screen door was Uncle Marlin Harrison. At forty-one, he was a dark-brown, muscular man with a few gray hairs streaking through the black curly mass on his head.

"You're here!" cheered Malcolm. He flung the door open and latched onto his older brother.

"Falcon...," grumbled Uncle Marlin, tensing up under his brother's display of affection.

"Alright, alright," said Malcolm, releasing his brother from the un-reciprocated hug. He motioned to Derek and said, "You know my son."

"Yo," said Uncle Marlin, holding up a few fingers as part of his greeting.

Derek found that he could not respond. His tongue was stuck as he gazed into the cold brown eyes that paralyzed him.

"I think the cat got his tongue," joked Malcolm.

Uncle Marlin was silent. He stood there with his hands in his pockets, his eyes trained on his nephew. They seemed to examine Derek, almost as if they were learning all they could about him just from look-ing. The brow above the eyes furrowed, and the mouth far below them set into a frown. Derek detected some hint of emotion in his uncle's eyes, but what exactly it was he could not place.

"Marlin," said Malcolm, cutting through the awkward silence. "You can either have my room or the couch in here."

"Keep your room, Falcon," answered Uncle Marlin. He had turned his eyes away from Derek when he said it, and Derek realized he was no longer stricken.

"D...Dad," said Derek, finding his voice.

"Oh, he does speak," laughed Malcolm.

"I... I'm going out."

"You are?" replied Malcolm. "But your uncle just got here."

"I just need to go out right quick."

"Alright," sighed Malcolm. "But don't stay out too late."

Derek had never escaped from somewhere so fast in his life. He stood in his front yard, sucking in large quantities of air as he tried to process what had just happened. As he gathered his wits, he turned on his favorite song and let the music carry him away from his problems:

It cost a bag to bag her,
and I don't know what to do
Spending up my money,
buying clothes, hair, nails, and
shoes.
My baby's in my bag,
so, she can look how I want her to.
She put that pressure on me,
got me wrapped up like a fool.

"Dee!" yelled someone, causing him to pause his music. Derek recognized the girlish voice belonging to his own proverbial baby that had him 'wrapped up like a fool'. His girlfriend, Adrianna Brown, ran down the street waving at him to get his attention. He watched as his little ballerina came to him and leaped into his arms.

"How's my baby today?" said Derek, hugging Adrianna.

"Wishing April would hurry up and get here so I can turn sixteen and drive myself places instead of having to walk everywhere," said Adrianna annoyedly.

"Is that so?" said Derek. He motioned to his truck and said, "Want to go for a ride?"

"You know my dad doesn't let me ride around with you without his permission."

"Well, go ask him."

"I can't," said Adrianna. "He's out with Gretchen."

"So, he can go out with his fiancée whenever he wants, but you can't even get into a car with your boyfriend?"

"Yes."

"Well, where are you going?"

"I'm on my way to my society meeting but I wanted to see how you were doing first."

"You could've called me for that."

"I wanted to *see*."

"Well, do you like what you *see*?"

"Always," said Adrianna. "But really I want to know how you feel."

"As good as I can all things considered," said Derek. "So, where's the meeting today?"

"At Charmaine's."

"Isn't that near your mom's house?" asked Derek. "I could walk you there."

"Uh uh," said Adrianna. "You know the rule. No boys allowed."

"If that's the case, what do you do when it's your turn to host meetings? Because there's no way your father is agreeing to that."

"I host them at Mom's house," said Adrianna. "Forrest is a very agreeable stepfather."

"I'll bet he is," said Derek. "But I'm not very agreeable with you walking to Charmaine's house by yourself."

"She lives right around the corner from my dad," said Adrianna.

"No, *I* live around the corner from your dad," said Derek. "It takes fifteen minutes to walk from his house to your mom's house, and even longer to walk to Charmaine's."

"I walk all the time. It's not a big deal."

"It is to me," said Derek. "Either you let me walk you or you call your dad and ask him to let me give you a ride."

"Oh alright," said Adrianna, removing her phone from her purse. She dialed a number and waited for the other person to pick up. "Hello? Dad? Can I get a ride with Derek to Charmaine's house?"

Derek listened as Mr. Torrance Brown's voice faintly spoke to Adrianna on the other end of the line.

"That's what I said!" exclaimed Adrianna, agreeing with whatever her father said. "But he insists that he drive me there."

The father-daughter pair exchanged a few more words.

"Okay bye," said Adrianna, hanging up the phone. "He said yes."

"That was a very long-winded 'yes'," said Derek as he held the passenger door open for Adrianna.

"You know he had to finish fussing about it first," said Adrianna as she got in the car.

"I know," answered Derek when he started the car. "Your dad is good at four things: fussing, yelling, throwing shoes, and music."

"Well, he isn't throwing shoes anymore," said Adrianna. "And now instead of randomly freestyling, he randomly freestyles and sings all over the house at any given time."

"Isn't that a good thing?"

"Not at five in the morning when I'm awakened from *my sleep* because *he* wanted to hit a random high note while getting ready for work! But if I wake him up out his sleep, I'm suddenly the least favorite child of the day!"

"You know what you need," said Derek. "You need some music."

Derek turned on his radio and continued playing the song he was listening to on his phone.

Vincent on the beat
And I want to have fun,
So I got my notepad
And I made a little song,
I ain't really got a girl
I just needed a hook,
Embedded in your brain
You can call me a crook
Because I stole your mind
Ha! I made you look!
But I've got your tongue
So now you're my rook!
Cause you're spitting my rhymes
And singing my chimes
And behind that other guy
I ain't doing no time
I got money to make
I ain't selling my soul

Or wasting my life
On a broke down joke
I'll punch your lights out
Then I'll lift you back up
Cause that's who I am
Who I've been from jump
Oh I hate that song
If you didn't know
I'm not for violence
It was all for show
Now back to this song
That I went and wrote
Cause I was bored
Yeah, bored and alone

"Let me just…," said Adrianna, turning the volume down.

"Hey!" whined Derek. "That's my song!"

"Sir, it is entirely too loud," said Adrianna. "I don't know why you and your cousin insist on vibrating the whole town with your cars, but I want no parts of it."

"You disrespected me, Matty, and my man Knokout," said Derek, arriving at the Townsend home. "Now, you got to get out."

"Alright," said Adrianna. "Unlock the door and let me out."

"Aren't you forgetting something?"

"What?"

"Where's my kiss?"

"I could ask you the same thing."

Derek and Adrianna stared at each other. Adrianna tilted her head sassily, indicating that she would not be giving Derek the kiss he wanted. If he wanted to share a moment of love with her, he would have to initiate it.

"Alright, I'll kiss you," said Derek, relenting.

"And no games either," said Adrianna.

"When have I ever played games?"

"Last time you licked me on the face like you were a dog."

"I mean that *is* how dogs kiss..."

"Are you a dog, Derek?"

"Oh alright," said Derek. He kissed Adrianna on the cheek and said, "There. I kissed you normally."

"Thank you," said Adrianna. She kissed him on the cheek and got out of the car. "Have a good day."

"You too."

Derek ensured Adrianna got safely inside the house and then drove to his grandparent's house. The sun hung in the sky, slowly descending to the earth to allow for the night to take over. When he arrived, he found his grandmother in the living room cleaning while Jordan sat on the couch, flipping through television channels.

"Hi," said Derek.

"Hey," said Nanna Kiana. "What are you doing here so late?"

"I just wanted to get out of the house."

"Well, I'll never object to seeing you."

"Is Auntie Leya here?" I want to say hi to her."

"She's in her room, but don't stay in there too long," advised Nanna Kiana. "Your aunt needs time to herself."

"Okay."

Derek made his way to where Aunt Soleya was staying. He knocked on the door and waited for a reply.

"Come in," said Aunt Soleya softly.

A morbid and stifling air filled the atmosphere on the other side of the door. Shadows clung to the walls, directing curious eyes to their origins at the window, providing the sole source of light. It was by this window that Aunt Soleya Harrison sat with a mug in hand, staring out at life beyond the panes.

"Hello Auntie Leya," greeted Derek.

"Hello De–!" began Aunt Soleya, stopping herself upon realizing the name she was about to speak. She sighed and said, "Hello Nephew."

"I uh... I just wanted to say hi and see if you were doing alright."

"I'm doing well," said Aunt Soleya, followed by a sip from her mug. "Thank you for asking."

"What's that you're drinking?"

"Black coffee."

"This late in the afternoon?"

Aunt Soleya nodded and took another sip of coffee, returning her tired eyes to the window.

"Tell me, Nephew," said Aunt Soleya. "Have you seen my husband today?"

"Yes ma'am," answered Derek. "He'd just arrived at our house when I left."

"I see."

Derek shifted nervously as an uncomfortable silence filled the room.

"I'll um... I'll go now," he announced.

"Okay."

The fever of embarrassment burned Derek's face as he left the room. His aunt had not even been able to call him by name. As he walked along the hallway, Derek looked up at the family photos on the wall. He stared at the big family photo on the wall and focused on the faces of himself, his grandfather, and his missing cousin.

Derek had tried everything to carve out an identity for himself separate from his namesake and his eponymous cousin. Growing his hair into an afro had not worked, as it reminded the community elders of his grandfather in his youth. He and his cousin had the same nose and lips as their grandfather. Their physiques resembled one another, with Derek's being more muscular due to his athletic activities. Not even the tiger stripe tattoo snaked around Derek's right wrist helped his cause, as his grandfather also had a tattoo on his chest.

And yet, there was one feature that distinguished him from the other two. One feature that allowed him to be irrevocably Derek Drumaine Harrison: his eyes. Though they were dark-brown in color like the others, their shape was of a foreign origin. They did not resemble those of anyone in his family but instead were entirely and uniquely his.

Derek had one explanation for the phenomena: they were the eyes of the woman who birthed him.

They were the eyes of the woman who had shoved him into his grandfather's arms almost as soon as he was out of her womb. The woman who, at seventeen, left him behind to start a new life elsewhere without him in it. Derek did not mind the rejection though. She had left him with a family who loved and cared for him. As he entered the kitchen, he came upon the patriarch of this loving and caring family sitting at the kitchen table. His mouth was set in a line, and his eyes scrunched as if he were battling some terrible thought.

"That's a scary face you're making, Granddad," said Derek. "What's on your mind?"

"I don't know what I'm going to say tomorrow," said Granddad Derrick, still glaring into space. "I've been working on this sermon all day and I have nothing."

"Hmm," said Derek. He looked around the room and spotted a deck of cards on the table. Brightening up with an idea, he said, "I know what you need."

"What?"

"A break," said Derek, sitting down at the table. He picked up the cards and said, "Let's play a game."

His grandfather looked at him and frowned. Derek knew why. Granddad Derrick saw his resemblance to Derik as did everyone else in town. He dealt the cards and began their card game without saying anything.

"Auntie, can you get me a snack?" Derek heard Jordan ask from the living room.

"Do I look like a maid to you?" remarked Nanna Kiana. "And please take your feet off my table."

Nanna Kiana passed through the kitchen to join her sisters on the back porch while Derek and his grandfather continued their card game. Derek was about to take his turn when he noticed his grandfather peering into the living room.

"Go get my belt," instructed Granddad Derrick, an unspoken rage burning in his eyes. Derek obeyed and as he passed through the living room, noticed that Jordan still had his feet on the table. It became clear what would soon take place, and Derek retrieved the large leather belt from his grandfather's room without any sympathy for his cousin.

"Where are you going with that?" asked Jordan as Derek passed through the living room again.

"Granddad asked for it," answered Derek.

"You must've really pissed him off for him to whoop you at your big age."

"Someone pissed him off alright."

Derek returned to the kitchen and handed the belt to his grand-father. The latter entered the living room, leaving a silence that was soon broken by the leather strap cutting through the air.

"YOW!" yelped Jordan. Derek watched as his cousin flew from the couch to escape the punishment. Jordan grabbed at the belt, saying, "Stop! Stop!"

"Didn't your aunt tell you to take your feet off the table?!" shouted Granddad Derrick. "Huh?!"

"Yes sir!" cried Jordan.

"So, why are they still up there?!"

"I don't know!"

"Don't make me have to come back in here!" threatened Granddad Derrick. He returned to the card game and said annoyedly, "Derek, take your turn."

"What's going on in here?" demanded Aunt Nancy as she bustled into the room. "Why was Jordan yelling?"

"Get your grandson, Nancy," said Granddad Derrick as he placed his belt on the back of his chair. "I'm low on patience."

"What did you do?"

"I whooped him."

"Why?!"

"Because Kiki told him to take his feet off the table and he put them right back up there after she walked away."

"Derrick, Jordan is too old to be getting whoopings."

"No one is ever too old," said Granddad Derrick. "And if he doesn't want it to happen again then he better do as he's told next time. I'm not playing with him, Nancy."

The look in his grandfather's eyes was one Derek was not used to seeing. At least, not on his grandfather's face. It was the look that confirmed that Uncle Marlin was just as much Granddad Derrick's son as Malcolm was. His eyes were cold and emotionless in the same manner Uncle Marlin's usually were, and Derek chose to keep quiet, hoping to avoid being paralyzed again. He stayed quiet until he was home again where Uncle Marlin sat on the couch watching television. Gathering his courage, Derek decided to confront his uncle and stood in front of the television, blocking his uncle's view.

"Do you think you're made of glass?" asked Uncle Marlin.

"Let's get one thing straight," said Derek. "If we're to live under the same roof, then we need to get to know each other better."

Uncle Marlin cut the television off and stared at his nephew.

"What'd you say?" he said.

"I... I... I think we need to... get to know each other better," stammered Derek, losing what little courage he had built. "Dad said I could ask you anything... and you'd answer..."

"As long as the question's not stupid," said Uncle Marlin. He patted the seat next to him. "Sit."

The youth obeyed his uncle, being sure to leave distance between them should he need a quick escape.

"Ask away," said Uncle Marlin.

"Um...," said Derek. He looked at his uncle's jawline and followed it up to his ear, taking notice of the hole in his earlobe. "Do you wear earrings?"

"Sometimes."

"Wow, I didn't know that!"

"Is that what you wanted to ask me?"

"No... uh... um... how many jobs do you have?"

"Three. The barbershop, my tech repair, and I manage the gym at the community center."

"Wow. How does your tech repair work?"

"People bring me their devices and I repair them. Of course, now I've got to get all new equipment because my equipment was in my house."

"So, you worked from home?"

"Yeah."

"Wow. Where does most of your money come from?"

"Never ask a man how he makes his money."

"Matty got that from you."

"Actually, he got it from Bernard. But it was good advice, so I took it too."

"Oh."

"Is *that* what you wanted to ask me?"

"No," said Derek. "Uh... are you mean?"

"That's subjective. Some say I am, some say I'm not."

"Do you think you're mean?"

"No."

"Would you ever beat me up?"

"Have you given me reason to?"

"But would you?"

"If you put me in a position where I have to."

"Do you like me?"

"If you're scared of me, Derek, just say that."

"I... I'm not... I'm not scared!"

"Okay," said Uncle Marlin, shrugging. "I'm just trying to 'get things straight' like you said."

"I just want to know who I'm living with, that's all."

"Your father and your uncle."

"You say that as if we have a close relationship."

"If you want me to leave then I'll leave."

"Th...that's alright!" laughed Derek nervously. He did not want to upset his father by making his uncle uncomfortable enough to leave. "I just want to know who I'm living with."

"What've you heard about me?"

"What?"

"Tell me what you've heard about me, and I'll tell you if it's true or not."

"I heard...," began Derek. "I heard that you beat up people you don't like."

"That's false," said Uncle Marlin. "I defend myself against people that attack me. If you don't attack me, you don't get beat up. It's pretty simple."

"Interesting," said Derek, starting to feel more comfortable. "You know, there's something that's always bugged me."

"What?"

"Why did you give Dee-Three the same name as me?"

"Your father and I had a rocky relationship during the time you and my son were born."

"So, you did it to spite Dad?"

"Yeah," said Uncle Marlin. "Not my finest moment, but it's too late to do anything about it now."

"Did you really tell Dee-Three you didn't want him?"

"Yeah."

"Why?"

"Because he asked."

"You know, that really hurt his feelings."

"He shouldn't have asked then."

"So, you don't care that you hurt his feelings?"

"My job is to provide for them," stated Uncle Marlin. "I can't help it if their feelings get hurt because they asked for an answer they didn't really want."

"That's not a good father."

"What do you know about being a good father, Derek?"

"I know what my father has shown me."

"And I know what my father has shown me."

"I refuse to believe that Granddad only provided for you and didn't care about your feelings."

"You'd be surprised what type of father your grandfather was."

"Granddad wouldn't do that."

"To you," said Uncle Marlin, standing up. "But I know who my father was, and those two people aren't the same person. Stand up so I can make up this couch."

Derek did as his uncle asked and watched as he prepared the couch to sleep on.

"Was Granddad really that mean when you were younger?" asked Derek.

"Oh yeah," Marlin said. "But I don't blame him. He had to be mean with a son like me."

"What's 'a son like you'?"

"Stubborn and rebellious like a wild horse. That's how he described it. I'm your grandfather's wild horse that he never tamed. And I hated him for trying to tame me until I was old enough to understand he did his best the only way he knew how."

"What made you understand?"

"Life," grumbled Uncle Marlin, laying his suitcase on the couch to search through it. "My father was trying to make a man out of me, and I didn't appreciate it until it was too late."

"Do you think you're a good father?" asked Derek.

"My kids are all taken care of, aren't they?" replied Uncle Marlin, removing a durag from the suitcase.

"Yeah, but...," began Derek, slowly letting the statement die. He did not feel it was his place to tell his uncle what his children thought of him.

"But what?" said Uncle Marlin, turning to him while tying the durag onto his head. "The most important job a father has is making sure everyone is clothed, fed, and has a roof over their head. Nothing else matters if those things aren't taken care of."

"Do you care that Dee-Three is gone?" asked Derek, veering to another topic.

"That's a stupid question."

"No, it's not!"

"Yes, it is."

It was only for a second, but Derek saw it. His uncle had glared at him and then quickly looked away. The expression on his face was as if he had seen a ghost.

"Do I remind you of him?" asked Derek.

"Who?"

"Derik."

"In some ways," said Uncle Marlin. "All three of you are somehow the same and somehow different all at once. Any more questions?"

"No."

"Then, I'm going to sleep."

Derek went to his room feeling unsatisfied. The conversation with his uncle had given him new insights and generated more questions in him. Yet, one thing was clear to him: nobody looked at him and saw only him. Instead, everyone saw three people. He was the walking phantom of Creeke, reminding everyone of the missing boy and the past youth of the elderly pastor. And it was clear to him that he would never get to be just Derek Drumaine Harrison.

-

Chapter Five: Allison

It was the crying that woke Allison up. Soft agonized sobs that moved Allison to seek out their source at two in the morning. Allison felt her way along the dark hallway, not wanting to alarm anyone else by turning on a light. Her first guess to the source of the crying was her mother's room. Pressing her ear to the door, she listened and discovered she was wrong. As she crept through the house, she realized the crying came from the living room. Granddad Derrick sat alone there with nothing but the television as his sole companion and light source. Tears streamed down his face as he miserably looked up at the ceiling with sullen eyes.

"Granddad?" said Allison. "What are you still doing up?"

"I couldn't sleep," sighed Granddad Derrick, quickly wiping his face. "Every time I try, all I think of is your brother being out there all alone."

Allison watched as her grandfather's serious face slowly contorted into a pained, chuckling one.

"It's ironic, isn't it?" he continued. "I have to encourage everyone else later today and yet here I am struggling myself."

"It only means you're also human."

"You're so sweet, Queenie," said Granddad Derrick. "It's moments like this that make me hopeful that I haven't completely ruined the family with my rottenness."

"You're not rotten," reassured Allison. "You made mistakes, just like everyone else."

"And now I'm reaping what I've sown," muttered Granddad Derrick. "The whole family is a mess and it's all my fault."

"You couldn't have done any worse than my parents have."

"Don't say that."

"It's the truth," complained Allison. "Mother probably only cares about how this will affect her reputation, while Dad probably doesn't care at all."

"I'm going to let you in on something," whispered Granddad Derrick. "I didn't always like your mother because I thought she was just a shallow, pretty face. But as I got to know her, I realized she and I had lived similar lives. She's been told all her life that her reputation is *the* most important thing she has, and she has to protect it at all costs."

"And you agree with that?"

"Of course not," explained Granddad Derrick. "But like I said, I understood it because I've been in her shoes. All someone had to do when I was younger was call me 'Bishop's son' and that was it. People would make me feel like my whole life would be ruined if I damaged 'Bishop's' reputation."

"But you're different from Mother."

"Not really," said Granddad Derrick. "It only took me meeting her once to see her for who she truly was. Your mother isn't the heartless woman you're making her out to be, Queenie. She's human like the rest of us, dealing with life the only way she knows how. If she 'ruined the family' as you claim, she probably didn't mean to. I know I didn't mean to."

"And what about Dad?"

"I...," began Granddad Derrick. "I shouldn't be worrying you up with this. These are my burdens to carry."

"You don't have to carry them alone."

"You're right," said Granddad Derrick, standing up. He placed his hands on Allison's shoulders and said, "But I'm also not going to saddle you with them either. Now, off to bed with you."

"Yes sir."

"And Queenie?"

"Sir?"

"Don't tell your grandmother about this," instructed Granddad Derrick. "I don't want to worry her."

"Yes sir."

"Goodnight."

"Goodnight."

Allison was going to strangle Derik when he was finally found. Instead of being nice and curled up in a warm house, she was out in the cold listening to Mayor Perry urge anyone with information about Derik to come forward. She fidgeted around, trying not to focus on how little help her stockings were at keeping her legs warm.

"Stand still!" chastised Mrs. Harrison.

Allison rolled her eyes at her mother. She was struggling against the cold December wind with nothing but a long-sleeved yellow wool dress and a coat from her Nanna's closet. Nanna Kiana had given Allison some of her old clothes, but despite the nice gesture, most of them were too old-fashioned and unflattering.

"Please," said Mayor Bernard, scrunching his face up as if he were going to cry. "If you know anything... anything..."

He paused to sniffle and pulled out his handkerchief to dab at his eye.

"Please," mumbled Allison, trying not to laugh at the horribly over-acted role of the worried grandfather Mayor Bernard performed for the people of Creeke. "There aren't even any tears coming out his eyes."

Mrs. Harrison nudged Allison and gave her a sharp look.

"I'm sorry," apologized Mayor Bernard. "I don't think anyone can imagine how hard it is to be up here like this knowing my grandson is missing. I'm going to ask that Pastor Harrison leave us with a word of encouragement during these troubling times."

Mayor Bernard wiped his face again as he stepped back into his wife's arms, allowing Granddad Derrick to take his place before the congregants. He placed his bible on the podium and looked out over the crowd. A pair of sunglasses obscured the sleepless eyes of the elderly man, but they could not hide the aura of heaviness he carried in his heart.

"Good evening, everyone," began Granddad Derrick "I want to begin by saying I stand before you solely as a messenger from The Lord sent to encourage you. These past few days have been very troubling for me and my family, and quite honestly, I didn't even want to speak today. But as the time drew near, I heard The Lord drop in my spirit the word 'distress', and I think that perfectly sums up how we're all feeling. Distressed.

"Distress is defined as being in pain... suffering... affliction. Our community is in pain. We're suffering and afflicted by the trials and tribulations of this life. And many of us are like David in Psalms Fifty-Five, saying 'Oh that I had wings like a dove! for then would I fly away and be at rest'. But I want to let you know that running from your trials and the hard times is not the way to handle it. We don't have to endure these burdens alone. We have a Helper who assists us. A Comforter who comforts us and wants us to lean on Him in our weakness so he can be our strength. A Deliverer who saves us in our direst moments.

"The sixth verse of Psalms eighteen says that 'In my distress I called upon The Lord, and cried unto my God: he heard my voice out of his temple, and my cry came before him even into his ears'. And if we skip down to verse seventeen, it tells us that 'He delivered me from my strong enemy, and from them which hated me: for they were too strong for me'. Verse nineteen tells us 'He delivered me, because he delighted in me'.

"If we take our definition and apply it to the verse, it now reads 'in my pain, in my suffering, in my affliction, I called upon The Lord, and cried unto my God'. And the Word of God says He heard me. He heard my cry of pain, He heard my cry of suffering, He heard my cry of affliction. And He delivered me from what caused me pain, and suffering, and affliction. He delivered me from the spirit of depression, from the spirit of anxiety, from the spirits of worry and shame. I can't save myself from those things. Only God can save me. And He does it because he delights in me. Because He desires me to have a spirit of power, love, and sound mind. So, I want to encourage you all to have hope and lean on The Lord in your time of need. Take the time to form a relationship with Him if you haven't already. Let him take the reins and rest in knowing that no matter what happens he has it all worked out. Let us pray."

After the town hall meeting ended, many of the townsfolk stood around socializing. Most conversations centered on Granddad Derrick's sermon or Mayor Perry's speech, but some focused on the family and its drama. Allison overheard such an exchange when she passed by Mrs. Tasha Lee and Mrs. Rachel Payne.

"I always knew it was something wrong with that family," gossiped Mrs. Lee. She was medium-brown like her daughter Danielle and had the same negative attitude too. Pushing a strand of hair from her face, she said, "No one in the world has it together THAT well."

"I knew something was off when they put the oldest boy out," responded Mrs. Payne, who looked like an older, less pretty version of her daughter Priscella. Her thin, arched black eyebrows raised as she said, "Because why would they put him out if everything was all good?"

"I heard they put him out because he was on drugs."

"I wouldn't be surprised considering who Marlin's best friend is. Marlin himself might be on drugs for all we know."

"If he is, it's got to be steroids."

"Right? But I heard they put the son out because he got someone pregnant."

"I believe it. The way the second son acts behind these girls he had to have learned it from someone. And who better than his older brother?"

"And they probably learned it from their uncle. Let's not forget about him having a whole baby at fourteen."

"Who you telling? And that boy of his will probably follow in his father's footsteps and get the little Brown girl pregnant too.

"I wouldn't be surprised. And they probably all learned it from the grandmother! Remember at the women's conference when she admitted she used to get down back in the day?"

"I sure do," said Mrs. Lee. "And they all sat up there in church at the revival looking down at us like everything was all good. The whole family is a mess! I'm glad Danielle is nothing like those kids."

"Right?" giggled Mrs. Lee. "My Priscella would never even dare to embarrass me like that. Every single one of those kids lack home training."

"The only ones who lack home training are you and your trifling daughters!" snapped Allison, tiring of the false accusations against her family. "Don't you have anything better to do than stand around and gossip about others?!"

"Well, I never!" declared Mrs. Lee.

"Come along, Allison," said Mrs. Harrison to her daughter. "I won't have you further disgrace us by engaging with charmless gossips."

"Further?" questioned Allison, following her mother. "When did I first disgrace us?"

"When you chose to wear such an unflattering dress to a public event."

"It's the only dress Nanna had that didn't look like a shirt on me."

"And what excuse do you have for your hair?" countered Mrs. Harrison, looking at the bun sticking out from the back of Allison's head. "You could've done something to it before we left."

"You're right!" exclaimed Allison sarcastically. "I should've dug through the ashes of the house and found a wig to put on, even if it was a little burnt. Why didn't I think of that before?"

"Why do you always have to argue with me, Allison?"

"Because you don't make sense! I'm trying to find my brother – your son might I add – and all you care about is my hair!"

"Because you should still be presentable. You don't have to look like you're going through a hard time just because you are!"

"Oh my goodness!"

"Ladies," chimed in Nanna Kiana, placing a hand on each of their backs to calm them down. "Let's not fight today. There's too much going on already."

"You talk to her, ma'am," sighed Mrs. Harrison. "I just can't deal with her today."

Mrs. Harrison walked away, leaving Allison alone with her grandmother.

"Queenie," sang Nanna Kiana as she eyed her granddaughter.

"She started it," said Allison, forming her lips into a pout. "It's like nothing I do is ever good enough for her!"

"Allow your mother some grace," encouraged Nanna Kiana. "She's under a lot of stress right now."

"And I'm not?" argued Allison. "All she cares about is what other people think of her!"

"Can you blame her? Her son goes missing and the first thing people do is talk about her like she's the reason why."

"Who cares what other people have to say?" said Allison frustratedly. "They don't even know us like that!"

"Your mother cares."

Allison dropped the subject. For as long as she could remember, her mother had always cared too much about what other people thought. And she had begun imposing her beliefs on Allison, trying to conform her to her idea of a proper lady.

The July sun beat down on Allison's head as she sized up her opponent. Derek may not have played on sports teams like the other Harrison men, but his acrobatic background made him more than able to beat her in street football. If Allison wanted to win against him, she needed a strategy.

"Queenie Harrison's got the ball and she's going for it!" said Grand-dad Derrick, mimicking a football game announcer as he watched from the porch. "She's running the ball! D-Money tries to tackle her, but she dodges him! She's at the fifteen! The ten! The five! TOUCHDOWN!"

Granddad Derrick ran off the porch and high-fived Allison.

"That's my girl!" he cheered. "Keep it up and you could be Creeke High's first female football player!"

"You think I could do that, Granddad?" asked nine-year-old Allison.

"Of course, you can," said Granddad Derrick. "You can do anything you put your mind to as long as it's in The Lord's will for your life."

"I can do anything I want?"

"Yes."

"Good," giggled Allison. "Because I don't want to play football."

"Okay," said Granddad Derrick. "There's other sports out there."

"I don't want to play sports at all."

"My heart," said Granddad Derrick as he clutched his chest. "You're breaking my heart."

Granddad Derrick tilted his head and stuck his tongue out the side of his mouth. With his eyes closed, he did not see Mrs. Harrison drive up the path. Allison watched as her mother walked up to her grandfather with a puzzled expression on her face.

"Mr. Harrison?" asked Mrs. Harrison, lowering the designer sunglasses on her face. "Are you alright?"

"I'm fine, Leya," said Granddad Derrick, straightening up. "Queenie broke my heart, that's all."

"I hope she didn't give you too much trouble," sighed Mrs. Harrison as she glared at Allison.

"I never have any trouble out of her," laughed Granddad Derrick. "Now, her brothers on the other hand..."

"What did Derik do?"

"Dee-Three's fine. I was actually referring to Matty and Cornbread. They're competitiveness is getting out of hand."

"I'll talk to them about it," said Mrs. Harrison. She looked her daughter over from head to toe and sucked her teeth. "Look at you. You're covered in dirt."

"A little dirt never hurt anyone, Leya," joked Granddad Derrick.

"Unless it's thrown on your name, of course."

"I see you're still one of the sharpest tools in the shed."

"Is Mrs. Kiana inside?"

"Yeah, she's here. Go on in."

Allison followed her mother into the house.

"Hello?" called Mrs. Harrison. "Mrs. Kiana?"

"I'm in here!" answered Nanna Kiana from the kitchen. When Allison and her mother arrived in the kitchen, Nanna Kiana hugged Mrs. Harrison. "My Soleil! Long time, no see!"

"I'm sorry," apologized Mrs. Harrison. "I've just been really busy with the salon lately and Marlin's trying to get his tech repair business going and..."

"You don't have to explain anything to me," said Nanna Kiana. "I'm glad to see you're both doing so well."

"Thank you."

"What brings you by?"

"I came to pick up the children."

"Do we have to go already?" whined seven-year-old Derik.

"Yes," said Mrs. Harrison. "Go put your shoes on."

"Okay," grumbled Derik, leaving the room.

"He was such a great help today," said Nanna Kiana gleefully. "We made chocolate-chip cookies. Would you like one?"

"No, thank you," declined Mrs. Harrison.

"Nanna!" yelled nine-year-old Derek as he ran into the kitchen. He almost collided with Mrs. Harrison and cried, "Whoa!"

"Derek, please watch where you're going!" fussed Mrs. Harrison. "You almost knocked me over!"

"Sorry Auntie Leya," apologized Derek. "Nanna, Granddad wants to know if the cookies are done yet."

"Yeah, they're done," said Nanna Kiana.

"Okay!" said Derek, running back outside to relay the message to his grandfather.

"Give these to my grandsons," said Nanna Kiana, putting some of the cookies in a plastic bag, and handing them to Mrs. Harrison.

"Yes ma'am," said Mrs. Harrison. "Derik were leaving! Come say goodbye to your grandmother!"

"Bye Nanna," said Allison and Derik when he returned.

"Bye bye!" said Nanna Kiana. "Be good for your mother!"

Once they were all in the car, Mrs. Harrison began unloading her complaints.

"How did you get so dirty?" she asked Allison.

"We were playing football," said Allison.

"Football," scoffed Mrs. Harrison. "Why can't you and your grandfather play something less dirty? Like chess! You love chess and it doesn't require you getting all dirty to play it!"

"Granddad doesn't like chess," said Allison. "He says it's too hard."

"All I want is for you to be a lady," griped Mrs. Harrison. "Is that too much to ask for?"

"Can't ladies play sports?"

"They can, but they should also be presentable. They shouldn't be walking around with dirt on their clothes and their hair sticking up all over the place. You don't see me walking around looking disheveled."

"Who cares?" complained Allison.

"I care," said Mrs. Harrison. "No child of mine is walking around this town looking unkempt so people can talk about me being a bad mother behind my back."

"That's all you care about," griped Allison.

"A good reputation is important to maintain, Allison," said Mrs. Harrison. "You'll understand when you're older. Just wait and see."

Allison was older, and she still did not understand. Mrs. Harrison had always complained about Allison not being ladylike, and Allison was tired of it. Her hair and nails were always done, she wore cute clothes and makeup, and she did her best to have good manners, good grades, and be respectful to everyone, but none of it was good enough for her mother. And it was not lost on her that her mother judged her on a different standard from her brothers. She expected less from them, and Allison thought it unfair. Seeing eye to eye with her mother was impossible because they and what they valued were too different.

The family reconvened at the grandparent's house after the town hall meeting. Mayor Bernard stopped by to give his thoughts on the whole situation, much to Allison's chagrin. She watched as he made a show of himself, pacing across the living room furiously while a frustrated harangue escaped his lips.

"How could this happen?" complained Mayor Bernard Perry. "Do you know how this will make me look?"

"How terrible," snorted Granddad Derrick. "My grandson is missing and all you care about is how this makes *you* look."

"With all due respect Pastor Harrison, Derik is my grandson too."

"When it suits you."

"How could you let this happen, Soleya?" asked Mayor Perry, ignoring Granddad Derrick's quip. Despite being the mayor and richest man in Creeke, Mayor Bernard was not well-regarded by the townspeople. He instead relied on his marital relation with the 'founding family of Creeke' to keep him socially relevant and silence any accusations of corruption. Because of this, he hoped to establish a kinship with Granddad Derrick and tried to avoid stepping on his toes whenever possible.

"I..." said Mrs. Harrison, unsure of how to answer.

"Why do I even bother asking you," muttered Mayor Perry under his breath. "All I wanted was one son and instead I get idiots for daughters."

"You should leave, Bernard," said Granddad Derrick as he stood up. "I'd much rather spend what time I have left in my life searching for my grandson than listen to you insult your daughter."

"I'm sorry to have offended you, Pastor," apologized Mayor Perry.

"I'll see you out," said Granddad Derrick.

After Mayor Bernard left, Mrs. Harrison fled to her room. Granddad Derrick returned to the living room with a new guest in tow: his best friend, Mr. Damian Parker. Mr. Damian looked like an old, nearly identical version of his son Terrence, but his usual demeanor was calmer and more lighthearted than his son's.

"What was he doing here?" asked Mr. Damian.

"What he always does when he comes around," answered Granddad Derrick. "Sowing discord and hoping I'd approve of it."

"One of these right under the chin would put an end to all that," said Mr. Damian, holding up a fist. He performed an uppercutting motion, saying, "Real quick. Just *UH!*"

"I wish," laughed Granddad Derrick. "But then your son would arrest me for knocking that viper's head clean off his shoulders."

"My goodness!" cried Aunt Nancy. "That's the first time he's laughed since I've been here!"

"Then it seems I've done some good," said Mr. Damian. "Shoot, you'd be doing Noah a favor. Bernard practically has his walking papers all ready to go if he makes even the slightest mistake with this case."

"No one in their right mind in this town would accept Terrence being fired as police chief," said Granddad Derrick. "He's been the most effective and most efficient chief in the history of this town. If Bernard didn't want him in charge, then he should've kept his pride in check and appointed a new chief instead of letting the town choose who they wanted."

"No one takes that clown seriously anyways," said Mr. Damian. "He's only still mayor because he runs unopposed. You should be the mayor of this town, not him. This town was literally founded by your family and you're more likeable than him. The way everyone responded to your sermon as opposed to his speech today is proof enough of that."

"Careful, Damian," warned Granddad Derrick. "That sermon was God's handiwork not mine, and it was meant to encourage the people, not wage a political war. Besides, my track record with leadership positions is not that great."

"You're at least a better leader than Bernard is," said Mr. Damian. "He should be ashamed of himself, standing up there playing a role like that. There weren't even any tears coming out of his eyes!"

"At least someone agrees with me," muttered Allison under her breath.

"Queenie, did you say something?" asked Granddad Derrick.

"I was just talking to myself," answered Allison. "Mr. Damian, could you tell us a story like you used to when we were kids before you leave? I think we could all use the distraction."

"I don't know if that would be appropriate," said Mr. Damian.

"It's alright, Damian," encouraged Nanna Kiana before slipping out the front door.

"I don't mind either," said Granddad Derrick. "You can even use my chair if you like."

"Okay then," said Mr. Damian with a grin. He sat in Granddad Derrick's great armchair and said, "Gather around and let Uncle Damian tell you a story."

The younger family members gathered around the great armchair to listen to the elderly man who would weave a tale for them.

"There once lived four young princes and one princess who were burdened down with the trials of life," began Mr. Damian.

"What have I done?" mumbled Allison.

"Don't count me out yet, Queenie," said Mr. Damian. "Now, one of the young princes disappeared and his family and their whole village was distraught. The younger family members desperately wanted to find him and therefore asked the village elders for advice on what they could do. One of the elders spoke up and said, 'You must take up your burdens'."

"What burdens?" questioned Derek.

"Each one had a burden they had to contend with," answered Mr. Damian. "The two eldest brothers struggled with honoring not only the commitments they'd made but also their brotherhood."

Deidrick looked at the wall.

"Their sister struggled in her relationship with her parents, unwilling to grasp their view on things."

Allison blushed.

"And their cousin had his own struggles that only he knew about."

Derek avoided Mr. Damian's gaze.

"You might be asking, 'Mr. Damian, what did these burdens have to do with finding the missing prince?'," said Mr. Damian. "Well, my young people, it had everything to do with it. In order to find the missing prince, the others would have to cooperate and work together as a family. But they couldn't do that if the family was broken. And they certainly couldn't help anyone else if they themselves needed help. The missing prince would need to return to a strong and loving family, and that could only happen if the others take up their burdens and came to terms with them."

"That's a nice story, Mr. Damian," said Deidrick, standing up. "But that's all it is: a story."

"Oh well," said Mr. Damian. "Can't please everybody."

Deidrick walked away to his room.

"Do you really believe what you told us, Mr. Damian?" asked Derek.

"I do," said Mr. Damian. "If the others put their differences aside and worked together, I truly believe they'd stand a good chance of helping the missing prince when he returns."

Mr. Damian looked at his watch.

"I should get going," he said, standing up. "It's getting late."

"Thanks for coming, Damian," said Granddad Derrick.

"You know I've always got you," said Mr. Damian, engulfing his friend in a hug. "I'll call later to check up on you."

"Okay."

"And Derrick?"

"Yeah?"

Mr. Damian whispered something in Granddad Derrick's ear and left. What he said, Allison did not know. All she knew was that whatever it was, it was enough to cause her grandfather to shed a few more silent tears.

-

Chapter Six: Matthias

Matthias had done a good job avoiding his parents. He had rarely seen them in eight years, and when he did have to see them, he made sure to stay as far from them as possible. But as he stood on his grandmother's porch, he wondered how long he could avoid them. His mother was in the house, and Matthias was unsure whether he had enough self-control yet to face her. Therefore, he stood on the porch with Nanna Kiana, wanting to quickly get through their conversation and leave.

"Alright Nanna," said Matthias. "Lay it on me."

"What?" said Nanna Kiana confusedly.

"What did you want to talk about?"

"I wanted to talk about Dee-Three. I saw him the day he disappeared."

"You did?"

"Yes," said Nanna Kiana. "I went to your parents' around five-thirty that evening and he was dressed like he was going out. He wasn't expecting to see me, and I smelled... I smelled cigarettes on him when I went over there."

"Cigarettes?" said Matthias, crinkling his eyebrows. "He doesn't smoke."

"That's why I wanted to talk to you," said Nanna Kiana. "Matthias, tell me the truth. Did you give your brother cigarettes?"

"Of course not!" cried Matthias. "I'd never do something like that, Nanna!"

"I didn't want to accuse you," said Nanna Kiana. "But I know what I smelled and you're the only one I know who... do you know anyone else who would give them to him? Because I'm almost positive that's what caused the fire since most of the damage was to his room."

Matthias only knew one person who could have given Derik a cigarette: the same person who gave them to Matthias when he himself was a teenager.

"It's alright if you don't," sighed Nanna Kiana. "Thank you for putting up with an old woman's suspicions."

"Anytime," said Matthias half-distractedly.

"And Matty?"

"Ma'am?"

"Please don't tell your grandfather about this," said Nanna Kiana. "He's already worked up as it is, and I don't want to add onto it."

"Sure thing."

Matthias's gut told him he knew the culprit's identity. As he left the house, Matthias looked at the patch on his arm and grimaced. He was fourteen when he first started smoking cigarettes. Fourteen and sitting in his room at his parent's house on a hot day, allowing the culprit to influence him.

"Are you sure we won't get in trouble for this?" asked fourteen-year-old Matthias.

"Yeah, as long as you keep quiet," said the culprit with a grin. Those charming brown eyes glowed amber as a flame burst from the lighter. "Hold the cigarette between your lips and I'll show you how to light it."

Matthias obeyed and positioned the tobacco stick in his mouth. He had always seen people smoke to deal with their problems, and Matthias had many problems. Trying to uphold the perfect family image took a toll on him, and he needed a way to cope. So, he inhaled the cigarette smoke and quickly realized how unprepared he was for it.

"Ack!" coughed Matthias.

"You'll get used to it," said the culprit.

It had started with cigarettes and soon festered into a life of reck-lessness that Matthias still struggled with. He was not the culprit's last victim either. That silver tongue had charmed Deidrick into the same lifestyle, had enthralled Allison into getting a tattoo at sixteen, and might have started in on Derik before his disappearance. And it angered Matthias. As he arrived home, he found the culprit sitting on the couch with the thing that started it all tucked between his medium-brown fingers.

"Cell," said Matthias, narrowing his eyes at his older cousin. "I know you gave Dee-Three a cigarette."

"And?" answered Marcellus nonchalantly. "How was I supposed to know he'd burn the house down with it?"

"Why'd you give it to him?"

"To calm him down. He was nervous about going to meet this person and–!"

"What person?"

"Someone he'd been talking to online. I assumed it was a girl. They were meeting at a sandwich shop in the city, so I agreed to take him and scope out the scene with him."

"You just took him out there and left him?" accused Matthias.

"Of course not," argued Marcellus. "Whoever he was meeting wasn't there when we got there, so I dropped hm off and told him I'd swing back around when he was done. When I didn't hear from him, I went back, and he was gone."

"What do you mean he was gone?"

"Just what I said. He was gone. I assumed he took off with his little girlfriend and let him do him."

"He's sixteen!" cried Matthias in disbelief. "Why would you assume that?"

"I mean, when you think about the stuff we did at sixteen..."

"Dee-Three isn't like us! He wouldn't even consider doing half the stuff we did at his age!"

"You sure about that?"

"Do you know the girl's name?" asked Matthias annoyedly, ignoring Marcellus's insinuations.

"No. Like I said I just assumed it was a girl."

"So, you've known this whole time about this and just decided to lay low while my brother might be out there fighting for his life right now?"

"Man, you know it isn't like that, Playboy," said Marcellus defensively. "I just can't be the main suspect in a missing persons case."

"What did you tell the police then when they questioned you about him?"

"I told them that he had gone on a date, and I didn't know anything other than that."

"And conveniently left out the fact that you were his ride to the date," griped Matthias. He had an epiphany and accusingly exclaimed, "Is that why you got your car detailed all of a sudden?! To erase the evidence that he'd been in your car?!"

"Why are you yelling at me like I'm the one to blame?"

"Because you are the one to blame! You're possibly the last one to see him alive and you said nothing!"

"Look, I told you everything I know."

"The only thing keeping you safe right now is the fact that you're my cousin," declared Matthias. "But Dee-Three better turn up alive or you'll be the first person I come after."

Matthias could not believe what his cousin had done, and yet he was not surprised by it. When Matthias was younger, Marcellus was the coolest guy he knew because he did what he wanted without consequence. And after Matthias came to live with his Aunt Soriah and Uncle Quincy, Marcellus included Matthias in all his adventures. But as an adult, the admiration of his older cousin had faded, leaving behind disappointment with the way Marcellus conducted himself.

Learning that Marcellus had information about Derik and kept it to himself angered Matthias. He decided it was in both of their best interests that he temporarily lay his head elsewhere. Avoiding his parents sometimes threw hitches into his life as he could not go to his Uncle Malcolm's or his grandparent's homes. Instead, he found himself on Alexander's doorstep, hoping that he could stay there for the time being.

"Hey Matt," said Mr. Jeremy-Micah Brown, Alexander's father, when he answered the door.

"Hey," said Matthias. "Can I stay on your couch tonight?"

"Have a fight at home or something?"

"Something like that."

"Well, you know my couch is always open whenever you need it but let me check with the Missus first to make sure," said Mr. Jeremy-Micah. He turned his head inward and yelled, "Hey Franny! Come here real quick!"

"What is it?" called Mrs. Francine Brown.

"Come here!"

"I can't right now!"

"Why not?!"

"Jeremy-Micah, what do you want?!"

"I want you to come here!"

Matthias heard footsteps stomp through the house as Mrs. Francine walked to the front door. He watched as Mr. Jeremy-Micah's face went from a normal one to one of horror.

"Franny, what is on your face?!"

"It's a beauty mask," answered Mrs. Francine, staying out of sight. Matthias imagined Mrs. Francine's dark-brown face covered in some green or white goop and stifled a chuckle. "Now what do you want?"

"Do you mind if Matt crashes on the couch tonight?"

"You made me come all the way out here to ask that?"

"I didn't know you were beautifying yourself. Not that you need it."

"Why can't he sleep in the guest room? That's what it's for."

"He asked for the couch."

"He's sleeping in the guest room and that's final. Now if you'll excuse me..."

"Sorry," said Mr. Jeremy-Micah when Mrs. Francine left. "You'll have to sleep in the guest room."

"That's fine," said Matthias. "Thanks."

"No problem."

Creeke mayor holds town hall meeting, addresses concerns
by Arnold Green, Creeke Courier

Creeke mayor Bernard Perry held a town hall meeting on Monday.

Mayor Perry addressed community concerns about missing teenager, Derik Harrison. Perry stated during the meeting he planned to do "all he could" to find Harrison. Many citizens are in support of Perry and are hopeful he will succeed at finding Harrison.

"We miss our grandson very much," the mayor's wife, Sophia Perry said in a statement to the Creeke Courier. "We fully support Chief Parker and local law enforcements efforts to find him and we're praying that we'll soon have answers about what happened to Derik."

Anyone with information regarding Derik Harrison is asked to contact Creeke police immediately.

"It's exactly what he wanted," griped Matthias, throwing the newspaper aside. "He's managed to spin this whole thing for his benefit!"

"How do you know he's not serious?" asked Alexander, picking the newspaper up and placing it neatly on the kitchen table.

"I can show you a grandfather who's actually worried if you want," said Matthias. "This man is only doing this to protect his precious public image."

"If this has you riled up, I can't imagine how you'll feel when I tell you what the mayor has planned for today," said Alexander. "He's gathering up a group of volunteers to go searching for Derik outside of Creeke."

"It's brilliant!" complained Matthias. "First, he garners public sympathy. Then he makes himself look like he's doing all he can. And then when he comes back unsuccessful, he'll spin it again to convince people in some way to support his 'efforts' by giving him money. At this point, I wouldn't be surprised if he's holding Dee-Three somewhere until the time is right and plans to bring him back and keep the money."

"Do you really think he'd do that?"

"I put nothing past him," said Matthias. "He's a hustler."

"So are you."

"I hustle with integrity," said Matthias, going to the refrigerator. He opened it and cried, "Where's the beer?!"

"I told Dad to throw it out. It tempted me every time I opened the fridge."

"Alex!"

"He didn't drink it anyways," said Alexander. "It was only in there for guests who wanted it."

"I'm a guest and I wanted it!"

"Oh well," said Alexander. "You didn't need it anyways."

"You and your morals," complained Matthias.

"My morals keep us out of trouble," said Alexander. "The last thing you need is to return to old bad habits."

"Man, why can't you let me slide every once and a while?"

"Because that's not what friends do," said Alexander. "We said we were going to do better. So, we're going to do better."

Matthias grumbled under his breath as he went to finish his breakfast. It seemed like the weight of the world was on his shoulders, and he had no way to cope with the strain. He could not smoke, he could not drink, he could not distract himself with pleasure. Every coping mechanism Matthias had learned under Marcellus's tutelage had been swept away by Alexander's insistence on living right. And for the first time in his life, Matthias questioned if living right was worth the pain and discomfort that came with it.

Chapter Seven: Deidrick

With Nisha giving him the cold shoulder over Sharon, Deidrick found himself needing something fresh and new. Late that Tuesday afternoon, he accompanied Nanna Kiana to the grocery store. He was not looking for anything serious, just someone to have fun with. And he found it standing behind the counter at Brewer's. The beautifully chocolate twenty-one-year-old Mikayla Brewer sat at the cash register, reading a magazine. Deidrick eagerly settled across from her to pay her some attention.

"Hey Beautiful," said Deidrick.

"Oh boy," chuckled Mikayla. "Deidrick, what you want?"

"How's my favorite salesgirl today?"

"Your favorite salesgirl?" laughed Mikayla. "Does your girlfriend know you have a favorite salesgirl?"

"What girlfriend?"

"Now Deidrick."

"I'm serious. What girlfriend?"

"Aren't you seeing someone right now?"

"I see a lot of people every day."

"Just terrible."

"What? I'm a single man."

"A single man that's for everybody."

"Not everybody," corrected Deidrick. "Just the pretty ones."

"I must be ugly then because you certainly aren't for me," said Mikayla. "You are for the community."

"You're not my type anyways," grumbled Deidrick.

"Shh!" shushed Mikayla, putting a finger up. "Do you hear that?"

"You mean that group of girls yelling?" said Deidrick. "Yeah, I hear them."

"It's always something!" complained Mikayla, coming from behind the counter. Deidrick followed her through the maze of aisles to the makeup aisle where the commotion came from. Priscella stood arguing with Danielle and the two Garza sisters, Mariana and Mariella. A few customers witnessed the spectacle, including Deidrick, who stood beside Diana and Althea.

"I'm not stealing from these people's store!" declared Priscella. "Just because you can't afford your stuff doesn't mean I can't afford mine!"

"Shhh!" said Mariana, noticing the new arrivals to the aisle.

"It's too late to be shushing each other now," said Mikayla, approaching the girls. "Show me your purses, ladies."

Priscella obeyed and opened her purse for Mikayla to search.

"Okay Prissy, you're all clear," said Mikayla. "Next."

"I'm not showing you anything," argued Danielle. "You don't have any right to search our stuff!"

"Okay ma'am," said Mikayla. "If you would like for me to call Creeke PD and have them come out here, I can do that."

"Dani!" whispered Mariana. "If she calls the police on us, Uncle Terrence might show up!"

"So?" said Danielle. "I'm not worried about *Cousin* Terrence."

"You might not be, but we are!" replied Mariella. "He'll make sure we get in trouble!"

"You guys are so scary," complained Danielle.

"Have we reached a decision, ladies?" asked Mikayla.

Danielle and the Garza sisters begrudgingly opened their purses. As Mikayla searched through them, she removed stolen items from the bags.

"I see we had some sticky fingers in the makeup aisle," stated Mikayla. "I'm going to have to ask you ladies to leave."

"That's fine!" said Danielle. "I didn't want to shop here anyways! Let's go girls!"

The girls stopped to glare at Priscella.

"You can find your own ride home," declared Danielle. "And some new friends too!"

The three girls shuffled through the crowd and out of the store.

"Now, they ought to be ashamed of themselves," said Diana. "You should've called their parents, Miki."

"What for?" sighed Mikayla. "Their parents won't do anything but give them a slap on the wrist anyways. And they might not even do that!"

"It's alright, baby," said Deidrick, patting Mikayla's back. "It's nothing to get all worked up over."

"Oh, leave me alone, Deidrick!" huffed Mikayla, shoving Deidrick's hand away. "Go flirt with someone else!"

"Someone's touchy," said Deidrick as Mikayla walked away.

"Hold on now," said Diana. "That's my future sister-in-law you're talking about."

"Don't you think you're rushing things, Diana?" said Deidrick. "You and Ralphie just started dating."

"No," replied Diana. "Ralphie and I are getting married one day. I can feel it."

"You're eighteen," said Deidrick. "Don't you think you should live your life a little first?"

"No offense Deidrick, but I don't want to hop between guys like you hop between girls," said Diana. "Ralphie is serious about me, and I'm not jeopardizing that."

"It's not my fault I like to live life to the fullest," said Deidrick.

"Well, you do that," said Diana. "You got everything, Thea?"

"Huh?" said Althea, looking up from her book.

"You and these books," huffed Diana. "Did you even get what you were supposed to get while you're sitting up here reading?"

"I was waiting on you to finish looking at the nail polish."

"Oh my–!" griped Diana.

The sisters walked away, leaving Deidrick by himself. He went in search of Nanna Kiana. Aisle after aisle passed by until he saw his favorite pair of honey-colored legs in the fruit aisle. Twenty-seven-year-old Beverly looked at different brands of canned fruit, determining which one she wanted. She had been Deidrick's crush since he was a boy, and he could remember always trying to catch a glimpse of her beauty from as early as thirteen.

He sat at the living room window, staring at her. She was standing at her mailbox, looking over the envelopes that had been placed inside. The summer heat had caused her to dress in a way that made Deidrick's view enjoyable. His eyes pored over her nineteen-year-old body, drinking in every inch of her beauty.

"What are you looking at?" asked fourteen-year-old Matthias, standing next to him.

"Nothing," said Deidrick, blushing.

"Nothing huh?" said Matthias, smirking. "You sure you weren't checking out Beverly?"

"Man, I don't blame you, Cornbread," added seventeen-year-old Marcellus, licking his lips. "Beverly is bad. I wouldn't mind getting a piece of that myself."

"Why don't you go talk to her then, Cell?" asked Matthias.

"I don't feel like it."

"She's out of your league anyways."

"Nah," said Marcellus. "No girl is out of my league. I can bag any girl I want when I want."

"You can?" asked Deidrick.

"Of course, I can," declared Marcellus. His phone began to ring. "Here goes one of my girls now."

"One of them?" repeated Matthias.

"What's up, baby girl?" said Marcellus, placing the call on speakerphone.

"Cell where are you?" asked the girl.

"Where I'm at!" snapped Marcellus. "What do you need to know for?"

"Dang, you don't have to be mean," said the girl. "I'm just trying to see what you're up to."

"Why?"

"Because I want you to come over."

"I'll think about it," barked Marcellus, before hanging up the phone.

"Why'd you talk to her like that?" asked Deidrick. "Don't you like her?"

"Only when she sneaks me in her mama's house," joked Marcellus.

"But you just said she was your girl," said Deidrick.

"She's ONE of my girls," corrected Marcellus. "But I'm a single man."

"How does that work?"

"Simple," said Marcellus. "I get what I want and go. And when one of them doesn't give me what I want, I get it elsewhere. And when they start missing Cell and want to act right, I come back around."

"Man, you're a trip," laughed Matthias.

"I'm just being honest," said Marcellus. "When it comes to dealing with girls, you always make sure you're the one in control. You've always got to be three steps ahead of any girl you deal with. Because if not, they'll play you like a fool."

"Sounds like you're speaking from personal experience," teased Matthias.

"Nah," said Marcellus. "Ain't no girl smart enough to fool Cell. Every girl I've been with has given me sweet love and made me a man. Those were the best moments of my life."

"I want to become a man too," said Deidrick.

"I can make it happen if you want," said Marcellus. "Just say the word and I'll set it up."

The memory left Deidrick's eyes, a small smile on his face. His moment came at sixteen, and Marcellus had been right about it being the best moment of his life. Since then, he had a craving that he filled wherever he could. Whether the chosen girl was single or taken did not matter to him. All that mattered was that she gave him what he needed. But Nisha was different.

"I'm not doing anything until I'm married," she had declared on one of their dates when the topic had come up. Nisha held up her hand and wriggled her ring finger. "A ring is required for this lady."

So, Deidrick intended to wait her out. Nisha was a challenge to him, and he would do whatever it took to get what he wanted, even if it meant promising her a relationship. But as time passed, Deidrick became comfortable with Nisha, and he began wondering what a life with her would be like. And she helped his imaginings by demonstrating how much she cared for him and would hold him down. She did almost everything he wanted his girl to do and yet, no matter how much she asked and no matter how much he imagined, he just could not follow through. The thought of giving up his freedom scared him. There were too many beautiful women in the world to confine himself to only one forever.

He glanced again to get another peek at Beverly. But instead of finding her, he found one of the Ms. Nelsons, the one not engaged to Mr. Brown, struggling to reach a can on the top shelf. She was attractive to Deidrick too, but she had too much attitude for his tastes. He considered helping her, but Mr. Bud Vaughn beat him to it.

"Hey Greta," said Mr. Bud. His curly red hair was cut short, and his bronze face was devoid of facial hair. Curiosity glinted in his green eyes as he watched Ms. Greta, his physique towering over hers.

"Hi," said Ms. Greta, still straining to reach her item. She did not seem to notice who was talking to her.

"Here, let me get that for you," said Mr. Bud. He reached over her and pulled the can into her hand.

"Oh," said Ms. Greta, looking up to see who her helper was. Her eyes focused on his face, and realizing how close Mr. Bud was to her, she blushed and looked down. "*Oh.*"

"Is everything alright?"

"Ye...yeah," said Ms. Greta. "I didn't realize it was you. Th... thanks Bud..."

"No problem."

"So, were you here because of those girls?"

"No, just shopping," said Mr. Bud. "Boss doesn't let me do anything outside the station."

"Sounds about right," said Ms. Greta. "He's a control freak just like his brother."

"Yeah, but it's not a big deal to me."

"Plan on baking something?" asked Ms. Greta as she looked in his basket.

"Yeah. I was thinking lemon-frosted cookies."

"You'll have to let me try some."

"Only if you help me bake them. Jana told me you're a great baker."

"I only baked like one cake that I shared with her."

"She really liked it. She's always telling me stuff about you."

"She is?!" exclaimed Ms. Greta, her cheeks turning red.

"Well, yeah. She really likes you and your sister."

"Oh," laughed Ms. Greta nervously.

It was clear to Deidrick that she crushed on Mr. Bud, but he did not think the latter could tell. The pair walked away, still talking. Deidrick resumed his search for his grandmother and found her in one of the food aisles.

"There you are, Nanna," said Deidrick. "Did you hear that commotion back there?"

"I heard that and more," said Nanna Kiana. "Do you mind if I tell you a story about my younger days?"

"Go ahead."

"When I was sixteen, I liked this older boy and I thought he liked me too," said Nanna Kiana. "He kept telling me he wanted to see just how much I liked him, and I liked him enough to let him sneak me into his mother's house one night. I thought I was so cool and mature, but by that next day, the whole school knew every detail about our night together. Everyone had labeled me as 'easy'."

"Nanna why are you telling me this in the middle of the grocery store?" asked Deidrick.

"Because you need to hear this while it's still on my mind," said Nanna Kiana. "Now, where was I?"

"You were easy."

"That's right," said Nanna Kiana. "I was easy, and that older boy didn't pay me any mind anymore. The only boys I attracted after him were guys who wanted my body and nothing else. After a while, I started to believe I really was easy and so I got with guy after guy, telling myself that these were the only men who would ever value me."

"Nanna, I already know all this about you," said Deidrick. "You were living life."

"I was living life, but it wasn't the right one," said Nanna Kiana. "Your grandfather was the first man who didn't try to get with me physically. He was so naive about those types of things back then, and the more I fell in love with him, the longer I wanted to keep him in the dark. He was the first man I'd truly loved in a long time, and I was scared that he would leave me if he knew the truth about me. I was so ashamed of myself that I couldn't work up the nerve to tell him. But he found out anyways. When your grandfather confronted me about it, I just knew it was over. I just knew he wouldn't have someone that was 'used' and 'unpure'. But I was wrong. He not only told me he didn't care, but that he loved me to the point of wanting to marry me. But most men aren't like your grandfather. They wouldn't accept a girl they deem as 'used'."

Deidrick did not respond, but he silently agreed with her. He knew that he personally would not want to settle down with a girl who had been with other guys. That was why Nisha was special to him. She was saving herself all for him.

"Cornbread, do you understand why I've told you my story?" asked Nanna Kiana as she stopped walking to look at her grandson.

"Not really."

"Deidrick, I'm afraid I have to agree with Mikayla about you being 'for everybody' as she put it."

"You heard that?" laughed Deidrick.

"I did, and I don't find it funny," revealed Nanna Kiana. "Deidrick, when I look at you, I don't see a man who would make the decision your grandfather made. You behave like those guys from my past. Lying and deceiving, and not caring about the pain you leave behind when you've gotten what you were after."

"Who have I hurt?"

"Nisha," said Nanna Kiana. "You've given her the expectation that you will be together, but really you're off doing your thing with no intention of being with her."

"Nanna, I–!"

"Don't bother trying to hide it," said Nanna Kiana. "I'm old, not dumb."

"I'm not ready for a relationship yet."

"In my experience, when a man says that but he's steady doing relationship things, what he really means is he's just waiting until he gets to the girl he really wants to be with."

"Dang Nanna," said Deidrick. "You make me seem like a bad guy."

"Because I want you to do better and stop living in sin," said Nanna Kiana. "I can't force you to do right, but I can hope that what I've told you will cause you to think about what you're doing. Especially before someone seriously gets hurt. Sooner or later, you'll have to decide what's more important to you."

"Well, when that time comes, I'm sure I'll make the right decision."

"I'm not so sure," said Nanna Kiana.

"Mrs. Kiana! Deidrick!" cried Mikayla. She ran toward them, waving a newspaper frantically.

"What is it dear?" asked Nanna Kiana.

"Ralphie just dropped these off!" exhaled Mikayla. "Fresh off the press! Look!"

Mikayla handed the newspaper to Nanna Kiana, and she and Deidrick looked over the front page.

Surveillance video shows 16-year-old leave sandwich shop, enter car

by Ralph Brewer

New details emerged Monday in the search for a missing 16-year-old.

Surveillance footage shows Derik Harrison leaving a city sandwich shop around 7:30 pm. Harrison then got into a black sports car that left the parking lot heading north.

Harrison is 5 feet 6 inches tall, is dark-brown, and has black shoulder-length curly hair. Surveillance footage from inside the restaurant showed him wearing a black coat, red polo, black jeans, black and red sneakers, and a necklace with a black circular accessory. Anyone with information regarding Harrison's location is urged to contact local law enforcement immediately.

"Lord, have mercy," gasped Nanna Kiana. "Have these already gone out?"

"To my knowledge," answered Mikayla.

"We've got to get home," said Nanna Kiana, handing the newspaper back to Mikayla. "Come on, Cornbread."

"What about the groceries?" asked Deidrick.

"I'm not worried about that right now! Let's go!"

"I'll hold them for her," reassured Mikayla. "Go on."

"Thanks," said Deidrick.

Nanna Kiana sped up the road, just barely obeying the traffic laws. Reading the paper had undoubtedly focused her on Granddad Derrick. His whole demeanor had been off since Derik disappeared, and Deidrick knew his grandmother worried he might go and do something without thinking first. When the pair arrived home, Aunt Nancy and Aunt Paulette stood in the living room arguing with each other.

"We have to go out there and search for him!" said Aunt Nancy.

"We need to wait and see what Danette says first!" argued Aunt Paulette.

"Why? All she'll do is agree with me and we're wasting time!"

"You don't know that!"

Aunt Nancy was the first to see Nanna Kiana. She grabbed the newspaper off the table and rushed over to her.

"Danette, did you see the paper?" asked Aunt Nancy.

"Nancy, let the girl get all the way in the house first," said Aunt Paulette.

"Paulette, will you be quiet? You are not my mother."

"Who do you think you're talking to?!"

"You!"

"Both of you, QUIET!" hollered Nanna Kiana. Her sisters quieted and looked at her. "Where's my husband?"

"In his study," said Aunt Nancy.

"Has he seen the paper?"

"I think but I'm not sure," said Aunt Paulette.

"Okay," said Nanna Kiana. "I'm going to go check on him. And both of you, please stop arguing. Nobody wants to hear all that."

Nanna Kiana left for the study. While his aunts occupied themselves, Deidrick decided to take action. Mr. Damian's words replayed in his head as he thought about what he could do to find his brother. If Mr. Damian was right, then he would need the help of his other brother. He would need to work with Matthias. Deidrick drove to the Campbell residence and found Marcellus standing alone outside with a cigarette.

"Where's Matthias?" asked Deidrick.

"Don't know," said Marcellus. "He stormed out of here yesterday and I haven't seen him since."

"What happened?"

"He got mad at me over something stupid," explained Marcellus. "He'll probably be back when he cools down."

"I need to find him now."

"I don't know what to tell you," said Marcellus. "He might be down at the court. I know he used to go there a lot when he got pissed about stuff."

Deidrick followed Marcellus's suggestion and went to the park's basketball court. There he found the Parker brothers, Terrence Jr. and Michael, having a one-on-one match.

"Hey!" called Deidrick.

"Hey!" answered nineteen-year-old Michael. "You trying to join?"

"Not today," said Deidrick. "Have either of you seen Matthias?"

"He's at Uncle Mikey's," said twenty-two-year-old Terrence Jr.

"Don't go over there starting trouble, Deidrick," warned Michael. "We may be cool, but my family comes first."

"It's nothing like that," said Deidrick. "I just need to talk to him."

"Alright," said Michael skeptically.

"But if something does go down, call me so I can come watch," joked Terrence Jr.

"Junior, shut up," griped Michael. "Always instigating."

"I'm just saying," said Terrence Jr. "Deidrick versus Matt is one of those pay-per-view type of matchups. Like Dad and Uncle Torrey levels of going at it. You never leave disappointed."

"You're just as bad as Mariana and Mariella," said Michael. "Always starting stuff."

"Nah, I'm not as bad as those two. I just watch what's already going on. Those two actually start trouble."

"All three of you are troublemakers in my eyes," muttered Michael. "Did you need anything else, Deidrick?"

"No, that's it," said Deidrick. "Thanks."

"No problem," said Terrence Jr.

Deidrick went to Alexander's house and knocked on the front door. Alexander opened the door and looked at Deidrick with surprise upon seeing it was him.

"I need to see Matthias," said Deidrick.

"Are you planning on fighting with him?" asked Alexander.

"No."

"Then come in."

Alexander led Deidrick to the guest room where Matthias was staying. A newspaper sat in his hand, showing the same front page that had caused mayhem at home. When Matthias saw Deidrick, he scowled.

"Matt, you've got a visitor," said Alexander. He left the room, adding over his shoulder, "Please don't fight."

"What do you want?" asked Matthias.

"I need to talk to you about Dee-Three."

"What about him?"

"I've been thinking about how Mr. Damian told me that we have to work together if we want to find Dee-Three."

"And?"

"And I want my brother back and I know you do to. We don't have to be friends, but if we have to work together to do this, then I say we be grown men about it and do what we have to do."

Matthias closed his eyes as if he were contemplating Deidrick's proposal. Then he looked at the newspaper again, inhaled, exhaled, and then looked back at Deidrick.

"I'm only agreeing to this for Dee-Three's sake," said Matthias. "If it's not about him, then don't speak to me."

"Fine by me," said Deidrick. "That news article says he was last seen at this sandwich shop in the city. I say we start there."

"Nah," said Matthias sarcastically. "Why didn't I think of that?"

Deidrick let out a quiet sigh as he realized working with Matthias would not be easy. The unresolved issues between them made it barely possible for them to be around each other. But finding Derik was more important to them so Deidrick bore with it. An hour later, they were on the road to stay with James in the city. Matthias would stay indefinitely, while Deidrick would only stay the night. They would begin their search the next day.

-

Chapter Eight: Derek

He had the dream again. Stood amidst the flames of the house, watching as they licked away the walls to reveal the stormy sky above. But it was not him standing in the mirror crying in agony. It was the older one, then himself, then the youngest. All of them morphing into each other, writhing until the mirror broke. The flames stretched forth their gnarled fingers from the shattered glass and rooted themselves in and around him. Their painful touch forced him to his knees. Forced him to watch as the fire tore through the town, claiming home after home, burning his beloved town to ashes.

"How long?!" he cried. "How long will this last?!"

Then the flames ceased. Their pain no longer tortured him, replaced with a sense of peace. Derek awoke from the dream. It stormed outside, and his hand was joined to someone else's. Starting at that hand, he moved his eyes up the arm to the body that owned it. Uncle Marlin knelt beside his bed, his face buried in Derek's covers while faint words escaped his lips. He squeezed Derek's hand, and Derek did not know what to make of it. Closing his eyes, he allowed himself to be carried off into another dream. Later that morning, he visited Adrianna at her father's house. They whispered together on the porch while her father sat just beyond the screened window playing his piano.

"I think...," whispered Derek. "I think my uncle was praying over me when I was sleeping."

Mr. Torrance Brown snorted. Derek could only see his mouth as the upper half of his caramel-colored face was obscured by the shadow of the porch.

"Dad," chastised Adrianna through the window. "Are you eavesdropping?"

"No," uttered Mr. Torrance without missing a note. "Why should I care about what Marlin was doing?"

"It's not nice to eavesdrop, Dad."

"I already told you I wasn't!" snapped Mr. Torrance, cutting his piano playing short. "And even if I was, this is my house and I'll do as I please. If you don't like it, that's too bad."

"You won't let us come inside, and I don't like the idea of you sitting here listening to our private conversation."

"There are no boyfriends or girlfriends allowed in the house unless I say otherwise," said Mr. Torrance. "That's the rule and you know it. If you don't like it, once again, that's too bad."

"But why?"

"Because I said so."

"But Dad–!"

Mr. Torrance's mouth became gritted. Adrianna turned her head away and released a quiet, frustrated breath.

"That's what I thought," said Mr. Torrance, resuming his piano playing.

"I think I'll go now," said Derek.

"Alright," sighed Adrianna. She hugged Derek and whispered in his ear, "I'm sorry about him."

"It's fine," said Derek. He knew Mr. Torrance's abrasiveness was fueled by regret. Anytime the man looked at Derek, he did not see the boy dating his daughter but the lingering phantom of the now-missing student he had berated in September. Derek knew this and reassured Adrianna that he had no hard feelings against her father by saying with a smile, "I'll see you later, okay?"

"Okay."

"Goodbye sir," said Derek.

"Bye," muttered Mr. Torrance.

By the afternoon, Derek had traded the Brown's porch for his grandfather's, sitting with him while they watched his grandmother and aunts rock in a chair swing under one of the trees. Derek had explained his dream to his grandfather, leaving out the part that happened when he woke up.

"This is the same dream you had back in the fall?" asked Granddad Derrick.

"Yes sir," said Derek. "But this time I wasn't just me. I was me, you, and Dee-Three. I don't understand it, Granddad."

"Sometimes, The Lord gives us dreams to tell us about ourselves," explained Granddad Derrick. "And sometimes he gives them to us so we can intercede for others. And sometimes their attacks of the enemy. Just ask him and he'll tell you what it means."

"Is that what you did when you had your nightmares?"

"Several times," said Granddad Derrick. "And it took decades before I got an answer I understood."

"Decades?"

"It could take your whole life to get an answer to that dream, Derek," said Granddad Derrick. "Or you could get one tonight. It's all in The Lord's timing. All I can tell you is to keep your cousin and your family in prayer."

"But it wasn't just the house that caught fire," said Derek. "It was the whole town. Everything was burning."

"That's because Creeke is one big family," said Granddad Derrick. "Everyone here is connected in some way and when one of us is hurt, all of us are affected. Like in my dream. The rot didn't just stay on the tree I touched. It spread everywhere. Fire is the same way, spreading and consuming everything in its path."

He frowned. Nanna Kiana was talking to Mrs. Marianne Brown, who had just arrived.

"And it's the same with pain too," continued Granddad Derrick. "You hurt one person and that pain you caused spreads to other people too."

Mrs. Marianne came onto the porch and stood before Granddad Derrick.

"Hey stranger," said Granddad Derrick. "Haven't seen you in a while."

"You know how it is," said Mrs. Marianne. She looked at Derek and said, "Hello."

"Hello."

"I brought you a cherry pie," said Mrs. Marianne, holding out a wrapped-up pie to Granddad Derrick. "I know it's not what you want right now but–!"

"Thank you," said Granddad Derrick, accepting the pie.

"I'm sorry I didn't come around sooner. I just figured..."

"You don't have to explain anything to me," said Granddad Derrick. "How is he?"

"Fine," answered Mrs. Marianne. "He's become acquainted with Mary."

"Mary?" said Granddad Derrick confusedly. "And Torrance is okay with that?"

"I don't think he knows."

"Is he... treating her right?"

"Seems to be. I don't think he wants to mess this up because she's the only one willing to talk to him."

"Not even Mikey or Marie's kids?"

"Won't even acknowledge he exists. Mikey and RieRie stay distant from him too."

"Then you don't ever get to see any of them?"

"I go and visit them, but I do wish sometimes they would come to me," sighed Mrs. Marianne. Realizing who she was talking to, she said, "I'm sorry. It's selfish of me to talk about this considering..."

"I brought it up."

"I know but..."

"Can you take this in the house, please?" said Granddad Derrick, handing the pie to his grandson.

"Yes sir," answered Derek.

He carried the pie into the kitchen, where his father fixed a sandwich.

"Can you hand me that?" asked Malcolm, pointing to the lunch meat near Derek.

"Why can't you get it?" said Derek.

"Because you're closer."

"No, I'm not," said Derek, moving away from the lunch meat.

"Did you know they used to stone rebellious sons to death in the Old Testament?" joked Malcolm.

"Granddad told me that once," chuckled Derek as he handed his father the lunch meat. The mention of rebellious sons made him think of his previous conversation with Uncle Marlin. He wanted to find out his father's thoughts on being a father. "Dad?"

"Yeah?"

"What's the most important job a father has?"

"Where are you going with this?"

"No, you are not going to be a grandfather."

"Okay good," Malcolm sighed with relief. "I'm only thirty-two. I'm too young for that."

"Can you answer my question now?"

"I'd say the most important job a father has is loving their child," said Malcolm. "He's willing to sacrifice everything for his child's well-being."

"Hmm..."

"You don't agree?"

"It's just that when I asked Uncle Marlin this question, he said his job was to provide and that was it. And when I pressed him on it, he said that's what Granddad taught him was important and that Granddad was mean."

"He's right," said Malcolm. "Your uncle insists though that your grandfather did what he had to do and didn't know any better. And who am I to argue with him over his experience?"

"Was that your experience too?"

"Nope," said Malcolm. "Your grandfather was way more patient and lenient with me. If it weren't for his help, I don't think I would've been able to raise you properly."

"What would you have done if I wasn't born?"

"Probably be a lawyer like I wanted."

"Why don't you pursue it then?"

"Nah," chuckled Malcolm. "It's too late for me."

"You just said yourself that you're still young. Plus, I'm not a child anymore. I can handle myself."

"I'm not questioning whether you can take care of yourself or not," said Malcolm. "What I'm saying is college and law school cost money. Money I don't have. Besides I barely graduated high school because I was working two jobs to support you."

"But you just said Granddad and Nanna helped you out though."

"I mean, they didn't put me out," said Malcolm. "And they kept you fed and watched you when necessary. But they made it clear you were primarily my responsibility. Everything you needed came out of my pockets."

"Well, I'm not a child anymore. You can pursue your dream now."

"My dream now is to see you grow up and be successful. Besides, I don't mind being a mechanic. It pays my bills."

Derek returned to the porch conflicted. Mrs. Marianne was gone.

"Why the long face?" asked Granddad Derrick.

"Granddad, I'm afraid I see you in a new light now and it's not a very good one."

"What did I do?"

"You were a mean father to Uncle Marlin."

"That...," began Granddad Derrick, slightly confused. "That was a long time ago."

"That's all you have to say?"

"What do you want me to say?"

"I don't know. I guess I was hoping it wasn't true."

"If I said that, then I'd be lying to you."

"Granddad, how could you?"

"As your grandfather, I reserve the right to not have to answer to you."

"But Granddad–!"

"Listen," interrupted Granddad Derrick. "I don't need you to remind me that I've messed up along the way. All you need to do is tell me whether I'm being a good grandfather or not."

"How can I know whether you're doing a good job or not if I don't know your track record?"

"You don't need my track record to know that I love you."

"But I do need it to know how you choose to show it. For all I know you could just be pretending to love me."

"Well, that hurt," said Granddad Derrick. "I don't want you to be set against me."

"I don't either," said Derek. "But I'm afraid I don't know you anymore."

"To be fair, you never really knew me like that to begin with."

"Now, *that* hurt."

"Let's stop this, Derek," pleaded Granddad Derrick. "It's nonsensical and all we're doing is hurting each other."

Derek did as his grandfather wished and silently sat down. But there was a feeling of uneasiness between them, and he did not like it. He did not like it at all.

The rest of Derek's day had been uneventful. He met up with Samiel Dow Jr., one of his best friends. Samiel would be turning eighteen in March and had recently had his braces removed. Therefore, he wanted to celebrate by eating at the hometown favorite, Patty's.

"Are you okay?" asked Samiel as they walked through Patty's parking lot.

"I'm fine," Derek said with a small smile. "Dee-Three is still missing, and I ruined my dad's life, but it's nothing I can't handle."

"Run that by me again."

"What?"

"The part about you ruining your dad's life."

"It's nothing really," said Derek. Although his father's life decision bothered him, Derek had purposely mentioned it to avoid explaining his confrontation with his grandfather. "I was born and now his life is ruined."

"He told you that?" gasped Samiel, his hazel eyes widening.

"Well, no," admitted Derek. "But it's obvious that's what happened."

"Are you sure it's not a misunderstanding?" said Samiel teasingly.

"Hey," griped Derek. "Don't use my words against me."

"Look, you helped me through my dad crisis, so now I'm going to help you through yours."

"I'm not having a dad crisis."

"Yes, you are."

"No, I'm not," declared Derek as they approached the counter.

"Yes, you are," chimed in Charmaine Townsend. She was the sixteen-year-old daughter of the Townsend family, with medium-brown skin, big brown eyes, and curly hair.

"Charmaine, you don't even know what we're talking about," said Derek.

"That's true," said Charmaine. "But I *do* know that you two are customers in line, so I have to ask you what you would like."

"Usual," said Derek.

"One chicken tender basket, please," said Samiel.

"No Scammi Special?" said Derek, surprised.

"Not today."

"Well, this is a first," said Charmaine, ringing the order up. The boys paid for their food and sat at a table near the counter. When the food was ready, Charmaine announced it by calling for her brother. "Benjamin! Food's ready!"

"CAN I GET TO IT FIRST, CHARMAINE?!" bellowed eighteen-year-old Benjamin Townsend. He was Derek's other, shorter best friend. Benjamin had recently dyed the tips of his dreadlocks red, making Derek wish he had dyed his own hair red for his birthday as he wanted.

"You don't have to yell at me about it!" said Charmaine, poking her lip out. "I was just making sure you knew!"

"Some things never change," said Derek, watching as Benjamin went to get their food.

"No, they don't," agreed Samiel.

"Two chicken tender meals," said Benjamin, setting down the food on the table.

"You should be ashamed of yourself, Benji," teased Samiel. "Yelling at poor Charmaine like that."

"Oh, she'll get over it," griped Benjamin, sitting down.

"Of course she will," said Derek. "Because you're going to apologize to her as soon as you leave us."

"I am, am I?"

"I'm not forcing you to," clarified Derek. "You're going to take one look at her sad little face, and that iceberg you call a heart is going to melt. It happens every time you yell at her."

"I can't help it," sighed Benjamin. "Sometimes I just get so worked up, and before I even realize it, I'm screaming at her."

"Benji with Da Bad Attitude," said Derek, christening Benjamin. "That should've been your rap name like I suggested."

"It was too long," said Benjamin. "Besides, I can't go shooting myself in the foot by labeling myself as having a bad attitude. No one would want to work with me."

"You'll do the same type of damage by publicly hurting your sister's feelings," chastised Samiel. "Everyone here is so used to it that it's an expected part of eating at Patty's."

"He's right," agreed Derek. "That's also not a good look for your parent's *family business* to have their *family* fighting in front of customers."

Charmaine rang the front bell, signaling that more food was ready.

"See?" noted Derek. "She doesn't even announce the food anymore because you made her upset."

"Go ahead and apologize, Benji," said Samiel. "You know you want to."

Benjamin stared at Charmaine. He shot from his chair and marched over to her.

"Charmaine," said Benjamin. "I'm sorry I yelled at you."

"I don't accept," said Charmaine. "You always apologize and then you yell at me again. I'm over it."

"What if I pay for your dress to The Perry's ball?" proposed Benjamin. "Would you forgive me then?"

"Will you really?" cried Charmaine, lighting up with excitement.

"Get whatever dress you want," said Benjamin. "It's on me."

"Oh, thank you, Benji!" said Charmaine, hugging her brother. "Does this mean I'm forgiven?"

"Only if you don't yell at me anymore."

"I won't," said Benjamin. "Now, put your smile back on."

"Yes sir!" chirped Charmaine.

"Told you you'd apologize to her," teased Derek when Benjamin returned.

"Oh, shut up," griped Benjamin.

"But why buy her a dress though?" questioned Derek. "There's no way the Perrys are still having their winter ball this year."

"Oh yes they are," said Samiel. "Kamie is dying to go since it'll be her first time."

"They can't be serious," said Derek. "Continuing on with the winter ball while their grandson they supposedly care so much about is missing?"

"They've labeled it a 'winter charity ball' this year," said Benjamin. "All proceeds are supposed to go toward helping the family find Derik."

"The only family receiving the money is them," said Derek. "This is so dirty and low-down, even for them."

"Even if their motives for finding him are selfish and shady, any effort put toward finding him is better than no effort at all," said Samiel. "The Perrys are the richest people in Creeke and if anyone has the resources to find Derik, it's them. What matters is that he's found, preferably safely."

"Yeah," agreed Benjamin. "Who cares about money if it means a better chance at finding Derik?"

"I care because it's my family being used to line their pockets," said Derek. "I'm not going and that's final."

That evening, Derek ate dinner with his father when a knock on the front door alerted them. Samiel's father, Samuel Dow Sr., stood on the porch, still dressed in his police uniform. Malcolm answered the door.

"Hey Mr. Sam," said Malcolm, slightly concerned. "Is everything alright?"

"I'm not sure how to answer that," said Mr. Samuel. "I'm here to give you a heads-up about what we found today."

"A heads-up?"

"Derik's phone was found on the side of the road north of the city," explained Mr. Samuel. "It was badly damaged, but it still worked."

"That's great, right?"

"Yeah," said Mr. Samuel. "But... um... it was discovered that uh... one of the people he was talking to... um..."

"Mr. Sam, what is it?"

"He was talking to someone named Monique Evans."

Derek perked up. His cousin had communicated with someone named Monique Evans. Possibly, the very same Monique Evans who birthed and abandoned Derek eighteen years prior. The same woman who had left his father with a bitter taste in his mouth against her and the people who judged him.

"I'm sure more than one person with that name exists," said Malcolm.

"Based on the conversations they were having, it's definitely someone who knows about your history with her," said Mr. Samuel. "It's possible he was lured to the city by someone using Monique as an alias."

"Like a catfish?" said Derek.

"Exactly," said Mr. Samuel.

"Are you saying he was kidnapped?" asked Malcolm.

"It's possible," said Mr. Samuel. "That's why I wanted to give you a heads-up just in case you get called in for questioning."

"Why would I get called in for questioning?"

"Any number of reasons. Terrence is leaving no stone unturned with this case."

"But why would someone want to kidnap him?"

"There are plenty of terrible reasons why some sick person would do it. I just didn't want you to be blindsided by it."

"Well, thanks."

"You're welcome," said Mr. Samuel. "Have a good night."

"Do you think it's her?" asked Derek after Mr. Samuel had left.

"It can't be," said Malcolm. "Why would she suddenly show an interest in you all these years later after leaving the way she did? It's probably someone pretending to be her like Mr. Sam said."

Malcolm's words stung Derek. Derek knew his father meant well by what he said and was probably also right. But he could not help but wonder. He wondered what it would be like if Monique really did want to meet him one day. What it would be like if she one day returned and became his mother and maybe reignited her flame with his father. Or if she had possibly already married someone else and birthed brothers and sisters Derek knew nothing about. Not having a mother had never bothered him, but he still sometimes wondered. For as long as he could remember, there were periods when it crossed his mind, and with those periods came constant reminders of what he lacked.

That summer when Allison beat him at street football, Derek watched his Aunt Soleya drive away with his cousins. He had always watched her interact with his cousins and be a mother to them. Derek wanted to know why he did not have one. So, he asked his grandmother when they were watching television.

"Nanna, why don't I have a mom?"

"Who said you don't have a mom?" asked Nanna Kiana angrily.

"No one," answered Derek. "But Queenie and Dee-Three have one and I don't. It's not fair."

"Well grandson, sometimes people just don't have their moms."
"But why?"
"For many reasons."
"Why don't I have one?"
"She had to go away."
"Dad said she didn't want me."
"Your father shouldn't have told you that."
"Why didn't she want me?"
"Well, I don't think she was ready to be a mom yet."
"So, when she's ready, she'll come back?"
"I don't know," said Nanna Kiana. She hugged Derek and said, "But until then, I'll be your mom."
"But you're my Nanna," laughed Derek.
"So?" said Nanna Kiana. "Nannas are moms too. And we're better because we're nicer."

Nanna Kiana had been a great stand-in for the mother role to Derek. But it did not change the fact that he knew he had no mother. Those periods of reflection always came and went, and life would return to normal after their departure. The revelation of Derik's conversations began another period for Derek. He knew reality was probably closer to Mr. Samuel's theory and that the real Monique was living her life without ever thinking of him. Despite it all, Derek in his heart still could not help but wonder about what he never had.

-

Chapter Nine: Allison

The winter charity ball was the buzz of the town. Allison despised how the mayor had encouraged people to attend the ball and make donations after he had 'failed' to find Derik. She wanted nothing to do with the whole affair, but despite her protests, her mother insisted they would be attending. Therefore, she sat in Althea's room, watching as Althea showed off the gown she would wear that fateful night.

"Isn't it lovely?" asked Althea.

"Yeah," answered Allison.

"What are you going to wear?"

"Nanna's been making my dress since November," said Allison. "But honestly, I don't want to go."

"You don't?"

"No," said Allison. "I'm only going because we go every year and Mother wants to keep it that way. Honestly, I'm appalled that the crooked mayor and his wife are going through with their ball with everything going on right now."

"You call your grandparents, 'the crooked mayor and his wife'?"

"They aren't my grandparents," declared Allison. "As far as I'm concerned, the only grandparents I have are Granddad and Nanna."

"Pastor Derrick and Mrs. Kiana would hate to hear you speak like that."

"Well, it's the truth."

"Hmm...," said Althea. "Want to see something interesting?"

"Interesting?"

Althea went to her closet and began pushing on the wall.

"What are you doing?" asked Allison.

"You'll see."

The wall moved. Allison thought her eyes were playing tricks on her, but they were not. Althea had pushed the wall in, revealing it to be a door.

"What did you do?"

"It's a secret room. I stumbled on it a few months ago."

"Your family has lived in this house all these years and you never knew it had a secret room?"

"No. I'm thinking of maybe turning it into a hidden library where I can go and read in peace."

"That would be cool. Your own little reading room."

"Yeah. I need to make sure I install a handle on both sides though, so I don't get trapped in it."

"That's definitely a must."

"Thea!" called Diana. "Come here!"

Allison followed Althea into the living room. Ralph Brewer sat on the couch next to Diana, holding a plate of chicken nuggets while listening to her rant.

"Honestly Ralphie, some of the prices at Brewer's are outrageous!" complained Diana.

"I don't make the prices," said Ralph. "I just help out when necessary."

"The least you could do is convince your family to give your girl-friend a discount."

"And the least you could do is give your boyfriend something that doesn't taste like straight up frozen mush," said Ralph, scrunching his face as he held up a chicken nugget. "I'll have to teach you how to cook these properly."

"You don't have to teach me anything!" declared Diana, snatching the plate from him. She walked to the trash can and dumped the unap-preciated food in it. "That's the last time I make anything for you!"

"Diana, did you need something?" asked Althea.

"Yes," answered Diana. "Well, no. Ralphie wanted to see you."

The girls turned their attention to Ralph.

"Thea, there's no easy way to say this," said Ralph. "But your Uncle Arnie needs you to take over Derik's column at the paper. He wants to maintain the youthful perspective of it and you're the only other teenager he knows that can write in the required style."

"He wants me to replace him?" asked Althea.

"No, just..." said Ralph, glancing between her and Allison. "Just stand in for him until he comes back. What do you say?"

"Allison?" said Althea, looking at her friend. "Are you okay with that?"

"Why are you asking me?" asked Allison.

"He's your brother."

"Girl," said Allison. "It's fine."

"Well, as long as it's fine with you I'll do it."

"Glad that's settled," said Ralph. "I've got to get back to the office."

"The nerve of him insulting my food like that!" said Diana after Ralph left. "Just like his grandfather! That's probably why he's named after him!"

"Diana," said Althea.

"What?"

"You're ranting again."

"So?" said Diana, settling down. She looked at Allison and asked, "Did your brother break up with his girlfriend?"

"Who?" said Allison. "Deidrick?"

"Yes, Deidrick."

"He doesn't have a girlfriend."

"Then him and Nisha aren't together?"

"Not to my knowledge."

"Then that makes sense because he sure was flirting up a storm with Mikayla the other day at Brewer's."

"Oh boy," groaned Allison. "The last thing we need is more drama."

"Maybe it was nothing," suggested Althea.

"Maybe," agreed Diana.

"With him, it was definitely nothing," said Allison.

"Well, if Ralphie Brewer keeps it up, it'll be definitely nothing between us too," said Diana.

Later that day, Allison went to work. She had been the receptionist for Miss Leya's since November, having taken on the job when her parents could not find a suitable replacement for Sharon. Allison liked the job and earning her own money, but even that small joy was dampened by her brother's disappearance. The door bell chimed to announce a customer and Allison mustered up her best smile.

"Welcome to Miss Leya's Beauty and Barbershop where you'll leave feeling just as good as you'll look," said Allison, espousing the greeting she was supposed to give every customer. "How may we help you today?"

"I'd like to book a hair appointment," said the woman. She slid her sunglasses off her medium-brown face, and Allison lit up with recognition.

"Cynthia?"

"In the flesh," giggled twenty-two-year-old Cynthia Green. She was the eldest sister of Diana and Althea.

"I thought you were studying abroad."

"I just got back a few days ago."

"How was it?"

"It was fun," said Cynthia. "You'll have to try it when you go to college."

"Is Gloria coming home too?" asked Allison, referring to the second-born Green sister.

"No," snorted Cynthia at the idea of her younger sister coming back to Creeke for a visit. "That girl is off living her life. I doubt we'll be seeing Glo anytime soon."

"That's too bad. Does Matthias know you're back?"

"Not yet. But there will be more than enough time for us to catch up since I'm taking this semester off."

"Why?"

"I need a break from school. My scholarship allows me one break without losing it, and I'm using it on this semester."

"He'll probably be glad to hear that. I still think you two would make a cute couple."

"Ew, that'd be like dating my brother."

"I was just saying."

"Listen, does your mother have any open appointments for next week? The closer to the winter ball the better."

"Nope."

"You didn't even look."

"Cynthia, you are far from the first person to come in here trying to book an appointment with Mother for this ball," said Allison. "She's all booked up."

"You're lying!" cried Cynthia "What am I going to do?"

"Nisha has some availabilities."

"Yeah, but Nisha isn't Mrs. Leya," whined Cynthia. "Nisha has two years of experience while Mrs. Leya has over two decades worth. I want Mrs. Leya!"

"Miss Green," said Mrs. Harrison, coming to the front when she heard her name. "Is there something the matter?"

"No ma'am," said Cynthia, settling down. "I was just expressing my disappointment that you have no available appointments."

"I'm sure that can be distressing," said Mrs. Harrison. "But Nisha has some availabilities and I assure you her work will turn out just as great."

"Yes ma'am," said Cynthia. "Thank you."

Mrs. Harrison walked away.

"Book me with Nisha as close as possible to the ball," sighed Cynthia.

"Will do," said Allison.

"Thanks Alli," said Cynthia.

"You're welcome," said Allison.

Cynthia left and was soon replaced by a new group of customers.

"Welcome to Miss Leya's Beauty and Barbershop where you'll leave feeling just as good as you'll look," said Allison. "How may we help you today?"

"Miki and Nicki are here to get their hair done," said twenty-one-year-old Brianne Lewis, motioning to Mikayla and sixteen-year-old Nicole Brewer. She lowered her voice and whispered, "I'm just here to get away from my parents."

"Oh yeah," said Allison. "Didn't they move back in together?"

"Yes," grumbled Brianne. "My dad decided to take another stab at acting by joining a play in the city. Ever since I've been home, he's been asking me to run lines with him, and my mom is encouraging it!"

"Well Bri, you *are* a theater major and an aspiring actress," said Mikayla.

"Okay, but I am on *break*," said Brianne. "I knew I should've stayed on campus, but my parents were all 'We want to see you! It'll be our first holiday as a family again!' I should've known it was trap! This break needs to hurry up so I can go back on campus."

"Don't speak that," said Allison. "I need my two weeks off."

"Oh yeah," said Brianne. "I forgot high schoolers only get two weeks off for winter break."

"You don't have to rub it in," grumbled Allison.

"You're almost there."

"That's right," agreed Mikayla. "A few more months of easy torture and then life cranks it up a notch."

Allison noticed Nicole had not said anything during the conversation. In fact, she seemed to be actively avoiding Allison. The bell chimed again, and all the girls looked at the new arrival to the shop.

"Welcome to Miss Leya's Beauty and Barbershop where you'll leave feeling just as good as you'll look," said Allison. "How may we help you today?"

"I'm here to get my hair done," said Priscella.

"You can wait over there," said Allison, motioning to the waiting area.

"Thank you," said Priscella.

"Does she have to be here while I'm here?" complained Nicole.

"You guys didn't here this from me," whispered Brianne. "But I heard that she and the other little girl – Principal Lee's daughter – I heard they fell out."

"I'm the one that told you that Bri," said Mikayla.

"I was just making sure we were all caught up. Apparently, she doesn't have any friends now."

"Priscella, I'm ready for you!" called Nisha.

Allison watched as Priscella got up and went to Nisha's chair. The situation between Priscella and Danielle was unsurprising. And yet, she could not help but empathize. She knew what it was like to not have friends outside of her brothers. They had been her friends until she met the ones she had now. But Priscella was an only child and was truly alone. And as Allison looked at her, she could not help but pity her.

That evening, Allison visited church with her family. Her church attendance before living with her grandparents had been inconsistent, but since coming to live with them, they made sure she attended every service. Therefore, she along with Jordan, Deidrick, her aunts, her mother, and her grandparents all sat listening to Pastor Forrest Hall give his sermon to the congregation. Pastor Hall's preaching had improved since the revival, and it was evident in how the congregation responded to him. But despite how good the service was, there was still one person dedicated to trying Allison's patience, even in the house of The Lord.

"How long is this supposed to last?" whispered Jordan.

"Until it's done," answered Allison annoyedly.

"Well, when is that?"

"When he's finished preaching."

"Man, this is boring!"

"Shut up Jordan!"

Allison felt a tap on her arm. Her mother glared at her, and Allison settled into her seat. She only glared at Allison. Only Allison did her mother chastise, criticize, and complain about. Never any of the boys. Even when she was on her best behavior, her mother always found something to point out about her. The boys got to be rowdy, rude, and reckless and faced virtually no consequences. But Allison had to be a lady, always biting her tongue and hiding her feelings away lest she be the bane of the family. It annoyed Allison, and she felt that way through the rest of the service until Nanna Kiana approached her.

"Queenie," sang Nanna Kiana.

"Ma'am?"

"Do you want to do something for me?"

"What do you need?"

"You see Priscella over there all by herself?"

Allison looked to where her grandmother indicated. Priscella sat alone in a corner of the church, waiting for her parents to be ready to leave.

"Yes."

"I need you to go over there and talk to her."

"Nanna, please no," begged Allison. "Anything but that."

"She looks like she could use a friend."

"Why does it have to be me?"

"You know, I knew a little girl with no friends once," said Nanna Kiana. "All she had were her siblings, because all the other neighborhood kids teased her and gossiped about her and made her feel lonely. All that little girl wanted was one person, *just one person*, to be her friend..."

"Okay Nanna, I get it," uttered Allison. "I'll go talk to Priscella."

"That's all I ask."

Allison begrudgingly did as her grandmother asked and approached Priscella. She did not know how she would explain why she was talking to her. For as long as they had known each other, Allison had never liked Priscella. To Allison, Priscella was just Danielle's dumb shadow that followed her around, doing what she was told without thinking for herself.

"Hello Priscella," said Allison. "Mind if I sit here?"

"Go ahead."

"I noticed you sitting here all alone, so I thought I'd join you."

"You mean your grandmother made you come talk to me."

"I–!" began Allison, shocked by Priscella's perceptiveness.

"You don't have to admit it," said Priscella. "My mother used to make me do the same thing with Dani when we were younger."

"She did? You mean you didn't like being her friend?"

"We became friends because her mom and my mom are best friends."

"Really?" said Allison. "What caused you two to fall out?"

"She only cares about herself!" complained Priscella. "All she does is complain, gossip, insult, and try to run everyone!"

"If we're being honest Prissy, you also did those things with her."

"I know," sighed Priscella.

"Well, if it isn't Little Miss Brutus," said Danielle, mocking Priscella as she approached her with the Garza sisters in tow. "I see you wasted no time aligning yourself with the Queen of the Losers."

"If Priscella is Brutus, does that make you Caesar?" asked Allison. "Because I'd be more than happy to get the party started and put us all out of our misery."

"Are you threatening me in church?" snorted Danielle. "How sad!"

"So sad!" said Mariana.

"Very sad!" said Mariella.

"Very, very sad indeed!" mocked Allison. "Don't you three have anything better to do other than be embarrassments to your families?"

"I'd rather be a so-called embarrassment than a certified loser," said Danielle

"Well as the only veteran that got cut from the cheer squad, I'm sure you're doing a great job at both," retorted Allison. "I guess Daddy couldn't help you out with that one, huh?"

"At least my father likes me."

"At least my father makes sure I have money, so I don't get caught stealing out of Brewer's."

"Hmph!" muttered Danielle. "Come along girls! We've wasted enough time on these losers!"

"Who's Brutus?" whispered Priscella once the girls were gone.

"Don't worry about it," said Allison. "Honestly, I say you're better off not having them as friends. Especially if she treats you more as a follower than as an equal."

"It doesn't matter anyways," said Priscella. "All she'll do is replace me with some other girl like she did with Latasia and Nicole."

"Prissy!" called Priscella's father, Mr. Jacob Payne. "Let's go!"

"Coming!" answered Priscella, standing up. She looked at Allison and said, "Bye."

"Bye."

"How'd it go?" asked Nanna Kiana after Priscella was gone.

"Okay," answered Allison. "But you didn't have to pull up my past to get me to talk to her."

"Your past?" said Nanna Kiana. "I was talking about me."

"You?"

"Yeah, me," said Nanna Kiana. She scrunched up her face and said, "Who's been picking on my baby?"

"Nanna, you know I don't get picked on," declared Allison. "But who's been picking on my Nanna?"

"Child, they don't matter now. Some of them are even dead."

"Okay," said Allison. "Jordan was getting on my nerves all night."

"What was he doing?"

"Just complaining about how he was bored and ready to go."

"Lord, have mercy," sighed Nanna Kiana. "Why can't that boy ever act right?"

"I don't know," said Allison. She glanced at her mother, who was talking to First Lady Leilana Hall. "And then Mother sat up there and blamed me like it was my fault he didn't know how to act."

"I'm sure it was a misunderstanding."

"She's always blaming for everything while her sons run around like a bunch of wild hyenas."

"Queenie, don't say that about your brothers."

"It's the truth," said Allison. "They barely ever get in trouble for anything or told to do stuff around the house. It's always me and I'm tired of it."

"Have you told her this?"

"As if she'd listen to me," ranted Allison while pouting. "All she cares about is me 'being a lady'."

"Well Queenie, you can't expect things to change if you don't speak up."

"I doubt they would even if I did," grumbled Allison. And she meant it too.

-

Chapter Ten: Matthias

While Derek spent his Wednesday learning new information about his family and Allison spent hers making new acquaintances, Matthias had started his Wednesday off in the city. Before leaving Creeke, Alexander had asked him to check on Drake. Matthias liked Drake, so he did not mind obliging Alexander. He knocked on the door to the apartment that Drake shared with Andrew, waiting to be let in.

"Matt!" exclaimed Andrew when he opened the door. "What are you doing here?"

"I'm here to see my son," answered Matthias.

"Your what?"

"I'm here to see Drake," clarified Matthias. "Is he here?"

"Yeah," answered Andrew, letting Matthias into the apartment. "Why'd you call him your son?"

"Inside joke."

"I didn't realize you guys were close like that."

"You don't have to be close to have an inside joke," laughed Matthias. He noticed that Andrew had company over. A lanky, medium-brown guy with a blonde-tipped mohawk sat playing one of Andrew's video games. Matthias motioned to him and said, "Who's your friend?"

"That's Quentin," said Andrew, introducing his friend. "Que, this is my friend, Matthias. We go way back."

"What's up?" said Quentin, keeping his eyes on the screen.

"What's up?" said Matthias.

"If you ever see someone playing with us with the tag SuperGentlemanQue or SuperGentleman12, it's Que," said Andrew. "But yeah man, Drake's in his room."

"Thanks," said Matthias. He knocked on Drake's door.

"It's open," called Drake.

Matthias opened the door and found Drake laying on his bed.

"Hello son," said Matthias.

"I don't have your money," said Drake.

"*Hi, hello, nice to see you too,*" joked Matthias. "We don't do that anymore?"

"I just figured we get to the point."

"Well, you got to the wrong point," said Matthias. "I'm not a loan shark today. I'm here because Alexander wanted me to check on you while I was out here."

"Oh."

"Are you enjoying your freedom?"

"I wish you wouldn't describe it like that," sighed Drake, sitting up.

"Why not?" questioned Matthias, taking a seat in Drake's desk chair. "That's what I lent you five-thousand dollars from my savings for when you left your father's house."

"I know," said Drake. "But I just don't like the way that sounds."

"Alright, whatever you want," said Matthias. "Do you need anything?"

"I can't ask you for anything else," said Drake. "You've already given me enough as it is."

"Suit yourself," said Matthias. "So, how long do you think it'll take you to pay me back?"

"How long do I have?"

"I don't know," said Matthias. "When's the next time you'll be in Creeke?"

"March," answered Drake. "That's when my dad's wedding is."

"Then I'll give you till then," determined Matthias. "The next time you show up in Creeke, I expect five-thousand dollars to show up with you. After that it's no longer a friendly loan."

"Okay."

"Come on, Drake," said Matthias, slapping Drake on the arm. "Liven up. You make me feel like I'm hounding you or something."

"It's not you," said Drake. "I've just got a lot on my mind."

"Well, tell me about it," said Matthias. "That's what Alex sent me here for."

"Well...," began Drake. He looked at his closed room door and lowered his voice. "For one, I'm concerned about Andrew. You know it's getting to be about that time of year..."

"Oh yeah," sighed Matthias. "March will mark four years since his baby brother died."

"Yeah," said Drake. "And I think your brother going missing is reminding him of that. Of course, he's trying not to let on, but I know when he's upset about something, especially when it reminds him of Simon."

"And I know how he feels," said Matthias. "The only difference is there's still a possibility for my brother to come back."

"And that's another thing: my brothers," said Drake. "Simon was Andre's best friend, and Derik was Antoine's, and now both of those boys aren't around, and neither am I. And on top of that, Tamela's mother is sick again, and I'm just out here living my regular life while she's running around trying to finish school and care for her mother all at once."

"You couldn't have predicted all this stuff would happen."

"I know, but if I had just kept my cool and stuck around..."

"Then you'd either be locked up right now for snapping and killing your father, or dead because he snapped and killed you," joked Matthias.

Drake was silent.

"I'm just kidding," said Matthias. "You can't shoulder everyone's problems man. Try to lighten up a little."

Drake let out a quiet sigh.

"I've got to get going," said Matthias. "Take care man. Alright?"

"Alright," said Drake, showing Matthias out of the room. "Bye."

"Andrew, I'm heading out," said Matthias, patting his friend on the shoulder as he passed him. "You need anything?"

"I'm straight," answered Andrew. "You?"

"I'm good."

"Let me know when you get home, alright?"

"Okay."

After fulfilling his promises to Alexander and Andrew, Matthias picked up Deidrick and commenced their search for Derik. They silently rode to James's gas station to fill up on gas, and Deidrick went inside to purchase snacks. James joined Matthias in his car during his break, and the two reminisced on old times.

"Remember when you guys would come up here to visit and we'd go around the neighborhood exploring?" asked James.

"How could I forget it?" laughed Matthias. "You ditched me all the time and I had to find my way back to Aunt Nancy's alone."

"You were supposed to be right behind me," said James. "I turn around and you're nowhere to be found. You got yourself lost."

"Man, whatever helps you sleep at night."

"We used to have such fun times," sighed James. "I wonder what happened to us."

"We grew up," said Matthias. "And some of us grew apart."

"It shouldn't be like that though," complained James. "We're all family."

"Being blood doesn't automatically make us all family."

"You're right," agreed James. "It's love that makes us a family. I love my grandfather even though he's gone, and my Nanna, and my parents too even though they're working abroad right now. I love my aunts and uncles and my cousins too. Jordan may get on my nerves a lot, but he's the only brother I have so I love him too. And I know that you feel the same way too. You love your family even though you're trying to act all nonchalant about it."

"I care for majority of the people I'm related too," said Matthias.

"What about Deidrick?"

"It's complicated."

"How is it complicated? You either love him or you don't."

"I can't explain it."

"Try."

"I can't."

"What did he do to you to make you feel this way towards him?"

Matthias thought back to that day when it all began. That summer day when he was weeks from being fifteen and Deidrick was a month from being fourteen and they were still thick as thieves.

It had started with a street basketball game, where Matthias was teamed up with Andrew and Alexander against Deidrick, Terrence Jr., and Michael. Matthias had bet Deidrick that he could beat him at a game of twenty-one, and Deidrick had accepted. They battled it out on the park's court, sinking bucket after bucket in a close competition to be the first to score twenty-one points.

A group of girls had gathered to watch the game, and Matthias felt a sense of pride being able to show off his skills for a crowd. But there was one girl in particular who always showed him support on the court, whether he played in the street, at the park, or in a school gym. Cynthia stood on the sideline with her sister Gloria, jumping up and down excitedly when he got the ball.

"Score one for me, Matty!" cheered Cynthia.

Dribbling the ball, Matthias winked and pointed at her. Not wanting to disappoint his number one fan, he decided to try and dunk the ball. He had done it before on his hoop at home, but the park's hoop was higher. As he got closer, Deidrick prepared to defend against him and try to steal the ball. Matthias kept his eyes on the goal, and before he knew it, he crashed into Deidrick and knocked him to the ground.

"Bro!" shouted Deidrick. He stood up and cried, "Really?!"

"What?" said Matthias. "We're playing basketball."

"Nah!" yelled Deidrick as he shoved Matthias. "You're sitting up here cheating!"

"If you can't handle it then get off the court!" replied Matthias, shoving Deidrick back. "Don't get mad at me because I play better than you!"

"Bro how are you playing better than me when you're cheating?!" said Deidrick, shoving Matthias again.

"Bro, quit shoving me before you really make me mad," said Matthias, shoving Deidrick again.

Deidrick swung at Matthias. Matthias dodged the punch and wrestled Deidrick into a headlock.

"You really want to do this right now?!" yelled Matthias. "You really want me to embarrass you in front of all these people, Cornbread?!"

"Bro, quit grabbing!" shouted Deidrick, trying to break free from Matthias's hold.

"Come on guys," said Andrew, getting between them. "Break it up."

"Nah Andrew, let them get it out their system!" laughed Terrence Jr.

"Matthias, let him go," said Andrew, pulling Matthias's arm.

"Nah, because if I let him go and he punches me, it's going to be a problem," said Matthias.

"Just let go."

Matthias obeyed and released Deidrick, who seized the opportunity to punch Matthias in the face.

"Ooooooh!" instigated Terrence Jr.

"NAH, NAH!" yelled Matthias, trying to escape Andrew's grip. "I told you, Andrew! Let me go!"

"Come on!" said Deidrick, egging Matthias on. He was being held back by Alexander. "Come over here and get it!"

"Let me go, Andrew!" demanded Matthias.

"No!" said Andrew. "Calm down!"

"Andrew, let me go before I fight you too!"

"Fight me if you have to but I'm not letting you go until you calm down."

"Andrew, come on!" huffed Matthias. "He punched me in my face!"

"Bro, don't act like Andrew's holding you back!" yelled Deidrick.

Matthias fought to get free from Andrew but was unsuccessful, for Andrew was stronger than him.

"I'm going to take you home," said Andrew.

"Don't think this is over!" screamed Matthias.

"Yeah, whatever," called Deidrick.

Matthias continued to wrestle with Andrew for freedom until he got tired and allowed himself to be walked home.

"Andrew, why didn't you let me get him?!" said Matthias, when they were out of the park.

"Matt, you don't need to be fighting him. That's your brother."

"He punched me in my face! I told you what would happen if he punched me!"

"He's still your brother. You shouldn't be trying to beat him up like he's some dude on the street."

"So, if Simon punched you–!"

"Simon is nine, his punches wouldn't hurt. And even if he did punch me, I wouldn't try to hurt him because he's my brother."

"I just want my round," said Matthias. "That's it."

"Try to calm down," said Andrew. "I'm sure you and Deidrick will work it out just fine."

Matthias tried to take Andrew's advice and calm down. But every time he came close to being okay, he remembered how Deidrick punched him after Matthias tried to let him calm down, and he became mad all over again. He soon realized he would not be able to move on until he and Deidrick fought it out. So, Matthias stood at the front door, waiting for Deidrick to walk through it.

"Bro, what are you doing?" asked Deidrick, when he came home that evening.

"I'm waiting for you so I can get my round."

"Man whatever," said Deidrick as he passed Matthias to enter the kitchen. "I'm not fighting you."

"Why?" asked Matthias, following him. "Because there's no one around to save you?"

"Bro, I'm not fighting you over a basketball game."

"*You punched me in the face over it earlier.*"

"*Because you tried to clown me in front of everyone.*"

"*Yeah, and I tried to spare you the first time you swung on me,*" *said Matthias, inching closer to Deidrick.* "*But you wanted to be bold and swing again, so I want my round.*"

"*Bro, get away from me,*" *said Deidrick, putting his arm up to keep Matthias away. It offered little protection against Matthias, who returned the punch Deidrick gave him earlier. They swung wildly at each other, and within seconds Matthias stood over Deidrick, pummeling his face and body while Deidrick did his best to cover himself, crying out* "*Bro, okay! You got it!*"

Matthias could not control himself. Every punch provided Matthias a release for all his pent-up frustrations about his life. Deidrick was no longer his brother Deidrick, but instead a destination to receive all the rage built up inside of him.

"*Matty, stop!*" *screamed Deidrick.* "*HELP!*"

"*Hey!*" *someone yelled.* "*Get off of him!*"

Matthias felt himself being dragged away from his relief.

"*No!*" *yelled Matthias, trying to continue swinging.* "*Let me go!*"

"*Cut it out!*" *yelled the intruder, pinning Matthias to the wall.*

Matthias kept his eyes on Deidrick, looking over his handiwork. Deidrick's face was bloody, and he sat on the floor whimpering as he stared at Matthias.

"*I'm not done with you,*" *threatened Matthias.* "*You ain't never going to be safe around me!*"

"*You shut up!*" *said the intruder. Matthias looked to see who had separated them and discovered it was his father. Those cold brown eyes bore into Matthias's, and his lip turned up into a snarl.* "*What do you think you're doing you little psychopath? You trying to kill your brother?*"

Matthias did not answer. All he felt was rage. He had been the one wronged, and yet he was the one getting screamed at. His father locked him outside while he tended to Deidrick, and when he was done, he took Matthias to stay with his Aunt Soriah for what ended up being forever.

"Matty?" said James. "What did Deidrick do?"

"He got me put out the house," said Matthias. "I beat him up after he hit me first and *I* got put out. If that wouldn't have happened, I wouldn't have turned out the way I did."

"Matty, you can't blame him for the things you did after you were kicked out. And you really can't blame him for you getting kicked out either. You had the choice to let it go."

"I tried but he kept trying me," complained Matthias. "Plus, he did the same things I did but no one looked at him differently. Nobody called him a psycho, or threw him out the house, or acted like he didn't exist. How come I get treated worse than him and we've done the same things?"

"It sucks that those things happened to you," said James. "But it's been almost eight years since then. You've got to let this go and move on."

"Whatever."

"My break is almost up," said James. "Hopefully, you guys find something relating to Dee-Three. And don't be afraid to try to fix things with Cornbread either. He's still your brother and you both shouldn't be at odds like this."

Matthias did not reply. James returned to the store, and Deidrick came out with his snacks. He opened a box of candy and held it up to Matthias.

"Want one?" asked Deidrick.

"No," said Matthias.

"Okay," said Deidrick, shrugging his shoulders. He threw a handful of candy in his mouth and said, "So, what's the game plan when we get to the sandwich shop?"

"We ask the management if they know anything."

"And what if they don't cooperate?"

"Then we figure something else out."

"That's not much of a plan."

"Do you have something better in mind?"

"Nope."

"Then shut up."

That was the end of the conversation. They arrived at the sandwich shop and went inside. But before they could make it to the counter, Deidrick stopped and stared at a couple sitting together by the window. Matthias could not see who the guy was, but he knew the girl. It was Nisha. And when Matthias saw her, and then saw the rage-filled look Deidrick was giving her, he knew then that what they had come there to do had been sidetracked.

Chapter Eleven: Deidrick

Nisha was sitting with a man. A man that was not Deidrick. His skin was medium-brown, black hair braided down, and he had a scar on the back of his neck. All physical attributes that did not belong to Deidrick.

"Who is that?" growled Deidrick.

"Don't know, don't care," said Matthias. He snapped his fingers in front of Deidrick's face. "Remember what we're here for. It's probably a friend or something anyways."

"You're right," said Deidrick, trying to calm himself. Nisha noticed him, and her eyes widened. He realized it was not a friend and stormed over to the pair, determined to get answers.

"Deidrick," said Nisha, meeting him before he reached the table. "What are you doing here?"

"I'm looking for my brother!" shouted Deidrick. "What are *you* doing here?! And who is that?!"

"Deidrick, please don't make a scene," pleaded Nisha.

"Who. Is. That. Nisha?!"

"Don't bring that in my store!" commanded the store manager. "Take it outside!"

"Come with me," groaned Nisha, leading Deidrick out of the restaurant. She positioned herself between the door and Deidrick to block him from getting back inside.

"This is what you're doing?" accused Deidrick. "You're messing around on me?"

"I'm just weighing my options like you are," said Nisha nonchalantly. "What's the problem?"

"Bro!" laughed Deidrick as he took a few steps away from Nisha. When he got a hold of himself, he walked back to her and said, "Tell me who he is, or I'll go in there and find out myself."

"Why?" asked Nisha. "We're not together, remember?"

"Alright," said Deidrick, freeing himself from his hoodie.

"What are you doing?"

"I'm not leaving till I know who this is disrespecting me," explained Deidrick, removing the diamond stud in his right ear. "Everyone knows we're seeing each other. I'll wait out here all day if I have to."

"No!" whined Nisha. "I was just trying to make you feel how you make me feel, alright?"

"I don't care about that right now, Nisha," said Deidrick dismissively. "You wanted to get back at me. Okay, mission accomplished. I want to know who this man is."

"We have to leave," said Matthias as he exited the restaurant. "If we don't the manager will call the cops on us."

"They can call who they want to call!" yelled Deidrick. "I'm not leaving until I know who this man is disrespecting me!"

"You're going to have two men disrespecting you in a minute if you don't get in the car," threatened Matthias.

"Please do what he says," begged Nisha. "Get in the car."

"No!"

"Get in the car," said Matthias through gritted teeth.

Deidrick contemplated whether fighting with Matthias was worth the man's identity. After a few seconds, he decided to get in the car. But his anger did not subside. Nisha had messed around on him. The girl that had always been loyal to him had gone out with another dude behind Deidrick's back. He felt he could not trust her anymore.

The task of getting information fell on James, who took care of it after work. While Deidrick waited for James, he tried to determine the man's identity by matching his neck to photos of his previous customers. None of them had the scar he looked for, and it angered Deidrick.

"Who was that dude at the restaurant?" ranted Deidrick. He knocked a pillow off the couch and yelled, "Bro!"

"Cut it out," said Matthias.

"I want to know who he is! He disrespected me!"

"Deidrick, I don't care about your little love triangle," said Matthias. "What I care about is that we couldn't get any answers about Dee-Three because you couldn't control yourself."

"You're the last person who should talk about controlling themselves!" argued Deidrick. "If you were in my position, you'd be mad too!"

"I would never be in your position because I'm not stupid like you."

"You were stupid enough to get yourself kicked out of the house!"

"Yeah, because you laid on the floor and played victim," said Matthias. "You probably went crying to Mommy to convince her not to let me come back."

"I did not!" cried Deidrick. "I tried to apologize to you, and you threatened to stab me!"

"Sure did," agreed Matthias. "Like I said, you won't ever be safe around me."

"You're a demon!" declared Deidrick. "Just straight-up evil!"

"And whose fault is that?" countered Matthias, growing angry. "You jacked up my life! I hate you!"

"I hate you too!" replied Deidrick. He did not want to be bothered with Matthias, Nisha, her mystery man, or anyone else. Deidrick needed an escape from it all. So, he slammed the front door behind him and went where he knew he could shut his mind off for a while. The cold nipped at him as he stood outside Sharon's apartment, banging on her door.

"Deidrick?" asked Sharon when she answered. "What are you doing out here?"

"I was in the neighborhood," muttered Deidrick.

"I would let you in, but...," said Sharon, wincing at something behind her.

"Whatever it is, I'm sure I can handle it."

"I uh..."

"Let me see it," said Deidrick, smirking as he looked Sharon up and down.

"Alright," said Sharon, leading him into the apartment.

Deidrick let his mind drift. This time his thoughts did not focus on the younger brother but on the older one. He remembered how Matthias had beat him up. And he remembered the look Matthias had when they were pulled apart. But Deidrick also remembered how he had tried to set things right and let himself drift into the memory.

His forehead was scraped where Matthias had drawn blood. It had been a week since the fight, and Matthias had been sent to stay with the Campbells to cool down. Home had seemed empty to Deidrick without his brother there. He needed his best friend back, so he went with Mr. Harrison to make things right and bring Matthias home. Deidrick's stomach twisted in knots as he contemplated what to say to his brother. But when Matthias turned and scowled at him, he knew he had to say something.

"Matty," said Deidrick.

"Go away," said Matthias.

"Just listen for a second."

"No. Leave me alone."

"I just want to say sorry."

"I don't care. Go away."

"Bro, just listen!"

"I said leave me ALONE!" yelled Matthias, picking up a kitchen knife. He clutched it, eyeing Deidrick with the intent to use it on him.

"Alright, I'm leaving," said Deidrick. When he reached the front door, he saw his father leaning against the wall with his arms crossed. He kept his eyes trained on the kitchen, and a word fell from his lips, followed by a dismissive grunt.

Psychopath. That's what Mr. Harrison had called Matthias. And Deidrick could not disagree. He did not want to believe that his brother would ever consider using a knife on him. But he had. Matthias had threatened to stab Deidrick. The realization sunk in, and Deidrick accepted that he had lost his best friend.

"Sharon!" called a man's voice, breaking Deidrick from his trance.

"Shoot!" squeaked Sharon. It was her boyfriend, Malik. "You've got to get out of here!"

"I'll just hide until he leaves."

"You can't!"

"Why not?"

"Because he's not going to leave!"

"Well, I can't go out the front door!"

"Sharon! Where are you?!"

"I'm in the room!" called Sharon. She looked around the room and pointed at the window. "There!"

"We're on the third floor!"

"What other option do we have?"

"Why is the door locked?!" bellowed Malik, banging on the door. "Sharon!"

"Hold on!" yelled Sharon. She whispered to Deidrick and said, "You go out the window and I'll stall him."

"What about my shoes?" asked Deidrick. He did not care about his hoodie all that much. But his new baby blue and white sneakers were the first shoes he had bought since the fire, and he refused to leave without them.

"Sharon, open this door before I break it down!" threatened Malik.

"We don't have time!" whispered Sharon. "I'll give them back to you later! Now go!"

It was not Deidrick's first time leaving through a girl's window. Nor was it his first time leaving through a window not on the first floor. But it was his first time leaving with only half his wardrobe on. He slipped himself through the window, and the cold air stung his exposed chest.

Deidrick eased himself off the ledge and hung onto it, while Sharon opened the room door to appease Malik.

"Whose shoes are these?!" shouted Malik. Deidrick could hear him stomping around the room and slamming doors. "You have somebody in here, don't you?! Where is he?! I know he's in here!"

"Don't be ridiculous!" argued Sharon. "There's nobody in here except us!"

"Then why does it smell like a man was in here, Sharon?!"

"Because this is your room too! You're the only man in here!"

"Liar!" yelled Malik, throwing stuff around. "I knew I shouldn't have agreed to that stupid plan of yours! Because now look! You bringing other dudes around and got them chilling in our spot like it's theirs! It's probably his and not mine!"

"It is not, Malik!"

"You're lying! And when I find him, he's dead!"

Deidrick felt that his life was in danger. He had to escape, and the only way out was down. Below him were two bushes, and they would have to suffice for a soft landing.

"Lord, please don't let me die," prayed Deidrick.

He inhaled and let go of the ledge. The branches of the bush scraped into his bare back as he landed on them, causing a cry of pain to erupt from his lungs. But he could not stop. Deidrick rolled off the bushes and ran to his car in nothing but his pants.

"Hey!" yelled Malik, looking out the window.

Deidrick did not stop to see if Malik followed him. He dove into his car and sped off. Malik stood in his rearview mirror yelling and throwing stuff at him, but Deidrick was sure Malik had not seen his face. As his adrenaline calmed down, the pain of the scrapes on his back set in. But it was a minor inconvenience to what Deidrick was really concerned about.

During the argument, Malik had accused Sharon of claiming something was his when it was really another guy's. Deidrick did not like the sound of that. If it was what he thought it was, then Deidrick's days of fun with Sharon could be ending. Sharon had potentially signed him up for something he was not ready for, but he had to be sure it was true. Therefore, he resolved to return soon to get answers and his shoes back.

"What happened to you?" asked James.

"Nothing," said Deidrick. "Did you learn anything about Dee-Three?"

"All the manager could tell me was what the surveillance footage showed," said James. "Dee-Three left the restaurant after waiting about fifteen minutes and got into a black sports car that had pulled up. He didn't order anything either."

"This is just great," griped Deidrick. "It's not like we're in a big city with tons of black sports cars to help narrow it down."

"Don't give up yet," said James. "Maybe something about him will turn up that can help us."

-

Chapter Twelve: Derek

The rest of winter break had been a gloomy one. Gift exchanges on Christmas were dampened by unopened 'To Derik' presents still under the tree at the end of the night. Entering the new year rang hollow for the family because Derik had not been there to enter it with them. Not to mention, Derek was still processing the information he had learned about his grandfather's past. His only bright spot during the dark times was practicing his routines for the upcoming spring showcase at his dance studio.

"One, two, three, four, one two, three, four," counted Derek as he danced around his room. It would be his final showcase before graduating, and he wanted to make the most of it. Once graduated, he planned to attend a performing arts college and was preparing for his eventual audition. He had, however, applied and been accepted to a few backup colleges under an undecided major to appease his father's concerns.

As he flowed through the motions of his routine, a sound made him pause. Two knocks at the top of the door. The beginning of the special code he and his cousin had come up with in middle school. He was thirteen then, while Derik was eleven, sitting in their grandparent's kitchen with nothing to do.

"I have an idea," said Derek.
"An idea?" repeated Derik.
"You know how people act like they can't tell us apart?"
"Yeah."

"Well, what if we started using that against them? Something only we would understand."

"That's sounds cool. But what would we do?"

"Hmm...," said Derek, thinking. He looked up and saw the hallway mirror and got an idea. "What if we acted like a mirror?"

"A mirror?"

"Yeah. Anytime someone says they can't tell us apart we start acting like each other."

"Like monkey see, monkey do."

"Yeah. Except we're not monkeys."

"That sounds cool."

"Here, do what I do," said Derek, holding up his right hand.

"Like this?" asked Derik, holding up his left hand to match Derek's right.

"Yeah. Now repeat after me. I am you and you are me."

"I am you and you are me."

"And now," said Derek, joining his hand with Derik's. "We are each other."

"And now," said Derik, repeating the motions. "We are each other."

The boys sat there, holding each other's hands and staring. Then they laughed.

"This is going to be fun," said Derek.

"This is going to be fun," said Derik.

And it was fun. It was fun forming a shared bond and identity with Derik. They had created all types of tricks and gimmicks for their mirror game, including a secret knock. He heard it again. Two knocks at the top of the door. Derek inched toward it, unsure if he should repeat the code back.

"Derek?" said Uncle Marlin, causing Derek to sink. It was not Derik. After opening the door, Uncle Marlin said, "I'm going over to my parent's house. Did you want to ride along?"

"Sure."

The car ride was a silent one. Derek watched as the barren trees of Creeke whizzed by, pointing to the edge of town where his grandparents lived. When they arrived, they found Allison in the kitchen reading a book.

"Is your mother here?"

"In her room," answered Allison.

"Thanks," said Uncle Marlin. Before he could move, however, Aunt Soleya appeared in the kitchen.

"Marlin," said Aunt Soleya annoyedly. "What are you doing here?"

"Leya, I need to talk to you."

"About what?"

"I'm about to take a large sum of money out of our savings account."

"What's a large sum of money?"

"About ten-grand."

"Ten-grand?!" cried Aunt Soleya. "Why are you taking so much out of our account?!"

"Because I need it."

"For what?!"

"For what I need it for!"

"What? Are you spending it on some girl or something?"

"Leya, don't piss me off today."

"Don't piss you off?" snorted Aunt Soleya. "My child is missing, my house is destroyed, my reputation is in shambles, you're trying to take all this money out of our savings account without telling me why, and *you don't want me to piss you off*?"

"Yes," Uncle Marlin declared. "Because I've given you everything you ever wanted, and you repay me by not trusting me."

"What do you expect when a girl young enough to be your *daughter* offers herself to you knowing that you're married?"

"I didn't do anything!" argued Uncle Marlin. "She came onto me, and I shut it down because I'm married to you! In fact, *I'm* the one that told you about what happened and supported your decision to fire her!"

"But she wouldn't have any reason to think that was okay unless you gave her a reason to believe it was."

"Soleya," said Marlin. "If I wanted that girl, I would have had her."

"No!" whispered Derek distressfully. "Why would you say that?"

"Are you serious?!" cried Aunt Soleya.

"Yes, because you're tripping over nothing!" ranted Uncle Marlin. "I've never disrespected you and I've given you everything you ever wanted! I married you when I wasn't ready because that's what you wanted. I gave you four kids when I didn't want any at all because that's what you wanted. I built you that house because you wanted it. *I* paid for that salon because *you* wanted it. And yet somehow, I'm still the bad guy!"

"So, you finally admit it," said Aunt Soleya. "You never loved me."

"Did you hear anything I just said?"

"I heard you loud and clear. You didn't want to marry me, and you didn't want a family with me."

"But I still gave them to you though. I gave you what you wanted."

"That's not what I wanted, Marlin! I wanted us to be happy to-gether! I wanted you to love me!"

Derek watched his uncle, awaiting his next move. Uncle Marlin glared at Aunt Soleya, then whisked her off her feet and began walking toward her bedroom.

"What are you doing?!" cried Aunt Soleya.

"Isn't this what you want?" asked Uncle Marlin.

"No!" bellowed Aunt Soleya. "Put me down!"

"You're confusing me, Leya," said Uncle Marlin, setting Aunt Soleya back on her feet. "What do you want?"

"I want you to leave me alone!" said Aunt Soleya, running to her room.

"I don't get it," said Uncle Marlin to Derek and Allison. "First, she says she wants me to love her and when I try, she rejects me!"

"She wants you to love her," said Derek. "Not *love* her."

"What's the difference?"

"Oh boy," sighed Derek.

"What is going on in here?" asked Granddad Derrick.

"Hi Granddad," said Allison.

"I was just talking to Soleya," explained Uncle Marlin.

"It sounded more like you were arguing with her to me," said Granddad Derrick. "Is everything alright?"

"Everything's fine."

Derek did not feel like talking to his grandfather. So, he disappeared onto the porch to wait for Uncle Marlin to be ready to leave. But it was not Uncle Marlin who came out the door. It was Granddad Derrick.

"Derek, what's the matter with you?" asked Granddad Derrick.

"Nothing."

"Then why are you being weird?"

"How am I being weird?"

"You didn't say anything to me."

"Do I always have to speak to you?"

"When you're in my house, yes."

"Well, I'm sorry, but I'm still shocked by what I've learned about you."

"Shocked about what? That your grandfather isn't perfect and had a life of mistakes before you were born? Like I told you before, I don't have to explain myself to you."

"And you think that's fair?"

"Yes, because it doesn't concern you. You're acting like I did something to you personally, and to make matters worse, you're disrespecting me over it now."

"No, I'm not."

"You don't think deliberately not speaking to me as a guest in my house isn't disrespectful to me? I don't care about you feeling how you feel, but you're not going to disrespect me."

"Wow," snorted Derek. "You really did tell Uncle Marlin you didn't care about how he felt."

"Yes, I did," said Granddad Derrick. "But I keep telling you that's all in the past now."

"How is it in the past if you just said it to me?" argued Derek. "I never thought you could be so cruel to do something like that."

"Cruel?" repeated Granddad Derrick. "You think I'm cruel?"

Derek did not answer, nor did he look at his grandfather. Granddad Derrick accepted his silence as a response and returned to the house. After a while, Uncle Marlin came out, and they both returned home feeling unhappy.

"And that's why I didn't want to stay over there," said Uncle Marlin, breaking the silence.

"Why?"

"Because all Leya and I have done for months is argue about Sharon," said Uncle Marlin. He handed Derek his coat and said, "Hang this up for me, will you?"

"Sure thing," said Derek. He started to hang his uncle's coat in his closet when he noticed a paper sticking out of the pocket. Derek failed to resist temptation and peeked at the paper. Pasted onto the page in blocky letters was the following note–

IF YOU WANT TO SEE YOUR SON AGAIN, BRING THE MONEY TO THE PREVIOUSLY MENTIONED LOCATION ON SATURDAY AND LEAVE. TELL ANYONE ABOUT THIS AND THE BOY DIES.

It was accompanied by a picture of Derik staring fearfully into a camera. His face was tear-stained and bruised, while his mouth and hands were bound with tape.

"Oh no!" gasped Derek.

"Derek," said Malcolm. "I need to talk to you."

"What about?" said Derek, quickly stuffing the note back into the coat pocket.

"What did you say to your grandfather earlier?"

"We had an argument."

"Okay but what did you say? Because your uncle told me that your grandfather went outside to talk to you and came back in the house a few minutes later and burst into tears."

Derek froze.

"My father rarely cries. So, what'd you say?"

"I uh...," stammered Derek. "We were talking about him being a mean father, and I expressed my disappointment and uh... we had an argument over it. I didn't mean to make him cry."

"Well, you did," said Malcolm. "You need to apologize."

"You told me to never apologize for how I felt."

"When you're right," said Malcolm. "You're not right this time. You're acting just like those people at the church, holding stuff against people even after they've grown and atoned for their mistakes. You don't think your grandfather doesn't already feel bad or regret how he was?"

Derek did not answer.

"I'm sure learning the truth has been a shock to you, but the way you're going about processing it is starting to hurt other people. Do the right thing and tell the man you're sorry."

Derek felt ashamed. He had accused his grandfather of being cruel and in turn, had become the cruel one. In the same way his grandfather had hurt others trying to prove a point, he had hurt his own grandfather to prove his own point. They had become one and the same, hurting those they cared most about. And Derek was ashamed.

-

Chapter Thirteen: Allison

The day of the winter charity ball had arrived. That morning, Allison sat in the kitchen with her aunts and Nanna Kiana, the latter sewing the final touches onto Allison's gown. In and out weaved the needle, each stitch bringing the two fabrics together as one. It was in this same manner that Allison explored the family photo box. Each picture she drew brought past memories to present recollection, reminding everyone of a happiness they had not felt in two weeks.

"Who are these two guys?" asked Allison, holding up a photo of three smiling teenage boys in football uniforms. The two guys she referred to smiled toothy grins, one mouth full of braces and the other crooked teeth. But the boy in the middle, who Allison easily recognized as her father, only smiled a little as if he were forced to for the camera.

"Those were Marlin's best friends, Kasey Ferguson and Zack Graham."

"Were? What happened to them?"

"Zack moved away after high school. And Kasey..."

"Yeah?"

"He made a mess of his life," sighed Nanna Kiana.

"Hmm...," murmured Allison, staring again at the photo. She had never known her father to have any friends besides her Uncle Malcolm. He always seemed like the antisocial type to her. Allison wondered what he would have been like had his friends still been around and then slowly returned the photo to the box.

The next photo she drew was a sepia-colored one of a smiling family. A medium-brown man dressed in a nice suit hugged a dark-brown woman closely. Beside them, an older light-brown woman stood with two dark-brown little girls at her side and a third on her hip. On the bottom was written, 'Barry and Kim, Danette (age 8), Lettie (age 6), and Nanna Ana with Cece (age 4)'.

"Where was this taken?" asked Allison.

"I think that was an Easter Sunday because Papa has on his Sunday suit and he only went to church for Easter and Christmas," said Aunt Paulette. "But our mother and grandmother used to wake us up early every Sunday and make us go with them."

"The sun wouldn't even be out yet either," whined Aunt Nancy. "And now Danette acts the same way."

"So?" said Nanna Kiana. "What do you have going on that's more important than being in The Lord's house on His day, Cece?"

"She even sounds like Mommy!" cried Aunt Nancy.

Allison pulled out another sepia-colored photo. This photo was a close-up of the woman labeled as 'Kim' in the previous photo. She seemed to possess a quality of all her daughters in her face. Nanna Kiana's observant eyes, Aunt Paulette's cool expression, Aunt Nancy's cheerful smile. But Allison saw some of herself in Kim's photo too. Underneath the neatly kept hair and stylish clothes, Allison felt the personality of Kim transcend beyond the page. Her aura radiated that she had been a force to be reckoned with, much like Allison herself.

"Nanna, did you have a good relationship with your mother growing up?" asked Allison, showing her grandmother the picture.

"I sure did," said Nanna Kiana. "Of course, I had my grievances with her, like my name for example. But overall, I loved my mother and I miss her too."

"What's wrong with your name?"

"Nothing," said Nanna Kiana. "But everyone always used to tease me about it because it was uncommon."

"Kiana isn't an uncommon name."

"Now, it isn't," said Nanna Kiana. "But when I was growing up it certainly was. I used to always wish my father had gotten his way and named me Danette instead. But I guess I should be grateful because if he had gotten his way, me and your aunts would be Danette, Paulette, and Nanette."

"Nanette," gagged Aunt Nancy. "I can't believe he wanted to give me such an old lady name!"

"You're not exactly a spring chicken, Nancy," said Aunt Paulette.

"So?" said Aunt Nancy. "You're closer to old age than I am."

"Nancy, stir that pot on the stove for me please," said Nanna Kiana.

"Why can't Queenie do it?"

"Because I told you to do it."

"There she goes acting like Mommy again," griped Aunt Nancy. "Alright Mini Mommy, I'm on it."

Allison pulled another photo from the box. Two teenage girls sat smiling side by side in matching school uniforms. The description read 'Lana & Leya – Friends 4 Life'.

"Mother and First Lady Hall really meant it when they wrote 'friends for life'," said Allison.

"It's nothing short of a miracle they survived this long," said Nanna Kiana. "From feuding husbands to Sophia's meddling. Those two's friendship has really been tested."

"Did Mother have any other friends?"

"I would imagine so. She was a very popular girl."

"Do you remember what she was like growing up?"

"Let's see," said Nanna Kiana. "I met your mother when she was about thirteen or fourteen. She would come to girl's bible study with Soriah and sit in the back. I never really spoke to her that much until one day when she had to be about sixteen or seventeen, because Soriah was already married to Quincy and your mother was driving by that time. That day, I was out in front of the church greeting all the kids with your grandfather when all I see is your father and his friends being chased down the street by your mother. From what I understand, your mother had asked your father to hold her purse, and he got it in his mind to prank her and took off running with it!"

"I can't imagine Dad playing a prank."

"He was always provoking people to get a reaction," sighed Nanna Kiana. "You should've seen the poor thing flying down that road after them. Your father was standing on the church steps waiting for her with a smirk on his face and as soon as she caught up with him, she marched right up to him and smacked your father so hard across the face, you could practically hear it across town."

"She smacked him?"

"Left her handprint on his face," confirmed Nanna Kiana. "Then she called him 'insolent', and snatched her purse, and ran off into the church in tears."

"What was she crying for?"

"Oh, she was embarrassed," said Nanna Kiana. "Apparently, it was unladylike for her to be running, and then her hair was a mess due to the wind, and she felt like everyone was laughing at her."

"She was worried about what everyone else thought, even back then," sighed Allison. "What ended up happening after that?"

"I helped her get herself together, and that was that," said Nanna Kiana. "Then not even a week later, your father comes and tells us that he and Soleya are going on a date."

"After he stole her purse?!" cried Allison.

"That's what I said," said Nanna Kiana. "Apparently, your father tried to apologize and your mother would only forgive him if he took her on a date."

"She saw an opportunity and took it."

"That's what your grandfather said but I didn't see it that way," said Nanna Kiana. "Your mother took it all in stride and I liked her for that. Any girl who could manage your grandfather and your father at the same time without skipping a beat automatically had my respect."

"Mine too," said Aunt Paulette.

"And definitely mine," said Aunt Nancy, taste-testing a bit of food with the spoon she had been using to stir. "This is good, Danette. I need to try some more."

"Nancy, don't you put that spoon back in that pot after you had it in your mouth!"

"Oh hush! I know how to cook!"

"Give me that!" demanded Nanna Kiana, going to take the spoon from Aunt Nancy.

The two sisters fought over the spoon to the amusement of Allison. She continued digging through the picture box and came across a stack of handwritten notes. Removing the rubber band holding them together, Allison commenced reading the first one.

> *Derrick,*
> *"Because of the savour of thy good ointments thy name is as ointment poured forth, therefore do the virgins love thee." -Songs of Solomon 1:3*
> *- Kiana*

"What are these?" said Allison.

"Those look like the love notes your grandparents used to send each other," said Aunt Paulette.

"Love notes?" repeated Allison. "Nanna, Granddad wrote love letters to you?"

"Well, I wrote one to him after he got back from the army, and he just went along with it...," explained Nanna Kiana, throwing the used spoon she successfully wrestled from her sister into the sink. She returned to the table with flushed cheeks, and Allison could not tell if she was blushing about the notes or just hot from wrestling with Aunt Nancy.

"How did you understand what these verses meant?"

"I used a dictionary," teased Nanna Kiana. "I know you young folks don't know anything about that since you all just look everything up on the internet now."

"Haha very funny," said Allison at her grandmother's playful jab. "Can you explain them to me?"

"Okay," agreed Nanna Kiana, taking the first note in her hand. "This was the first one I sent him. I told him he was cute, and all the girls must like him."

"What'd he say to that?"

"When I first met your grandfather, I'd already messed up by calling him cute and asking if he was single," explained Nanna Kiana, rolling her eyes. "None of that was new to him and he always avoided answering why he was single. But this time his response surprised me."

Allison watched as her grandmother pulled out the next note in the series of her grandparent's love affair and handed it to her. It read:

Kiana,
"The glory of young men is their
strength." -Proverbs 20:29
- Meathead Derrick

"Your grandfather was basically like 'I've resisted all the girls' and trying to be all smooth," laughed Nanna Kiana.

"That's just like him too!" exclaimed Aunt Nancy.

"Come to find out, none of the girls were paying your grandfather any mind," revealed Nanna Kiana. "Thelma told me nobody wanted to date him because he was the Bishop's son, and it was too much pressure. So, I sent him this note."

Meathead,
"My beloved is [black] and
ruddy, the chiefest among ten thou-
sand. His head is as the most fine gold, his
locks are bushy, and black as a raven."
-Songs of Solomon 5:10-11
- Kiana

"Then he sent me this back."

Kiki,
"Thou art all fair, my love; there
is no spot in thee." -Songs of Solomon 4:7
- Derrick

"Basically, he said I looked good too," said Nanna Kiana, beaming. "After he sent this, we went on our first date. I took him to this little roller rink in the city and we had a great time, except for that moment when he skated his butt straight into the wall."

Everyone laughed.

"We went on two more dates before he sent his next note," said Nanna Kiana. "Our second date was at the city library. Your grandfather was trying to prove to me that he was smart because I had insinuated that he wasn't when we first met."

"Did he prove it?"

"He did, actually," said Nanna Kiana, playfully shaking her head. "Of course, he got a little too excited about a particular theology book that he really wanted and got us put out the library, but he did prove he was smart. And then, our third date was a picnic out at the creek. That man lugged this big old picnic basket around like he had a feast in there. I open it and all that was in there was two measly peanut butter and jelly sandwiches."

"Sounds just like him," whispered Aunt Paulette.

"I guarantee you the real reason he took me out there was so he could show off his body," giggled Nanna Kiana. Her cheeks became rosy as she thought back on her youth. "It was so hot that day and your grandfather was out there looking all fine with the sun shining on those big, oily muscles of his..."

"Danette," said Aunt Paulette, waving her hand in front of Nanna Kiana's eyes. "Come back."

"Huh?" murmured Nanna Kiana, snapping out of her nostalgic haze.

"She even daydreams about her man the way Mommy used to too," teased Aunt Nancy.

"Oh, hush Nancy," said Nanna Kiana. "Where was I?"

"Your date at the creek," reminded Allison.

"Oh right. That was the date we'd had our first kiss and a few days later, this was the next note he sent me."

Kiana Danette Barnett,

"Full name?" said Allison.

"Mmmhmm," said Nanna Kiana.

Kiana Danette Barnett,
"I charge you, O ye daughter of
Jerusalem, by the roes, and by the hinds
of the field, that ye stir not up, nor
awake my love, till he please." -Songs of
Solomon 2:7
- Derrick Jermaine Harrison
P.S. He pleaseth.

"Aw, he was in love," giggled Allison.

"He sure was," agreed Nanna Kiana. "I was nervous about dating him seriously at first because of some... things I still hadn't told him at the time. But when it all came out, he didn't care about it. He accepted me as I was and we're still together all these years later."

"Was this the last note?"

"No," said Nanna Kiana, resting her head in her palms. "I didn't write it down, but my response was *'I am my beloved's, and his desire is toward me'* from Songs of Solomon 7:10."

"And what was his response?"

"*I am my beloved's, and my beloved is mine*," spoke a new voice. Allison turned to see Granddad Derrick standing in the kitchen doorway. "*Songs of Solomon 6:3.*"

"How long have you been standing there, Granddad?"

"Long enough to hear about my oily muscles," said Granddad Derrick seriously.

"We were just looking at pictures, Meathead."

"I see that," said Granddad Derrick. He grabbed a photo from the box and showed it to Allison. "Here's one of me."

Allison looked at the photo her grandfather retrieved. It was a school picture. Granddad Derrick wore his school uniform and had a big afro on his head.

"You used to have a lot of hair," said Allison.

"Yeah," sighed Granddad Derrick. "But the army got me used to keeping it short."

"You also look like... everyone here," said Allison. "Dad, Uncle Falcon, Matty, Cornbread, D-Money, Dee-Three. You somehow look like all of them."

Allison rifled through the box for pictures of all the men in the family and arranged them all to compare to her grandfather's picture.

"See?"

"I see," said Granddad Derrick. He pointed to the photo of Derik and said, "I remember this one. He said it was his favorite."

Derik's smile transcended beyond the paper. He wore a navy-collared white polo with a single red stripe positioned diagonally across the shirt like a sash. It made him look like a prince who was only missing his crown. Allison had picked that shirt out for him a few years ago, and it had been his favorite for a while. She still remembered sitting in the fitting room area, waiting for him to show her how it looked.

"How do I look?" asked twelve-year-old Derik, coming out of the fitting room.

"It looks good on you," said fourteen-year-old Allison. "You look like a prince. Especially with the way you're growing your hair out."

"A prince, huh? I like that."

"You should wear that on the first day of school."

"I think picture day would be better."

"Why?"

"Because if I wear it on the first day of school no one will remember that I looked like a prince," explained Derik. "But if I wear it on picture day, I'll be a prince forever."

Derik had been right. The image of him as a prince was a reminder that he had existed. Everything of his was gone, and so was he. Every polo he had cherished had burned up with that first one. But the photo, the princely image of him, remained.

"Oh dear," said Nanna Kiana. "I think I might need some more thread."

"I'll get it for you," volunteered Allison.

"That's okay," said Nanna Kiana. "I'll get it."

Nanna Kiana left the kitchen.

"Queenie, I think we've cherished enough memories for now," said Granddad Derrick.

"You're right," said Allison. She put all the photos back in the box and returned them to her grandparent's closet. There, she found Nanna Kiana crying. "Nanna?"

"Oh!" cried Nanna Kiana, wiping her face. "I didn't hear you come in."

"I was putting your picture box back," said Allison.

"Kiki, what's the matter?" asked Granddad Derrick, coming in behind Allison.

"I was just thinking about Derik is all," admitted Nanna Kiana. "I didn't want to seem obnoxious to everyone, so I thought it best just to step away for a bit."

"Kiana, you're my wife," said Granddad Derrick, hugging Nanna Kiana. "You don't have to hide your feelings from me."

"I know," sighed Nanna Kiana. "But I just didn't want you to be worried."

"And I didn't want you to worry either," admitted Granddad Derrick. "But all that's done is made us both suffer in silence. From now on, let's be honest with each other, okay?"

"Okay."

Allison left the couple alone and went out on the porch. It was a sunny day made cold by the January wind. Everyone in town was preparing for the ball, treating it like a regular party instead of the repurposed 'charity event' it claimed to be. Life had continued on without Derik, and Allison felt guilty for becoming used to it.

That afternoon, Allison stood in the middle of her room as Nanna Kiana sewed her dress onto her. Allison had done her own hair and makeup beforehand, choosing a silver wig and frost-inspired cosmetics. Nanna Kiana's best friend, Mrs. Thelma Parker, had come over to help with the sewing, and both women put their decades of experience as seamstresses to work to have Allison ready in time to leave with her mother.

"Honestly Nanna, I don't see why it's necessary to sew me into my dress," joked Allison.

"You agreed to do things my way if I made your dress for the ball, remember?" said Nanna Kiana.

"I didn't know that included being sewn into it," said Allison. She looked down at the gown and said, "You could've at least made it red like I wanted."

"A red dress at an all-white ball?" snorted Nanna Kiana. "Do you hear this girl, Thelma?"

"I sure do," said Mrs. Thelma, her medium-brown skin glowing under the sunlight. "Trust me, Allison. You're better off wearing this white one."

"What's the problem?" questioned Allison. "Shouldn't I be allowed to wear what I want?"

"I don't want you to do something you'll later regret," said Nanna Kiana. "You step into that ball in a red dress and the whole town will be calling you Jezebel within the hour."

"The only Jezebel attending the ball is the one hosting it," scoffed Allison.

"Allison Queen!" chastised Nanna Kiana. "Whether you like her or not, Sophia is still your grandmother, and I won't allow you to disrespect her."

"You're my grandmother, Nanna."

"All I know is you better be on your best behavior tonight," said Nanna Kiana. "You be polite to Sophia, and don't make things difficult for your mother."

"And remember to turn the other cheek too," advised Mrs. Thelma.

"Okay," sighed Allison.

"You're all finished," said Nanna Kiana.

"I'd say this is our best work yet, Kiki," said Mrs. Thelma.

Allison went to look at herself in the mirror.

"Do you like it?" asked Nanna Kiana.

"I love it," said Allison.

"Let's go show your grandfather."

Allison followed her grandmother to the living room, where the rest of the family was.

"Well, aren't you just the prettiest little thing, Queenie?" said Aunt Nancy.

"Gorgeous," said Aunt Paulette.

"Oh, I don't know about all that," said Allison, blushing.

"I do," said Granddad Derrick. "My little Queen is all grown up."

"Jordan, don't you think Queenie looks nice?" asked Aunt Nancy.

"Yeah sure," uttered Jordan, his eyes remaining on the television.

"You didn't even look at her!"

"She looks fine," said Jordan, glancing at Allison before returning to the television.

"This boy," griped Aunt Nancy.

"Do you mind if I get a few pictures?" asked Granddad Derrick.

"Go ahead," said Allison.

A few photos later, Mrs. Harrison entered the room. Her dress was plain.

"Oh, you look nice!" exclaimed Aunt Nancy.

"Can I get a few pictures of you two together?" asked Granddad Derrick.

"Only a few because we need to get going," said Mrs. Harrison.

Allison marveled at the size of the Perry's house and land. She had been there before when she was younger, but the memories of that time were scarce. As they drove up the driveway, Allison took in the full beauty of the house. The two-story, brown, antebellum-styled home was held up by white Tuscan columns that boasted a wraparound porch fenced in by iron banisters. It was a shame to Allison that such a beautiful home was wasted on such terrible people.

"Hello Mrs. Soleya," said the butler when the women entered the front door. "It's so nice to have your radiant smile light this place up again, ma'am."

"Thank you, Jack," said Mrs. Harrison. "Could you let Mother know Allison and I are here?"

"That's Allison?!" gasped Mr. Jack. "Well, I'll be! The last time I saw her she was just a cute little baby!"

"She's certainly not a baby anymore," said Mrs. Harrison.

"Hello Miss Allison!" said Mr. Jack, addressing Allison. "Do you remember me?"

"I'm sorry, I don't," answered Allison.

"That's alright," said Mr. Jack. "I'll let Lady Sophia know you've both arrived."

"Thank you, Jack," said Mrs. Harrison.

"How long has he worked here?" asked Allison when Mr. Jack was gone.

"Since before I was born," answered Mrs. Harrison. "He's the longest-lasting staff member in this house."

Allison followed her mother into the parlor where Aunt Soriah sat.

"Where's Mother?" asked Mrs. Harrison.

"She'll be down any minute," said Aunt Soriah. "Daddy is at his bar with Quincy and Marcellus. Are any of the Harrison men coming?"

"Not to my knowledge."

"Daddy won't be too happy about that," said Aunt Soriah. "I hope you don't mind my suggesting camellias as the main decor for the ball. I would've had roses since they're Derik's favorite, but they're not in season."

"It's fine," said Mrs. Harrison with a sad smile. "What's important is that they're an appropriate reminder for what this year's ball is about."

"If it isn't my favorite aunt and cousin," said Marcellus, entering the parlor with a glass in his hand.

"Is that mine?" said Aunt Soriah.

"If you want," said Marcellus, handing the glass to his mother. "You want one too, Auntie?"

"No, thank you," said Mrs. Harrison.

"What about you, Queenie?"

"I'm eighteen," answered Allison. "I can't drink that."

"So?" said Marcellus. "Didn't stop me when I was eighteen."

"And that's why you're a hot mess now."

"I can't help it that I like to have fun," said Marcellus. "Life's too short not to experience everything it has to offer."

"I don't think I want to experience it the way you do."

"Suit yourself."

"Florence!" yelled an older woman's voice. "FLORENCE!"

"She's coming in hot," said Marcellus. "You sure you don't want that drink?"

"I'm sure," said Allison.

"Where is that useless maid?" griped Lady Sophia Perry as she strode into the room. Her dark-brown face was caked in makeup, and a gaudy purple and gold day dress adorned her petite frame. She surveyed the room with her brown eyes looking for her maid, Florence. Allison noticed Aunt Soriah glance at Marcellus, who slightly shook his head at her.

"Hello Mother," said Mrs. Harrison.

Lady Sophia did not answer her daughter. Instead, she looked her over from top to bottom, and her face changed to one of mild disdain.

"Is that what you plan on wearing tonight?" asked Lady Sophia.

"No Mother," said Mrs. Harrison. "I have another dress for tonight."

"Good," said Lady Sophia. She glanced at Allison and asked, "What about her?"

"Allison?"

"Yes her."

"Yes, that's what she's wearing tonight."

"I guess it'll have to suffice," said Lady Sophia unimpressed. "You better go and change now. The guests will be here soon."

"Yes Mother," said Mrs. Harrison. "Come along, Allison."

Allison obeyed her mother, following her through the house. Her mother led her to a room where a hand-painted portrait of her mother as a teenager hung on the wall. Trophies and achievements littered the space, giving the impression that the room had been undisturbed since her mother last occupied it.

"Unzip me please," requested Mrs. Harrison.

"This was your room?" asked Allison, obliging the request.

"Yes," answered Mrs. Harrison as she slipped out of the dress. "I didn't spend much time in here though. I used to sneak and play with Leilana in the servant's quarters while Mrs. Ernestine cleaned the house. Then when I got older, I used to sneak out and go hang out at her house."

"Why did you have to sneak around so much?"

"Mother didn't want us to be too familiar with the staff and their families."

"So... she wasn't rich enough to be your friend."

"That's one way of putting it," said Mrs. Harrison. She handed her dress to Allison, saying, "Take this, please.

"Why are you changing dresses?"

"That's my decoy dress."

"Your what?"

"It's something Soriah came up with," explained Mrs. Harrison. "If I show Mother a less flattering dress first, then when she sees the one I actually want to wear, by default she'll like it because it's the better dress."

"Why not just wear the dress you want to the first time?"

"Because then she'll find something wrong with that one and I'll have to wear something else."

Mrs. Harrison disappeared into the closet to put on her new dress while Allison looked around the room.

"This certificate is awarded to Soleya Naima Perry for Outstanding Academic Performance at the Willard Academy for Girls," said Allison, reading one of the certificates on display.

"Do I look okay?" asked Mrs. Harrison, exiting the closet. Her new dress was form-fitting and glittering. It looked way better than her first one.

"Yes," answered Allison. "Where's this school?"

"It's a private institution in the city," explained Mrs. Harrison. "Your aunt graduated from there."

"Why didn't you?"

"I didn't like it there," said Mrs. Harrison. "It took a rather embarrassing tantrum when I was fourteen to get my parents to withdraw me so I could attend school here in Creeke with the other kids."

"I'm surprised you didn't send me to a school like that," remarked Allison.

"You wouldn't have fit in," stated Mrs. Harrison. "Willard prides itself on producing a certain quality of refined young ladies."

"Are you saying I'm not refined?"

"I'm saying you wouldn't have fit in there," said Mrs. Harrison. She looked at the clock and said, "The guests will be arriving soon. Let's head back downstairs."

As Allison followed her mother through the house, she wondered what it was like for her mother to grow up there. She imagined her prancing around the hallway with her sister. Sneaking out into the garden to frolic in the sun with a young First Lady Hall as they stifled their joyous giggles to avoid rousing the ire of Lady Sophia. Presenting herself atop the staircase as a young lady to a visitor, gently gliding down with graceful step until she reached the bottom to present her hand for a kiss. Her mother's origins were in that house, and possibly the answers to why she was the way she was were too.

The ball began at six o'clock sharp. From Allison's understanding, guests would be introduced by Mr. Jack by their level of importance in the community. Nanna Kiana was the guest of honor and would be the final person introduced. Toward the end of the ball, the Perrys would present all the donations to Nanna Kiana. It was all very organized, and Allison figured it was to cast the Perrys in the best possible light.

Allison took note of every guest that attended the ball. The Townsends, the Greens, the Dows, the Brewers, the Lees, the Paynes, the Vaughn siblings, the Ms. Nelson that was not engaged who came with Mr. Vaughn, Mr. Lewis and his wife Mrs. Hall, Brianne, Mr. Haynes, Chief Parker's children and their cousin Naomi, and the Garza sisters. To every guest was Allison hospitable, and only one family remained to be introduced.

"Presenting Mrs. Kiana Danette Harrison, accompanied by Mrs. Nancy Mae Keaton and Ms. Paulette Jean Barnett."

Everyone watched quietly as Nanna Kiana and her sisters approached the Perrys.

"Hello Bernard," said Nanna Kiana. "Sophia. Quincy. Soriah. Marcellus. Soleya. Allison."

"Hello Kiana," replied Lady Sophia. "So nice of you to come."

"Will Pastor Harrison be joining us this evening?" asked Mayor Perry.

"I'm afraid not," answered Nanna Kiana.

"That's too bad," sighed Mayor Perry.

"I'm sure his absence will be greatly missed," said Lady Sophia. "May I trouble you to acquaint us with these ladies you've brought with you?"

"These are my younger sisters, Paulette and Nancy."

"Pleased to make your acquaintance," said Aunt Paulette.

"You have a beautiful house," said Aunt Nancy. "Very spacious."

"Thank you," said Lady Sophia, arrogantly holding her head up.

"I believe we've taken up enough of your time," said Nanna Kiana. "I hope you'll take good care of my granddaughter. I'm sure she's glad to be here. Isn't that right, Allison?"

"I couldn't miss it even if I tried," muttered Allison, earning sharp looks from Nanna Kiana and her mother.

"I'm sure Allison will have plenty of enjoyment tonight," said Lady Sophia. Once Nanna Kiana was out of earshot, Lady Sophia muttered just loud enough for Allison to hear, "Even if she is a charmless child."

Mrs. Harrison glared at Allison, quieting any opportunity she had to respond to the insult lodged against her.

"My wife and I would like to thank you all for attending this evening," said Mayor Perry. "We hope you all enjoy yourselves, and if you can find it in your heart to give even a little to the cause of finding my grandson, we'd greatly appreciate it. No donation is too small, nor too big. With that being said, let the fun begin."

Everyone clapped and broke off into groups to mingle amongst themselves.

"Money," scoffed Allison. "That's all they care about."

"Be mindful of our guests, Allison," said Mrs. Harrison.

"You're always so worried about what everyone else thinks," argued Allison. "But I don't care what they think. They can talk all they want, but I'll always hold my head high with dignity."

"I guess the old saying is right, Leya," teased Aunt Soriah. "The apple really doesn't fall far from the tree."

"But the question is which tree did the apple fall from?" remarked Mrs. Harrison.

"Yours, clearly," chuckled Aunt Soriah. "Mother's in one of her nit-picking moods, so I'd make sure all my hairpins were in before I went near her if I were you."

"Must you always bring that up, my dear?" said Mrs. Harrison with a matching smile.

"Only because I care," said Aunt Soriah. "I better go make sure Marcellus doesn't empty the bar all by himself tonight."

"A little late for that," mumbled Allison.

"Come along, Allison," said Mrs. Harrison.

"Where are we going?" asked Allison.

"We have to make sure everyone is having a good time," said Mrs. Harrison. "Remember to smile but not too much, and don't say anything rude."

"Must you have so little faith in me, Mother?"

"And don't be argumentative either."

Allison rolled her eyes. Had she known she would be playing hostess, she would have tried harder to get out of going to the ball. She made her way to Danielle and the Garza sisters to get the hard people out of the way first.

"Hello girls," said Allison, forcing a smile onto her face. "You all look lovely this evening."

"We know," said Danielle haughtily.

"It was a compliment, Dani," said Allison, maintaining her smile.

"As if I need your compliments," snorted Danielle.

"See Dani, I only have so much time to spend with each guest tonight and I want to make sure the Garza sisters get a chance to speak to me too," said Allison. "Anything you two would like to say?"

"I don't have anything to say to you," stated Mariana.

"Me either," said Mariella.

"As you wish," said Allison, smiling so hard she felt her face would rip in two if she smiled any wider. "It's been wonderful talking to you all, but I mustn't keep myself from the other guests. If you'll all excuse me."

"Yeah, you do that," said Danielle as Allison walked away.

The next group she went to was Latasia, Kameryn, Charmaine, and Nicole.

"Hello ladies," greeted Allison.

"You can drop the façade," said Latasia.

"I wish," said Allison, maintaining her smile. "I have to be nice to everyone."

"Well, we're your friends so that shouldn't be too hard," said Latasia. "Right Nicki?"

"Ri...right," uttered Nicole, once again refusing to look Allison in the eye.

"I can't stay too long," said Allison. "But are you guys having fun?"

"I am," said Kameryn.

"Do you like my dress?" asked Charmaine. "Benji bought it for me."

"Oh," said Allison. "Benji's got it like that, huh? It's cute."

"Thanks," said Charmaine.

Allison made her way around the room, greeting everyone. She answered questions about school, work, and what she planned to do after graduation. But the one topic everyone stayed away from was Derik. No one mentioned him at a ball that was advertised to be about him. Eventually, she found her way to Nisha, who stood near the wall by herself.

"Nice wig," said Nisha when Allison approached.

"It better be since it cost a 'nice' amount of money," said Allison. "I'm surprised you didn't get Deidrick to come with you."

"He's mad at me," sighed Nisha.

"What happened?"

"I went on a date with another guy, and he found out and went ballistic."

"Dang," said Allison. "I didn't know you got down like that Nisha."

"I was just trying to make him feel how he makes me feel, but it backfired," said Nisha. "Now he won't return any of my texts or calls or speak to me at the shop either."

"I don't know what to say," said Allison. She liked Nisha, but Deidrick was still her brother, and she did not want to have to take sides in their relationship drama. After ending her conversation with Nisha, Allison looked out the windows overlooking the gardens and noticed Priscella standing outside by herself. Priscella and her had talked a few times since their first conversation at church, and Allison realized Priscella was not that bad.

"What are you doing out here all by yourself?" asked Allison. From where they stood, they had a good view of the fountain in the center of the gardens. Ms. Greta stood near it, looking at the water.

"Nobody in there likes me," said Priscella.

"So?" said Allison. Mr. Bud had joined Ms. Greta at the fountain, and Allison's interest was piqued. "Lots of people in there don't like me either, but I'm not going to let that affect me having a good time. You shouldn't either."

"Why do you even care?" griped Priscella. "You only talk to me because your grandmother makes you."

"That's how it started," said Allison. The conversation between Ms. Greta and Mr. Bud seemed to have become heated. He tried to take her hand, but she pulled away and turned from him. "But now I talk to you because I want to."

"Why?" said Priscella, turning to Allison. "I'm an outcast."

"Because I don't treat people according to their popularity," said Allison. "That's Danielle's thing."

"And if Dani did it, then that means I did it too," sighed Priscella.

"Yeah, you did," said Allison, wincing. "But you're trying to do better, so that counts for something."

"Yeah," snorted Priscella. "Now instead of three bad friends, I have no friends at all."

"Dang," said Allison. "And here I was thinking we were starting to become friends."

"Seriously?" said Priscella. "You want to be my friend?"

"Well, don't make it sound like a curse or something," joked Allison. The conversation between Mr. Bud and Ms. Greta seemed to lighten up. She faced him again and drew near to him. "If someone had told me a year ago that we would be getting along, I would've laughed in their face and called them a liar. And who knows? Maybe once people get to know you like I did, I'm sure they'll come around and give you a second chance."

"Yeah right," said Priscella. "Why would anyone want to give me a second chance?"

"Because you're not a bad person," encouraged Allison. Her heart began to race as she watched the couple near the fountain. They were drawing closer and closer to each other.

"You really think so?"

"I do."

"And you really do want to be my friend?"

"Well, yeah," confirmed Allison. "I'd say that I want us to be friends."

"I have a friend," said Priscella, a smile slowly spreading across her face. "I have a friend!"

"Mr. Bud and Ms. Greta kissed.

"Did you see that?!" gasped Allison.

"What?" asked Priscella.

"Mr. Bud and Ms. Twin kissed!"

"Really?! Where?!"

"There you are!" said Mrs. Harrison, coming up to them. "They're about to open the dance floor."

"Finally!" said Allison, losing sight of the couple. "Something fun to do!"

"You're not dancing."

"Seriously?" cried Allison. "I don't get to dance?"

"Mother prefers that the hostesses refrain from dancing."

"I don't care what she wants!"

"Allison."

Allison could not believe it. The very essence of a party was being able to dance and socialize. But her socializations all evening had been brief and polite. And while Marcellus made a drunken fool of himself on the dance floor, she had to sit off to the side like some delicate flower that should not be disturbed.

"Marcellus and Quincy really seem to be full of spirit this evening," laughed Lady Sophia, fanning herself gingerly with a white folded fan.

"They're full of spirits alright," snorted Aunt Soriah.

"It's a shame Marlin couldn't be here too, Soleya," said Lady Sophia. "I hope everything's alright."

"Marlin's fine, Mother," said Mrs. Harrison. "He just doesn't like parties."

"It seems there are many things he doesn't like," said Lady Sophia, eyeing her daughter. "You know, I'm glad you chose to wear this dress. That other one did nothing for your figure."

"Thank you, Mother."

"Perhaps if Marlin saw you in this one, he would've been more inclined to come."

"Perhaps, Mother."

"Soriah, who did your hair?"

"Soleya, Mother."

"Really?" said Lady Sophia. "It was so well done, I almost mistook it for a professional stylist's work."

At this, Allison raised her eyebrow. Regardless of how she felt about her mother's personal priorities, she never decried her mother's abilities as a hairstylist. Allison expected her mother to say something to defend her profession, but Mrs. Harrison remained quiet. But her expression turned from complacent to surprised, and Allison looked to see what had caused the change.

"Presenting Mister Derek Drumaine Harrison."

Allison watched as her cousin entered the ball. His lithe, muscular figure was adorned with a silver, rose-patterned polyester blazer and white slacks. He strode confidently through the crowd right up to where Allison sat.

"Hello Auntie," said Derek to Mrs. Harrison. He turned to Aunt Soriah and Lady Sophia and said, "Auntie's sister and mother."

Allison stifled a laugh at the titles Derek had bestowed upon Lady Sophia and Aunt Soriah. He turned to Allison and grinned, revealing himself to be wearing the golden grill he had received as a birthday present.

"Good evening, milady," said Derek in a proper-ish tone, bowing before Allison. He extended his hand to her and said, "Might I have this dance?"

"Why certainly, my good sir," said Allison, emulating Derek's tone. She took his hand and allowed herself to be led to the dance floor. "Now I must inform you that I have no idea how to waltz."

"Then I guess it's a good thing you have an expert on the matter as your partner," laughed Derek heartily. "All you have to do is follow my lead."

Derek took Allison's hand in his and began to walk her through the waltz. They glided around the dance floor amongst the other dancers.

"Hanging in there?" asked Derek.

"Barely until my knight in shining armor showed up," answered Allison. "They really wanted me to watch everyone else dance while I sat up there looking like some stuffy royal princess looking down on her peasants enjoying themselves."

"Well, I'm glad to be of service to my big cousin," chuckled Derek.

"Why are you here anyways? I thought you didn't want to come."

"I didn't. But I then I imagined how bored you'd be without me, so I came anyways."

"And you didn't want to bring your girlfriend along with you?"

"She didn't want to come," said Derek. "She doesn't like the Perrys very much."

"Can't say I blame her."

"I do have something to share with you though," said Derek. He dropped his voice to a whisper and said, "I found a ransom note in Uncle Marlin's coat pocket."

"A what?!" shouted Allison.

"Shh!" hushed Derek, covering Allison's mouth with his hand.

"What did it say?" whispered Allison, swatting her cousin's hand away.

"I don't remember exactly, but Uncle Marlin got it yesterday."

"So, Dee-Three was kidnapped."

"Seems like it."

"But why would someone take him?"

"More like who," said Derek. "Whoever took him knows your parents have money and also knew about Monique Evans."

"You think it was someone in Creeke?"

"It could be," said Derek. "But who could benefit from this?"

"May I have everyone's attention please?" said Mayor Perry as the waltz ended. "We'd like to take this time to thank everyone who donated to our cause."

"There's your prime suspect right there," grumbled Allison. "He's benefitted greatly from this situation."

"I would like to call our guest of honor Mrs. Kiana Harrison up here," said Mayor Perry.

Allison watched as her grandmother went to stand with Mayor Perry.

"Mrs. Harrison, we want to present this check to you," said Mayor Perry. "We hope and pray that it be more than helpful in the search for our grandson."

"Thank you," said Nanna Kiana. The pair posed for a photo that would be featured in the Creeke Courier.

"This whole thing is so fake and forced," said Derek. "I can't believe Nanna agreed to this."

"Neither can I," said Allison. "The whole thing is just sad."

"Is there anything you would liked to say?" said Mayor Perry to Nanna Kiana.

"Yes, there is," said Nanna Kiana. "The Bible in First Peter Three verse Eight tells us to be of one mind, to have compassion, to love one another as brethren, and to be sympathetic and humble. I want to thank you Mayor Perry and Lady Sophia for being courteous enough to ensure that my family had the means to locate our grandson by putting on this event because you didn't have to. And I want to thank you all who showed up tonight and donated to this cause. We are very appreciative of what you all have done for us not only financially but also with moral support. Our family continues to ask that you keep us in your prayers. Thank you."

"I shouldn't have done this," yawned Nanna Kiana as she undid the seams on Allison's dress after the ball. "Because now I'm sleepy and I can't go to bed until it's done."

"I told you," said Allison.

"Did you enjoy yourself tonight?"

"After D-Money showed up, I did."

"Yeah, I didn't really want to be there either. But your grandfather told me it was a good opportunity to preach The Word, and we both thought it would be better that the money be presented to me than to your mother. But she told me after I accepted it to give it to Marlin. I thought it was a good idea because the last thing she needs is another reason for people to talk about her badly right now."

"Even her own mother talks badly about her," complained Allison. "She was repeatedly disrespected the whole night by that woman for no reason and I don't like that."

"Don't involve yourself in it," advised Nanna Kiana. "Let Soleil deal with her mother as she sees fit."

"I just don't like to see people mistreated, that's all," said Allison. "But it shocks me that Mother would allow herself to be treated like that. I expected her to speak up for herself."

"If that's what you expected, you don't know your mother as well as you think you do," said Nanna Kiana. "If you spent less time fighting her and more time embracing her, you would understand a lot better the reasons your mother does what she does."

"Are you sure you're not just saying that because you're biased towards your "precious Soleil", Nanna?" teased Allison.

"She's precious to me for a reason," said Nanna Kiana. "You're so much like her and you don't even realize it. But I can't force you to see that. You'll have to discover it for yourself."

Chapter Fourteen:
Matthias

"Derik, what do you want for your birthday? You'll be the big one-six, man."

"Wings."

"Wings? Like chicken wings?"

"No, wings like a dove."

"What poetry book did you pull that from?"

"The Bible."

"Maybe that's what I'll get you."

"What?"

"A poetry book.

"A poetry book?"

"You've always been good with words."

"Hmm..."

"Not something you want?"

"It could be cool. I've already got the first line for one."

"Cool. What is it?

"Would you turn your music down please?"

"Nah. This is my car. You know how I roll."

"It was worth a shot. How about another one?"

"Okay."

"You ready?"

"Yeah."

"Will you miss me when I'm gone?"

Yes. That was his answer to Derik's first line of his poem. Matthias thought of Derik as he weaved between cars on the city highway. One month ago, his brother had been with him in his car, and now he was gone. He had learned no new information about Derik since that day at the sandwich shop. The city was too big for him to cover alone, and he did not even want to consider the possibility of Derik not being in the city at all. Therefore, Matthias begrudgingly accepted he could do nothing more and had to wait along with everyone else for new information.

However, Matthias was not keen on returning to live with the Campbells because he was still mad at Marcellus. He needed a moment to get his mind right and decided to take advantage of being in the city to finally help his grandfather's best friend, Richard Anderson, with his car. Mr. Richard lived in a two-story house in the suburbs with his wife, Kate. Their daughter Kaitlyn lived down the street from them with her husband, John.

When Matthias arrived, he found his grandfather standing with Mr. Richard in the front yard tossing a football and laughing. Matthias had not heard his grandfather laugh at all since Derik had disappeared. His grandfather's visage had been perpetually grim, and his eyes tired and almost completely devoid of life. Seeing his grandfather have fun, hearing him laugh, had been almost like a return to normalcy for Matthias.

"Granddad?" said Matthias. "What are you doing here?"

"I was bringing Jordan back home and came to see about you," said Granddad Derrick. "James said you came here, but you weren't here when I got here and Rick pulled out the old football, and now here we are."

"And I won too," laughed Mr. Richard.

"You did not," said Granddad Derrick, laughing just the same.

"Yeah, I did," said Mr. Richard. "I got you to laugh. That means I won."

"Oh alright," relented Granddad Derrick. "You won."

"I'm going to go see what John is doing to my car in the garage," said Mr. Richard. "You guys come join us when you're ready."

Mr. Richard walked away, leaving Matthias to talk alone with his grandfather.

"I guess you couldn't straighten Jordan out after all," said Matthias.

"There's nothing to straighten out," said Granddad Derrick. "Jordan wants to learn the truth about life the hard way, and I came to an understanding with your Aunt Nancy that he can do that at home. His antics were putting me at risk of letting out a side of me that I don't to come out anymore."

"I get what you mean," said Matthias. "Once the monster is out, he's hard to get back in his cage."

"And when he's out, he's cruel and wrecks everything," said Granddad Derrick, his mouth setting into a frown. "Even when he's caged back up, he still wrecks stuff."

"That's why you find others to help keep him controlled," said Matthias. "He can't come out if others help you keep him in check. For example, you help me keep my monster controlled."

"I do?"

"Yeah," said Matthias. "Whenever you come around me, you make me want to do right."

"That's not me," laughed Granddad Derrick. "That's The Lord shining His light through me."

"Well, The Big Guy is a big help then."

"The Big Guy," chuckled Granddad Derrick. "I remember when I taught you and your brother that to make things easier for you both to understand."

There was a silent pause.

"You know, that monster of yours really tore up your relationship with your brother," said Granddad Derrick.

"I just can't get along with him," sighed Matthias. "It's like any time I'm with him I just get mad at him, and everything goes wrong."

"Unforgiveness," said Granddad Derrick. "I've been there. Unforgiveness will have you acting completely out of character and hurting people you didn't mean to hurt."

"Hmm," muttered Matthias.

"I don't know all of what happened back then, but I know hardened spirits when I see them," said Granddad Derrick. "You and him both are hardened with pride. If you both set your pride aside, you guys could set things right."

"You think so?"

"I know so," said Granddad Derrick. "Now, what do you say we go see what Rick and John are trying to do with this car."

"Okay."

Mr. Richard stood in his garage with John. The car in question was an old-school brown car. Matthias began running diagnostics on it while Granddad Derrick, Mr. Richard, and John stood aside watching.

"John, if you didn't know what you were doing, you should've just said so," said Mr. Richard.

"Dad, you just need to get a new car," said John.

"I've had this car for a long time, John, and it still runs perfectly fine!"

"Well, it's not running now."

"And that's why Matt is here," said Mr. Richard, acknowledging Matthias. "He's going to fix it because he's good with cars."

"That depends on what's wrong with it," interjected Granddad Derrick. "But I agree with John, Rick. You just need to get a new car."

"Ricky, you're supposed to be on my side!"

"I am on your side, Rick. What'll you do if you break down on the side of the road?"

"That's how we ended up here in the first place," muttered John.

"The only opinion here I'm interested in is Matthias's," declared Mr. Richard. "Matt, can you tell what's wrong with it?"

"Sure," said Matthias. "It needs a lot of maintenance, but the reason it's not running is because your battery's dead."

"Richard," grumbled Granddad Derrick, rubbing his temples. "How did you let that happen?"

"I didn't," said Mr. Richard. "John handles all that for me now."

"Oh sure, blame it all on me," said John sarcastically. "It's not like it's your car, Dad."

"Either way, looks like I'm putting up money for a new battery," sighed Mr. Richard. "Thanks for your help, Matt."

"No problem."

After determining the issue with Mr. Richard's car, everyone gathered in his house to watch the football game. Matthias watched as the players ran back and forth across the field, reminiscing on the days when he would watch the game at his grandparent's house. His grandparents would cheer and rage at the screen in the same manner that his grandfather, Mr. Richard, Mrs. Kate, Kaitlyn, John, and even himself were doing then. It made him glad to see his grandfather behaving like himself again.

"Want a beer?" asked John when they both went into the kitchen during a commercial break.

"No thanks," said Matthias. "I try not to drink in front of my grandfather out of respect."

"Got it," said John. "That's a nice car you've got out there,"

"Thanks," said Matthias. His candy red car was his greatest accomplishment. Imagining the stares he got when the speaker in his trunk bumped music loud enough to shake the car made him laugh. He loved leaning his seat all the way back while blue decorative light not only filled the car's interior but lit up the road under him too. But what he loved most was that he had paid for everything. No one else could hold his car over his head, and it was that feeling of independence that Matthias loved most.

"Do you work on it yourself?" asked John.

"Yeah," answered Matthias. "My uncle taught me everything I know about cars."

"You'd probably make a great mechanic."

"I used to be one, but I quit."

"Oh?"

"John, Matt!" called Kaitlyn. "The game's back on!"

The men returned to watching the game. Back and forth the players ran, drawing forth mixed emotions from the spectators who watched them. In the fourth quarter, Mr. Richard's favorite team was five yards away from the victory touchdown. This was their last chance to win. With less than a minute left on the clock, the play went into motion. And everything went well until the final hope was taken down without reaching the goal line.

"Oh!" cried Kaitlyn. "So close!"

"Darn it!" exclaimed Mr. Richard. "There's no way we'll win now!"

"Richie," said Mrs. Kate. "Calm down."

"I am calm!" declared Mr. Richard. "But these boys nowadays don't know what they're doing! Back in my day we would've never let an opportunity like that get away!"

"Oh boy," said Kaitlyn. "Here he goes talking about the good ol' days again."

"I was a good player back in my day," said Mr. Richard. "The rush I used to get whenever I was on the field was awesome. I miss that feeling."

"Me too," said Granddad Derrick. "I know I shouldn't, but I miss those days when life was simple."

Gone were those days, and Matthias knew it. The illusion of normalcy, of everything being as it was before, was gone. He looked at his grandfather and realized he was also gone. His funny, warm-hearted grandfather was gone, and the tired, lifeless shadow that had filled his place for the past two weeks had returned. And gone was the kind, younger brother that Matthias loved. Derik was still gone.

Chapter Fifteen: Deidrick

"Cornbread, can I ask you advice on my hair?"

"You want me to cut it off, Dee-Three? Because I still can't believe you let Mom convince you to grow it that long."

"No, I like my hair this length. I was thinking of dyeing it blonde for my birthday."

"Like the blonde highlights you did a few years ago?"

"No, fully blonde. What do you think?"

"I don't specialize in coloring, but you do realize coloring your hair is a big change, right?"

"Maybe that's what I want. A big change."

A big change. Derik had talked of making a big change a month before he disappeared, and now Deidrick would possibly experience his own big change. Deidrick sat in the parking lot of Sharon's apartment complex, contemplating how he would go about confronting her. He suspected she was pregnant and wanted to know if the baby was his.

His baby. The thought made Deidrick queasy. Children were not a part of his immediate life plans, and he hoped Sharon could ease his mind by telling him the baby was Malik's. As he gathered the nerve to exit the car, he saw Sharon rush from her apartment with Malik. They seemed to be having another argument.

Deidrick did not know why, but he followed them. Following a girl was not ordinary for him, but Sharon was no longer an ordinary girl to him. He needed answers and figured he would get them if he stayed patient. In his mind, they were going to a pregnancy clinic or something like it. But Sharon and Malik drove north of the city to a trailer in the woods and Deidrick, unsure of what was happening, hid his car behind some trees a few feet away. A few minutes later, a tall third person exited the trailer and joined them in the car. The trio sped off, and after waiting to ensure they were gone, Deidrick exited his car and crept up to the trailer. After failing to find a spare key to get inside, he took a hairpin from his pocket and began working at the lock.

"Always keep a few handy," said Deidrick, mimicking Marcellus. "You never know when you'll need to pick a lock or two."

Once inside, Deidrick first noticed a necklace with a circular-shaped accessory on the floor. Deidrick picked it up and upon closer inspection, realized the accessory was a poker chip. Etched into the bottom were the letters 'MH'. It was the necklace he had gifted to Matthias years before.

"Why is this here?" questioned Deidrick.

He inspected the rest of the trailer. The living room was a mess, while the bathroom trash can contained clumps of black curly hair and bloody tissues. In the bedroom, the bedsheets were tousled as if someone had lain in them, and a money-filled envelope lay on the nightstand. However, there was nothing in the trailer to explain how the necklace had gotten there, and Deidrick returned home unsatisfied.

It was clearly Matthias's necklace because Deidrick remembered Matthias etching those initials into it. But Deidrick had not seen Matthias wear that necklace since their falling out. It was always possible that Matthias had worn it since then, but Deidrick entertained another possibility. He found the newspaper that mentioned Derik's last known appearance and re-read it.

"...*and a necklace with a black circular accessory,*" read Deidrick.

There it was. Derik had been wearing the necklace when he went missing, which meant Derik had been at that trailer. Deidrick was more anxious than ever to question Sharon. He wanted to know why she went to that trailer and whether she was pregnant with his baby. But before he could further investigate, a knock at his door caught his attention. Nisha stood in his doorway, looking at him.

"How did you get in here?" asked Deidrick.

"Your grandmother let me in," explained Nisha.

"What do you want?"

"To talk," answered Nisha. "You haven't called me."

"Why should I?" snorted Deidrick. "You found yourself a new man, right?"

"He's not my new man."

"Then who is he?"

"I don't know."

"You don't know?"

"We met online. That was the first time I'd ever seen him."

"He didn't give you a name?"

"Hak."

"That's his name?"

"That's what he told me it was."

"Last name?"

"He didn't say."

"So, you were going to make me jealous with a guy you don't even know?" questioned Deidrick. "How long would this have gone on if I didn't catch you? How did you even plan on me finding out?"

"I invited him to the shop to get his hair cut."

"You were going to bring him to my job?!"

"First of all, it's my job too," said Nisha. "And it wasn't going to become anything serious. Deidrick, you have to believe me when I say you're the only one I want."

"You have a funny way of showing it."

"You're so selfish!"

"I'm the selfish one?"

"Yes," said Nisha. "Don't you get why I've resorted to this to try and get your attention? I've been waiting three years for you Deidrick, and it's because I love you and see so much in you."

"Okay."

"Okay?" repeated Nisha. "That's all you have to say?"

"What do you want me to say?" asked Deidrick.

"Deidrick please," begged Nisha.

"Just go."

Nisha sighed and left. A few seconds later, there was another knock on his door, and Deidrick became irritated.

"I thought I told you to go!" barked Deidrick. But when he turned around, it was not Nisha in the doorway. It was his mother. "Oh. I thought you were Nisha."

"Did you two have an argument?" asked Mrs. Harrison, sitting on the bed.

"Something like that," answered Deidrick.

"Well, at least I'm not the only one having relationship issues around here."

"She tried to make me jealous by flirting with another guy."

"She did?"

"Yeah. And when I caught her doing it, now I'm the bad guy."

"That's just like with me and your father," ranted Mrs. Harrison. "I'm the bad guy because I'm mad about the fact that Sharon came onto him. In fact, he thinks I should be applauding him for rejecting her!"

Deidrick remained silent. The last thing he wanted on his mind was Sharon and her possible pregnancy.

"But my thing is, Sharon should not have even been comfortable enough with him to do that in the first place," continued Mrs. Harrison. "So, now I'm wondering what he did or said to make her feel like she had room to do that. He probably was flirting with her just like Nisha was flirting with that other guy. If I were you, I'd dump her."

"We're not together."

"So, that talk just now was you breaking up with her?"

"We were never together."

"You weren't?"

"No."

"This whole time I thought you two were in a relationship," said Mrs. Harrison. "If you two were never together, then why are you mad at her?"

"Because I'm the only guy that she's supposed to be dealing with."

"So... you're not together, but you don't want her to be with anyone else?"

"Not when she's dealing with me."

"You're selfish," said Mrs. Harrison, standing up.

"Dang Mother," said Deidrick. "I thought you were on my side."

"I thought I was too," said Mrs. Harrison. "But you're just like my father. Everything has to be your way and that's it."

"I'm just saying," said Deidrick. "If we're supposed to be working toward a relationship, then why is she flirting with other guys?"

"How long do you expect her to work toward the relationship?"

"Until I'm ready!"

"See? Selfish."

"Man, whatever," said Deidrick. "Any girl that deals with me shouldn't be flirting with other guys."

"And that should go the same for you too," said Mrs. Harrison. "You shouldn't be flirting with other girls either."

Those were his mother's parting words. She was supposed to be on his side but instead had sided against him. Deidrick realized he was alone in facing the big changes happening in his life. Big changes that he was unprepared for and did not want to happen.

-

Chapter Sixteen: Derek

"Do you ever regret getting a tattoo?"

"No. I plan to get more when I'm grown."

"You do?"

"Yeah."

"You can do anything you want when you're grown. But when you're a kid, it's like you can't do anything."

"Well, what are you trying to do that's so special that you can't wait two more years?"

"Nothing. I was just talking."

"You'll be sixteen in a few weeks. That means you'll be old enough to drive by yourself. That's something to look forward to."

"You'll be eighteen and you don't drive."

"That's because I don't have a car. But I do have a license."

"What are you going to do when you get a car and graduate?"

"I don't know. Go wherever my feet take me, I guess. As long as I'm able to dance, I'll be okay."

"You're so optimistic."

"Sometimes you have to be. You to have hope even when you don't want to."

"I guess you're right. Sixteen is something to look forward to, right?"

"Yeah. Because it's one year closer to adulthood."

"Yeah. Okay."

Winter break had ended, and the start of the final stretch of senior year was upon Derek. In six months, he would be free of the chains of high school and enter adulthood. As he entered the kitchen for breakfast, he found Uncle Marlin reading the Creeke Courier at the table.

"Hey Uncle Marlin."

"Yo."

Derek chuckled.

"What's funny?"

"You always say 'yo' as your greeting."

"So?"

"I think it suits you," said Derek. He sniffed the air and said, "Something smells good."

"I made breakfast."

"I didn't know you cooked!"

"I don't usually but I know how to."

"Well, what made you do it this time?"

"I was hungry."

Uncle Marlin had cooked French toast, bacon, sausage, and scrambled eggs. Derek made himself a plate and thought it tasted delightful. He had become more comfortable with having his uncle around and was glad his pre-judgments about him were wrong.

"What smells good in here?" asked Malcolm, entering the kitchen.

"Uncle Marlin cooked."

"I love when you cook," cheered Malcolm. "That summer you spent working with Uncle Damian was the best thing to ever happen to you."

As Derek ate his breakfast, he looked at the newspaper Uncle Marlin held, and a headline caught his attention.

'It's on sight': KV, Knokout arrested following nightclub brawl, shooting

"Can I see that?" asked Derek.

"Sure," answered Uncle Marlin, handing him the paper.

'It's on sight': KV, Knokout arrested following nightclub brawl, shooting

Rappers KV and Knokout are facing several charges after a violent nightclub brawl that left three people injured on Saturday.

A viral video clip captured the fight and subsequent shooting at Sepia nightclub. According to Sepia's social media pages, Knokout was the headliner for their pajama-themed 'Jamma Jam' event. A witness who wished to remain anonymous stated the brawl started immediately after KV entered the club around 12:30 am.

"It was no words," the witness said. "KV and his crew walked in, and he took off on [Knokout]. Knokout caught hit him with that bottle and it went from there."

Footage from the fight shows KV rush at Knokout, who picks up a beer bottle and smashes it against KV's head. The two then wrestle and punch each other. The man with Knokout, identified as his cousin Zion Cartwright, 27, tries to break up the fight before being attacked by KV's security and entourage. Cartwright wrestles one of the men, D'Marko King, 18, to the ground who subsequently pulls out a gun and shoots it. The witness says the shooting caused a mass panic among clubgoers.

"It was chaos," the witness said. "Complete and utter chaos."

Police say that one man not involved in the fight was shot in the leg. The other two injured in the brawl were KV, who sustained a head injury, and Zion Cartwright, who sustained minor injuries. The witness says Sepia security is to blame for the incident and that the whole thing was avoidable.

"Security didn't do their job and put us all in danger," the witness said. "There's no way a man should've been able to get a gun in the club. There's no way KV should've gotten in when they knew Knokout was there."

It is believed the fight stems from an August incident where KV accused Knokout of stealing from him. Knokout denied these allegations and claimed in a diss track that the thief was a member of KV's entourage. Issues between the two have heated up since August, with KV stating multiple times it was 'on sight' when he encountered Knokout. Knokout stated that he had no desire to fight KV, and instead wanted to focus on his music.

Those arrested include:

Ra'kaveon King (KV), 22

Vincent Cartwright (Knokout), 22

Duke Layton, 30
Eugene Ellis, 21
D'Marko King, 18
Jaden Gray, 24
Zion Cartwright, 27

"I'm glad I didn't go to that," said Derek, returning the paper to Uncle Marlin.

"To what?" asked Malcolm.

"Knokout's performance. There was a fight that led to a shooting, and Knokout and KV got arrested."

"That's what they get for fighting in a public place," said Malcolm. "They should've taken it to the ring."

"Malcolm, what do you know about taking something to the ring?" asked Uncle Marlin.

"I'd say I know more than you do, Mr. I-got-arrested-for-throwing-down-in-the-middle-of-a-high-school-hallway."

"Arrested but not charged," clarified Uncle Marlin.

"Only because Mr. Arthur begged Chief Parker to have mercy on you," teased Malcolm. "I still can't believe you did that. That was so stupid."

"I was having a bad day and he made it worse," grumbled Uncle Marlin. "He always makes things worse."

"Have you always disliked Mr. Brown?" asked Derek.

"Always?" repeated Uncle Marlin. "No."

"Really?" said Derek. "I heard you never liked him."

"It's the other way around," explained Uncle Marlin. "I was pretty indifferent towards him until he kept getting me in trouble. He's the one who never liked me."

"I remember when Kasey said you were both two sides of the same coin," said Malcolm. "Even though he was acting a little weird when he said it, I think it's the truth. I feel like you two could honestly be friends because you have a lot in common."

"Brown and I being friends will happen when Hell freezes over," declared Uncle Marlin. "Until that time comes, we won't have any issues as long as he stays away from me."

"That shouldn't be too hard," said Malcolm. "All you have to do is avoid him the same way D-Money avoids anything above a C in school."

"Sir," whined Derek.

"Your grades could be better," said Malcolm. "It needed to be said."

"I'm passing all my classes."

"Barely," said Malcolm. "You're supposed to do *better* than me, not similarly to me. You should be an honor student like your uncle was."

"Which uncle?"

"Marlin," said Malcolm, motioning to his brother. "He was an honor student and a good athlete, and he threw it all away to be a thug. Marlin, how could you let yourself fall off like that?"

"The same way you fell off before you even got on," said Uncle Marlin.

"You didn't have to go there."

"You asked."

"I did ask, didn't I?" mumbled Malcolm.

"Plus, I wouldn't say I fell off since I own two successful businesses and still manage a third one quite well," added Uncle Marlin. "I just had an irresponsible moment."

"I guess," said Malcolm. "Everyone has an irresponsible moment at some point."

Derek silently agreed with his father. His biggest irresponsible moment was permanently roped around his wrist in the form of tiger stripes. But it was not an irresponsible moment he regretted. That moment was reserved for his latest one when he had made his grandfather cry. They had not spoken since their argument, and Derek was too embarrassed to face him again.

He went to school pondering his embarrassment. Derek did not care that everyone stared at him because he reminded them of Derik. In fact, he was glad because it reminded them of what they had forgotten. Derik was still missing, and everyone had sympathized and moved on.

With Derek still around, they were forced to remember. The school day dragged on for Derek until his final period, when he got to see Adrianna for a few minutes between classes.

"Derek," said Adrianna when he came to her locker. "When you see my father in class today, do not react."

"What's wrong with him?" asked Derek.

"Nothing bad," said Adrianna. "Gretchen has just encouraged him to try something... new."

"Did he dye his hair or something?"

"Something."

"Hmm...," said Derek, trying to guess what the 'something' could be. "So, he's done something in addition to taking off his eyepatch. Interesting."

"How did you know about that?" gasped Adrianna.

"About the eyepatch?" asked Derek. In response to Adrianna affirming him, he said, "Everyone knows. It's the big topic for the day."

"Oh no!" cried Adrianna. "What are they saying?"

"Just that's he's not wearing it," answered Derek. "Some people are saying he looks adorable without it. Personally, I'm interested in this scar he's been hiding."

"No!" objected Adrianna. "Bad Derek!"

"Why are you talking to me like I'm a dog?"

"Because!" said Adrianna. "Dad is insecure about his scar. If he feels people are talking about it, or even worse making fun of it, he's going to put the eyepatch back on and we don't want that. That's why you can't react!"

"Alright, alright," relented Derek. "But I still want to see it."

"Listen to me," commanded Adrianna, pulling Derek closer to her by his shirt. "Do not stare at him."

"You know, you holding me like this makes me want to kiss you," flirted Derek.

"I'm not playing with you, Derek," said Adrianna. "Do not stare and do not lick my face!"

"But I *can* kiss you?"

"Is that all you think about?"

"Come on," begged Derek. "This is the only time I see you during the day. Just a quick one? Please?"

"Dria, why do you have your boyfriend all gripped up like that?" asked Andre, approaching them.

"You couldn't have worse timing, Rockstar," begged Derek.

"I'm trying to get him to understand how important it is that he doesn't stare or react to Dad today," explained Adrianna.

"Listen to me," said Andre, taking hold of Derek from Adrianna. "You do not stare. You do not react. You do not ask questions. You do not make a nickname. You do not make a joke. You do not–!"

"Okay, I get it!" cried Derek, wrenching himself free of Andre's grip. "Let me go before you tear the shirt off my back Andre. Dang!"

"Getting a taste of our medicine today, are we?" teased Benjamin. "I like that."

"You would like seeing me be roughed up," grumbled Derek.

"I enjoy it," said Benjamin. "You ready to go to class?"

"Yeah, let's go before these Browns start throwing shoes at us and create another Brown-Harrison feud."

"Just for that you don't get a kiss today," said Adrianna.

"Aw man," whined Derek.

"And for the last time," said Adrianna. "Do. Not. Stare."

"Or else me and all my siblings will hunt you down," said Andre.

"Alright, I won't," said Derek.

"Welcome back, class," said Mr. Torrance. "Did everyone have a good break?"

No one answered. They were all too stunned. Derek himself could scarcely believe his eyes. Rather, he could scarcely believe whose eyes he saw. He knew he was not supposed to stare, but he could not help it. It was the first time he had seen Mr. Torrance Brown without his eyepatch. The scar Mr. Torrance was so insecure about split his eyebrow in two and made him look mischievous.

"Are you guys alright?" asked Mr. Torrance, growing concerned.

"Are you?" responded Mariana.

"Mariana, what kind of question is that?" said Mr. Torrance.

"I'm just asking because you showed up with no eyepatch on."

"Leave it to the dummy to bring it up," grumbled Nicole.

"Dummy?" repeated Mariana. "Last time I checked, I'm the only one in here who fluently speaks more than one language."

"Yeah," said Latasia. "English, Spanish, and Stupid-ish."

"You know what," said Mariana.

"Children," said Mr. Torrance. "Like I told you all before the break, leave the drama in theater class."

The class settled down.

"This is a new year, so we're trying new things," said Mr. Torrance. He added more quietly, "And that apparently includes changing your seating assignments because I'm not listening to this for the rest of the year..."

"Mr. Brown," said Ms. Nelson over the loudspeaker. "Can you send Derek to the guidance counselor's office please?"

"He's on his way," said Mr. Torrance, rolling his eyes.

"Thank you."

"Interrupting my class," grumbled Mr. Torrance.

"I heard that!"

"Then take your hand off the button!"

"Don't tell me how to do my job!"

"Girl, take your hand off the button! You're holding my class up!"

Derek wondered what Ms. Nelson wanted with him in the guidance counselor's office. He wondered if maybe he had had a schedule change that he was unaware of. On the way there, Derek ran into Allison.

"You got called out of class too?" asked Allison.

"Yeah," said Derek. "I wonder what this is about?"

"Who knows?" said Allison. "Did you hear about the new girl today?"

"What new girl?"

"Her name's Jada and she's a senior," said Allison. "Apparently, her dad is Zack Graham, and he moved the whole family back here."

"Dang, I feel bad for her," said Derek. "Imagine having to move school's during your senior year."

"I know right."

"But where'd you learn all this from?"

"From Stacy," said Allison. "But that's not all. Apparently, Jada's already acquainted herself with Danielle and her minions."

"That clique has run through six girls in less than a year," joked Derek. "At this point, Dani is running a girl group. How does she already have a replacement for Prissy in less than a month?"

"She works fast," laughed Allison. "I'm surprised the Grahams are back in town though. I wonder if they'll try to put Mother out of business."

"I don't know," said Derek. "Weren't Zack and Uncle Marlin best friends?"

"That's what Nanna said," recalled Allison. "But to some people, friendship means nothing when money is involved."

"True."

The cousins arrived at the counselor's office. Ms. Greta sat at her desk, writing something down. Derek easily told her apart from her sister by their attitudes. Ms. Greta was less patient and more outspoken than her sister, but also was very nice and tended to be more interactive with the students than Ms. Gretchen. She looked up when Derek and Allison entered and smiled.

"Hello," said Ms. Greta. "Come in and sit down please."

"Hi, Ms. Nelson," greeted Derek.

"Hi, Ms. Twin," said Allison.

"Queenie," said Derek, looking at his cousin annoyedly. "We've been over this. They have the same last name."

"And we also went over how one of them is getting married soon which means they won't have the same last name anymore," said Allison. She looked at Ms. Greta's finger and added. "And it's not her."

"Well, maybe if you learn to tell them apart, you wouldn't have this problem."

"They're identical."

"I'm practically identical to Derik and you can tell us apart."

"Because there are differences to distinguish between you two. She and the other Ms. Twin look exactly the same."

"Okay, but *she* doesn't like being called Ms. Twin."

"Oh, you don't?" gasped Allison, looking at Ms. Greta. "I'm sorry."

"It's alright," said Ms. Greta.

"You are so dumb," uttered Derek.

"Says the person with a C in English," retorted Allison. "How do you have a C in a language you speak?"

"Okay guys let's reel it back in," said Ms. Greta. "I just wanted to talk to you both because I know this is a hard time for your family right now, and I wanted to see if there was anything I could do to help."

"I'm fine," said Derek.

"Me too," said Allison. "But thank you for asking."

"Hey Greta!" said Mr. Bud, bursting into the room waving a brown paper bag around. He noticed Allison and Derek, and his cheeks became red. Running a bronze hand through his hair, he awkwardly laughed saying, "Oh! I didn't realize you had someone in here."

"That's alright," said Ms. Greta, also blushing. "What did you need?"

"I... was just... uh...," said Mr. Bud, also blushing. "Bye."

"Um...," said Allison. "Can we go?"

"Ye... yeah," said Ms. Greta. "You guys can go."

"Okay, have a good day," said Derek.

After leaving the office, Allison looked around to make sure she and Derek were alone in the hallway.

"I think those two are dating," whispered Allison.

"Why do you think that?" asked Derek.

"They kissed at the ball," said Allison. "Now he shows up here acting all friendly. And did you see how flustered they both got when they saw each other? I'm telling you they're dating."

"If you say so."

After school, Derek danced around the living room when someone knocked on the front door. An unfamiliar man stood on the porch. He was a bald medium-brown man, and when he saw Derek, he smiled awkwardly, showing his crooked teeth.

"Uh... hi," said the man. "I'm looking for Marlin Harrison. I was told I could find him here."

"Uncle Marlin's not here yet," said Derek. "But he usually gets back around this time."

"I see," said the man. "Could you tell him his old buddy Zack stopped by to see him?"

"Zack?" repeated Derek. "As in Zack Graham?"

"Oh, you know who I am?"

"I've heard of you."

"You have?" said Mr. Zackariah. "What's your name?"

"Derek."

"They said you were missing!"

"That's my cousin. I'm Malcolm's son, Derek. We're both named after my grandfather."

"Oh," said Mr. Zackariah. He looked Derek up and down and said, "You look a little old to be Malcolm's son. How old are you?"

"Eighteen."

Mr. Zackariah began doing the math, and his eyes widened when he got his answer.

"Fourteen?!" gasped Mr. Zackariah.

"Yeah."

"Wow! Who's your mom?"

"I don't have one."

"Oh shoot, my bad," said Mr. Zackariah, wincing. "Well... my kids are around your age. My daughter Jada just turned eighteen and my son Tyler is nineteen. Of course, if you decide to be friends with Tyler, you'll have to be a bit patient with him since he can't hear."

"He can't hear?"

"Yeah, he's deaf."

"Oh wow," said Derek. "Would you like to come in and wait?"

"Sure," said Mr. Zackariah. "It's crazy to me that Malcolm had a child that young. Last I saw him he was this big and practically attached to Marlin's side."

Mr. Zackariah bent over and placed a hand next to his thigh to demonstrate Malcolm's height as a child.

"He's definitely grown since then," said Derek.

Uncle Marlin entered the house. He looked at the guest and crinkled his eyebrows.

"Zack?"

"Marlin!"

"Yo!" said Uncle Marlin with a smile, causing Derek to notice the gold cap he had not previously seen. It occurred to him that he had never seen his uncle smile. Uncle Marlin dapped Mr. Zackariah up and said, "What are you doing here?"

"I moved back."

"You did?"

"Yeah," said Mr. Zackariah. "Had to come back to take care of my old man because I'm the only one willing to do it."

"That's ironic."

"Yeah, I know. Riley Jr. being taken care of by Zack the baby of all people. But he's still my old man and made sure I was straight growing up, so now I'm returning the favor."

"Makes sense."

"I was just talking to your nephew here and telling him how shocked I was that Malcolm had him so young. Was he really fourteen?"

"Yeah."

"That's crazy!"

"Yeah..."

"You still keep up with Kasey?"

"Like a hawk."

"That's cool. How is he?"

"He's doing okay."

"That's good to hear. When's the last time you spoke to him?"

"Last week. He's excited about March."

"What's in March?"

"Can't say yet."

"Why not?"

"I'm legally bound to silence until March."

"Why bring it up then?"

"You asked."

"Same old Marlin. How are you? I heard your son is missing."

"He is."

"Dang man. What happened?"

"I don't know. I was on vacation when it happened."

"Man, that's crazy."

"Yeah."

"How's Leya taking it?"

"Horribly. She's mad at me right now."

"Because of your son?"

"No. Something else. Ruined our vacation and everything. Money just wasted because she wanted to argue the whole time."

"Dang."

"Zack, I know you didn't come over only to say hi."

"Same old Marlin. Never misses a thing."

"What did you want?"

"Well, like I said, I just moved back to town. I was hoping you could hook me up with a booth at your barbershop."

"I don't see why not as long as you're not trying to stage a coup to take over."

"Why would I stage a coup?"

"It was a joke."

"You really are the same old Marlin," laughed Mr. Zackariah. "Bad jokes and all. I wonder if you're still just as hotheaded too."

"You should know that the shop is more Soleya's territory than it is mine," said Uncle Marlin, ignoring the question. "So, if you work there, she would be your day-to-day boss and not me."

"No problem," said Mr. Zackariah. He winked and added, "And you don't have to worry about me trying to get with her either. I have my own wife now."

Uncle Marlin grimaced.

"Everything's all settled?" said Mr. Zackariah.

"You'll have to sign a contract and pay your first month's rent, of course," said Uncle Marlin. He extended his hand to Mr. Zackariah. "Once that's handled you'll be good to go."

"I'm glad," said Mr. Zackariah, readily shaking his friend's hand. "I would say we celebrate over drinks, but you don't drink."

"Why should I?"

"Same old Marlin."

Chapter Seventeen: Allison

"Dee-Three, what do you think about this outfit for your party tomorrow?"

"A lady doesn't wear that, Allison."

"Ugh, you sound like Mother."

"That was the point. But no, it looks fine."

"She always scrutinizes every little thing I do! She never does that to you."

"Because she doesn't care about me."

"You think so?"

"The most important things to her are her reputation and her husband. And now both of those are out of wack and she's taking it out on us. She doesn't care about us. I bet if I disappeared tomorrow, she wouldn't even notice or care. Neither would Dad. Nobody would care."

"I'd care."

"You say that now."

"Okay, rude much."

"Whatever."

The first week back at school had been an awkward one for Allison. There were pitying looks and sympathetic affirmations from everyone when Allison was nearby, but overall, life for everyone had continued in Creeke. New changes and new people had overshadowed the mystery of the missing boy. Only a few families still offered active support to the Harrisons during the troubling times, and the Greens were one such family. Allison spent more and more time at their home, often staring out the window at the ruins of her own home. It was this very thing she did that Saturday while visiting Diana, who was painting her toenails a deep red.

"Did you hear about the break-in at Brewer's?" asked Diana.

"No," said Allison, turning from the window. "What happened?"

"I don't know. Ralphie said the door was forced open when he went down there this morning to open up. Whoever broke in stole some food and clothes, and left money on the counter, but the security camera didn't catch their face."

"They must've been desperate if they couldn't wait until the store was open."

The sound of giggling came from Althea's room.

"What's going on in there?" asked Allison.

"They're having their Little Sister Society meeting," answered Diana. "You don't like it?"

"Huh?"

"You called it their little Sister Society meeting."

"That's the name of it," said Diana. "The Little Sister Society because they all happen to be little sisters."

"Oh," said Allison. "So, why aren't you in there then?"

"Girl, I'm about to be nineteen in May," said Diana. "I am too old for that."

"Well, I'm going to go sit in on the meeting."

"Go ahead. I won't stop you."

Allison went to the room and slipped quietly inside. Adrianna stood toward the front, surrounded by a group of girls listening to her speak.

"Hi Allison," greeted Adrianna. "Are you joining us today?"

"I guess...," uttered Allison. She had not intended to bring attention to herself.

"Okay," said Adrianna. "Sit wherever you like. We were just going over what are priorities for this month are. Our first order of business is a prayer for our fellow Little Sister, Em. As we all know, her mother's cancer has returned and we're all believing that she'll be healed in Jesus' name."

"Amen," said all the girls.

"The second order of business is the review of our tenets," said Adrianna. She displayed a poster with what seemed like rules written on it in different inks and fonts. "Allison, as our newest member–!"

"Already?" asked Allison. "There's no screening process? No background check?"

"A background check on you would be unnecessary," said Althea.

"How do you know?" questioned Allison. "You guys can't possibly know everything about me."

"Your name is Allison Queen Harrison," said Althea. "You're eighteen, a senior at Creeke High School, slated to be valedictorian, a member of the student council organization, the school's honor society, President of the school's chess club and currently employed as a part-time receptionist at Miss Leya's Beauty and Barbershop. You have three brothers – two older, one younger – and you're the only girl, and your family is the founding family of the town. Your hobbies include reading, chess, and math, and upon graduation you plan to go to college for engineering."

"Why do you know so much about me?"

"Because you're Allison," said Althea, smiling. "We already know who you are. Like I said, a background check on you would be unnecessary."

"Ahem," said Adrianna, calling the attention back to the meeting. "As I was saying, Allison, if you're going of be a part of this, then you'll need to contribute a tenet. It can be something that you already do in your everyday life, or something you wish to work on."

"Can I get an example?" asked Allison.

"Sure," said Adrianna. "My tenet is courageous. A little sister is never afraid to speak up for herself or others."

"Oh, that's good," said Allison. "What are the other ones?"

"I'll go next," said Latasia. "My tenet is smart. A little sister always uses her brain and never lets others think for her."

"Mine is gracious," said Althea. "A little sister extends to others the grace that she wishes bestowed upon herself."

"Helpful," said Charmaine. "Little sisters lend a helping hand to those in need when they can."

"Honest," said Nicole. "A little sister speaks the truth, even when it's hard to do."

"And Em's is positive," said Adrianna, accounting for Tamara's tenet. "A little sister doesn't tear down others, but instead uplifts and encourages those around her. Those are the tenets that we founded the Little Sister Society with. Now, we'll ask the members who are not founders to share theirs."

"That's us," whispered Kameryn. "Mine is respectful. A little sister respects those who respect her."

"Hmm," said Allison, thinking. "I don't know what to say."

"Well, what do you think is important when helping the community?" asked Althea.

"To be authentic," said Allison, thinking of the Perry's. "You can't help the community if you're always changing yourself to fit in and get people to like you."

"There you go," said Adrianna. "Your tenet is authentic. Write it on here."

Allison did as she was requested. When she finished, her tenet read, 'Authentic (Allison): A little sister remains true to who she is and does not alter herself for the approval of others'. The girls went over the rest of their priorities and adjourned the meeting.

"Did you have fun?" asked Diana when Allison returned to the living room.

"It was cool," said Allison.

There was a knock at the door, and Althea answered it. The girl at the door was unfamiliar to Allison. She had the biggest smile Allison had ever seen.

"Hey!" said the girl to Althea. "Am I too late for the meeting?"

"Yes, it ended," said Althea. "But there's still someone here I want you to meet."

Althea led the girl over to Allison. She was light-brown and had big, curly, brown hair on top of her head. Her ears held multiple piercings, and her style of dress seemed casual.

"Allison, this is Jada Graham-Hernandez," introduced Althea. "Jada, Allison Harrison."

"Nice to meet you!" greeted Jada, extending her hand to Allison excitedly.

"Hi," said Allison, accepting the handshake.

"You're Mr. Marlin's daughter, right?"

"Yeah, that's me."

"I knew it!" cried Jada. "My dad told me his friend Mr. Marlin had a daughter around my age."

"How do you know Althea?"

"We have a class together," explained Jada. "She invited me over for this meeting she was hosting so I could meet more people, but I got lost and I guessed I missed it."

"Well, that's unfortunate," said Allison.

"Yeah," agreed Althea sulkily. She brightened up and then said, "I got it! You both should come to the slumber party here at my house next Saturday!"

"Who all is going to be there?" asked Allison.

"The same people that were here at the meeting," said Althea.

"And me because I live here," said Diana sarcastically.

"I'll see, but I can't guarantee anything," said Allison.

"Well, I'll definitely be there," declared Jada.

"Great!" said Althea.

"I should get going," said Allison. She looked at Jada and said, "It was nice meeting you."

"You too!"

Allison left and was barely out of the driveway before she dialed Stacy's number.

"Hello?" answered Stacy after two rings.

"Stacy, guess who I met?" said Allison.

"Who?

"The new girl."

"Really?" asked Stacy. "What was she like?"

"She seems cool, definitely has *a lot* of energy," said Allison. "But I'm still going to keep my eye on her. I don't know how I feel about being friends with someone who's all buddy-buddy with Danielle and her minions."

"I know that's right," said Stacy. "Speaking of minions, I still can't believe you tried to replace me with Prissy! I was only gone for two weeks for vacation! I was coming back, girl!"

"Now Stacy," said Allison. "You know you're my girl. The only reason I even started talking to Prissy was because Nanna asked me to. But honestly, I actually kind of like her though. She's not that bad of a girl."

"I could've told you that," said Stacy. "Me and her were cheerleaders together, remember? At least we were until she up and quit, following behind Dani who couldn't even make it on the team again."

"That is so embarrassing," cackled Allison.

"It really is," agreed Stacy. "But no, Prissy is really a sweet girl when she's *not around Dani*. Dani just brings the worst out of her."

"That girl brings the worst out of everyone," said Allison.

"So, what are you doing today?"

"I'm on my way home," said Allison. "Mother's going to visit Lady Sophia later, and I'm going with her."

"Oh boy," said Stacy. "Don't let her get under your skin, okay?"

"I'll try," said Allison. "What about you? What are you up to?"

"Just cleaning my room while I wait on my friends to hop on the game with," said Stacy.

"What game?"

"*The Well*. It updated with some new DLC so my guildmates and I are going to check it out."

"I haven't played that game since sophomore year."

"I know. We were playing it together and then you abandoned me, remember?"

"Life happened. Who do you play with now?"

"Some friends I made online."

"You don't know them?"

"Uh... not exactly."

"Stacy, you've got to be careful with stuff like that. Those people could be creeps."

"Nah, these guys are cool. If you ever decide to hop back on, you could join the guild and meet them yourself."

"Girl, I don't have time for that. I'm trying to be valedictorian and get into a good college."

"I already got my college acceptance letter to my dream school."

"That's great," said Allison. "I'm still waiting on mine."

"I narrowly missed the GPA requirement for a full scholarship because of stupid biology," sighed Stacy. "I know you won't have these problems, Miss Valedictorian. You're definitely getting a full scholarship."

"Girl, Miss Valedictorian is looking more and more like Miss-I'm-Just-Happy-I-Graduated every day," whined Allison. "Biology is not being kind to me either and Andre is not playing. The only thing keeping me in first and him in second in the ranking is his procrastination and tendency to get easily distracted. If it weren't for that he'd have easily overtaken me by now."

"I wish I had Andre's brain," said Stacy. "He literally waits till the very last minute to do assignments and still manages to get an A on everything. Meanwhile I'm over here studying diligently and putting in effort, and I'm barely hanging on to a B."

"And I'm literally fighting to keep an A," said Allison. "Andre is just naturally smart."

"And he's musically talented too," whined Stacy. "It's just not fair."

"Well, I mean, he is a Brown," said Allison. "Music is their thing, even though some of them try to pretend like it's not."

"I know," said Stacy. "But you have to hear him play the guitar sometime. That is literally his instrument."

"I'll ask him to play for me some time," said Allison, arriving home. "I got to go. I'll call you later."

"Alright, bye."

"Bye."

The visit to the Perry residence was an uninteresting one. Allison sat quietly beside her mother, half-listening to the conversation between Lady Sophia, Aunt Soriah, and Mrs. Harrison. Every now and then, Lady Sophia made a snide remark, but Allison ignored them because Nanna Kiana had instructed her to once again be polite.

"Young lady," said Lady Sophia, snapping her fingers at Allison to get her attention. "Accompany me to the garden."

Allison looked to her mother, who nodded her silent assent. The brisk air nipped at Allison's face as she followed the elderly woman about the garden. There were no eye-catching plants to be seen during the wintry season, but the vast view of the Perry's property was more than enough to compensate for it. She spotted the guest house on the other side of the garden. Her parents had lived in that house when they first married. It was far enough to have privacy from the main house but close enough to fall under the big house's rule.

"Let me be frank, Allison," said Lady Sophia as they traveled one of the garden paths. "I don't like you."

Allison bit her tongue, resisting the urge to confirm the mutual feeling.

"I find you to be a very ill-mannered, ill-tempered, disagreeable girl," continued Lady Sophia. "Still, you are a Perry, which means you can still be useful to this family."

"Useful?" said Allison.

"You are of age," explained Lady Sophia. "It's time you start considering your prospects."

"My prospects?" said Allison. "After I graduate high school, I'm going off to college, and then I'm getting myself a job."

"A job," snorted Lady Sophia. "You are the culmination of the best families in this town, and you want to waste it all on a job?"

"It's not a waste."

"It is," said Lady Sophia. "My mother had a job. Had me working and cleaning houses with her for people who didn't care anything about us. And what did she have to show for it? Nothing. Nothing at all. She had to marry me off just to pay her bills! And yet, you and my ungrateful daughter have everything handed to you and you both want to work! How ridiculous!"

"It's not ridiculous!" argued Allison. "There's more to life than just marrying well!"

"You're wrong," said Lady Sophia. "I can have a life *because* I married well. I don't have to stress about finances or worry about where my next meal is coming from. Why would anyone want to throw that away just to make a few measly dollars that'll be gone before you even realize it was there?"

"Because if I get married, I want it to be to someone I want to marry and not out of some ridiculous duty to a family I don't even care about!"

"You better wake up, little girl," snapped Lady Sophia. "This family you don't care about could be the one to keep you taken care of. It's taken care of me very well and I plan to keep it that way. That's why you need to do your duty and maintain its legacy. If you play your cards right, you could live out the rest of your days without ever having to lift a finger."

"That's for me to decide."

"Ungrateful just like your mother!" declared Lady Sophia. "Here I am trying to help you out, and you just act stubborn like you have it all figured out! This is why I don't like you!"

Allison held her peace. Marrying based on family connections was not her plan for life. In fact, marriage was not anywhere close to being on her radar. There was a life full of possibilities that Allison wanted to explore before even considering tying herself down to someone else.

"How was the visit?" asked Nanna Kiana when Allison returned home.

"Horrible," grumbled Allison. "Lady Sophia tried to convince me to marry well."

"Child...," uttered Mrs. Thelma under her breath.

"So, you had a conversation with her Queenie?" asked Nanna Kiana.

"Yes," said Allison. "We walked around her gardens, and she told me I needed to marry well instead of getting a job because I'm a Perry. Of course, this was after she told me she didn't like me."

"*Child*...," said Nanna Kiana. "Queenie, do not listen to any of that woman's advice. You get married if and when the time is right."

"That's right," said Mrs. Thelma. "There's nothing wrong with waiting a little longer to get married like I did."

"And there's nothing wrong with not being married at all," said Aunt Paulette. "I was married for one week and that was the worst week of my life. I realized after that that married life wasn't for me and haven't looked back since."

"And it didn't help that your husband was sorry," ranted Aunt Nancy. "No ambition, no initiative, no nothing! Just wanted to lay around the house all day and have you take care of him!"

"This isn't about me Nancy," said Aunt Paulette.

"Yes, it is!" cried Aunt Nancy. "Don't you end up with a man like that Queenie! When you get married, marry someone who is compatible with you, steps up to the plate to lead the family, and is willing to go through thick and thin with you. That's what my Joseph was like, and I was with him to the very end."

"That's right," agreed Nanna Kiana. "Your grandfather and I have definitely had some thin moments, but I honestly couldn't have asked for anyone better to go through them with by my side."

"You can say that again," said Mrs. Thelma. "Damian and I started out thin. I had to wade through the hurt left behind by another woman and gain his trust before we could even have our relationship. During our dating stage, sometimes I got frustrated with him and would leave. Sometimes he got frustrated with me and would leave. But every time we left, we always came back together and picked up where we left off and I'm glad we did."

"And as for being a working woman," said Nanna Kiana. She motioned to her sisters and said, "I worked hard to help my family and I don't regret it. But marriage and work aren't the end all and be all of life. You only get to be young once Queenie and I don't want you wasting your life on trying to find 'the one'. Find yourself first and let the one find you if it's meant to happen. Okay?"

"Yes ma'am," said Allison.

That evening, Allison went to talk to her mother about the day's events. Her mother sat at her vanity, preparing herself for bed.

"Mother?" said Allison. "Can we talk?"

"Yes, we can," said Mrs. Harrison. "What do you wish to talk about?"

"You," said Allison. "I don't like that your parents treat you like you're stupid. How can you be stupid when you're running a successful business?"

"My mother does not like that I run a business."

"Trust me, I know," griped Allison. "What would she prefer that you do?"

"Be married to someone of high standing in the community."

"Is that why you married Dad?"

"It's complicated."

"How is it complicated?"

"Your father and I were eighteen when we married," explained Mrs. Harrison. "And a big reason we married when we did was because my parents encouraged it."

"They forced you to marry him?"

"Well, I was in love with him too, so it wasn't hard to get me to agree to the idea," said Mrs. Harrison. "But looking back on it, my parents highly influenced the match."

"Let me guess: you had to do what was right for the family?"

"How did you know?"

"That's what your mother and I talked about this afternoon in the garden. She wants me to do the same."

"I'm not surprised," sighed Mrs. Harrison. "My mother married my father when she was eighteen and he was twenty-seven. Her and her mother were poor, and my father made a good amount of money, so her mother encouraged a marriage between them. Then when Soriah was eighteen and Quincy was thirty, our parents encouraged her to marry him because he was a promising real estate agent."

"Um...," uttered Allison, coming to a realization. "Is this your way of telling me you're about to marry me off to some rich man?"

"Don't be silly," said Mrs. Harrison. "Who would you even marry?"

"I was just asking because I noticed a pattern," said Allison. "The parents seem to marry the daughters off young. How old was your grandmother when she got married?"

"She was never married."

"She wasn't?"

"No." Mrs. Harrison looked around, then whispered, "But between you and me, I didn't like that woman. She had a nasty attitude. Mother tolerated her because that was her mother, but she didn't like her all that much."

"Sounds like you, me, and your mother."

"Don't misunderstand me, Allison," said Mrs. Harrison. "I don't hate my mother. Sometimes I even wish we had a closer relationship, especially because she couldn't have any more children after I was born. That's kind of why I wanted a daughter of my own. So, I could have the relationship with her that I never had with my mother."

Allison was silent.

"I wanted my life to be different from my mother's," revealed Mrs. Harrison. "My parents don't love each other, and my father has total control over everything because everything revolves around him and his desires. They're only still together because it benefits them both. I wanted things to be different with me and your father, but I guess I hoped for too much."

"Well, at least Dad doesn't control your money."

"Yes," agreed Mrs. Harrison. "Your father isn't controlling like my father is and he's provided for us very well. I'm grateful for that. But I could've married anyone for that. I married him because I loved him."

"Did Dad ever show you he loved you before you married him?"

"I'm not sure anymore," sighed Mrs. Harrison. "My parents had me so focused on just securing him as a match that I never really thought about whether he actually loved me or not. He could've been paid to marry me for all I know."

Mrs. Harrison looked at herself in the mirror and sighed.

"I don't know why I'm telling you all of this. Maybe it's because I want someone to talk to."

"You can talk to me about anything," said Allison.

"That's what I should be saying to you," chuckled Mrs. Harrison. "It's funny. I wanted a daughter so badly and now I have one and...!"

"And?"

"And we don't have the relationship I wanted either."

"Well, if you would let be myself."

"I do let you be yourself."

"No, you want me to be this prim and proper lady that's always quiet and keeps her thoughts to herself like you. But that's not who I am though. I speak up and make it known how I feel."

"I...," began Mrs. Harrison. She stopped to think, then sighed. "Your Aunt Soriah was right. The apple really didn't fall far from the tree. My mother wanted me to be a supportive wife for the rest of my life, but I wanted more, so I went after more. And now, here I am years later with my own daughter, and she's having the same experience but now I'm the mother trying to hold her back."

"Well, you're not as bad as your mother."

"Aren't I though? I wanted you to be a lady because I was worried about my own reputation. I was worried what people would think if I had an unruly daughter instead of a quiet, subdued one."

"Am I really unruly?"

"Sometimes. But you're different from me like you said."

"I am different from you. I may not be the type of lady you are, but that's because I'm trying to be my own type of lady."

"I see that now," said Mrs. Harrison. "Everything I've done with my children has been because I was worried about my reputation. Your brother is missing, and our last conversation was when we argued, and I slapped him. And then we went to bed angry, and I left for vacation the next day and came back and he was gone. And then Matthias doesn't ever talk to me. He won't even come near me. And Deidrick only speaks to me when he wants something. I'm not close to any of you. You all probably hate me."

"I don't hate you, Mother," said Allison. "In fact, I love you very much. And for the first time tonight, I feel that I understand you a little better."

"You do?"

"Yes. And I believe Derik will come back safely."

"How do you know?"

"Hope," said Allison. She kissed her mother on the cheek and said, "Goodnight."

"Goodnight."

-

Chapter Eighteen: Matthias

Matthias had no idea what to do anymore. He had nothing new about Derik, but he did not want to admit defeat and return home. No one could help him either because he and Deidrick were not talking again, James had to work all the time, and Jordan annoyed him with complaints. All Matthias could do was wait for something to happen, and he did so reluctantly. The only thing that kept him going was the few people who were in his corner, supporting him.

"Bro, did you hear Cynthia was back in town?" asked Andrew as they played a game of twenty-one at the city gym. Jordan had come with them but had disappeared to exercise elsewhere.

"Andrew, don't try to distract me with small talk," said Matthias.

"Distract you," laughed Andrew. "Matt, I've already dropped nineteen points on your head and I'm the one with the ball."

"So?"

"You know what," said Andrew. Before Matthias could process anything, he found himself lying on his back while Andrew yelled, "Twenty-one!"

Matthias stared up at his friend, who swung back and forth on the rim. Andrew had dunked on him. His friend dropped to the floor and stood over Matthias triumphantly,

"Good game," said Andrew, holding out his hand to help Matthias up.

"Good game," laughed Matthias, accepting the hand. "Is that really how I look when I do that?"

"Sure is," said Andrew. "Now like I was saying, did you hear Cynthia is back? She's taking the semester off."

"That's cool."

"Come on, Matthias. This is your chance."

"Cynthia and I are just friends, Andrew."

"You want me to believe all that flexing and showing off on the court for her is 'just friends'?"

"Just friends."

"If you say so," said Andrew. "You know, this reminds me of old times when we all would be out in the street hooping without a care in the world. Those were the days."

"You make it sound like we're old or something," laughed Matthias.

"We're not old but I miss those days," said Andrew. "All you guys were like my extra bros and now we all barely hang out anymore. Everything's changed."

"That's life," said Matthias. "You lose people, and you gain people."

"Yeah, I know," sighed Andrew. "The losses suck the most. Especially when they're permanent."

Matthias did not reply, knowing that Andrew was referring to Simon.

"Man," said Andrew, sucking his teeth. "I would give anything to have my brother back."

"I know he'd be proud of you if he could see you now," said Matthias. "That boy was your biggest fan."

"Yeah," agreed Andrew with a chuckle. "Remember when he'd show up to all our games holding that big sign with my name?"

"Sure do," said Matthias. "He'd be all in the bleachers hollering your name at the top of his lungs."

Andrew laughed softly. He closed his eyes and took a deep, shaky breath.

"Matt, you got to get right with Deidrick, man," said Andrew, wiping a tear from his face. "You got to do it before it's too late. If I had known Simon was going to die when he did, I would've spent more time with him. I would've loved him harder, wouldn't have gotten annoyed about how he was always up under me. I would've given him the world before he left. You've got to get right with Deidrick because you never know when life will change. God forbid, but something could happen to either one of you, and it would be too late. Take Derik for example. He's missing and you don't know when, or even if he's coming back."

"He's coming back," declared Matthias.

"Matt, I'm not trying to be discouraging or break your faith, but you've got to be real with yourself," said Andrew. "It's possible he might not come back."

"I'll believe it when I see it," said Matthias.

"Hey Matty," said Jordan. "You ready to go?"

"Yeah, I guess," said Matthias. "Thanks for the games, Andrew."

"No problem," said Andrew. "And remember what I said. Don't let it become too late."

"I'll think on it," said Matthias. "Next time, we'll hit the bags so you can show me what you've learned in those boxing lessons of yours."

"Yeah, alright."

Matthias and Jordan left the gym.

"I had a good workout," said Jordan. "You win?"

"You kidding?" answered Matthias. "I was up against Andrew. He could've gone all the way to the league if he wanted but chose to be a boxing video game and anime nerd doctor instead."

"Wow," said Jordan. "He must really want to do that if he gave up possibly making it to the league."

"Yeah," said Matthias. "Probably doesn't want anyone to die the way his brother did."

"How'd his brother die?"

"He got sick and was misdiagnosed. By the time they realized what was really wrong it was too late."

"Dang, that's messed up. It really shows you how unpredictable life is."

"Yeah. Makes you want to have your life in order, doesn't it?"

"Yeah."

Matthias pulled his car into James's gas station to refill it. While he waited, Jordan went inside to get snacks, and James came outside to talk to him.

"Why the long face?" asked James.

"Just thinking," answered Matthias. "You on break?"

"I'm off," said James. "I'm ready to go home and put my feet up."

"I bought you some candy, Matty," said Jordan, returning to the car. He handed Matthias a chocolate bar, then held up a bag of chips. "And I got these for me."

"Jordan, you don't eat hot chips," said James.

"I'm grown," said Jordan, opening the bag. "I eat what I want."

"Are you sure you can handle those though? I heard they're really spicy."

"I wouldn't have bought them if I couldn't handle them, James."

"But–!"

"Just let it go," said Matthias, placing a hand on James's shoulder. "He'll learn."

Matthias noticed a man at another gas pump looking at them. The man was rotund and dressed in all black. A ski mask obscured his face, but Matthias thought nothing of it since it was cold.

"Hot!" hissed Jordan. "Hot!"

"I thought you said you could handle it," teased James.

"I can!" exclaimed Jordan, tears forming in his eyes. "But I didn't know they'd be this hot though!"

"You're such an idiot," said Matthias.

"Hey you!" said the man, charging at them.

"Me?" said Jordan, pointing to himself.

"Yeah, you! You sleeping with my girl?!"

"What?"

"Oh, you want to play dumb?! I saw you with my own eyes!"

"I don't know what you're talking about, man," scoffed Jordan. "But you better get from around here."

"Or what?" challenged the man.

"You really want to find out?" threatened Jordan.

It happened so fast. One minute Jordan was standing next to Matthias, and the next he was on the ground covered in blood. The man fled, leaving chaos in his wake. Some patrons fled the area, while others panicked over what to do. James crawled over to Jordan, holding a hand over his own bleeding shoulder.

"Jordan!" cried James. "Someone call for help!"

Matthias realized he also was on the ground. All he remembered were the sounds of the bangs and shoving Jordan away from them. There had been six bangs. Two of them were in Jordan. Another two in a nearby car. One in James's shoulder. But the last one was missing. Matthias could not find it. He tried to stand to search for it and fell back down.

"Matty, stay still!" sobbed James.

Matthias did not understand why he could not push himself up. As he looked down at himself, he saw he was also bloody. Streams of red flowed down his arm onto the concrete, mixing with the spilled chips. Then came the pain. Excruciating, searing pain in his arm. That's where the sixth bang had gone. Into his arm. He was shot.

-

Chapter Nineteen: Deidrick

Jordan had been shot. James had been shot. Matthias had been shot. His brother had been shot.

"Get out the way!" hollered Deidrick as he drove passed a slow-moving car. He could not get to Aunt Nancy's house fast enough. Turmoil had taken hold of the family when they first heard the news. Aunt Nancy's chilling screams of despair and disbelief haunted Deidrick. 'They shot my babies,' was all she could say between sobs as she clung to Aunt Paulette.

Curiously to Deidrick, aside from Aunt Nancy, almost none of the women had broken down. Not Aunt Paulette, who had comforted Aunt Nancy, nor Nanna Kiana, who had cared for Granddad Derrick through his panic attack. Allison had quickly wiped away the few tears she did shed and did whatever she could to help.

But the weirdest reaction was his mother's. Upon hearing the news, Mrs. Harrison walked outside and stared at the sky. She stood out there for a while, her eyes trained on the starry sky, no words passing through her lips. Just looked at the sky without a single tear falling from her eye.

Waiting for answers hurt the most. But by Tuesday, Matthias was out of the hospital, and Deidrick sped up the road Wednesday to see him. He had no idea what he would say to Matthias. His only desire was to see him. Entering the room, he saw Matthias sitting up in bed with gauze wrapped around his bicep, and their eyes met.

"They said you were shot," said Deidrick, the words tumbling quickly off his tongue.

"Grazed," said Matthias, holding up his arm. He winced and set it back down. "Hurts too."

"What about James and Jordan?"

"James got nicked on the shoulder, but he's fine," said Matthias. "All I know about Jordan is that he got hit twice and that's only because I saw it with my own eyes."

"Dang. Do they know who did it?"

"Not yet, but I swear I know who it is."

"You saw them?"

"He was a big guy with a mask on," said Matthias. "But I recognized his voice."

"What did he say?"

"He accused Jordan of sleeping with his girl. They argued, and then he started shooting."

"Jordan slept with his girl?"

"I don't know. He hadn't left the house since Granddad brought him back, but it could've been before then."

"Do you think the guy got Jordan mixed up with someone else?"

"I'm not sure," said Matthias. "Like I said, he sounded familiar. I just can't place where I know his voice from."

The brothers sat silently for a moment. They were alone together for the first time since their argument.

"I didn't mean it," said Deidrick, breaking the silence. "When I told you I hated you. I didn't mean it."

"I didn't mean it either," said Matthias, looking at Deidrick. "I was just mad."

"How did we get like this?" sighed Deidrick.

"Pride," said Matthias. "Back then, I got mad at you because I felt like you were trying to fight me to show out in front of those girls."

"I thought you were trying to do the same thing with the basketball game and that's why I got mad."

"Man," said Matthias, sucking his teeth. "We fell out over a group of girls!"

"Bro!" cried Deidrick. "Some girls neither of us even got with!"

"Shoot, I could've pulled them all if I wanted to!"

"So could I!"

"Ain't this some crap?" laughed Matthias.

"Bro, it really is," laughed Deidrick. After settling down, he said, "I don't think I can explain what I felt when I heard you were shot. I just kept thinking how our last conversation was us yelling that we hated each other, and I didn't want those to be my last words to you."

"Me either."

"What were we even mad at each other for?"

"I just felt like we both did the same stuff and I got punished while you got away with it," said Matthias. "You got to stay in the house and still be their son and be part of the family while I was handed off to Aunt Soriah without a second thought and basically disowned. And this past year, I've really just been reflecting on the bad choices I've made over my life, and it pissed me off even more because I felt like it could've all been avoided if I hadn't been kicked out."

"Was being kicked out really that bad?" said Deidrick. "You and Cell could do whatever you guys wanted and no one over there cared."

"Exactly," said Matthias. "No one over there cared. I could do and say what I wanted, and go where I wanted, and no one over there ever cared."

"Sounds like paradise to me."

"Yeah, until you wake up one day and realize you've amounted to nothing. Nothing but an angry man stuck in a dead-end job and nothing to show for yourself."

"I think you're thinking a little too deeply about this."

"That's all I've had time to do for the past few days," said Matthias. "What if I hadn't been shot in the arm, but somewhere more critical and died? What kind of legacy would I have left behind? How would people remember me? Take you and me for example. We wouldn't have been on good terms, and you just said you didn't want that."

"Even if that had happened, you still would've been my brother."

"Your brother," repeated Matthias. "After everything I've done to you, you'd still call me 'your brother'."

Matthias looked at the wall.

"I feel like I've messed up my whole life," admitted Matthias. "That's why I've been so hard on Jordan over his antics, and why I'm so glad Dee-Three isn't as wild as we were. I don't want them turning out the way I did."

Deidrick did not respond. But the mention of Derik made him remember the necklace.

"Can I ask you something?" said Deidrick.

"What?" replied Matthias.

"What happened to the necklace I gave you?"

"The poker-chip one? I gave it to Dee-Three."

"When's the last time you saw it?"

"I don't know. He wore it a lot though, so he probably had it on him when he disappeared."

"Then you don't know anything about a trailer in the woods north of the city?"

"What trailer?"

"Never mind."

"Do you know something about what happened to Dee-Three?"

"I don't know," answered Deidrick. "But I'm going to find out."

"Alright," said Matthias. He looked down at Deidrick's shoes and exclaimed. "Dang! You were that worried about me?!"

"Bro!" cried Deidrick. "Don't look at them!"

"I ain't never seen you with some busted shoes on," said Matthias. "You must really have hit rock bottom."

"These are the only shoes I've got. All my other ones got ruined in the fire, and I had to leave my new ones behind at someone's house!"

"Got a little too distracted, huh?" laughed Matthias. "I remember those days. Alex was a great wingman, but he was a terrible lookout."

"Alex Brown?" asked Deidrick in disbelief.

"Yeah," said Matthias. "Well, the old Alex anyways. That Alex was a wild party boy. This new and improved one is trying to get us both into Heaven."

"I always thought of Alex as the quiet, innocent type, especially since his dad is so loud."

"Alex may be quiet but he's far from innocent."

"That explains why you two are so close."

"He's like a brother to me," said Matthias. "He's seen me at my best and at my worst."

"Like a brother," repeated Deidrick.

"Yeah," said Matthias. "But you are my brother. You've experienced my best and my worst, and you're still around."

"Because I'm your brother," said Deidrick. "I'm not leaving you behind no matter how mad we get at each other."

"Brother," said Matthias. He looked out the window and said, "Our brother is out there somewhere."

"And I'm not giving up on finding him," said Deidrick.

"Neither am I."

Chapter Twenty: Derek

The dream was different. Derek was not in a burning house but instead in his moonlit room. Someone stood beside his bed, staring at him. As Derek looked closer, he realized who it was. Standing under the moonlight was Derik. He seemed ethereal, with his hair cut shorter, and he was noticeably skinnier. Derik did not say anything. He simply smiled.

"Am I dreaming?" questioned Derek.

"I don't know," said Derik. "Are you?"

"I don't know," said Derek. "What happened to you? I miss you."

"I miss you too."

"We're going to find you."

"I hope you do. A boy almost never defers one's never-ending duty."

"What's that mean?"

"It's a reminder for you to find me."

"I'll remember it then."

"I know you will," said Derik. He turned to look at himself in the mirror. "You know, I kind of see it now. We do look alike."

"It's like we said," said Derek. "I am you, and you are me."

"I am you, and you are me," repeated Derik. There seemed to be a sadness in his voice. "I should let you get back to your dream now. Here, I'll tuck you in."

Derek allowed his cousin to draw the blanket up to his chin.

"Goodnight," said Derik, touching a hand to Derek's cheek that made him shiver.

Before Derek knew it, his dream had changed. He dreamt of himself and Derik being together again, having fun like they used to. Playing all their little games, pretending to be each other until it was no longer clear who was who. Later that morning, his father and Uncle Marlin looked at him peculiarly when he sat down to breakfast.

"What is it?" asked Derek.

"Did you go somewhere last night?" questioned Malcolm.

"No. Why?"

"Your uncle said he heard you talking and then saw you leave."

"I didn't go anywhere."

"Huh," said Uncle Marlin. "Maybe I was dreaming."

"Yeah...," said Derek. "Maybe you were."

There was a silent pause.

"Marlin, have you been to see Matty yet?" asked Malcolm.

"No," said Uncle Marlin.

"Are you going to see him?"

"No."

"But he's your son."

"And?"

Malcolm let the subject drop. After breakfast, Derek met with Allison at the library. She and Andre were supposed to be studying together, and Derek was there to get help with his homework. But the two of them were instead waiting for Andre to show up.

"Where is this boy at?" griped Allison.

"Probably still trying to escape the dungeon," joked Derek.

"Well at this point, he'll be better off staying there. If he doesn't show up within the next five minutes, I'm leaving."

"Give him some time," said Derek. "Besides, I need to tell you something."

"What?"

"I think Dee-Three was in my room last night," revealed Derek.

"What?!" said Allison, her eyes widening. "Are you sure?"

"Not really," said Derek. "Uncle Marlin said he heard me talking last night and then saw me leave the house. But I know I didn't go anywhere."

"And it was him you were talking to?"

"Yeah, but I thought I was dreaming," said Derek. "When I asked what happened to him, he told me to remember a phrase."

"What phrase?"

"A boy almost never defers one's never-ending duty."

"What does that mean?"

"I'm not sure," recalled Derek. "He told me to remember that for us to find him."

"Maybe it's some kind of code?" guessed Allison after writing the sentence down.

"But how do we figure it out?" asked Derek.

"Well, he told it to you," said Allison. "Did you guys have any secret codes or languages?"

"We had our secret knock and our mirror game," said Derek. "He also tried to teach me morse code once, but I couldn't catch on."

"I don't think it's any of those," said Allison. "Maybe it's an anagram."

Allison worked at the letters trying to make different phrases. Her many attempts produced phrases such as 'stables don't die forever even roads guy men yen e', 'bay toast melds severed dung over neon eye n fire', and 'toads give alms due to fenders born every eye nnn'. After 'sender smote vale sonnet during body fever nay e', Allison shook her head and gave up.

"I don't think it's an acronym," said Derek.

"A what?"

"An acronym. That's what you said, right?"

"I said an *anagram*."

"Same thing."

"No, it's not," griped Allison. "Anagrams rearrange phrases to make new ones. Acronyms are words made up of the first letter of each word in a title or phrase. For example, if we take the first letters from this phrase here and put them together, they make... abandoned."

"Abandoned?" repeated Derek. Realizing that he and Allison had stumbled upon the answer, he cried, "That's it! It's an acronym!"

"Shhh!" shushed another library patron.

"Sorry," apologized Derek.

"I never thought you having a C in English would come in handy," remarked Allison.

"I told you I was smart," said Derek triumphantly.

"So, this was his answer to where he was?" said Allison. "Abandoned?"

"Yeah," said Derek. "He must be talking about the abandoned building by Brewer's. Dad told me someone spotted him messing around near that building once."

"You think he's been there this whole time?"

"Either that or he's got something in there he wants us to know about."

"Let's check it out then."

"What about Andre?"

"What about him?" said Allison. "This is way more important. I can always study with him some other time."

The abandoned building in question had no indication of what it previously was. All that remained of the building were the wooden floorboards damaged in certain spots parallel to the roof that undoubtedly leaked when it rained. Graffiti clung to the walls, colorizing the once-blank spaces with the imaginings of artists who used the world as their canvas.

"What could he possibly have in here?" asked Allison, swatting away the dust floating in the air.

"I don't know," answered Derek. "But whatever it is, we need to find it."

"What are we even looking for?"

"Something that explains to us where he is."

"All I see is dust and dirt."

"Well, he wanted us to come here, so there must be something here," said Derek. "Now if I were Dee-Three, what would be valuable to me in a place like this?"

Derek looked around the building. In a corner, something caught the sunlight and bounced it onto the walls above it. It was to this corner that Derek went and found himself looking down at his fractured face. Rather he was looking at himself in the reflection of a broken hand mirror. Beneath his reflection was a box that, when opened, contained a notebook. Opening it to the first page, Derek discovered the paper was covered in Derik's cursive handwriting.

> <u>August</u>
> This is my hideout journal in case some nosy person discovers my home journal in my room. I like this building. It's the perfect place to go and hide when I need a break from my life. Nobody would ever think to look for me here, and if they did, they wouldn't be brave enough to come inside after me. I might have to use this place a lot more now that Mother and Dad are arguing.

"Hey!" called Derek. "I found something!"

"What is it?" asked Allison, joining him.

"It's a journal," said Derek. "Should we read this? There could be personal info in here he doesn't want us to know."

"He's the one who led us to it," reasoned Allison. "If he didn't want us to read it, he wouldn't have done that."

"True," said Derek, flipping to the next entry.

<u>August</u>
Dad told me today he didn't want me. He didn't come right out and say it though. I had to ask him first. He was sitting on the couch reading a book about finances, and I had to know. So, I marched right up to him and said, 'Tell me the truth: do you like me?'. And he said, 'Why?'. Not yes, not no, but 'why?'. So I said, 'I want to know because you treat me like you didn't want me or something'. And without looking up from his book, this man said, 'I didn't'."

"Wow," snorted Allison.

"Do you want me to stop?"

"No, keep going," instructed Allison, crossing her arms. "I want to hear this."

I'm not sure why I was so surprised. He's never been all that affectionate toward me, nor has he paid me any mind beyond when I make him mad. But I guess I didn't expect him to actually say it. Naturally, I wanted to know why so I asked. And he said, 'I didn't want kids at all'. He wouldn't go into any further detail beyond that. It's only now I realize he never answered whether he liked me or not. Given this revelation though, I think it's safe to say that he does not.

But now I have even more questions. Why didn't he want kids? Why have them knowing he didn't want them?"

"Now I want to know too," said Allison.

"Me too," said Derek. "And I'm going to ask him when I see him."

The sound of something falling caught their attention. Derek stuffed the journal in his coat and turned around to see Ralph entering the building. He had knocked over a wooden plank that had been leaning against the wall.

"What are you guys doing in here?" asked Ralph.

"Uh...," said Derek, trying to come up with an explanation.

"We were looking for clues about Derik," said Allison. "He liked to hang around here a lot, so we thought maybe he'd left something behind."

"What are you doing here Ralphie?" asked Derek.

"I uh...," stammered Ralph. "I was doing the same."

"You knew about this place?"

"We came here one day after an assignment because he was curious about it," said Ralph. "I told him it was dangerous to be in here because there could be mold, sharp objects, and holes in the ground, but he didn't care. This place drew him in."

"What was this place?" asked Derek.

"I don't know," said Ralph. "It's been abandoned for as long as I can remember."

Ralph looked around the building and shook his head.

"He didn't know but I could see him from the grocery store sneaking in here," laughed Ralph sadly. "I would give anything now just to see him sneak in here again. Honestly Derek, when I saw you, I thought you were him."

"Oh," uttered Derek.

"You really cared about him, didn't you?" said Allison.

"Yeah," said Ralph. "Honestly, I saw a lot of my younger self in him. That's why I took him under my wing. You guys know I don't have any brothers either, so Derik kind of felt like a little brother to me."

"If it makes you feel any better, I'm sure he liked you too," said Allison. "And I'm also sure he knew and understood how much you cared about him too."

"Thanks," said Ralph. "I think we should get out of here. It's still a dangerous place in my eyes."

"You're right," agreed Allison.

The three of them left the building and walked across the street to Brewer's.

"Some people think I'm crazy for continuing to believe he'll come back," said Ralph. "But I can't help it. I can feel it in my spirit that he's still alive, and that he'll come back one day."

"What if he already was back and we didn't know?" said Derek, thinking about the previous night's encounter.

"What do you mean?"

"I was just wondering out loud. I had a dream he was back and just hiding."

"Oh," said Ralph. He looked at the grocery store as if a new thought had entered his mind and then sucked his teeth and shrugged like he was dismissing it. "If that were the case, I'd be glad that he was back, but I'd also be peeved at him for making us worry like that."

"Well, Ralphie, we shouldn't keep you from the store," said Allison.

"Yeah," said Ralph. "Working two jobs is never fun kids, so stay in school."

"You stayed in school though," said Derek.

"Yeah, but I'm also a Brewer," grumbled Ralph. "That means no matter what I do, the family business will always be my job. But that's a me problem. See you guys later."

Ralph went inside the store while Derek and Allison returned to their cars.

"What should we do about this?" asked Derek, pulling the journal from his coat.

"I say we read through it, and if there's anything it that can help us find him, then we turn it in to the police," said Allison.

"Do you want to take it?"

"No, you keep it," said Allison. "I have the slumber party this evening, so I won't have time to read through it."

"Alright," said Derek. "I'll let you know what I find."

"Okay."

Derek sat in his room that afternoon, picking up reading from where he had left off.

<u>September</u>
Ms. Nelson appointed me the editor-in-chief of the Creeke High Gazette today. I guess volunteering at the Creeke Courier really paid off. Speaking of the Creeke Courier, I wish Ralphie would stop asking me so many questions about my home life. I know he means well, but good grief. The whole point of being at the office is so I don't have to think about home.

I just feel like no one understands me. I can't explain it, but I don't feel like my own self. It's like everything I do is always compared to someone else. I can never just be me. That's why I'm so excited about being editor-in-chief. Because it's finally something that I can do. And it's something only I can do without being compared to anyone else.

Derek did not need an explanation for who 'someone else' was because he knew it to be himself. He knew Derik's frustrations well. They
were interchangeable to the people of Creeke, and they had accepted it
to a certain extent. However, Derek had taken up dance to separate himself, and in that same way, Derik had taken up writing. But it seemed
like no matter how hard they tried to carve out their own identities,
Derik was Derek, and Derek was Derrick, and Derrick was Derik and
Derek until all that remained in everyone's mind was the mixed-up
image of one, singular dark-brown boy.

> <u>September</u>
> Mr. Shoe-Thrower yelled at me yes-
> terday. Then Dad went and fought
> with him. Then they both got arrested.
> Then D-Money called himself 'setting
> me straight' after school (like shut up,
> you're not Granddad, and this has
> nothing to do with you).

"Oh, he's definitely getting chopped in the neck for that," laughed
Derek.

> Then we had to have a 'mediation'
> this morning where they both basically
> said they were having a bad day yester-
> day. Just because they had a bad day
> doesn't mean they need to take it out
> on me. I had a bad day too, but
> you don't see me going around calling
> people an idiot and fighting, do you?

It's not my fault Mr. Shoe-Thrower's biological father was trash. And it's also not my fault that Dad keeps having bad days because of his arguments with Mother. He wouldn't even be having bad days if he'd just answer Mother's stupid question. How hard is it to tell her you love her? It doesn't even have to be the truth. Just tell her you do so we can all stop hearing about it. Every time she asks, he's always like, 'I've given you this' and 'I paid for that'. Then again, I guess I shouldn't expect much from them. Dad's never been the caring type, and I doubt he ever will be. Mother cares more about her reputation and being a lady than she does about us. Of all the people on this planet, why did I have to get these two as parents?

<u>October</u>

Something interesting happened today. D-Money's mom contacted me. She thinks I'm him and she wants to meet him. I'm going to ask him what he thinks about it.

I asked him what he thought about meeting her, and he didn't like the idea. I don't blame him, but just because he doesn't want to meet her doesn't mean she can't still meet him. I could take his place and pretend to be him. She might even consider letting me move in with her. Of course, I'd miss Granddad and Nanna, and everyone else, but it would be a necessary sacrifice. I just have to get away from that house. It's such a draining place. Dad didn't even want me in the first place, so I doubt he'd care that I was gone. Mother's so worried about her reputation that she wouldn't even notice I was gone. Cornbread and Queenie will probably be moving out soon, which means I'd be the only one left in that house. I refuse to be alone there, biding my time until I turned eighteen. I have to get out now.

<u>October</u>

D-Money and Adrianna pulled off their little revival plan. I'm just glad that Granddad got to preach again. I've also been getting to know Monique pretty well. I was a little skeptical about if she was who she said she was at first because there were some details about herself she seemed to forget. But after talking with her some more, I believe it's really her because she knows things only a person from Creeke would know. Like for example, she knows about all the drama with D-Money's birth, and she hates Uncle Falcon as much as he hates her. I'm hoping that one day I can meet her in person. I just know she would take me away if only she met me.

<u>November</u>

D-Money and I had our birthday party yesterday. Technically, my actual birthday isn't for another two weeks whereas his was actually yesterday. D-Money thinks I have a secret girlfriend, but he doesn't realize I'm actually studying him so I can become as much like him as possible. If I'm going to pull off this little switch-a-roo with Monique, I need to match him as close as I can because I don't know all of what she knows about him. I'm already at a disadvantage because he decided being an acrobat was his life's goal, so everything else needs to be almost perfect. Mimicking him isn't too hard because of our little game, but being him is a whole other story.

"This man is sneaky!" cried Derek. "No wonder he kept doing it so much around that time!"

I decided to put my efforts into practice today at the party. The first step was to dress like him, so I asked him to send me a picture of what he was wearing that day. His outfit was surprisingly simple. He had on a red candy-themed jacket, a black t-shirt with denim biker jeans. His jacket went well with Queenie's candy-themed two-piece outfit. I was surprised he didn't wear any half-and-half-colored pants because he's obsessed with them for some reason.

"Because they look good and I can pull them off," said Derek. "But no, I was trying not to outshine you on our big day."

The shoes he chose were these multi-colored shoes Queenie had bought him back in September, but the dominant colors in them were black and red. And in typical D-Money he wore a red cap to match his shoes. This time he had it sitting backward on his head, and I'm glad he didn't dye his hair red like he had wanted to. He also wore his name chain along with his new golden grill that had been an early birthday present from Matty.

His color scheme seemed to be black and his favorite color, red, so I decided to take it a step further and add my favorite color, blue. Matty had given me this comic-superhero themed bomber jacket, and I'd never had an occasion to wear it until today. I borrowed these blue and red sneakers from Deidrick and had to stuff tissue into the toe area so I wouldn't crease them (also because he has big feet, and I didn't want the shoes falling off my feet). I put them with jeans and a black t-shirt, and my poker chip necklace and I was good to go. D-Money took me, Sami, and Benji to the gym because he wanted to get right for the party.

D-Money's new truck that Uncle Falcon got him for his birthday is so cool. I guess it's a good thing he only has dance on Tuesdays and Thursdays because he'll definitely need the other days to work for gas money. But our time at the gym made me realize my plan to become him might have a serious hitch. D-Money is a lot stronger than I thought he was.

"Well duh," said Derek. "I do a lot more athletic activity than you do."

I did my best to keep up with him, but he has that Granddad energy. It never runs out! By the time we got done, he seemed like he was barely tired!

"Because it was a light workout...," said Derek. "It was just so I could look good for the party."

If I have to exercise the way he does, I just need to give up now. Because there's no way I'll be able to lift the kind of weight he did.

After the gym, we got ready for the party. Watching D-Money play around with Sami and Benji made me realize just how different we were. He's more outgoing and friendlier than I am. He's also a lot louder than I am too. Even though I can mimic his voice, style, and mannerisms almost perfectly, his personality is different. He's too unique.

"Because I'm one of a kind, baby!" laughed Derek.

The party was fun. Of course, Mr. Shoe-Thrower wouldn't let his kids come so that meant Andre, Adrianna, and Antoine weren't there. I'm cool with Andre and Adrianna, but Antoine is my best friend. Why can't I have my best friend at my birthday party? Why can't D-Money have his girlfriend at his birthday party? Especially when they live around the corner from D-Money's house, which is where the party was at!

Anyways, since Adrianna couldn't come, D-Money was kind of sulky. He didn't dance as much as he normally would've and kind of stayed off to the side with me. He did however do the little boxing tournament and won.

"Of course, I did!" said Derek. "Can't nobody beat me in the gloves!"

(In my opinion, he only won because Andre wasn't there).

"Wow!" laughed Derek. "That's foul! Now I'll have to challenge Andre one day and see if he can beat me all because you said that."

After that, he got super hyped up when Benji performed and asked him to do a dance he had him choreograph for the song. Benji's performance was cool. He's going to make it big one day, I already know it. And D-Money is going to be an amazing dancer. He's already really great. But of course, his mood was ruined when someone decided it would be a good idea to do this thing where the birthday boys got a kiss for our birthdays. D-Money was not having it. He said unless they found a way to get Adrianna over there to kiss him, he wasn't doing it. So, he didn't get kissed, and he was pissed off for the rest of the night.

"Because," griped Derek. "Why are people trying to get me to kiss some other girl when I have a whole girlfriend? What sense does that make?"

But I don't have a girlfriend, which meant I couldn't back out.

"You could've said no, and I would've held you down," said Derek. "And anyone who didn't like it could meet me outside with or without the gloves."

The girl I had my first kiss with tonight was Nicole Brewer. Cell has been telling me about girls and how to deal with them, but nothing he told me could've prepared me for tonight. I liked it. I liked it a lot. Honestly, I don't remember anything that happened after the kiss. Overall though, I had a good night. D-Money not so much...

<u>November</u>
I don't know if I want to go through with my plan anymore. Things still aren't any better at home, but the more I learn about Monique and her family, the more I feel like D-Money deserves to know about her. I know he said he doesn't want to meet her, but this is

his mother. It's not fair to him for me to take this from him just because of how I feel.

Also, things between Nicki and me have become awkward. She was delivering a birthday present to me from Ralphie. It was a reporter's hat. As she spoke, I stared at her lips, and an idea popped into my head. Nicki went to hand me the present, and I told her I wouldn't accept it unless she kissed me. Of course, she was shocked by my boldness, but I have been feeling rather bold lately as it is. I told her that as the man of the day, I wanted another kiss. And she couldn't resist the birthday boy, now could she? So, we kissed. Nicki's cheeks were red when we finished, and she ran off after handing me the present. Now, she avoids me like I've got the plague or something. I don't care because I only like her as a friend. I just wanted another kiss for my actual birthday. But I just hope Ralphie doesn't find out, or else he'll kill me...

<u>December</u>

I've made up my mind. I'm running away forever. I'll do it on the final day of school. I'm supposed to meet Monique that evening in the city, and I've already convinced Cell to take me so no one will suspect anything. I'll convince Monique to take her with me and be free of this place forever. No one will care anyways. All I did was tell Mother the truth about her relationship with Dad, and what do I get in return? I get slapped in the face! I'll leave for good, and she'll never have to worry about me again. I'll disappear from Creeke forever and never come back even if it's the last thing I do. <u>Then maybe, just maybe, I'll be happy for once in my life!</u>

After reading the final entry, Derek got on the phone with Allison to tell her what he had learned.

"Queenie," said Derek. "Did you know Dee-Three had a second kiss with Nicki?"

"What?!" hollered Allison. "No way!"

"It's true!" said Derek. "And he had been planning to run away since September."

"You're joking."

"I'm not," said Derek. "He was planning to pretend to be me and run away with Monique."

"Why?"

"According to his journal, he was unhappy here and felt like no one cared about him. The final straw was the argument with Auntie Leya where she slapped him."

"He has no one but himself to blame for that argument," said Allison. "He called her a viper that was finally showing its true colors, and then started going on this tirade and that's when she slapped him. Honestly, I would've slapped him too because he was just being way too disrespectful."

"He said the reason he got slapped was because he told the truth about her relationship with Uncle Marlin," said Derek. "What did he say?"

"That he didn't love her," answered Allison. "Knowing what I know now, that definitely struck a nerve in her. She feels like he could've been paid to marry her for all she knows."

"You know what," said Derek, getting up from the bed. "I'm getting to the bottom of this once and for all."

"What are you going to do?"

"I'm going to talk to Uncle Marlin and get some answers."

"Good luck with that," snorted Allison.

After ending the conversation, Derek marched into the living room to confront his uncle.

"Can I ask you something?"

"You know my policy," said Uncle Marlin. "But if I didn't know any better, I'd say you were the newspaper boy and not your cousin."

"He's the reason I have all these questions," said Derek. "You told him you didn't want any kids. I want to know why."

"I already told you why."

"No, why didn't you want kids?"

"What does this have to do with your cousin?"

"Uncle Marlin, just answer the question. Because I'm trying to let you make it, but it seems like every time I do, I learn something new about you that pisses me off."

"You're trying to let me make what?"

"I'm trying to give you a chance to explain yourself. Why didn't you want kids?"

"Because I didn't want to be the type of father your grandfather was."

"Then why did you have them?"

"Because Soleya wanted them."

"That's my next question. Why did you marry Auntie Leya?"

"Because she wanted to get married."

"Were you in love with Auntie Leya when you married her?"

"Why are you asking me all this stuff? And what does any of it have to do with your cousin?"

"Look," said Derek. "There's a lot of people in this family who feel like you don't love them. Like your kids, and they say they don't care. Then there are those like Nanna and Dad who say you do love them, and they care that you do. Auntie Leya loves you, but she doesn't know if you love her, and it's hurting her that she doesn't know."

"And what about you?"

"I'm not important right now," said Derek. "I want to know if you were in love with Auntie Leya when you married her."

"I..." began Uncle Marlin. "I don't know. I just remember wanting to be away from your grandfather for good, and Soleya and her parents provided a way out."

"So, whether she loved you or not didn't matter to you?"

"I never thought about it," said Uncle Marlin. "After she told me she wanted to get married, I agreed to do it. There was a moment when I considered calling the wedding off though because I felt like I wasn't ready. I tried to get advice from your grandfather, but he was so wrapped up in his own problems that he couldn't help me, so I had to figure things out for myself. So, I went through with it and let Bernard handle the rest. But just like anything to do with Bernard, what he provided came with a bunch of strings attached."

"What kind of strings?"

"Monetary strings," said Uncle Marlin. "We couldn't spend any money without his approval. Anything that had his name on the dotted line we couldn't use without his permission. I didn't like that, so I gave him back everything he ever gave us and got the first job I could find so I could make my own money."

Uncle Marlin's face curled into one of annoyance, and his voice turned venomous.

"Then, that spineless, bootlicking, cradle-robber Quincy tried to claim I married Soleya for her money!" ranted Uncle Marlin. "If I wanted her for her money I would've tried to get along with her awful family! The way Bernard and Sophia treated Soleya every chance they got disgusted me! And then they'd smile in my face and claim they were so happy to have me as a son and tell Soleya how good a job she did picking me! I've never wanted to choke so many two-faced people out so badly in my life! Living with those people was like living in Hell and it pissed me off so much that I got us out of there as soon as I could!"

"So, you married Auntie Leya because she wanted to get married, but you got married because it was a way to escape Granddad?"

"Yes."

"Then you didn't love her."

"I guess not when you put it that way."

"But what about now? Do you still not love her?"

"Now? Honestly, I don't see myself being married to anyone but Soleya. I'll do anything she wants to keep her happy."

"So, if she wanted a divorce, you'd go through with it?"

"If it would make her happy. I wouldn't be happy about it though."

"Why is it that you can say all this to me, but not to her?"

"Because you're easy to talk to."

"They're easy to talk to too. It can't be that hard to tell your family your feelings about them."

"Derek, my job as the man of the house is to provide for them," said Uncle Marlin. "If I let my feelings get in the way of that, they won't respect me as the man of the house. So, I let Soleya handle everything at home. What my feelings are doesn't matter as long as they're taken care of."

"It does matter!" argued Derek. "You and Auntie Leya keep arguing because she feels like you don't love her and were practically paid to marry her! Your family feels like you don't care about them! Dee-Three's whole reason for acting out was because he felt like you didn't love him! You're chasing everyone away!"

Uncle Marlin sat stunned. After processing what Derek said, he regained his composure.

"Derek, do you like me?"

"Yes," said Derek. "You're not scary or mean like I thought you were. In fact, I'd say you're the coolest uncle I have."

"Do you think I like you?"

"Honestly, I'm still not sure. Sometimes I feel like you do but then sometimes I feel like you're just tolerating me because I'm your nephew."

Uncle Marlin did not speak.

"I didn't mean to yell at you, but everyone is confused about how you feel," said Derek. "Everyone just wants you to be clear about your feelings."

"And what do you think being clear is?"

"Telling people," said Derek. "Dad says the best way to make people understand how you feel is to tell them. That's why he always wants me to say how I feel."

"Hey!" said Malcolm, entering the house. "It's cold out there!"

"Falcon, do you like me?" asked Uncle Marlin.

"Yeah...?" answered Malcolm confusedly as he took off his coat. "Why?"

"What do you mean 'why'?" laughed Malcolm. "You're my older brother, I'm always going to like you."

"Do you think I like you?"

"I would hope so considering I'm letting you stay with me," joked Malcolm.

"But you don't know for sure?"

"I'm pretty sure you like me," said Malcolm. "Did I miss something?"

"No," said Uncle Marlin. "I'll be back. I'm going to see Mom."

"Tell her I said hi," said Malcolm. After Uncle Marlin was gone, he turned to Derek and said, "What was that about?"

"I confronted him and told him he needs to be more clear with his feelings."

"That would be something to see."

"You don't think he can?"

"I'm sure he can, but will he actually do it is the question," said Malcolm. "I don't pretend to know everything about how your uncle, but I do believe how he shows his feelings tends to be misunderstood by the family."

"You do?"

"I believe he cares for us in his own way, but they don't understand what that way is."

"And you do?"

"I think I do."

"How?"

"Let me tell you a story," said Malcolm, sitting down. "When I was a kid, I got a really bad fever one day. Your grandparents couldn't afford to take off from work, so Marlin skipped school to stay with me. He spent that whole day taking care of me and making sure I was happy. It was the first time I saw his softer side, and as I grew older, it became easier to identify when he'd show that side of himself. That's how I know he cares. Because he wants to make people happy. Marlin's not this mean guy everyone makes him out to be. He's just guarded."

"He's not the only one."

"Who else is guarded?"

"You."

"Me?" said Malcolm. "I don't have a problem saying how I feel."

"Yeah, but any time the topic of church or Monique comes up, you close up."

"Because I have nothing to say."

"But you should. You should say how that situation made you feel."

"That's easy. That whole situation with how you came to be, pissed me off. Everyone turned their backs on me. Even Marlin."

"Is that why your relationship was rocky when I was a baby?"

"Yeah," said Malcolm. "Our relationship didn't get as bad as say Matty and Cornbread's, but I still felt betrayed. Like the one person who should've had my back didn't."

"How'd you get past it?"

"I had to trust him with you. One time you got sick as a baby, and Mom and Dad were out of town. I didn't know what to do so I called Marlin for help, and he came and took care of you until you were better."

"Why is it always me bringing people back together?"

"I don't know. I guess that's just what you do. Tear everything apart and then put it back together again."

"Not everything," sighed Derek. "Me and Granddad are still torn apart."

"Then put yourselves back together."

"And what about you?"

"What about me?"

"I still say you're guarded about church and Monique."

"I'm fine and my life is good right now. And I also know now that next time I go through something serious, not to expect any help from anyone else."

"That's not the way to be."

"But that's the way it is."

That night, Derek was practicing his routine when he received a text. Meet me at the burned-down house if you want to know the truth."

The text was from a blocked number. But Derek suspected he knew who it was from. He wanted to wrap his arms around his cousin and let him know everything was okay. Let him know that he understood and that he was not alone or unloved. Derek wanted Derik back.

"Uncle Marlin's not back yet?" asked Derek.

"Nope," answered Malcolm.

"Oh," said Derek. "Well, I'm going out for a bit."

"Be careful," cautioned Malcolm. "And don't stay out too late."

"I won't."

His heart thumped faster with every mile that brought him near the house. That house that caused the pain that split them apart would be the very place where they would reunite. As he neared it, he looked around for him. Walking up to it, he searched for that missing piece of his life that would soon be back with him. The last thing he remembered was a pair of headlights coming down the road toward him.

Chapter Twenty-One: Allison

It had started out as such a promising day for Allison. After leaving her brother's journal in Derek's care, Allison returned home to prepare for the slumber party. She would be meeting with the other girls later that afternoon to help them with some community service. After packing everything she would need, Allison sat at the kitchen table and practiced chess alone to pass the time. During this time, she received a video call from Andre.

"Video?" asked Allison.

"I'm testing my sign language," said Andre.

"Why?"

"To talk to my new friend."

"Well, hopefully I remember enough to help you."

"You should. We used to practice it together."

"Yeah, until you lost interest and gave up."

"Sorry."

"So, what's up?"

"You stood me up."

"You never showed."

"No, you never showed."

"We waited over an hour for you at that library, Andre."

"Why'd you leave then?"

"Because something came up."

"You couldn't tell a brother that you were leaving? My dad is literally mad at me and saying I wasted his gas."

"When is your dad not mad?"

"Who knows? What are you doing?"

"Playing chess until I go meet up with your sister and the rest of the girls."

"Playing by yourself again?"

"You know me well."

"Want me to play with you?"

"Sure, if you don't mind losing to a Harrison."

"Browns never lose to Harrisons."

"The Browns have lost to the Harrisons several times."

"Well, this Brown has never lost to a Harrison."

"You're behind me in the school ranking right now."

"Doesn't mean I'm dumber than you. Doesn't change the fact I've never lost to a Harrison."

"Got your chess board ready?"

"Almost."

"Don't get distracted."

"I'll try."

"You know how easily distracted you get."

"I can't help it."

"Ready?"

"Ready."

"I think Derek could beat you at dancing."

"Depends on what type of dancing it is."

"Some people think he can beat you in a fight."

"Some people also think you and I should be together."

"I don't want to be together."

"I don't either."

"Why are we talking about it then?"

"Because people don't always know what they're talking about."

"True."

"Check."

"You won."

"Told you I never lose to a Harrison. I captured your queen, Queen."

"Dork."

"Nerd."

"Bye."

"Bye."

Allison hung up and returned to playing by herself. She knew that many people thought she and Andre would make a cute couple, but she personally did not see it. Andre was her friend, and she saw no reason why their relationship had to change. Feeling a pair of eyes upon her, Allison panned her head to the kitchen doorway and spotted her father leaning against it, watching her.

"How long have you been standing there?" questioned Allison.

"I just got here," said Mr. Harrison. He looked at the chessboard and asked, "Are you playing by yourself?"

"Yes sir."

"Do you want someone to play with?"

"Like who?"

"I'll play with you," said Mr. Harrison, sitting down. "I like chess."

"You do?" asked Allison.

"Yeah. I bet you a thousand dollars I can beat you."

"I don't have a thousand dollars."

"If you win, I'll give it to you."

"Deal."

The chess match commenced.

"Why were you watching me?" asked Allison.

"I was interested," answered Mr. Harrison. "Why were you playing by yourself?"

"I had no one to play with," answered Allison.

"Hmm...," muttered Mr. Harrison.

The match continued. Allison realized for the first time she could see him up close. Her nose came from him, as did her forehead. She spotted the tiny holes poked through his earlobes and tried to remember a time she had seen earrings in them. A simple gold chain hung around his neck, and cologne radiated from his body. But the trait that held Allison's attention was his eyes. Those brown eyes of her father's missed nothing. They looked up at Allison, and she felt her breath hitch in her throat as they settled on her.

"Checkmate," said Mr. Harrison.

"Darn," sighed Allison. "Guess you can keep your thousand dollars."

"I'll still give it to you if you want."

"Why?" said Allison. "I didn't win."

"Why not? You want the money, right?"

"Yeah but...," said Allison. "No. We made a deal, and I don't go back on my word."

"As you wish," said Mr. Harrison, standing up. "This was enjoyable."

"Yeah, because you won."

"We can have a rematch if you want."

"Hey son," said Nanna Kiana. "I didn't know you were here."

"I came to see you," said Mr. Harrison. "I need to talk to you, Mom."

"Okay," said Nanna Kiana. "Let's go somewhere private."

"Alright," said Mr. Harrison. As he started to leave, he turned to Allison and said, "If you ever want to play again, let me know."

"Okay...," uttered Allison, slightly stunned. When she finally regained her senses, she looked back at the chessboard and said to herself, "What was that about?"

Around four that afternoon, Allison met with the other girls at Tamara's house. Because she and her older sister Tamela had been taking care of their mother, Tamara had hardly been able to leave the house for anything except school. Therefore, when the girls of the Little Sister Society showed up on her porch with food sent by their families, Tamara stood before them clad in raggedy, bleach-stained clothes and a headscarf with confusion written on her face.

"What's going on?" asked Tamara.

"We've come to check on you and see if you need help with any-thing," said Adrianna. Holding up the fried fish from her mother and the evenly and perfectly snapped green beans from her father, she added, "And we also brought food."

"Thanks," said Tamara, taking the dishes from Adrianna. "I'm trying to clean the house, but it's a bit much for only one person."

"Well, if you want us to, we'll help you clean up. Just tell us what to do."

"Okay."

Before long, Tamara had assigned every girl to a room in the house. Allison was assigned to help clean the kitchen with Adrianna and Tamara. She swept the floor while half-listening to the other two's conversation as they washed and dried dishes together.

"How's Mrs. Reesy's treatment going?" asked Adrianna.

"I don't know," said Tamara. "Tam is the one who handles all her medical stuff. They both just seem so tired, and I wish I could do more to help them."

"You're doing something right now by keeping the house clean."

"Yeah, but I feel like it doesn't compare," said Tamara. "Tam is the one really holding everything together. She won't even tell Drake how bad it really is because she doesn't want him to worry."

"Well, she doesn't have to worry about me telling him, that's for sure," said Adrianna. "All he'll do is go into fixer mode and stress her out even more."

"I'm sure she'd appreciate that," said Tamara. After a silent moment, she continued with, "I just want Mom to be okay. We've already lost Dad to cancer, and I don't want to go through that again."

Allison stopped listening after that. She did not want to seem like she was eavesdropping, especially when she had nothing important to add to the conversation. Instead, she moved into the living room where Nicole was, and continued sweeping in there. Once again, Nicole avoided looking at her, and Allison resolved to clear the awkwardness between them.

"Nicole," said Allison.

"Huh?" said Nicole.

"I just want you to know that I know."

"You know what?"

"About the kiss."

"*Who told you?!*"

"He did," said Allison. "Well, technically he wrote it in his journal and that's where I learned about it, but the point is it's not a big deal. Like, I was there when the first kiss happened."

"Yeah, but that was different."

"Do you like Derik?"

"Not like that," said Nicole. "He wanted another kiss for his actual birthday, and I was like 'Oh well, I've already kissed him once', so I went with it. And then when I handed him the present from Ralphie, I realized how close he was with my brother, and everything became awkward, and I didn't want anyone to find out."

"Well, I'm sure you'll be glad to know he didn't tell anyone," said Allison. "And your secret is safe with me and D-Money."

"*He knows too?!*"

"He was the one reading the journal."

"No!" cried Nicole. "You know he can't whisper to save his life!"

"He may not be able to whisper, but he can keep a secret," said Allison. "Trust me when I say no one else will know."

"Okay...," said Nicole.

"No one will know what?" asked Latasia.

"Nothing," said Nicole. "What's up?"

"Tell me why Althea just told me she invited that new girl to the slumber party," said Latasia.

"Seriously?" grumbled Nicole. "Why would she do that?"

"Too busy trying to be nice as usual."

"What's the big deal?" asked Allison.

"The big deal is that this is *our* slumber party," said Latasia. "And now Althea's gone and invited one of Dani's minions into our territory."

"You make it sound like we're at war with Dani," laughed Allison.

"We're not at war," said Latasia. "I just want her and her people to stay far away from me and my people because I'm still not over how they made fun of my brother back in the fall."

"Or how they tried to steal from my parent's store!" added Nicole. "That's taking money out of my pockets!"

"Jada didn't give me those vibes when I met her," said Allison.

"Of course, you'll defend her now that you're all buddy-buddy with Prissy," snorted Nicole.

"It's not even like that," said Allison. "I'm just saying she didn't give me that vibe."

"Well, she must be like them because she became friends with them very quickly," said Latasia. "And anyone that makes friends with Dani is not someone I want to be friends with."

"Me either," added Nicole.

The girls finished cleaning the house.

"Thank you, guys!" said Tamara. "You guys are the best!"

"You're welcome," said Adrianna. "And if you ever need anything, let us know."

"I will."

After visiting Tamara, the girls all went to Althea's house for the slumber party. Jada was there waiting for them, and although Allison was still a bit ambivalent about Jada, the same could not be said for the latter. Jada seemed to like Allison and wanted to be her friend.

"Did you have a good day?" asked Jada.

"Yeah," said Allison. "The other girls and I went to visit Em and Mrs. Reesy."

"Mrs. Reesy?" said Jada.

"That's Em's mother," explained Allison. "It's short for her middle name, Therese, because she doesn't like her first name the same way Em doesn't like hers either."

"What's Mrs. Reesy's first name?"

"Frances."

"I would go by Reesy too," giggled Jada.

"How do you like it here in Creeke?" asked Allison.

"It's cool," said Jada. "It's a lot different from where I'm from though."

"What's it like where you're from?"

"There's a lot more to do," explained Jada. "Also, the people there are more willing to get to know you. It seems like everyone here doesn't like me for some reason."

"Yeah...," said Allison, wincing. "It's because of the girls you've been hanging around."

"Who?" asked Jada. "Dani and the Garza sisters?"

"Yeah," answered Allison. "Nobody likes those girls."

"Why not?"

"Because they start a lot of drama," explained Allison. "Everybody assumed you were the same way because of how quickly you gravitated to them."

"So, people already don't like me because I'm trying to get to know everybody?"

"Yeah."

"That is so lame," complained Jada. "I like getting to know people for myself. I'm not going to dislike someone just because other people don't like them."

"And I respect that," said Allison. "I'm just letting you know why people are being kind of distant toward you."

"That's so annoying," griped Jada. "I've gotten along well with them so far, especially Mariana. Me and her have a lot in common."

"Really?"

"Yeah," said Jada. "We're around the same age and we have similar ethnicities. Of course, she's more into music and art while I'm more into math and science but that's okay. And then me and Mariella both like playing that *The Well* game. Honestly, I have more in common with the Garzas than I do Dani. I just hang around with her because she's their friend."

"Interesting," said Allison. "My best friend plays *The Well* too. I used to too, but I got too busy."

"You've got to get back into it! They've added so much new stuff!"

"Maybe I will. So, you like math and science too?"

"I love them," said Jada.

"It's so rare to find someone around here who likes them! Everyone usually complains about them because they say they're hard to understand."

"Right?! But they just don't seem that hard to me. If anything, the subject I like the least is history, and that's my brother's favorite."

"I don't really find history to be all that hard. My least favorite subjects are anything art related. I have no drawing ability whatsoever."

"Allison," called Latasia. She motioned for Allison to come near her. "Come here for a sec."

"I'll be right back," said Allison to Jada. She got up and joined Latasia and Nicole across the room, saying "What's up?"

"Girl why are you talking to her?" chuckled Latasia.

"Because I can," said Allison.

"I don't know how you do it," said Nicole. "First Prissy, and now Jada. You're like a mean girl magnet or something."

"Jada's not a mean girl," said Allison defensively. "And as for Prissy, she's honestly not that bad when she's not around Dani."

"You can be their friend if you want, but I want nothing to do with them," said Latasia.

"Me either," said Nicole.

"You know what Nicki, you're right, I am a mean girl magnet," said Allison. "Because before I attracted Prissy, I attracted you two."

"We're not mean girls," argued Latasia.

"You're both acting like it," countered Allison. "If I remember correctly, you *both* were the original members of Dani's girl group."

"Her what?" said Latasia.

"It's a joke D-Money came up with," said Allison. "The point is, you two were faithfully by her side too."

"That's different," said Nicole. "We didn't bully anyone, and we left when Dani started acting up."

"Dani's been acting up since her *freshman year*," said Allison. "You two were her friends up until *this past summer*. That's two years' worth of mean girl behavior that you both stayed friends with her through."

"Okay," said Latasia. "But why are you getting upset with us?"

"Because you two have been looking at me crazy and I'm over it!" ranted Allison. "Yes, Prissy was dumb for siding with Dani at first, but she's seen the light now! And sure, Jada is befriending them but that's because she's new in town! She's literally here at the slumber party right now trying to make friends with us and everyone's been rude by ignoring her!"

Everyone was silent. Allison had attracted everyone's attention.

"We've got to do better than this," said Allison, taking advantage of the spotlight thrust on her. "We can't claim to be any better than Dani and her minions if we're acting just like them."

"Um," interjected Diana, pausing from painting Kameryn's nails. "I know you're trying to get everyone to do better right now but uh... who is 'we'? Because me and Thea have *been* talking to Jada since she first got to town. That's you guys acting all weird."

"I didn't mean to be rude," said Charmaine, moving closer to Jada. "I'm sorry if I made you feel left out."

"Me too," said Kameryn.

"And me," said Adrianna. "I shouldn't have let my feelings toward my cousins affect how I acted toward you."

"I'm sorry too," said Allison. "I should've been more willing than I was to get to know you."

Everyone looked at Latasia and Nicole.

"I'm sorry for not giving you a fair chance," sighed Latasia.

"So am I," said Nicole.

"Thank you everyone," said Jada appreciatively. "No hard feelings."

"Hey Allison," said Althea. "There's someone outside your house."

"Who is it?" asked Allison.

Everyone crowded around Althea's bedroom window. It didn't take long for Allison to figure out the person's identity. The black space-themed hoodie made it obvious.

"It's Derek!" said Charmaine.

"What's he doing out here so late?" questioned Latasia.

"I know what he better *not* be doing," remarked Adrianna.

"I doubt he can see us from across the street, Adrianna," said Nicole.

"But what *is* he doing?" said Kameryn.

"Who is he?" whispered Jada to Allison.

"My cousin."

"Oh."

Nothing could have prepared Allison for what she witnessed next. A light shined on Derek, and he turned his head in its direction. Everyone watched as the light grew stronger until it morphed into a car. It sped up, jumped the curb, and threw itself into Derek. Gasps and screams filled the room as the girls watched the horror unfold before them. Derek floundered on the hood for a few seconds before falling off into the road below. Adrianna was the first to break from the shock.

"NO!" she hollered, dashing from the room.

"DEREK!" yelled Allison, following behind her.

Everyone poured out of the house to help the unconscious Derek lying in the road. The driver of the car knelt over him, seemingly going through his pockets.

"Hey!" hollered Allison. "What are you doing?!"

Allison could not tell who the driver was because their face was covered by a mask. Whoever it was looked her way, rushed back to their car, and drove off.

"Stop!" yelled Allison.

By the time Allison reached Derek, the car was gone. Allison stared down at her cousin's body. His leg was twisted into an unnatural position.

"Oh no!" cried Nicole. "His leg is broken!"

"Somebody call for help!" sobbed Adrianna as she held Derek's head in her lap.

Eventually, an ambulance arrived and carted Derek off to the hospital. By that time, he had regained consciousness, and silent tears ran down his face from the pain he was in. Allison did not know what to do. She paced back and forth in front of Ralph, who had been the first on the scene when Diana called him in a panic.

"You said it was a gray car that hit him?" asked Ralph.

"Yeah," said Allison.

"And the driver was going through Derek's pockets?"

"Looked like it."

"And they saw you?"

"Yeah."

"This isn't good," said Ralph. "If they purposely meant to run Derek over, and you all saw it, then they might come back to silence any witnesses."

"Ralph don't say that!" cried Diana.

"I'm serious," said Ralph. "This is a dangerous situation. I don't like the idea of you guys staying here alone. I'm staying until your parents get back."

Allison was thankful Ralph cared enough to want to protect them. But the only thing on her mind was Derek. Someone had meant to run him over and possibly kill him. And she wanted to know who and why.

-

Chapter Twenty-Two: Matthias

Alexander came to visit Matthias. It was not clear to Matthias why Alexander stayed away so long, but he was glad when his best friend finally showed up. When Alexander came into the room, Matthias greeted him and got no response. He watched as Alexander's eyes fell on Matthias's bandaged arm. A sob escaped his throat as tears flooded down his face.

"I'm sorry," apologized Alexander when he calmed down. "It's just when I heard you were shot, I was so scared you were going to leave me behind."

"Alex, when I finally leave you behind, I'm going out in style and leaving everything to you," joked Matthias.

"Don't joke like that."

"Alright," said Matthias. "You were that worried about me, huh?"

"You're like my only friend who isn't also my cousin," admitted Alexander. "I want to know who did this to you."

"I want to know too."

Matthias's phone rang. It was his grandfather.

"Hello?"

"Matthias," said Granddad Derrick.

"Hey, what's going on?" asked Matthias. He knew something was wrong because his grandfather had called him by his full name.

"We're on our way to the hospital," said Granddad Derrick. "D-Money's been hit by a car."

"A car?!" cried Matthias. "Is he okay?!"

"His leg is broken, but he's expected to live," said Granddad Derrick.

"Do you need me to do anything?"

"I need you to stay put," said Granddad Derrick. "You're still re-covering, and I don't want you over-exerting yourself."

"Granddad, you can't expect me to–!"

"Matthias," interrupted Granddad Derrick. "Please."

Matthias did not argue after that because he understood. His grandfather was tired. One grandson missing, one shot along with his two nephews, and now a third one ran over by a car. Five members of his family hurt in one way or another. It was becoming too much for his grandfather to bear, and Matthias understood.

"What's wrong?" asked Alexander when Matthias hung up the phone.

"D-money's been hit by a car," said Matthias.

"Oh no," gasped Alexander.

Matthias inhaled. He held in the air as long as he could, then released it.

"Bro, what is going on?!" screamed Matthias. He threw off his blankets and slipped into his shoes. "I've got to get out of here."

"Where are you going?"

"I don't know," said Matthias, grabbing his keys.

"Matt, are you sure you should be driving yet?"

"I don't care, Alex."

"I'm going with you."

"Come on then."

Matthias had no destination in mind. He only knew he could not stay put. All he needed was something to free his mind for a while. Something that would let him feel a sense of normalcy and security, even if only for one night.

"Matthias," said Alexander. "What are we doing here?"

Matthias looked up. While he was in his mind, his body had driven them to a bar. This was where normalcy was. Where he was comfortable. He did not say anything, but got out of the car and started walking.

"Don't," commanded Alexander. Matthias stopped but kept his back to Alexander. He did not want to see it. The look of disappointment on Alexander's face. "Don't go in there, Matt."

"I just want my life to feel normal."

"This isn't normal. This is just a distraction."

"So? What's wrong with that, Alex?"

"What's wrong with it is that the pain you're running from will still be there. It'll still be reality when you come back."

"I don't care."

"You do care," said Alexander, moving to stand next to him. "Otherwise, you wouldn't be here."

"Why can't you just let me do what I want?"

"Because then I'd be a bad friend."

"It'll only be one drink!"

"It won't, and you know it."

Matthias did know it. He wanted to drown it all away. To drown out the thoughts in his head, screaming at him about everything that had gone wrong. The temptation to walk through that door gripped him. And it was not until he saw a familiar face stumbled through that door that he felt that grip loosen.

"Cell?" said Matthias.

"Huh?" slurred Marcellus. "Oh, hey Playboy. What are you doing here?"

Anger. That was what Matthias felt. Angry because Marcellus had made this normal for him. Because he had tried to make this normal for Derik and lost him as a result. And then pity. Pity because Marcellus was still his big cousin who needed help. Still his big cousin who needed him because he had no one else. His big cousin who had been lonely in that house where he was only valued for what he would one day inherit. He had been lonely until Matthias had come along.

"He's not in any condition to drive," said Alexander.

"I'm perfectly fine," said Marcellus.

"No, you're not," said Matthias. "Where's your keys?"

"Uh uh," chuckled Marcellus. "I'm not telling you."

"Help me get him to the backseat," said Matthias.

"Where are we going?" asked Marcellus.

"Home," said Matthias.

"I don't want to go home."

"Cell, you're drunk."

"I'm not drunk," declared Marcellus. "I'm alive."

Matthias and Alexander laid Marcellus in the backseat. He looked up at Matthias and frowned.

"Playboy," said Marcellus. "Are you mad at me?"

Derik was still missing because of Marcellus's irresponsibility. Matthias knew that. But as he looked down at his drunken cousin, he could not find it in himself to be mad. He had been mad at everything and everyone for years, and he was tired. As he looked at Marcellus, all he felt was pity because he had been Marcellus and had lived Marcellus's life. Had lived the life of a boy in a man's body with a warped view of what manhood was. And he had almost walked into that bar and returned to that life until he saw what it had done to his big cousin.

"No," said Matthias. "I'm not mad at you."

"Okay," sighed Marcellus. It was a content sigh. One that he released because one of the only people who understood him had not deserted him. Marcellus needed him, just like Matthias needed Marcellus to remind him what he had escaped.

They drove home. No one was there to greet them as usual. Matthias laid Marcellus in his bed, then sank into the desk chair beside him. A smile formed on his lips as he watched his cousin's chest slowly rose and sank.

"I'm going to hang out here for tonight," said Matthias to Alexander.

"Alright," said Alexander. "I'll make myself comfy on that sofa out there."

"Take my room," said Matthias. "I'm not going to use it anyways."

"You sure? I don't mind sleeping on the sofa."

"My room and that's final."

"If that's what you want."

"I'll take you to get your car in the morning."

"Alright," said Alexander, turning to leave the room. "Goodnight."

"Goodnight," answered Matthias. "And Alex?"

"Yeah?"

"Thanks."

"No problem."

It was not just for his help with Marcellus. He had stopped Matthias from entering that bar. Had always been around even when Matthias felt he had no one else to count on. Alexander had been to him what he had been to Marcellus. Matthias was sure that he was a blessing sent to him straight from The Big Guy, and he would forever be grateful.

-

Chapter Twenty-Three: Deidrick

Sharon needed to explain to Deidrick why she went to a trailer where his brother's necklace was. She also needed to return his shoes and tell him if she was pregnant with his baby. But most importantly, Deidrick needed to discover what she knew about Derik. So, he banged on her door to confront her.

"Deidrick," said Sharon. "Why are you here?"

"I want my stuff back."

"Is that all you want?"

"Why? Are you going to give me something else?"

"What else do you want?"

"Just my stuff."

"That's all?"

"That's all. Can I come in?"

"Yeah... sure."

Sharon stepped aside, letting Deidrick in. He looked around the apartment, realizing how unwelcoming it seemed since the last time he had been there.

"I tried to come by the other day to get my stuff, but you were out."

"I was out with Malik."

"Go somewhere interesting?"

"Just out to eat," said Sharon.

"That's cool," said Deidrick with slight disinterest, knowing she lied. "So, Malik's been hanging around a lot more, huh?"

"Yeah. He claims I can't be trusted."

"Can't say I blame him."

"Wow, okay," snorted Sharon. "So, did you want your stuff now or...?"

"That's the whole reason I'm here."

While Sharon went to get the requested items, Deidrick put his master plan into action. He figured if Sharon saw the necklace, her reaction to it would answer his questions about Derik. So, he placed it on the counter, and when Sharon returned, her eyes went straight to it.

"You know, it's times like this when I really think about my brother the most," said Deidrick.

"Really?" said Sharon.

"Yeah," said Deidrick. "Sometimes I picture him just holed up in a trailer in the middle of nowhere or something."

"Why a trailer?" asked Sharon, tensing up.

"I don't know," said Deidrick. "I just do."

"Well, here goes your hoodie," said Sharon, changing the subject.

"Where's my shoes?"

"Malik has them."

"You gave him my shoes?"

"He said they're his now since you left them behind."

"Bro!" griped Deidrick. "Those were my new shoes! Where are they right now?"

"With him on his feet," said Sharon. "He practically sleeps in them now, because he wears them everywhere."

"I want my shoes back."

"I can get them back for you."

"Thank you," said Deidrick frustratedly.

"But what are you going to do for me in return?"

"What do you mean?"

"I mean... I'm the only one here right now," said Sharon, eyeing him suggestively.

"And how long is that going to last?"

"I'm not worried about Malik," said Sharon, running her fingers up Deidrick's arm. "In fact, I want him to catch us together."

"Sharon, don't tell me you've fallen for little old Cornbread."

"How can I help it?" sighed Sharon. "You give me what Malik doesn't. You make me feel... safe. He just yells at me and tries to control me and drags me into all his troubles."

"Really?"

"Yes," said Sharon, drawing Deidrick into an embrace. She relaxed her head on his chest and said, "If only you could just make all my problems go away."

"What, like kill Malik?"

"Deidrick!" gasped Sharon, letting him go.

"I'm joking," chuckled Deidrick. "But why not ditch the loser and join the winning team?"

"I can't," declared Sharon, turning dramatically away from him.

"Why not?"

"Because he's crazy," answered Sharon, her back still to him. "You don't know what he's capable of!"

"Like what?"

"You wouldn't believe me if I told you."

"Try me."

"Well...," said Sharon. She looked at Deidrick and said, "No. I can't let you get mixed up with him."

"You care about me that much?" asked Deidrick, approaching her.

Sharon wrapped her arms around Deidrick's neck and kissed him.

"Does that answer your question?" she asked.

"A little," said Deidrick, smirking.

"I can show you more if you like."

"Then show me."

Deidrick had come to get answers from Sharon, but he did not mind getting one last rendezvous for the road out of it. But even though he had had his fun, he still had a mission to accomplish. While Sharon was in the bathroom, he crept to her purse and dug through it. Inside was prenatal vitamins. It was the proof that Deidrick needed of Sharon's pregnancy. He pulled his pants on, and the last thing he heard was the toilet flush as he left the bedroom.

The necklace was gone from the counter. Sharon probably grabbed it when she seduced Deidrick and flushed it down the toilet during her trip to the bathroom. She was involved in Derik's kidnapping, and she knew Deidrick knew. That's why she tried to get Deidrick on her side and throw Malik under the bus in the process. But Deidrick was too smart for Sharon's tricks. He got what he wanted from her and left, just as Marcellus had taught him.

When he returned home, he planned to turn Sharon in for kidnapping Derik. He figured then they would be able to find him. But his plan halted when he walked in the front door. Sitting in the kitchen was Derik.

"Derik?" said Deidrick.

Derik looked at him. His hair was cut shorter, and he was skinnier. But it was Derik. He was back.

"Cornbread... I... I need your help," said Derik shakily.

"Bro, where have you been?" asked Deidrick. "How long have you been here? Does everyone else know you're back?"

"Deidrick, please," begged Derik. He put his head down and cried. Deidrick just stared, unsure of what to say or do. After Derik calmed down, he sat up, wiped his face, and looked at Deidrick. "I'm done. I'm sorry. I know you hate crying."

Deidrick could not respond because it was true. Crying irritated him. It was a sign of weakness to him, and Derik looked weak. But to Deidrick, Derik at that moment was not weak of his own accord. He had been weakened by someone else, and Deidrick wanted to know who had done it.

"What do you want to know?" asked Derik.

"Tell me everything from the beginning," said Deidrick.

"Okay," said Derik. "I wanted to run away because I was fed up with this family. I had been talking to someone named Monique over the internet, and I thought it was D-Money's mom. She said she wanted to get to know him, but he didn't want to get to know her, so I planned to take his place and convince her to take me with her. I convinced Cell to drive me out to the city by telling him I was meeting a girl and needed him to scope out the scene with me just in case. He agreed and gave me a cigarette to calm my nerves. I don't know why Matty liked those things so much because it was horrible. I took one puff and hated it, so I threw it in the trash. But I guess I didn't put it out correctly and it caught some of the papers on fire."

"That confirms what the fire department told us about it being started by a cigarette," said Deidrick.

"I didn't mean to burn it down," said Derik.

"What happened when you got to the city?"

"Monique wasn't there when we arrived. So, I told Cell I'd wait for her and that I'd let him know when I was ready to go, so he would leave. While I was waiting, Monique called and told me her husband would pick me up from the sandwich shop in a black sports car. I was skeptical but she said it would be easier that way for us to meet. The 'husband' came and got me and that's when everything went wrong. Once I was in the car, he pulled a gun on me and told me if I tried anything, he'd kill me. He threw my phone out the window and forced me to wear a blindfold. I was taken to this trailer where I was held captive at."

"What'd he look like?"

"He had on a ski mask, so I couldn't see his face," recalled Derik. "But his eyes were so dark and full of evil. I thought Dad's eyes were scary-looking but the 'husband's' eyes were way scarier."

"So, it was this 'husband' guy and 'Monique' who kidnapped you?"

"Yeah," said Derik. "And a third person was in on it too. I didn't see any of his features, but he was chubbier than the other guy. But I didn't see 'Monique' or the third guy until close to the time that I escaped. Most of the time I was at the trailer, it was the 'husband' who was there."

"Did he do anything to you?"

"He'd punch me anytime I did something he didn't like," said Derik. "And when I tried to escape the first time while he was out, he... he came back early and... and ripped some of my hair out."

"Is that why your hair is shorter now?"

"I cut it after I escaped to make it harder for them to find me," said Derik. "Those three wanted to ransom me and once they got the money, they were going to kill me. I'm sure of it. So, I had to escape. At first, the 'husband' let me roam around the house and would lock me in my room if he needed to leave because the knob only locked from the outside. But I messed with the door one day so that when he left, I could open it and escape. That's when he caught me by my hair and ripped some of it out. After my first escape attempt, he handcuffed me to a bedpost and installed bars on the windows."

"Then how did you escape?"

"I had hairpins in my hair," said Derik. "It took some time, but I was eventually able to unlock the handcuffs with them. And the door was still messed up from my first escape attempt, so I took his keys while he was asleep and drove off in his black sports car. At some point I lost the necklace Matty gave me."

"I would give you mine, but it's gone."

"It's alright," said Derik. "I was scared they would come after me. So, I stayed in hiding, and broke into Brewer's to feed myself while I slept inside the church. I tried to take what I could afford and left what money I had on the counter, hoping it would make up for having to break in. After that ran out, I got desperate, so I broke into Uncle Falcon's house to see if I could get food and clothes. But D-Money saw me, and I had to pretend he was dreaming so I wouldn't give myself away. I tried to get D-Money and Queenie to figure out who the kidnappers were by leading them to my old secret hideout. But then D-Money got hit by the car and–!"

"Wait what?" said Deidrick. "What car?"

"He got hit tonight by a car," said Derik. "I... I think it was the kidnappers trying to hit me. They must've been staking out the house and thought he was me."

"What the heck?!"

"I couldn't stay hidden anymore after that," said Derik. "This is all my fault."

"Do you have any idea who any of the kidnappers are?"

"I know who the girl is."

"Who is she?"

"It's Sharon."

"Sharon?" said Deidrick. "Nah, it can't be."

"It is," said Derik. "She was wearing that anklet she always wore at the shop. I'd know it anywhere."

"Any girl could have that anklet."

"I know it was her."

"I think the police are going need more than an anklet to prove it was her."

"Then you don't believe me?"

"I believe you," said Deidrick. "But I'm just saying what they might say when you tell them what happened. They might claim you made it all up just to cover up the fact that you ran away."

Mrs. Harrison entered the kitchen and stopped. She stared at the back of Derik's head.

"Hey Mom," said Deidrick. "Look who's back."

Mrs. Harrison did not say anything. She stared at Derik as she inched closer to him. Her hands cupped his face and slowly ran through his hair, confirming that he was real. Tears flowed down her face as she wrapped her arms around the son that had returned to them.

-

Chapter Twenty-Four:
Derek

New development in kidnapping case
by Ralph Brewer, Creeke Courier

One person was arrested Thursday in connection with the kidnapping of a local teen.

Authorities arrested Sharon Pierce, 21, in connection with the December kidnapping of 16-year-old Derik Harrison following an interview between Pierce and police.

"The tip came out of no where and led us right to her," an officer working on the case said.

The kidnapping happened after months of correspondence between Pierce and Harrison, in which Pierce communicated with the victim under a false identity. She then lured Harrison to a city sandwich shop and kidnapped him with the help of two accomplices. Harrison was held hostage in a cabin north of the city for a $50,000 ransom.

> Family members paid the ransom but
> saw no sign of Harrison's return.
>
> Harrison was reunited with his
> family Saturday. However, two of the
> accomplices are still at large. Anyone
> with any information is asked to con-
> tact law enforcement immediately.

The first thing Derek did when he left the hospital was dye his hair red as he had always wanted. Uncle Marlin helped him dye it. His uncle had taken on the responsibility of caring for him until his leg healed. One week had passed since the incident, and Derek was back home with no answer on who had done it.

"Hey," said Malcolm, coming into his room. His father had cried on that day when Derek was hit. Cried when he got the news, cried on the way there, cried in the waiting room when Derek's fate was uncertain and cried when he finally saw his son and knew for sure he would be okay. And Uncle Marlin had been his shoulder to lean on through all that crying.

"Hey," said Derek.

"I just spoke to your doctor," said Malcolm. "I have good news and I have bad news."

"Tell me the bad news first."

"You won't be healed in time for your audition for that dance program."

"That's alright, I can audition next year."

"Yeah... that's the bad news...," said Malcolm with a frown. "They um... they... they don't think you'll ever be able to dance again at all."

Everything stopped. The world stopped turning, only to recommence when Derek's heart resumed beating. His father stood before him, allowing the words to sink in and take effect before continuing.

"The way your leg broke...," uttered Malcolm. "It's a very slim chance you'll be able to dance again at the level you were before."

"A slim chance?"

"Yeah."

"That's better than no chance at all," said Derek. Those were the words that came from his mouth. Whether he believed them or not was still undecided. But those were the words that would ease his father's spirit, so he said them. "What's the good news?"

"You're not paralyzed or dead and will be able to walk again hopefully by the summer?"

"I guess that does count as good news."

"And Dee-Three is back."

"I know," said Derek. "How is he?"

"He's still adjusting to being back," said Malcolm. "Once he's more comfortable, I'm sure you'll get to see him."

"If I could, I'd go and see him."

"You need to focus on healing up your leg," said Malcolm. "However, there is someone here to see you."

"Who?"

"I'll send him in."

Malcolm left the room, and a few seconds later, Granddad Derrick appeared.

"Hi stranger," said Derek, lighting up with excited nervousness. "Haven't seen you in a while."

"I figured you didn't want to see me," said Granddad Derrick.

"It's not that I didn't want to see you," explained Derek. "I was just... I don't know."

"I know."

"You're looking a lot happier than you did before."

"Because everyone's okay," said Granddad Derrick. "The Lord heard my distress and answered my prayers."

"Are you upset with me for what I said?"

"I was never upset with you."

"You weren't?"

"Nope," said Granddad Derrick. "Maybe a little annoyed but never upset."

"I still could've behaved better."

"It's alright," chuckled Granddad Derrick. "You're my grandson, so I let you get away with a lot more."

"Granddad…"

"It's true," said Granddad Derrick. "When I look at you, and watch you grow up and be who you are, it's like I get to see the Derrick I never got the chance to be. You get to dress and wear your hair how you want. You get to speak your mind, and no one tries to shut you up or make you feel like an embarrassment to your family. Your father allows you your own opinions and never tells you they don't matter."

"Your father told you that?" gasped Derek.

"No, my mother did," corrected Granddad Derrick. "But my father didn't oppose it, probably because that's how he was raised by his father. My father wasn't really clear with how he felt about stuff. He'd always cover everything with a smile."

"Like you do," said Derek.

"Yeah," sighed Granddad Derrick. "And before I realized it, I'd done the same thing to Marlin."

"It's like Uncle Marlin said," said Derek, understanding the truth of the relationship between his uncle and his grandfather. "You didn't know any better."

"With him I didn't," said Granddad Derrick. "That's why I told you I didn't need you to remind me of what I'd done. Seeing him is reminder enough. But with Malcolm, I did my best not to repeat those same mistakes."

"And that's why they experienced two different fathers," said Derek. "Granddad, I'm sorry I judged you."

"Don't be," said Granddad Derrick, taking his grandson's hand. "I needed to hear it. It's only fair I be held accountable too like I've done to others."

"No, I have to make this up to you."

"You really don't."

"I've got it!" declared Derek. "I'll name my firstborn child after you!"

"Your firstborn child?"

"Yeah," said Derek. "Of course, he'll need his own nickname to differentiate him from us."

"But what if it's a girl?"

"Then she'll be called Derricka," said Derek. "The main thing is it'll be named after you."

"The way your mind works interests me sometimes."

"I brought soup," said Uncle Marlin, entering the room.

"Uncle Marlin, this is the perfect opportunity to practice what we talked about," said Derek excitedly. "Tell Granddad how you feel."

"Right now?" said Uncle Marlin.

"Yeah."

"Are you sick?" asked Granddad Derrick, looking at his son.

"No...," mumbled Uncle Marlin.

"Then what's D-Money talking about?"

Uncle Marlin looked away from his father, only to be face to face with Derek, who nodded his encouragement. He sat down and after a few contemplative seconds, took hold of his father by the shirt and pulled him closer to him.

"Marlin, what are you doing?" questioned Granddad Derrick.

"You remember when you'd get mad at me and hold me like this and yell at me?" asked Uncle Marlin.

"Yeah," said Granddad Derrick. "But why are you doing it now to me?"

"Because," said Uncle Marlin. "You're going to hear what Derek wants me to say. I've got you right where I want you, and I'm not letting go until I'm done."

"Okay..."

"I hated you."

"I don't want to hear this, Marlin," said Granddad Derrick, trying to break away from his son's grasp.

"Well, you're going to!" snarled Uncle Marlin, pulling his father back into place. "I hated you because you were hard on me. But then I got older and smarter, and realized everything you did was for my own good. So, I don't hate you anymore."

"But–!"

"Get it through your head, old man!" said Marlin. "It doesn't matter to me whether what you did was right or wrong. I don't hate you for it. Do you understand?"

Granddad Derrick nodded.

"Good," said Uncle Marlin, releasing his father.

"That was uncomfortable," said Granddad Derrick, smoothing out his shirt.

"How do you think I felt?" griped Uncle Marlin.

"But I'm glad you told me," said Granddad Derrick. "Damian told me last month I needed to forgive myself, but I've had a hard time doing so until now. I realize now the reason it was so hard, is because I needed you to forgive me first. Marlin, for the longest time I've regretted telling you I didn't care how you felt. I was wrong to say that, whether you care or not."

"You don't owe me anything," said Uncle Marlin. "You made me strong."

"I didn't make you strong," said Granddad Derrick. "I made you hardened, and I can't help but wonder what you'd be like if I hadn't done that."

"You think it's my fault Derik disappeared."

"No," protested Granddad Derrick. "That's not what I'm saying."

"Then what are you saying?"

"I'm saying I should've been a better father than I was."

"Why? You did what you had to do and now I'm successful enough to provide for my family. What's there to regret?"

"There's more to life than that, Marlin," said Granddad Derrick. "I shouldn't have set that kind of example."

"I don't want to talk about this anymore," said Uncle Marlin.

"But Marlin–!"

Uncle Marlin left the room.

"He does that sometimes," said Derek.

"I know," sighed Granddad Derrick. "I know."

"I'm working on getting him to open up more though."

"You shouldn't have to," said Granddad Derrick. He stared at the bedroom door and said, "I've made a lot of mistakes and bad decisions in my life, Derek, and I try not to regret them. But sometimes I do. Sometimes I do."

Chapter Twenty-Five:
Allison

Derik spent the past week inside the house like a caged bird. With two of his kidnappers still on the loose, it was determined that staying home was the safest option for him. Allison was tasked with bringing her brother's schoolwork home to him every day. Seeing his state saddened her. Her brother had always been more reserved, but since being back, he had become very jumpy. He seemed to always anticipate danger, and his mood swung from tranquil to irritable at random. Sometimes he would cry and then immediately apologize after he finished. It all reminded Allison of her grandfather.

They sat together in the kitchen. Derik worked on his math homework while Allison once again looked at family photos. Someone knocked on the front door, and it startled Derik.

"Who's that?" asked Derik.

"Let me see," said Allison. She went to the front door and peeked through the peephole.

"It's Priscella!" called Allison.

Derik did not answer. Allison opened the door and let Priscella in.

"Hey girlie!" said Priscella.

"Hey," said Allison. "What's up?"

"I baked some sugar cookies, but I made too many, so I brought some over to share."

"I didn't know you baked."

"Yeah," said Priscella. "I've started going to this baking class in the city and they teach us how to make so many things! I see Mr. Bud there too sometimes, and the last time I went, Ms. Nelson was with him."

"Ms. Nelson?"

"Yeah, the guidance counselor," said Priscella. "They baked cute little cookies together. Mr. Bud even got some flour on his face, and Ms. Nelson wiped it off and their eyes met, and they both started blushing. It was so cute!"

"Mhmm," uttered Allison, realizing that her dating theory was potentially more credible. She looked at the bag of cookies in Priscella's hand and said, "Can I try one right now?"

"Of course," answered Priscella, handing the bag to Allison. "They're for you."

Allison bit into the cookie.

"Oh wow," said Allison. "This is really good!"

"Is it?" questioned Priscella, brightening up.

"Yeah!" said Allison. "You might need to open a bakery one day."

"I don't know about all that..."

"I'm serious," said Allison, eating a second cookie. "If you don't believe me, then we'll ask Dee-Three what he thinks."

"Is he here?"

"Who Derik? Yeah, he's here."

Allison led Priscella to the kitchen.

"Hi Derik!" greeted Priscella.

"Hi," answered Derik plainly.

"Dee-Three, you have to try Prissy's cookies that she made," said Allison, holding the cookie out to Derik. "They're so good."

"What's in it?" asked Derik.

"It's a sugar cookie," said Allison. "Here, try it."

"Maybe later," said Derik.

"Alright," said Allison, deflating.

"I think I should be getting back home," said Priscella.

"I'll walk you out," said Allison.

The girls returned to the front door.

"Is he alright?" whispered Priscella.

"He's fine," said Allison. "Just focused on his homework, that's all."

"That's good. I thought maybe I'd done something wrong."

"No, you're fine."

"Okay. I'll see you at school on Monday."

"Okay. Bye."

"Bye."

Priscella left.

"When did you two become friends?" asked Derik when Allison returned to the kitchen.

"Over the break," answered Allison. "She's cool."

Derik shrugged. Allison pulled out the picture of Derik where he looked like a prince, and smiled.

"You know," said Allison. "While you were gone, I used to stare at this photo and wish you were still here."

"I hate that photo."

"Granddad said you loved it."

"I did," Derik explained, his eyes still fixed on the picture. "Now I can't stand the sight of it."

"Why?"

"Because...," said Derik. "I just don't like it anymore."

Granddad Derrick entered the kitchen and went through the drawers. Allison and Derik watched him, curiosity in their eyes.

"My gun is missing," said Granddad Derrick, failing to find it in the kitchen. "It's not where I normally have it."

"Did you move it?" asked Allison.

"No, I didn't."

"I'll help you look for it," volunteered Allison.

"Queenie, please be careful," begged Granddad Derrick. "That gun is loaded, and I don't need you accidentally hurting yourself."

"I'll be fine," said Allison. "The safety is on, right?"

"It should be," said Granddad Derrick. "But if someone moved it, there's no telling what they've done to it."

"I'll be careful, Granddad."

Allison was sure her grandfather had just misplaced his gun. Therefore, she figured the best place to start was his closet, where he usually kept it. As she searched, she noticed a plaque stuffed into the corner of the closet.

"What's this?" asked Allison, picking up the plaque.

"What's what?" said Granddad Derrick. Seeing what Allison held, he said, "Oh that? That's my degree."

"But this is a doctorate."

"I know."

"You know?"

"Like I said, it's my degree."

"Seriously?!" cried Allison. "This whole time I thought you had a bachelor's degree!"

"You didn't know that I had a doctorate?"

"No, I didn't know that. How dare you be smarter than I thought?"

"I'm not sure whether I should be insulted or flattered."

"Why would you keep this a secret?"

"Because it's just a title," said Granddad Derrick, shrugging.

"It is not!" cried Allison. "You can't just throw this to the side like it's nothing! You're the first Doctor in the family!"

"So?"

"See, you don't do right," sighed Allison. "Just for this, I'm going to get a doctorate so at least *someone* in the family will take the distinction seriously."

"Go for it," encouraged Granddad Derrick. "By all means don't let me be the only one."

"I will," said Allison determinedly. She and her grandfather searched the rest of the house and discovered the missing gun in his study.

"I didn't put this in here," said Granddad Derrick.

"Are you sure?" asked Allison.

"I may be old Queenie, but my memory still works," said Granddad Derrick. "This is not where I left this gun."

"Well, if you didn't put it in here, who did?"

"Hmm...," mumbled Granddad Derrick, pursing his lips as he stared at the gun. Although he did not answer her, Allison figured he knew who had moved it. He looked at her and said, "Thanks for your help, Queenie."

"You're welcome."

That afternoon, Allison once again accompanied her mother to visit Lady Sophia. They were shown into the parlor where Lady Sophia sat with Aunt Soriah. Nanna Kiana had once again instructed Allison to be polite, and Allison figured after the last visit that she could only be polite if she stayed quiet.

"Hello Mother," greeted Mrs. Harrison.

Lady Sophia did not answer. Instead, she glanced at Allison.

"She isn't well?" questioned Lady Sophia.

"Excuse me?" said Allison.

"Oh, she is well," said Lady Sophia, lifting a teacup to her face with her pinky extended. "She just doesn't have manners."

"*Excuse you?!*" cried Allison.

"My dear, when you walk into somebody's house you speak," said Lady Sophia, her tone full of pleasant malice. "Of course, I guess I shouldn't expect much of an apple from Soleya's tree."

Allison gathered her wits and looked at her mother, expecting her to address the jabs taken at them. Instead, Mrs. Harrison sat on the couch adjacent to Lady Sophia and engaged her in conversation.

"How have you been, Mother?" asked Mrs. Harrison.

"I've been wonderful," said Lady Sophia. "The ball was a success even though the Harrison men failed to appear."

"They were preoccupied," said Mrs. Harrison.

"Then you should've enticed them to become unoccupied," said Lady Sophia with the most disingenuous smile Allison had ever seen. "It never hurts to use your charm to your advantage."

"I know, Mother," said Mrs. Harrison. "I understand you've encouraged Allison to start thinking of marriage."

"Allison, marry?" laughed Aunt Soriah.

"Be quiet, Soriah Noelle," chastised Lady Sophia. She looked at Mrs. Harrison and said, "Yes, I encouraged her to begin thinking of her prospects."

"Mother, Allison is still young and–!"

"Still young?" snorted Lady Sophia. "Soleya, she's already eighteen. The sooner she gets married the sooner she can secure a better future."

Allison wanted to question who would benefit from the supposed 'better future' but instead held her tongue.

"I agree with Mother," said Aunt Soriah. "I haven't had to worry about anything in life since I married Quincy. Granted, I still don't think Allison would enjoy married life all that much because she's more independent-minded."

"Independence," scoffed Lady Sophia. "The only thing independence gives you is instability."

"Marriage can be unstable too," mumbled Allison.

"Speak up!" demanded Lady Sophia. "Honestly Soleya, did you not teach her that I hate mumbling?"

"I said, 'Marriage can be unstable too'," repeated Allison.

"Oh," laughed Lady Sophia. "It was nothing important. Just the delusions of a teenage girl who knows nothing about life."

"I'd say you're the delusional one," said Allison, losing her patience.

"Excuse you?" said Lady Sophia.

"Allison," whispered Mrs. Harrison, trying to get her to quiet down.

"For someone who claims to be such a lady, I am very appalled by your lack of decorum," said Allison, ignoring her mother. She would not allow herself to be disrespected any further. "As a hostess, you should be courteous to your guests. Not insulting them every chance you get."

"Do you know who you're talking to?" challenged Lady Sophia.

"A mean-spirited old woman who is bitter because her mother married her off to an older man for money," answered Allison. "And you did it to your daughters, and now you're trying to push me down the same path, claiming it's to 'secure a better future', when the only future you're interested in securing is yours."

"Allison!" cried Aunt Soriah.

"Who do you think you are to speak to me like this?" challenged Lady Sophia.

"Allison Queen Harrison," declared Allison, sitting forward while staring Lady Sophia in her eyes.

"You better be careful, little girl," warned Lady Sophia, mimicking Allison's body language. "I'm not one to be trifled with."

"Neither am I," retorted Allison.

"Are you really going to allow her to speak to me in this manner, Soleya?"

"I...," uttered Mrs. Harrison.

"Soleya!"

"I... uh..."

"Idiotic, useless girl!" ranted Lady Sophia. "Can't even manage her own brat of a daughter! Just a waste of a child! I bet if I'd had a son instead of you my life wouldn't be ruined like it is now!"

"Don't you speak to her like that!" argued Allison.

"I'll speak to my daughter how I want!" bellowed Lady Sophia.

"Not in front of me you won't!"

"Get out of my house! Both of you! NOW!"

Allison and Mrs. Harrison left the house. By then, Mrs. Harrison had regained her tongue and admonished Allison.

"How could you embarrass me like that?" complained Mrs. Harrison as they walked to the car. "All you had to do was sit there quietly like a lady."

"Sit there quietly while she says whatever nasty thing she wants?!" cried Allison in disbelief. "That would've been embarrassing to me!"

"It's her house! She can say what she wants!"

"That doesn't give her the right to be disrespectful!"

"You've disgraced me," said Mrs. Harrison. "I may as well be dead to them now."

"Good!" said Allison. "You don't need them!"

"Just get in the car."

Allison did as she was told, and they went home. When they entered the house, the pair found Granddad Derrick sitting in the living room watching television. He motioned for them to be quiet.

"What is it?" whispered Allison.

"Your grandmother is on the phone," whispered Granddad Derrick.

"Who is that coming in the door?" called Nanna Kiana from the kitchen, her usually sweet voice tinged with a hint of irritation.

"Queenie and Leya," said Granddad Derrick.

"Allison Queen, get in this kitchen *now*!"

"Uh oh," said Granddad Derrick. "Future Dr. Queenie is in *trouble...*"

"Hush, Dr. Granddad," said Allison. She entered the kitchen and found Nanna Kiana furiously pacing back and forth.

"I just got a call from Sophia," Nanna Kiana addressed Allison. "You may be eighteen, but you aren't grown just yet. Don't you ever, *ever*, in your life young lady, fix your mouth to disrespect that woman again. Do I make myself clear?"

"But Nanna–!"

"Allison," interrupted Nanna Kiana. "It is not your place to argue with Sophia, and even worse call her mean-spirited and bitter. Let your mother handle her mother. Not you. Am I clear?"

"Yes ma'am," sighed Allison.

"Now, get out of my face," Nanna Kiana griped, shooing her away.

Allison obeyed and exited the kitchen, passing her mother as she did. When she was out of sight, she hid behind the kitchen wall to hear the conversation between her mother and grandmother.

"Soleil," began Nanna Kiana, her temperament calmer than before. "What happened?"

"Everything would've been fine if Allison had acted like she had some sense," sighed Mrs. Harrison.

"You can't lay all the blame on Queenie," said Nanna Kiana. "I know my granddaughter. No matter how wrong she was, she wouldn't have done that unless she felt it was necessary. What did Sophia say?"

"We were discussing marriage and Allison just got upset. They argued and Mother said her usual 'Oh Soleya you ruined my life'. After that, she kicked us out."

"And you didn't say anything during all of this?"

"What could I say? I can't judge her for what's happened to her."

"Neither can I, but that doesn't mean I'm going to let her judge us either," said Nanna Kiana. "What standard has Sophia set that gives her the right to judge you against it? What has she accomplished?"

Mrs. Harrison didn't answer.

"I'll answer for you," Nanna Kiana said. "Nothing. She's accomplished nothing. You've far surpassed anything Sophia has ever done."

"What am I to do?" Mrs. Harrison sighed.

"Demand respect," said Nanna Kiana. "Isn't that right, Allison?"

Realizing she was discovered, Allison tried to duck out of sight.

"Don't bother trying to hide, I've known you were there all along. You've forgotten about the hallway mirror behind you."

"Dang it," said Allison. "Granddad, why didn't you warn me?"

"And miss all the fun?" joked Granddad Derrick.

"Just terrible."

Later on, Allison found herself in Stacy's room. Stacy was playing *The Well* while Allison filled her in on the day's events.

"Stacy," said Allison. "It went down today."

"What happened to 'I'm too cute to fight'?"

"Girl, please. I didn't fight anyone. I got into it with Lady Sophia."

"No, you didn't!"

"Yes, I did."

"What happened?"

"She had me messed up! I'm sitting there minding my business and she called herself being rude to me, so I called her out on it."

"That's what she gets."

"Yeah, but Nanna didn't like that and went off on me."

"Dang."

"I just don't like that lady though."

"What was the argument about?"

"She wants to marry me off."

"To who?"

"Someone with money."

"That wouldn't be too bad."

"Stacy, I'm not trying to be married at eighteen."

"I know. I'm just saying, it wouldn't be bad to be married to someone with money as long as you love him."

"I've got goals I want to accomplish before I get married though. Like going to college and starting my career. And now apparently getting my doctorate."

"That one's new."

"Yeah, well Granddad didn't do a good job representing as the first doctor in the family, so now I've got to do it."

"Your grandfather's a doctor?"

"My point exactly," said Allison. "Now Nanna wants me to apologize for how I behaved."

"Good luck with that."

"You know Jada plays that game too, right?"

"Does she? What's her username?"

"I don't know, I didn't ask. Maybe I should tell her yours, Sparkle_Princess13."

"I was thirteen!"

"You can't change it?"

"Not on this game."

"Dang."

"So, you and Jada are friends now?"

"Yeah, she's cool."

"Cool."

"You don't like that?"

"Like what?"

"That I've made friends with Prissy and Jada?"

"Why should I care?"

"I'm just asking. Some people get mad when their friends make other friends."

"Girl, we've been best friends since middle school. I'm not worried about you making other friends."

"Okay."

"Besides, it makes sense that you'd make friends with all the lonely girls, since you were the lonely girl once."

"Did you have to bring that up?"

"I'm just saying."

Allison shook her head and chuckled. She was glad that she was no longer the lonely girl and had friends she could count on. And she wanted to be that for others too, including her brother.

Chapter Twenty-Six: Matthias

Derik was back, and Matthias was thankful. His brother was skittish, but Matthias was sure that Derik only needed time to readjust. For the most part, Matthias was just glad to have his brother back. He tried to visit as much as possible, and that came with the added risk of running into his mother.

That Saturday, the risk became reality. Allison had returned from visiting Stacy, and they both sat in the kitchen with Derik when *she* entered. Matthias was at the sink filling a glass with water when he saw her in the reflection of an appliance. Clad in a robe, hair hidden in a bonnet, mug in hand. She stared at him while he watched her, his back turned to her.

"Matthias."

Matthias did not respond. He did not want to look at her, fearing anger would overtake him.

"How are you doing?" asked Mrs. Harrison.

"Why do you ask?" answered Matthias, keeping his back to her.

"I heard you were shot."

"Yeah. And?"

"Won't you look at me at least?"

Matthias again did not answer. He had wanted to say 'no', but he pictured Alexander calling him out for being disrespectful and instead lowered his head.

"Are you doing alright?"

"Why do you care?' asked Matthias, his anger slowly seeping out. He hoped she would leave soon.

"Because I'm your mother."

"My mother," spat Matthias. "What about when you put me out? Were you my mother then?"

"I didn't put you out," said Mrs. Harrison. "Your father did."

"Does it matter who actually did it? It was all done to avoid hurting your reputation."

"My reputation had nothing to do with it," said Mrs. Harrison defensively. "Your father figured it was best for you to live apart from your brother for everyone's safety. If anything, not having you in the house hurt my reputation."

"And we all know how much you cherish your rep over your children."

"Matthias, I never wanted you out of the house. I wanted you to come back. I've never stopped being your mother, but you won't let me in."

"It's everybody's fault but yours, huh?"

Mrs. Harrison did not answer. She filled her mug with fruit juice.

"I just wanted to know how you were doing."

"I'm fine."

That was the end of their conversation. Mrs. Harrison left the kitchen.

"You know she was worried about you right?" said Allison.

"Yeah right."

"She was," said Allison. "You didn't have to treat her like that."

"Since when did you become her number one cheerleader?"

"Since I realized I only had one mother and I'd better cherish her before it's too late."

"Could you two please not argue?" requested Derik.

Matthias and Allison settled down. They did not want to upset Derik and make him feel more uncomfortable than he probably already was. Someone knocked on the front door, and Granddad Derrick answered it. The visitor was Mayor Perry, who came to see Derik.

"Hello," said Mayor Perry, sitting across from Derik.

"Hello," said Derik.

"How are you?"

"I'm fine."

"That's good," said Mayor Perry. A smile spread across his face as he said, "I'm glad you're doing well."

"Why?" questioned Derik, narrowing his eyes.

"Well, because I know you had a rough time and I wanted to see how you were doing."

Matthias snorted.

"Is that your only reason for coming here?" asked Derik.

"Not exactly," said Mayor Perry. "I wanted to see what you thought of spending the day with me next weekend."

"Spend the day with you?"

"Yes," said Mayor Perry. "We could do whatever you like. Go wherever you want to go."

"And what's the catch?"

"No catch. I just wanted to see what you thought of it, is all."

"I'll get back to you."

"Better than no," said Mayor Perry. He stood up to leave. As he reached the kitchen entryway, he looked over his shoulder and said, "I look forward to your answer."

He walked out of the house, leaving the three siblings staring at the space he had occupied.

"The man is a snake," said Allison. "A straight-up evil snake. And I'm still convinced the kidnapping was his idea just to make himself look good."

"It wasn't," said Derik.

"How do you know?"

"He wouldn't have spent all that money just for publicity," said Derik. "The man with the evil eyes always taunted me about it, saying that the only thing keeping me alive was the ten-grand he was getting as his cut for holding me."

"Ten-grand," said Allison. "That's how much Dad told Mother he was removing from their savings. I wonder if he used it to pay the ransom."

"If he did it was a waste of money," said Derik. "But the ten-grand was just the evil man's cut. I'm sure the actual ransom was way more, and I doubt Dad spent that much on me."

"Matty," called Granddad Derrick from his study. "Come here!"

Matthias obeyed. He stared up at the picture of him and his siblings again on the way, but he did not feel uncomfortable looking at it anymore. They were all back together again, even if slightly altered. It made him glad.

"Sir?" said Matthias when he entered the study.

"I need to talk to you about your brother."

"Me and Deidrick made up already."

"I meant Derik."

"Oh."

"He's been messing with my guns."

"You mean T n' T?" joked Matthias, referring to the old nickname for his grandfather's arms.

"No," answered Matthias. "My handguns. He keeps moving them."

"Why?"

"I think he's testing how long it takes me to notice they're gone."

"You think he's trying to use it?"

"He's trying to feel protected. He's experiencing the same thing I did when I returned from the war, and he's scared. But I don't want him walking around with one of my guns on him. Not only is it dangerous, but it's also illegal."

"So, what's the plan?"

"I'm hiding my guns elsewhere. But I need you to talk to him about the ramifications."

"Why me?"

"Matty, I hate to put you in this position, but you've been shot. I haven't. I've only seen other people shot. You know more about what it does to a person than I do."

"I'll talk to him."

"Thank you."

Matthias returned to the kitchen.

"Derik."

"Yeah?"

"Let me holler at you for a minute."

"Okay."

They went to Derik's room, which he was sharing with Deidrick. Deidrick was out and about, which made it the perfect place for Matthias to talk to Derik alone.

"I'm just going to come out and say it," said Matthias. "Granddad knows you've been moving his guns."

Derik did not answer, but he looked away.

"He knows how you feel inside, but he doesn't want you to take them anymore."

"Why doesn't he tell me this himself?"

"Because he wanted you to get it from the perspective of someone that's been shot. It hurts. A lot. And it can tear whole families apart. And you could also hit people you weren't aiming to hit, like what happened to me. Not to mention, it's just plain illegal for you to have a gun on you because you're underage."

"What if I want it to hurt? What if I want them to feel what I feel? To pay for what they did to me?"

"That's not you and you know it."

"I don't know who is and isn't me anymore."

"Well, I do. And we both just want what's best for you. Leave his guns alone, okay?"

Derik did not answer. Tears rolled down his face as he looked out the window. The world beyond its panes was scary to him, and Matthias knew it. He wanted to protect his brother from all of it and also wanted those responsible to pay. But he also wanted his brother to be safe and he knew that Derik's current method for handling his pain was unsafe. Matthias was at a loss for what to do, but he knew he only wanted his brother to be okay.

Chapter Twenty-Seven: Deidrick

Sharon was in jail, and it was all because of Deidrick. He and his mother had taken Derik to the police station to give his statement, and within days, Sharon was arrested. But Deidrick still needed to know if Sharon's baby was his. So, even though he did not want to see her, he went to visit her. The beauty that had enraptured him for so long was gone from her, leaving behind only her inner ugliness that he had not noticed for so long.

"Deidrick, you have to get me out of here," said Sharon.

"Why?"

"Because I'm..."

"Pregnant?" said Deidrick. "Yeah, I know."

"You do? Then you understand why I need to get out."

"Is it mine?"

"What?"

"Is it mine, Sharon?"

"It might be."

"You're not sure."

"Of course I am! Now are you going to get me out or not?"

"No."

"Why not?"

"Because who do you think turned you in in the first place?" revealed Deidrick.

"You did this to me?"

"What can I say, baby?" said Deidrick. "Blood is thicker than water. Plus, I wanted to make sure I trapped you the way you tried to trap me."

"What are you talking about?"

"Simple," said Deidrick. "Remember when I had to escape your apartment through the window, and you and Malik started arguing while I was hanging on for dear life outside? Well Malik said something about 'it probably being his and not mine' and that got me thinking. What would be mine that wouldn't be his? And the only thing I could think of that both of us had in common, was you. So that made me suspicious. But see Malik also said that 'he shouldn't have agreed to that plan of yours because now I was chilling in his spot like it was mine'. And that made me wonder what that plan could be. Now this took me a little effort, but I think I've figured it out. See, we started our thing in October. But that was *after* you tried getting with my father in August. So, I'm thinking the original plan was for you to sleep with my father and maybe blackmail him, and Malik went along with it for the money. But when my father didn't go for it, you changed courses and got with me without telling Malik. But this time, instead of just sleeping with me, you planned to get pregnant and wanted to trap me into giving you hush money. But Malik wouldn't be okay with you being pregnant unless it was his baby, so you told him it was his baby, while also planning to cash in by secretly pinning it on me. That about right so far?"

Sharon glared at him.

"And you know," continued Deidrick. "You might've gotten away with it too if you hadn't gotten careless. I'll give you credit for that little performance you put on because you almost had me fooled that you really did love me. But that made me really suspicious because you've never claimed to love Cornbread before. I was just supposed to be your little side dish. What I think happened is you and Malik kidnapped my brother for revenge against my father rejecting you. Because only someone from Creeke would know about Monique and only someone familiar with my family's relationships would be able to use it properly to trap my brother. And who would know the family dynamics better than the receptionist that worked for them? But when Derik escaped from you, you were afraid that he had identified you to us. You knew that everything was coming apart. So, you tried to get ahead of things and convince me that you had nothing to do with what happened to my brother, and that you were also an innocent victim. That way when everything blew up, I could protect you and your little investment. And I might've believed you too if you hadn't taken the bait with my decoy necklace."

"Decoy?"

"Yeah," said Deidrick. "See when I bought that necklace for Matthias, I also bought one for myself. That's the one I left on your counter to see what you would do with it. And like a dummy, you got rid of it."

"You can't prove anything."

"I don't need to. You've personally given me all the proof I need of your involvement. But as to how you got here, well, let's just say that little anklet of yours got you more attention than you hoped for."

"I'll get you for this."

"Can't wait to see how," said Deidrick, standing up. "So long, Sharon. Enjoy your new life."

Deidrick acted like he was good, leaving out of that jail with his head held high. But inside, he was terrified. The baby was potentially his, and with Sharon locked up, it would fall on him to care for it. He needed to confide in someone who would not judge him. So, he went to the one person he knew had been through the same thing.

"Unc, I need to talk to you."

"What about?" asked Uncle Malcolm.

"I need advice on something."

"Okay..."

"So, there's this girl I've been dealing with."

"And... she's pregnant."

"How did you...?"

"Be real, Cornbread. Why else would you be talking to me about a girl?"

"Yeah, she's pregnant."

"Is it yours?"

"I'm not the only guy she's been with, so I don't know."

"Yeah, that's how it was with me too and we see how that turned out. Did you at least protect yourself?"

"She said she was on the pill."

"I'll take that as a no. That was dumb."

"Unc, you're supposed to be helping me."

"I am but I'm not going to sugarcoat it," said Uncle Malcolm. "Raising a child is hard, and it's a lot harder when you're doing it on your own. I suggest you maintain a good relationship with the baby's mother if it is yours."

"I can't."

"Why not?"

"I got her locked up."

"What kind of toxic mess do you have going on?"

"It's a long story but basically she's no good."

"Well, she can't be any worse than my baby mama," grumbled Malcolm. "Just handed my son off like a football and left. I hate that girl!"

"She's much worse."

"How much worse?"

"You know Sharon?"

"Sharon who?"

"Sharon Pierce. The one involved with the kidnapping."

"Her?" asked Uncle Malcolm, pointing to the newspaper.

"Yeah, her."

"You've got to be kidding."

"I wish I was."

"What were you doing messing with her?" said Uncle Malcolm. "Don't you have a girl?"

"Come on, Unc," said Deidrick. "You know how it is."

"Yeah, I used to," said Uncle Malcolm. "But I don't get down like that anymore though."

"What about those little dates you go on?"

"What about them?"

"Unc, you have a different girl every time."

"Because I'm... dating," said Uncle Malcolm. "I'm looking for someone to spend my life with. You're looking for someone to spend the night with. There's a difference."

"Dang Unc!"

"It's the truth!" said Uncle Malcolm. "You're a community man! A pass-around! These girls out here passing you around and now you might've gotten one of them pregnant. Trust me, I'm a retired community man and I know how this thing goes."

"So, you're a 'retired community man' and managed to have only had one child?" asked Deidrick skeptically.

"Because I protected myself after that first child. Something you obviously know nothing about."

"Man," groaned Deidrick. "What am I going to do Unc?"

"You've got to rip the bandage off and come clean to everyone. Especially your girl."

"Bro why?"

"Because it'll be better for them to find out from you than from someone else," said Malcolm. "Trust me."

"Ugh."

"And after you tell everyone, be prepared to be slapped by your grandmother," said Uncle Malcolm. He rubbed his cheek and added, "That lady has some strong hands on her, so don't underestimate her."

Deidrick returned home feeling even worse. He had not spoken to Nisha since their argument in his room because he was still mad at her. But with a potential child on the way, it would need a mother, and Nisha was his best option to fill that role. As he contemplated what to do, he noticed Matthias coming out of his room.

"Hey," said Deidrick. "What are you doing here?"

"Visiting Dee-Three," said Matthias. "We just finished talking and I'm about to leave."

"Can I talk to you first?"

"You trying to do another seven-year bid or something?" joked Matthias.

"Nah," said Deidrick. "It's not about us."

"Then what's up?"

"Bro, remember when I visited you and I told you I got caught up?"

"With the girl who stole your shoes?" laughed Matthias.

"Don't remind me," grumbled Deidrick. "Her man's been wearing them to taunt me. Probably stretched them out and everything."

"You trying to get them back?"

"I would like to, but he's disappeared!"

"What do you mean he's disappeared?"

"The girl is Sharon, and her man is Malik."

"Bro what? Why Sharon?"

"I didn't know about what she had done. But now she's pregnant and it might be mine."

"Bro!"

"Shh! No one knows yet."

"Then why are you telling me?"

"Because I don't know what to do. I've got to tell Nisha, but I don't know how."

"Just tell her."

"But how?"

"Are you trying to save the relationship?"

"We're not in a relationship."

"So, do you want the truth now or later?"

"What?"

"I don't think Nisha's going to want to be with you after this."

Deidrick shook his head. Matthias probably was right, but Deidrick still had to try. If he could make her understand that he did not mean for this to happen, then maybe she would still have him. He would have to suck up his pride, move on from what she did, and finally be in a relationship with her.

-

Chapter Twenty-Eight: Derek

Although Derek had used crutches to get around at school, his father was adamant that he stay off his feet as much as possible at home. So, all he could do was lay in bed and watch television. That Sunday, Derek had a heavy flow of visitors stopping by after church. His first visitors were the three younger Brown siblings.

"What's this?" joked Derek. "Mr. Brown let you guys leave the dungeon to go somewhere other than church or school?"

"Yeah, but I didn't know he was letting us go to a greenhouse," said Andre, looking at all the flowers in Derek's room.

"Andre," whispered Antoine, nudging his brother.

"What?"

"Hush."

"We can't stay too long," said Adrianna. "Dad gave us fifteen minutes to visit and two of them were already gone before we left."

"Why does he always have to be so strict?" said Derek.

"Because he is," remarked Andre. He picked up a pencil on Derek's desk and began twirling it between his fingers. Antoine grabbed a marker and began signing Derek's cast while Adrianna sat beside him on the bed.

"I don't know but I'm not trying to find out what'll happen if we're not back within fifteen minutes," said Adrianna. "Andre, how much time do we have left?"

"What?" said Andre.

"How much time do we have left before we have to leave?"

"I don't know."

"You don't know? You're supposed to be keeping track."

"I am?"

"Yes," huffed Adrianna. "I told you before we left to keep track of our time."

"You did?"

"Oh my–!" griped Adrianna. "Do you ever pay attention at all?!"

"Why couldn't you do it?!"

"Because I told you to do it!"

"You're not the boss of me!"

"It's called courtesy, dummy!"

"Who you calling a dummy?!"

"You dummy!"

"If I'm a dummy, then you're an ignoramus!"

"A what?!"

"Hey!" said Derek. "No fighting. Especially with big words I don't understand."

Adrianna and Andre settled down.

"I'm sure we can figure how much time you guys have left," said Derek.

"Yeah, and don't ask me to do it since I'm such a dummy," added Andre.

"Why ask you when we have Antoine?" retorted Adrianna. "He's good at math too."

"How'd I get in it?" whispered Antoine, putting the final touches on his signature.

"I don't know," answered Derek. "Just help them out so they'll stop arguing."

"Alright," agreed Antoine. "We had thirteen minutes when we left, and it took about two to three minutes to get here, so that's–!"

"Five minutes!" interjected Andre.

"Yeah," said Antoine. "Five minutes are already gone. How long have we been here?"

"About three minutes," said Derek.

"That's eight minutes," said Andre.

"Andre, I thought you weren't helping," joked Antoine.

"I'm not," said Andre. "I just knew the answer."

"Mhmm," said Antoine. "Anyways, we've already used up eight of our minutes and it takes two to three minutes to get back. If we factor in Dad wanting us to be back early like he usually does, that means we have to leave–!"

"Now," finished Adrianna.

"Now?" repeated Derek. "But you just got here!"

"I know," said Adrianna. "That fifteen minutes went by quick."

"Aw man," whined Andre. "I wanted to sign your cast!"

"Why don't you sign it, while I talk to Adrianna?" suggested Derek.

"You mean while you kiss and make googly eyes at Adrianna," muttered Andre, pretending to throw up.

"Shut up!" declared Adrianna, her cheeks turning red.

"Aw, she's blushing!" teased Andre. "Look 'Toine!"

"She is turning a little red," added Antoine.

"You two are so annoying!" griped Adrianna, rolling her eyes.

"Guys, leave her alone," said Derek.

"Oh alright," said Andre. "We've got to go anyways."

"It just isn't fair," huffed Adrianna. "I barely get to see you."

"Well, it's your dad's rules," said Derek. "I'm not trying to make him mad at us."

"Me either," said Adrianna.

"I don't want to interrupt, but can I ask you something?" said Antoine.

"Sure," answered Derek.

"How's Derik?"

"You haven't seen him yet?"

"Dad won't take me. He said I need to leave him be until he's ready to be seen. But no one is willing to tell me anything about how he is."

"He's doing okay," said Derek. "I'm sure you'll be able to see him in no time."

"Okay," said Antoine, releasing a sigh. "Thanks."

"No problem."

"I guess we've got to go now," said Adrianna.

"I guess you do."

"Bye," said Adrianna.

"Bye," said Derek.

Adrianna leaned down and let Derek kiss her on the cheek. The pair held onto each other's hands until it was no longer possible. Derek watched as Adrianna left the room, her seraphic form taking all the light out of the room with her. He hardly got to see her because of her father's strict rules, and when he did see her, it was never for long. It made him wonder how their relationship would survive. After the Browns left, Samiel and Benjamin came next to visit him.

"Oh!" cried Samiel upon entering the room. "Look at my boy Benji! Look at my boy!"

"I'm looking, Sami," said Benjamin.

"They done broke his leg!" continued Samiel. He fell to his knees and yelled at the ceiling, "Why?! Why?!"

"Boy, if you don't get up off the ground," griped Benjamin. "What is wrong with you?"

"I can't help it Benji," said Samiel. "They got my boy all sprawled out!"

"Right!" added Derek. "One minute I'm standing up minding my business, next minute I'm on the ground with my leg all twisted out of place."

"Oh!" said Samiel. "Man, they did you wrong!"

"So wrong!" said Derek.

"I'm about to smack both of you if you don't cut it out," said Benjamin.

"Benji, why do you always have to ruin the fun, man?" whined Derek.

"Seriously?" agreed Samiel. "Why can't you ever just let us be?"

Benjamin rolled his eyes and shook his head.

"Don't pay Benji any mind," said Samiel. "He's just a big softie trying to act all tough. You should've seen the way he was crying when he heard you got hit."

"Sami, you were crying harder than I was!" remarked Benjamin.

"Shoot, I probably cried harder than both of you combined," added Derek. "I wouldn't wish the type of pain I felt on anybody."

"Well, I'm glad you're alive," said Benjamin.

"Me too," said Samiel. "I don't want to lose another friend so soon, let alone my best one."

The boys got quiet at the mention of Simon.

"I got some surprises for you," said Benjamin, breaking the silence.

"I don't think I can handle any more surprises this year," said Derek.

"They're good surprises, I promise," said Benjamin, removing something from his bag. "The first is the hoodie I'm going to wear in my video. I had it customized, and I wanted you to sign it."

"Sure, if you'll sign my cast," said Derek.

"Deal," agreed Benjamin. He unfurled the white hoodie for Derek to see it in all its glory. Printed on the front amidst a sea of other supportive signatures were the words 'BENJI WITH DA BAD ATTITUDE' in big gold letters.

"Benjamin Raymond Townsend!" cried Derek in shock. "What is this?"

"That's my new name," declared Benjamin, smirking.

"You're telling me all I had to do was almost die for you to consider it?"

"I decided on this long before that happened. I was going to show it to you at the video shoot, but I figured this would be better."

"I guess you're right since I won't be in the video now."

"Who said you won't be in the video?"

"I'm going to be in a wheelchair or on crutches pretty much up until the summer according to the doctor."

"And?" said Benjamin. "The wheelchair will just make it more hype."

"You're serious?"

"He's serious," said Samiel.

"You're going to be in this video, Derek," said Benjamin. "Because you'll owe me some money if you don't."

"Why would I owe you money?"

"Because I had this made just for you," said Benjamin, producing a jersey from the bag. Printed on the back in big white letters was the name 'D-MONEY'.

"How much do your parents pay you to work at Patty's?"

"Enough to get jerseys made for everyone appearing in the video."

"Who is everyone?"

"My friends," said Benjamin. "The name of the song is 'Home Team' and I want my home team in the video."

"Aw Benji..."

"Yeah, yeah, I know," sighed Benjamin. "It's all sappy and sweet."

"You're just like my Uncle Marlin," laughed Derek. "A big softie trying to be tough, just like Sami said."

"Oh Mr. Marlin *is* tough... and scary," said Samiel. "He always looks at me weirdly whenever he sees me. I think he could probably lift me over his head if he wanted to."

"Maybe twenty years ago," snorted Benjamin.

"What do you mean he looks at you weirdly?" asked Derek.

"I don't know how to describe it," said Samiel. "It's not like a mean look. It's just... weird. Like he's seen a ghost or something. Maybe I remind him of someone. Or maybe it's something about my face. What if there's something on my face every time he sees me?"

"If Andre were here, he'd say it's epidermis," muttered Benjamin.

"Rockstar was here earlier," said Derek. "And he did use a big word."

"See?" said Benjamin.

"Whatever it is Sami, I'm sure it's nothing bad," said Derek. "Uncle Marlin's not a bad guy. Maybe you remind him of an old friend or something."

"Maybe."

After Samiel and Benjamin left, Derek had one final visitor. It was the person he had wanted to see most since he had left the hospital. The first thing he saw were the roses, and they made him smile.

"Roses," said Derek. "Your favorite."

"They're for you," said Derik. He looked around the room and said, "I'll put them with the rest of your flowers."

"Oh no," said Derek. "I want those in a vase, and I want them right there on my desk."

"They're fake."

"And?"

"Okay," said Derik. He set the flowers on the desk and sat next to Derek.

"Antoine was here earlier," said Derek. "He asked about you."

"I don't know if I'm ready to face other people yet," sighed Derik. "It took a lot just to come see you."

"Baby steps," said Derek. "How are you?"

"I'm so sorry," said Derik. "This whole thing is all my fault."

"How is it your fault? You didn't kidnap yourself."

"Yeah but–!"

"I read your journal like you wanted me to," said Derek. "I know why you wanted to run away."

"If I'd known this would happen, I wouldn't have done it."

"Derik, I'd get hit by a million cars if it meant having you back around."

"But then you'd be dead."

"True."

"I should've told you about her," said Derik. "I shouldn't have tried to take your place."

"You tried, remember? And I didn't want to listen."

"Yeah but–!"

"Dee-Three," interrupted Derek. Something felt stuck in his throat, and he swallowed it down. He smiled and said, "I'm not mad at you. Besides, it wasn't even her anyways."

"But what if it had been?"

"Well, it wasn't," said Derek. "Do you have any idea who either of the guys are?"

"No," said Derik. He shook his head and ranted, "But one of the guys kept calling me CJ from Sepia because I looked like some guy he'd met! What is Sepia?!"

"It's a nightclub. What did he look like?"

"He had on a mask, but he was kind of chubby."

"Malik."

"You know him?"

"Yeah. I'm CJ from Sepia."

"You are? What were you doing in a nightclub?"

"It's not important," said Derek. "Malik is Sharon's boyfriend."

"Who was the one guarding me like a watchdog?"

"I don't know."

"Whoever he was...," began Derik. He wrapped his arms around himself and shivered. "I'll never forget those eyes. It was like looking at death itself."

"They won't be able to run forever," said Derek. "They'll be caught sooner or later."

"Hopefully sooner," said Derik. "I just want to put this whole thing behind me."

-

Chapter Twenty-Nine:
Allison

It had been two weeks since Derik had returned, and the two men who helped kidnapped him still had not been caught. One of the men was Sharon's boyfriend, Malik, who was on the run. As to the identity of the other, Sharon refused to identify him, and the only thing anyone had to work with was Derik's description of his eyes.

"This whole thing is unsettling," said Althea. "Even with Ralphie here, I still don't feel very safe."

"I don't blame you," said Allison. "Ralphie's a good man, but he's not much of a fighter... or a cleaner apparently."

"Don't even get Diana started on that," sighed Althea.

"Shoot, Nicki could've at least warned you guys about how untidy he is," said Allison. "He might be Creeke's most untidy man!"

"I think that title belongs to Mr. Brown," said Althea. "I've heard his room is a nightmare."

"This doesn't make any sense!" declared Allison. "How do these people not know how to clean up after themselves?!"

"I don't know."

Allison looked out the window and noticed someone walking around. It was a medium-brown man with a scraggly beard. He had on a pair of shoes that looked like the new ones Deidrick had bought recently.

"There's a man walking up to the house," said Allison.

"A man?"

They both looked at the man. He went up to the door and rang the doorbell.

"Can I help you?" asked Diana when she answered the door.

"Do you have a phone I can use? Mine is dead and my car broke down."

"I could call a tow truck for you."

"That's okay. My brother can tow my car. I just need to call him."

"Well... uh..."

"If you can't do it, I understand."

"Uh... come inside," said Diana. "We have a house phone in the kitchen you can use."

"Thank you," said the man, entering the house. Allison heard them move to the kitchen.

"Uh... what did you say your name was?" asked Diana.

"I didn't."

"Right."

There was silence. Then the sound of running water.

"Is your brother not picking up?"

"Nope."

"That's too bad."

"Maybe you can help me."

"I can't tow a car," laughed Diana.

"Yeah, but you can tell me what I want to know."

"*How horrible*!" cried Diana loudly, followed by the sound of something shattering on the floor.

"Something's wrong," whispered Althea.

"Where's Ralphie?" asked Allison.

"He went to go help at Brewer's. He won't be back for hours."

"What do we do?"

"I don't know."

"Who else is in this house?" demanded the man.

"No one!" answered Diana quickly. "There's no one else here! I promise!"

"How about we look and see just to be sure?"

"We have to hide," said Althea, moving herself and Allison away from the door.

"Where?"

"Uh...," uttered Althea, looking around the room. Her eyes landed on her closet, and she led Allison to it. "The secret room. We'll be safe there."

"What about Diana?" asked Allison as they disappeared into the dark hidden room of the house.

"I don't know," said Althea, shutting the door just enough to hide them but leaving a crack for them to get back out. "The man must have a weapon. Otherwise, Diana would have hit him with a pan or something by now."

"Shh!" shushed Allison. "I think they're coming in here."

Allison and Althea peered through the crack in the door. They watched as the man rushed Diana into Althea's room and threw her to the bed. His right hand aimed a gun at Diana.

"I'm telling you there's no one else in here," said Diana

"Oh really?" said the man. He pointed at something on Althea's desk. "Then whose phones are these?"

"Oh no!" gasped Althea. "We left our phones behind!"

"They're mine," lied Diana. "I have two phones."

"Funny," said the man. "Neither of these girls on the lock screens look like you."

"So?" said Diana. "What do you want from me?"

"A boy got ran over out here," said the man.

"I didn't see anything."

"Don't play stupid. I heard there was a whole stream of girls that came running out of this house."

"I was having a slumber party."

"Aren't you a little old to be having a slumber party?"

"First of all, I'm grown!" argued Diana, shooting up from the bed.

"Yell at me like that again and you'll be grown and dead!" said the man, shoving Diana back down. He regained his composure and said, "Like I was saying, there was a boy that got ran over out here two weeks ago. You're going to tell me everything you and everyone else in this house saw and if I don't like your story, I'll kill you."

"I'm telling you I didn't see anything."

"And I don't believe you," said the man, aiming the gun at Diana's face. "You've got one more chance or else."

"I..."

The doorbell rang.

"Who is that?" asked the man. He peeked out the window and said, "There's a guy on the front porch."

Allison sighed with relief, thankful for the well-timed interruption.

"Get rid of him," commanded the man pulling Diana to her feet. "And if you make one wrong move, I'll kill you."

"Okay," said Diana. The man pushed her toward the door and out of the room.

"What are we going to do?" asked Althea.

"I don't know," said Allison. "Whoever is at that door may be our only hope."

-

Chapter Thirty: Matthias

Jordan had been discharged from the hospital and was in a rehabilitation center. He was expected to fully recover, but the road there would not be easy for him. Matthias decided to accompany James to visit Jordan to see how he had been since the incident.

"He's been a bit down since he got out the hospital," said James as they drove to the center.

"I'm just glad he's alive," said Matthias.

"Me too. I can't imagine how much worse things could've been if you hadn't pushed him out of the way."

"Me either."

They arrived at the center and after checking in, visited Jordan in his room. Jordan lay in bed staring at the television on the wall. Upon seeing James and Matthias, a smile spread across his face.

"Hey," said Jordan weakly.

"Hey," said James. "How are you feeling?"

"Okay."

"You had us worried for a minute there, man," said Matthias. "We were scared you weren't going to make it."

"Nah, I'm still here."

"And we're glad too," said James.

Jordan turned his head toward the window.

"I wish I wouldn't have said anything to him," said Jordan, the smile fading from his face. "Maybe then I wouldn't be in this position."

"Yeah, you definitely barked up the wrong tree," said Matthias.

"But that doesn't mean you should've been shot over it," added James. "Especially over a girl."

"That's the thing," said Jordan. "I don't know him or his girl."

"You're sure?" asked Matthias.

"I'm sure. I don't know if he got me mixed up with someone else, but I don't know him."

"Then that settles it," said James. "You were shot for absolutely no reason by some guy with no self-control."

"He had a reason even though it was a stupid one," said Matthias. "But since Jordan wasn't his intended target, that means whoever his actual target was is still out there messing around with his girl. And the shooter's just going to keep going after any guy that looks like that guy until it stops."

"Then he needs to be caught," said James.

"He does," said Matthias. "But no one knows anything. And anyone who does won't speak up."

"So, we all get shot and the shooter's just out and about like nothing happened," said Jordan. "This sucks."

"Yeah," said Matthias.

"All I remember are those baby blue shoes running away after he did it," said Jordan. "That's the last thing I saw before losing consciousness."

"And not much can be done with that," said Matthias.

There was not much left to say after that. James and Matthias left. Matthias had planned to visit Alexander that day but decided on a different course of action. He went to the Green residence when he arrived in Creeke to finally visit Cynthia. Everyone kept asking him about her, and he figured it was time he finally show his face and see where they stood. After waiting on the porch for a bit, Diana opened the door with a wide-eyed expression.

"Hey Matthias," said Diana. "What are you doing here?"

"I'm here to see Cynthia," said Matthias.

"She's not here," answered Diana a little too quickly for Matthias's tastes.

"How long is she going to be gone?"

"I don't know."

"Can I come in and wait for her?"

"No!"

"Why not? I've done it before."

"Because... the house isn't clean."

"You're lying. Mrs. Athena would never let the house get dirty."

"You can't come in," huffed Diana, grabbing the door to close it. "Now if you'll excuse me, I have some company."

"Company?" said Matthias, catching the door. "But you just said the house was dirty."

"Matthias, let go of the door."

"If you want to be alone with Ralphie just say that."

"Why are you in my business?" argued Diana.

"Because you're acting weird."

"No, I'm not."

"Let me say hi to Ralphie and I'll be on my way."

"He's not here."

"Then who is it then? A girl friend of yours?"

"No."

"Another guy?"

"Will you just leave?"

"Wow. You've got another guy here?"

"*How horrible!*" yelled Diana. "Why can't you just mind your business and *leave*?"

"Nah, I don't like this," said Matthias. "You're being weird and I'm not leaving until Ralphie or Cynthia gets back."

"Matthias," said Diana, blocking him from entering.

"Who is that?!" cried Matthias, pointing behind her.

"Who?!" shrieked Diana, turning around. Matthias took the opportunity to slip past her weakened defense into the house.

"I'm in," said Matthias, smirking.

"Please leave," begged Diana.

"Nope," said Matthias. "Not until I know why you're being weird."

"I'm telling you, nothing's wrong."

"Well, what do we have here?" said Matthias, spotting a man in the kitchen.

"What's up?" said the man.

"Nothing much," said Matthias. "Who are you?"

"Who are you?"

"Friend of the family," answered Matthias. He looked down at the man's baby blue shoes. "Nice shoes."

"Thanks."

"Where'd you get them?"

"My girl got them for me."

"That was cool of her. My brother had a pair like them, but he lost them."

"That's too bad."

"You know, you seem familiar."

"I do?"

"Yeah," said Matthias. "Something about your voice sounds familiar. Have we met before?"

"I don't think so."

"Hmm...," said Matthias. "What was your name again?"

"I didn't say."

"Yeah, you didn't," said Matthias. "I've got it! You're the guy from that one game!"

"Oh shoot," laughed Malik. "I thought you meant you knew me in person. Who are you?"

"I'm the step-pappy you said you were going to catch me one of these days. Well, here I am."

The man's face darkened, letting Matthias know he remembered their interaction.

"So, you ready to do this?" asked Matthias.

"You're seriously going to fight over a game?"

"Not just over a game," said Matthias. "You're the same guy who shot me and my cousins at a gas station. It was your voice I recognized. And now that I look at you, you look a lot like Sharon's boyfriend,

Malik Kelly. That means you helped kidnapped my brother. And those are my younger brother's shoes on your feet which means it was him you were trying to shoot over Sharon."

"Look man," said Malik. "You don't want any problems with me."

"I think I do," said Matthias, moving a chair out of the way.

"I'm telling you, you don't–!"

Matthias did not let him finish the sentence. The man responsible for shooting him and kidnapping his brother was before him, and Matthias had the perfect opportunity to let all his rage loose. Injured or not, he would not miss this moment and seized it by driving his fist straight into Malik's mouth to shut him up.

The gun fell from Malik's hand as he stumbled to his feet. It was not a fight but a battle for survival. Left, right, uppercut, took one to the face. Matthias kept swinging and dodging, using all the strength in his right arm to compensate for the missing strength of his left. They tore up the Green's kitchen, wrestling with each other for dominance, trying to overcome the other. But it was Matthias who came out on top. He knocked Malik out and stood over him, breathing heavily as he looked down at the man who had taken so much from him. His eyes went to Malik's baby blue shoes.

"Give me these!" ranted Matthias, snatching the shoes off Malik's feet. "You think you're going to steal my brother shoes and get away with it?!"

"You're bleeding!" cried Diana, coming to Matthias's aid.

"Aw, don't worry about it," said Matthias. "My stitches just busted, that's all."

"Here, let me bandage it for you," said Diana. She dug around in a cupboard and pulled out some gauze. As she wrapped it around Matthias's arm, she asked, "What are we going to do with him?"

"Lock him up until the authorities arrive," said Matthias.

"I was so worried," said Diana. "And I don't know what happened to Althea and Allison."

"Allison's here?"

"She was. But when he forced me to look for them, I couldn't find them. I tried to warn them as best as I could, so maybe they got it and escaped. But all their stuff is still here so I don't know."

"Queenie!" hollered Matthias. "Althea!"

There was no answer.

"Allison!" called Diana. "Thea!"

Once again, there was no answer.

"Stay here and call for help," instructed Matthias. "And hide that gun from him. If he comes to and tries anything, knock him out again."

"Uh...," uttered Diana, looking at the unconscious Malik. "Okay..."

Matthias searched the house for the girls, ending it in Althea's room. As he was about to give up and accept that they had managed to escape, he noticed a crack in Althea's closet door. He pushed it open to reveal Allison and Althea sitting inside, fear written on their faces.

"You didn't hear me calling you?" said Matthias.

"We didn't know if it was safe," said Allison. "We thought maybe he was forcing you to call us."

"Nah, I knocked him out."

"Is Diana okay?" asked Althea.

"She's fine. Not a scratch on her."

"Thank goodness," exhaled Althea.

"So, what is this? A secret room or something?"

"Yeah," said Althea. "I discovered it a few months ago."

"Is it escape proof?"

"I'm not sure. Why?"

"I think we'll use it to hold our little friend until help arrives."

"Fine with me," said Allison.

"Me too," said Althea.

Chapter Thirty-One:
Deidrick

While Matthias was rescuing Allison and the Green sisters from Malik, Deidrick was at the barbershop doing his job. Mr. Zackariah had come into the shop to meet with Mr. Harrison in his office and sign his contracts. Marcellus was in Deidrick's chair, ranting about the job he had recently lost.

"I'm pissed!" said Marcellus. "Sepia's temporarily closing down because whoever got shot during the fight between KV and Knokout is suing the club! They're trying to claim it's the security's fault the shooting happened! How is it security's fault?!"

"Because you're... security...," said Deidrick. "It was literally your job to make sure the club was safe."

"Man, I don't care about that job!" griped Marcellus. "I was just using it to get into places for free! But now, nobody will want to hire me after this!"

"Well, whatever you do at least you'll look good," said Deidrick, spinning Marcellus to face the mirror.

"I always look good," said Marcellus, placing his payment into Deidrick's hand. "Good looking out, cuz."

"No problem."

Marcellus left. While Deidrick cleaned his clippers, he heard the bell chime and saw Derek hobble into the shop on crutches with Mr. Harrison and Derik right behind him. The latter two went into the shop's back office, and Deidrick noticed Derik had a backpack with him. Meanwhile, Derek settled into one of the waiting chairs and exhaled.

"Look who's out of the house," said Deidrick.

"I know right!" said Derek.

"You getting a cut?"

"No, I just wanted to get out of the house. Uncle Marlin said he had some business to handle here at the shop, so I came with him and convinced him to bring Dee-Three too."

"Even on a broken leg, you still can't sit still," laughed Deidrick. "Enjoying your new hair color?"

"Yeah. It's awesome!"

"I still cannot believe you dyed it red because Knokout dyed his hair red in November."

"It looked cool to me," said Derek. "And I figured I'd do something to make me happy since I won't have use of my leg for a while."

Their conversation was interrupted by a guy entering the shop. He was medium-brown, tall, and strong-looking.

"You take walk-ins?"

"Yeah."

"I need a line up and a little off the top."

"Have a seat."

The guy sat down.

"You new in town?" asked Deidrick, starting work on the guy's wavy black hair.

"Visiting," said the guy. "A friend told me you were the best barber in town."

"I am."

"Cool."

Deidrick completed the haircut. But something bothered him about the guy. On the nape of his neck was a scar, and Deidrick was sure he had seen it before. He kept staring at it, wondering why it was so familiar to him when the guy was not.

"Am I done?" asked the guy.

"Ye... yeah," answered Deidrick.

"How much?"

"Forty," said Deidrick. "Have we met before?"

"Have we?" asked the guy. He looked at Deidrick with suspicious eyes, almost as if he were threatening Deidrick not to remember him. Those eyes creeped Deidrick out.

"I feel like I know you," muttered Deidrick. He concentrated on remembering where he had seen that scar before, and then it hit him. "You're–!"

"I suggest you shut up," whispered the guy, lifting the front of his shirt enough to reveal the hilt of a gun poking out of his waistband. He lowered it and said, "You said twenty, right?"

"Forty."

"You're sure it wasn't twenty?" repeated the guy, tugging the hem of his shirt.

"Yeah, you're right... twenty," said Deidrick uneasily. "My bad."

"Yeah, it is," said the guy. He handed Deidrick a twenty and said, "Thanks for the new look. Maybe I'll drop by again sometimes."

"You're not going anywhere," said Derik, pointing a gun at the guy. To Deidrick, it looked like one of his grandfather's guns. Before he could react, the guy grabbed Deidrick and put him in a chokehold.

"What are you doing?!" cried Deidrick.

"Shut up!" commanded the guy. Deidrick felt something metal pressed to his head and froze. The guy laughed and said, "Long time no see, Little Man."

"Why are you here?!" demanded Derik.

"Getting a cut. You like it?"

"Let my brother go!"

"Little Man's brother, eh?" said the guy. "What's up bro? I'm Hakeem. Sorry our official introduction couldn't be a little more... pleasant, but I'm sure you understand."

Deidrick did not respond. He feared any wrong word could end with his life being taken.

"I missed you Little Man," said Hakeem. "I've been looking all over for you. We had so much fun together until you stole my car and ran out on me. That made me a little angry, I'm not going to lie."

"Stop calling me that!" yelled Derik.

"Aw, come on Little Man," said Hakeem. "I know I said some mean things to you and punched you a few times, and accidentally ripped some of your hair out, but you shouldn't have made me mad."

"Let my brother go!"

"Why though?" said Hakeem. "I spared him once already and I don't like making the same mistake twice. And Nisha's such a nice girl too. I think I'll take her off his hands once I'm done here."

"You're not getting away!" declared Derik. "Move and I'll shoot!"

"Alright Little Man, if that's how you want it to be," said Hakeem. "You'll only get one shot though, because if you miss, I'll blow big bro here away. And once I'm done with him, I'll get you next. And this time I'll make sure it's you and not someone who looks like you."

Deidrick watched as Derek's eyes widened, the realization sinking in for all of them that it had been Hakeem who ran Derek over.

"So, go ahead Little Man. Take your best shot."

"Derik," said Mr. Harrison. "Give me the gun."

"No!" said Derik. "He's mine!"

"Go ahead then," said Mr. Harrison. "Shoot him. Get yourself locked away for the rest of your life."

"You'd like that, wouldn't you?" mocked Derik. "A nice, convenient way for you to get rid of me once and for all."

"You're right," said Mr. Harrison. "It would be a nice, convenient way for you to go away again if that's what you want. But it all comes down to what you do with that gun."

"Why do you care? You never wanted me!"

"Derik," said Marlin. "You wanted the truth, and I gave it to you. If it hurt you, then I can't help that. I was only answering your question."

"That doesn't change the fact that you hate me!"

"Is that what you think?"

"It's what I know."

"If you're so sure, then shoot. I won't stand in your way."

"Go ahead, Little Man," laughed Hakeem, daring Derik to shoot him. "I'm wide open."

Derik stood trembling. But he did not shoot.

"You're hesitant," said Mr. Harrison. He extended his hand and said, "You know you're not going to shoot so give it here."

"Why?" said Derik. "Why act like you care now?"

Mr. Harrison did not answer. He just stared at Derik, holding his hand out for the gun.

"Do you love me?" asked Derik. "Because if you love me then I won't do it."

"You're in luck, brother," Hakeem said to Deidrick with a chuckle. "You might just live, after all. Once he gets that gun away from him, you and I are going to move nice and slowly toward the exit. And if anybody makes any sudden movements it's all over for you. So go ahead, Mister. Set it in motion. Do you love your son?"

"How do I know you'll keep your word?" questioned Marlin, keeping his eyes on Derik.

"Little Man's still alive, isn't he?"

"Only because he escaped," said Marlin. "That didn't stop you from running me for fifty grand though."

"Whatever. Quit stalling and answer the question."

Deidrick realized his life hinged on his father admitting his feelings. And as he waited to hear his father's answer, he quietly accepted that he may be experiencing the final moments of his life.

Chapter Thirty-Two:
Derek

Derek watched with bated breath as he anticipated Uncle Marlin's answer. This was the moment where his efforts to get his uncle to express himself would either succeed or fail.

"Derik, why do you think I hate you?" asked Uncle Marlin.

"Because you do," said Derik. "You didn't care that I was gone. You went on with business as usual."

"How would you know if you were gone?"

"Because I know."

"Would you have rather I lied to you and told you I did want you? Is that what you would've preferred?"

"Why didn't you want me?"

"I didn't want to be a father."

"Then why have me?"

Uncle Marlin grunted. He glanced at Derek, and Derek nodded to encourage him to keep going. Closing his eyes and taking a deep breath, Uncle Marlin spoke.

"Honestly Derik, you were an accident. I thought after your mother had your sister we were done because what she wanted most was a daughter. So, when you came along, I especially didn't want you."

Derek's heart dropped. He knew the feeling well of being the unwanted accident that ruined lives. The feelings that stirred from that knowledge were something he did not wish on anyone, and it saddened him to know his cousin would feel what he felt.

"I know it's a terrible thing to say, but it's true," continued Uncle Marlin. "I didn't want you. And the worst thing Derik, is that I look at you now and see myself. You ask why I didn't want you, why I hate you. I wanted to ask my father those same things. Why did he hate me? Why was he always yelling at me? Why did he treat everyone else better than he treated me? What did I do to him? You want to know why I didn't want you Derik? It's because I didn't want to be like him. I didn't want to be the father he was. But now I know, I'm exactly how he was. And because I'm exactly how he was, I also now know exactly what he felt when he looked at me. I know you probably hate me, and I don't blame you. But I don't hate you. Just like I know now that he didn't hate me. You don't know how hard it is to accept that I chased you away. To know that I would've been the reason you were gone for good. I did everything I could to find you, to make you know I didn't want you gone. I searched, I took money from our savings, and even had to accept the donations the Perrys raised to pay that ransom. But no matter how hard I tried, you were nowhere to be found. But now that you're back, I want you to know I don't hate you. I don't want you walking around thinking I do or that I wish you'd never been born. I don't want you believing I feel like my life would've been better off without you. Whether I wanted you or not, you're here. You're here, and I took care of you, and I made you a part of my life. You're a part of my life now, and that's that."

Derek saw a tear slide down Derik's face in the mirror's reflection. The tear fell down his face, and onto Derek's hand. He looked at it, wondering how it managed to fall from Derik's face onto his own hand. Feeling his cheek, he realized he also was crying. Uncle Marlin's words touched him. To know it was possible for a parent to not want you and still include you in their life made Derek feel something. But he could not identify what it was he felt.

He was proud of his uncle. Uncle Marlin had loosened his guard and expressed what he felt for once. Derek thought the execution could have been better, but he was still proud. But that feeling of pride faded when his uncle slipped the gun out of Derik's hand. It hit him that everything his uncle said could have been false. Could have been empty words purposed solely to disarm Derik. Those words that had touched him could have been fake, just like the opportunity to meet his mother. That unidentifiable feeling came to Derek again as he eyed his uncle holding the gun.

"I've done my part," said Uncle Marlin to Hakeem. "Now you do yours."

"You have nothing to worry about as long as everyone stays where they are," said Hakeem. He inched toward the connecting door, dragging Deidrick along with him. "Nice and easy, big guy."

The connecting door swung open when Hakeem reached it. He and Deidrick disappeared through it, and all Derek saw were six legs lying sideways, kicking and twisting around. One pair of legs disappeared, then came running through the door in the form of Deidrick. Then another pair of legs stopped moving. They lay there, turned upward with the toes pointing to the ceiling. And the last pair of legs stood up and walked through the door with the gun in hand.

"It's a good thing I always get the entrances mixed up," said Mr. Bud. "Then, I wouldn't have been able to get the drop on him."

"How'd you know he was here?" asked Uncle Marlin.

"We got a call about a disturbance here," explained Mr. Bud. "Chief was on a call for the Green residence and Sam's out by the highway. That left me to check things out."

"Who called?"

"Not sure," said Mr. Bud. "I didn't recognize the voice."

"Is it safe to come out yet?" asked Mr. Zackariah as he peeked from the office.

"That's who called," said Uncle Marlin. "Yeah, Zack. It's safe."

"Is it always this exciting around here?" asked Mr. Zackariah.

"Not usually."

Mr. Bud arrested Hakeem and took him away. After the shock wore off, everyone returned to what they were doing before. But Derek did not feel happy like he had earlier. There was a new feeling in him, the unfamiliar twinge Derek shoved down every time he thought about his leg. And he felt it strongest when he looked at Derik. They looked at each other, saw each other's eyes, and knew they were the same again. He felt what Derik felt, and Derik felt what he felt. Derik was Derek, and Derek was Derik until all that remained in their minds was one dark-brown boy feeling a pain he could not express with words.

Chapter Thirty-Three: Allison

Final suspects in kidnapping case arrested
By Creeke Courier STAFF

The remaining suspects involved with the kidnapping of a local teen have been arrested.

Creeke Police arrested Hakeem Kelly, 27, and Malik Kelly, 24, Saturday. Both men are accused of helping Sharon Pierce kidnap Derik Harrison in December.

Police arrested Malik after he took hostage three young women in their home. He is also responsible for a January gas station shooting that left three injured. Authorities apprehended Hakeem after he took hostage customers and employees at Miss Leya's Beauty and Barber Shop. All victims involved with both incidents were rescued unharmed.

One week after the Kelly brothers were caught, life in Creeke was back to normal. It was February, and Derik could finally rest knowing that all his kidnappers were apprehended. Allison was happy for her brother, especially since he would be starting therapy soon. She knew it would take time and support for Derik to work through the traumatic experience, but for the most part, Allison was happy that her brother was safe and home. He had accepted Mayor Perry's offer to spend the day with him, and she hoped that he was okay. Meanwhile, Allison resumed her regular life at the beauty shop as a receptionist.

"Hey," said Jada, entering the building.

"Welcome to Miss Leya's Beauty and Barbershop, where you'll leave feeling just as good as you'll look," said Allison. "Here for an appointment?"

"No, just bringing my dad lunch," answered Jada, holding up a brown paper bag.

"He's on the barber side," said Allison.

"I knew I went through the wrong door," chuckled Jada.

"Still making new friends?"

"I'm always making new friends," said Jada. "But I had to drop some over the week."

"Who?"

"Dani told me if I was going to be friends with you and the other girls, then I couldn't be friends with them, and you already know how I feel about that."

"I do."

"Yeah, so I'm not talking to them anymore," said Jada. "It kind of sucks though because I did get along really well with Mariana and Mariella."

"Maybe it's for the best."

"Maybe."

"Hey! My best friend plays *The Well* too! I almost forgot to tell you."

"You told me. But what's her tag?"

"Uh...," said Allison, unsure if she should reveal Stacy's embarrassing username. "Maybe I can tell her yours and you two can go from there."

"Sure. Mine's Sweet_PatatoWato. I'll write it down for you to give to her."

While Jada wrote down the usernames, the front bell chimed.

"Welcome to Miss Leya's Beauty and Barber Shop, where you'll leave feeling as good as you'll look," said Allison. "How can I help you?"

"Hey girlie!" greeted Priscella. "I'm here to get my hair done."

"You're right on time," said Allison. "Jada, this is my friend Priscella. Prissy, Jada. You both already have something in common."

"We do?" asked Priscella. "What is it?"

"Dani."

"Aw," said Priscella. "She replaced you too?"

"Replaced me?" repeated Jada.

"Jada was your replacement, Prissy."

"Oh wow. You didn't last long at all."

"What do you guys mean 'replacement'?"

"Any time Dani loses a friend, she replaces them with a new one," explained Priscella. "So, when you see a new girl hanging with her, that's your replacement."

"Maybe it's a good thing our friendship didn't work out then," said Jada.

"It's definitely a good thing," said Priscella. "Because then I wouldn't have made friends with Alli."

"Aw," said Allison. "Girl, don't make me cry at work."

"Allison!" called Mrs. Harrison. "Come here!"

Allison went to where her mother was, leaving Jada and Priscella to form their own connection. Mrs. Harrison and Nisha were styling the Ms. Nelsons and gabbing about all sorts of topics.

"Ma'am?" said Allison.

"Sweep this hair up, please," instructed Mrs. Harrison, pointing at the hair on the ground.

"Yes ma'am," said Allison, going to get a broom. When she returned, she decided she had to know once and for all if she was right. She looked at the Ms. Nelsons and said, "Ms. Nelson?"

"Yes?" answered both women.

"Uh...," uttered Allison. She looked between the women, determined to identify them without looking for an engagement ring. Her eyes went back and forth between the two until she realized the one on the right had a near-invisible scar on her forehead that the one on the left did not. All she had to do was connect the scar to the correct Ms. Nelson, and she would be able to tell them apart. Looking at the Ms. Nelson without the scar, Allison pointed at her and said, "Ms. Greta...?"

"Yes," confirmed Ms. Greta.

"I got it!" cheered Allison. "I can tell them apart!"

"Girl," said Nisha.

"Yes Allison, what is it?" asked Ms. Greta.

"Are you dating Mr. Bud?"

"Allison!" shrieked Mrs. Harrison. "I'm so sorry, Greta. I don't know why she would ask you that."

"It's alright," said Ms. Greta. "We're considering dating, yes. We're still feeling each other out."

"Good luck with that," snorted Nisha.

"Why do you say that, Nisha?" asked Ms. Greta.

"Because it's like a free-for-all out here. No one wants to be committed to you these days."

"I used to think that way about relationships," chuckled Ms. Greta. "I swore I would be single for the rest of my life and now look at me, considering a relationship."

"Well, don't let him waste your time," advised Nisha. "Or else you'll find yourself three years later still asking him to make it official."

"I would never wait that long just to be a girlfriend," declared Ms. Greta. "I wouldn't even wait a year. Especially now that I'm older. I like Bud and I'm willing to take things slow, but not so slow that years are passing by with nothing to show for it."

"Not even if you loved him?"

"I've already been there and done that," said Ms. Greta. "When my ex-fiancé dumped me after a seven-year relationship, I realized how much you loved someone, how much time you put in, and even how faithful you were didn't matter if they didn't value it. I was so angry that I swore off romantic relationships forever. And it wasn't until this past summer that one of my friends helped me realize my ex did me a favor by leaving me. If I had married him, I would've been dissatisfied. And in my opinion, being satisfied in a relationship is more important than being in a relationship out of loyalty or because of time put in."

Allison glanced between Nisha and her mother.

"Bud makes me feel satisfied," continued Ms. Greta. "He's patient, and kind, and understanding..."

"So, when's the wedding?" joked Ms. Gretchen.

"Girl, we have to get through your wedding first," laughed Ms. Greta.

"All this wedding talk makes me itch," said Nisha.

"Nisha, how old are you?" asked Ms. Greta.

"Twenty."

"Oh," chuckled Ms. Greta. "Nisha, you have *way* too much life left to live to be trying to make a dead-end relationship work. If he is not serious, let him go and move on. Do not waste your life waiting around for someone to love you back. Trust me, it's not worth it."

Allison looked at her mother again, wondering if her mother agreed with the advice. She wondered if her mother regretted marrying her father and even if she considered leaving him. There was no hint for Allison to detect her mother's feelings on the matter. Mrs. Harrison just continued doing Ms. Gretchen's hair, smiling at the work that made her happy.

Sunday afternoon, Allison accompanied Mrs. Harrison to visit her parents again. She had been tasked by Nanna Kiana to apologize for her conduct during their previous visit. While Allison dreaded the idea of apologizing when she was not remorseful, Mrs. Harrison continued wearing the smile she had adopted the previous day at the hair salon.

Allison wondered what her mother was thinking that allowed her to continue smiling.

"Hello Mother," said Mrs. Harrison when she and Allison were shown into Lady Sophia's wing of the house. There was a sitting area with a bedroom beyond it closed off from view. A portrait of Lady Sophia hung on the mantle of the fireplace, looking down arrogantly on everyone who beheld it. Allison figured that Mayor Perry's wing was styled much the same. Mrs. Harrison hugged her mother and her sister and sat across from them.

"Have you come to apologize?" asked Lady Sophia, smirking at Allison.

"Yes," said Allison. "I apologize."

"For?"

"For my conduct during our previous visit."

"As you should," said Lady Sophia haughtily. "Soleya, your daughter certainly needs a lot more refining if you hope to turn her into a lady."

"Allison is already a lady, Mother," said Mrs. Harrison. The declaration shocked Lady Sophia and Allison alike. "She's not the same type of lady I am, but a lady nonetheless."

"Eh," muttered Lady Sophia, fanning herself with her folded fan. "If you think her manner will attract a good man, then I guess."

"Whether Allison marries or not is entirely up to her."

"Whether?" repeated Lady Sophia. "Soleya, are you feeling alright?"

"Perfectly fine."

"You know, it's very important that she make a good match."

"If she so desires."

"If she desires? Don't you think as her mother, you should do your duty and encourage her in that area?"

"If she wishes for me to encourage a match then I will."

"But what of her future?"

"Her future is hers to decide."

"Well, as her mother you could at least point her in the right direction like I did with you and your sister."

"And I appreciate your efforts."

"My efforts? Your father has no intention of leaving anything to any of us, but all of his fortune to his oldest grandson. I think my efforts deserve a little more credit at securing your futures for you."

"And what reward would you have for your efforts, Mother?"

"How dare you insult me?" said Lady Sophia. "After everything I've done for you, I–!"

"Mother, I'm tired of people telling me what they've done for me," griped Mrs. Harrison. "What about how you've treated me? How you've made me feel?"

"What does that matter?"

"Do you even care about our happiness in the futures you secured?"

"Happiness? I'm trying to weather the impending storm that is your father's eventual death because he plans to leave his whole estate in the hands of a buffoon, and you want to talk about happiness? What about my happiness? My whole life spent catering to that man and stupid, useless daughters who can't appreciate what's been given to them!"

"I think I've taken up enough of your time," said Mrs. Harrison.

"Don't you walk away from me!" demanded Lady Sophia.

Mrs. Harrison took Allison by the hand and led her to the exit. Lady Sophia walked behind them, ranting at Mrs. Harrison the whole time.

"You ungrateful child!" hollered Lady Sophia. "Everything I've done for you, and this is how you repay me?! My whole life spent on you and your sister, turning you into respectable ladies who could marry men worthy of you and this is what I get! My life ruined because giving birth to you ensured I'd have no more children! No chance of having a son to secure my place in this house! Everything I had will be left to that buffoon and it's all your fault! And that daughter of yours, oh...!"

Lady Sophia's rant was nonsense to Allison, so she did not bother listening to anymore of it. As they descended the stairs, Allison stared at her mother, wondering what had caused her to behave so differently.

"You walk out that door and I'll never speak to you again!" screamed Lady Sophia.

"If you so desire," said Mrs. Harrison, not bothering to look back.

"Soleya!"

"What's the matter, Mother?" said Mrs. Harrison. She stopped at the foot of the stairs and gazed at her mother. "Are you afraid that if I walk out the door I'll never come back?"

Lady Sophia did not answer. She looked down from the top of the stairs at her daughter, her lips pursed into an agitated line. Aunt Soriah silently stood behind her watching. Watching as her sister glared up at their mother, doing what she herself did not have the strength or will to do. Even Mayor Perry had come out of his bar with a glass in hand to see the commotion. His eyes were full of ire as he stared at his fussy wife. That man. Years of marriage, and he was just 'that man' to his wife. Nothing more than an owner who had purchased her freedom for the highest price. The disdain in Lady Sophia's voice when she said it had sparked a twinge of pity in Allison for Lady Sophia and the life that was forced upon her. But that spark was quickly doused by the insults lodged against her mother, and the reminder that for all her anger and all she had endured, Lady Sophia relished the benefits of the life she was so unhappy with.

"Come along, Allison," said Mrs. Harrison, turning away from her mother with that same smile on her face. She looked at her father and said, "Goodbye Daddy."

Allison wanted to add 'and good riddance'. She wanted to congratulate her mother for being strong enough to finally leave her dysfunctional family behind. But she did not. Instead, she followed her mother out of the house and asked the one question on her mind.

"Why?"

"Because I'm not wasting any more of my life waiting around for people to love me back."

Chapter Thirty-Four: Matthias

After spending over a month and a half in the city, Matthias was returning to Creeke. He would be living with his grandparents because they did not want him messing his stitches up again. Matthias was wary of living with his mother because he was unsure how he felt about her. Ever since Allison told him their mother had worried about him, he pondered whether she had really wanted him back in her life during their time apart. But even with his unsure feelings, he was sure he did not want angry grandparents. His grandparents had been through enough stress, and he did not want to add to it. So, he reluctantly agreed to move into their house.

"Once again, here I am chauffeuring you around," said Alexander.

"Well, you don't want me to overexert myself again, do you?" said Matthias.

"You should've called for help."

"There wasn't time. It was life or death, and I did what I had to do."

"What's today's itinerary, sir?" sighed Alexander.

"I'm moving all my stuff from the Campbells house into my grand-father's house. But first, I'm going to visit Cyn."

"Visit Cynthia?" repeated Alexander.

"I'm just checking on her and her sisters."

"Mhmm."

Alexander pulled up to the Green residence.

"You coming?" asked Matthias.

"And mess up your lover's affair?" joked Alexander. "I'm good."

"We're just friends."

"Mhmm."

Matthias went up to the house. Before he could ring the doorbell, Cynthia ran out onto the porch and grinned at him.

"I saw you coming up the drive," said Cynthia.

"So, you were waiting by the window for me?" said Matthias, smirking.

"No," said Cynthia. "I literally walked past the window, saw you walking up the drive, and came out."

"Alright, I'll believe it," said Matthias. "I came to visit you the other day."

"I heard," said Cynthia. "Ended up ruining your stitches and everything."

"And I'd do it all over again too," said Matthias. "Now Granddad wants me where he can see me so he can make sure I don't mess them up again."

"Well, I for one am glad you messed them up keeping my baby sisters safe."

"Glad enough to give me a hug?"

"Sure, I'll hug you."

Cynthia wrapped her arms around Matthias and squeezed him. While they held onto each other, Matthias figured it was a good time to ask the fated question.

"Cyn?"

"Yeah?"

"You trying to be more than just friends?"

"Matthias!" cried Cynthia, pushing Matthias away. "Why would you ask me that?! You know I hate when you flirt with me as a joke!"

"I'm trying to see where we stand."

"We're friends. Nothing more, nothing less."

"Alright."

"Were you... trying to be more than just friends?"

"Nope. I just asked because everyone won't leave me alone about it, and I figured you were running your mouth telling people that's what you wanted."

"I was not. If I wanted you Matthias, I could've been had you."

"And if I wanted you, I could've been had you too."

"Oh, you think I would've been one of those girls you snuck into your auntie's house?"

"I didn't have to sneak them in, they came right through the front door. You would've been the one sneaking me in."

"I think not. It's ring first around these parts."

"Well, just so we're clear, the ring's not coming from me."

"And I don't want it to come from you. You are like my younger brother."

"So, now I'm little bro?"

"I mean I do turn twenty-three this month, while you turn twenty-three in June so what would you call that?"

"I call it us being the same age."

"So, you came over here to pick with me?"

"I came to see how you and your sisters were doing."

"We're good. Diana's fussing at Ralphie, Althea's converting her newfound walk-in closet into a secret library, Gloria called to tell us she's still alive. We're good."

"That's good."

"And what about you and yours?"

"We're good. Me and Deidrick made up, Dee-Three's starting therapy soon, D-Money's recuperating, Queenie's good. We're good."

"How long is it going to be before you can make me proud on the court again?"

"Probably a month or two if I don't tear up these stitches again."

"Okay. Well don't let me hold you."

"And don't let anyone else hold you."

"See? I can always count on you to be the reason that I'm still single."

"Why me?"

"Because everyone treats me like you have an unsaid claim on me, and no one will approach me because of it."

"Maybe that's a good thing."

"And that's why I know I can count on you to keep me single. Because no one else will approach me, and I trust you not to try anything with me."

"Listen up world!" screamed Matthias. "Cynthia is single! I'm not her man! You can date her if you want! I won't stand in the way unless you treat her badly!"

"Oh my goodness," chuckled Cynthia.

"I made the PSA," said Matthias. "Now it's no longer my fault if no one dates you."

"You know what? Bye."

"Bye."

Matthias returned to Alexander's truck.

"Not her man, huh?" asked Alexander.

"Just friends," answered Matthias.

"Looked a little intense for 'just friends'."

"Just friends."

"Mhmm."

Matthias did not care what anyone else said. He knew he only saw Cynthia as a friend and nothing more. And he knew that she knew that he only saw her as a friend. Therefore, there was no reason for him to entertain thoughts of being in a relationship with her. Alexander drove to the Campbell house, and Matthias laid out the game plan for him.

"All my stuff is packed, so we should be in and out. Cornbread is helping us so it shouldn't take too long."

"I'm glad you guys made up."

"Yeah, yeah, whatever. Let's go."

Matthias entered the house and found Deidrick talking with Marcellus in the living room.

"Took you long enough," said Deidrick.

"I had to make a stop," said Matthias.

"A stop," scoffed Deidrick.

"Go grab a box while I talk to Cell," said Matthias.

"Go grab a box while I talk to Cell," mocked Deidrick, leaving the room.

"You're leaving," said Marcellus.

"Yeah, I'm leaving," said Matthias.

"I respect it."

"Listen Cell."

"You don't have to say anything. I know I screwed up by leaving him out there."

"Yeah, you did. But I just want you to know that whatever happens, I'm still here."

"That's what everyone says before they disappear."

"But I'm not everyone, am I?"

"No, I guess not."

"It doesn't take all day to talk to Marcellus," said Deidrick, walking through the room with a box.

"Let me help this boy before I end up punching on him again," said Matthias. "I'll see you around."

"See you around."

After they finished transporting all of Matthias's stuff to his grandparent's house, Alexander returned home, leaving Matthias and Deidrick on the porch alone.

"I got something for you," said Matthias.

"What?"

"Open that box right there."

"I was wondering why you didn't want to take it inside," said Deidrick. He opened the box and hollered, "Bro! Where'd you get these?! These look like the shoes I lost!"

"I took them off a guy I beat up," said Matthias. "No big deal."

"You stole them?"

"I retrieved what was rightfully yours from Malik."

"Man, you're alright with me," said Deidrick. "This is just the mood I needed to win Nisha back with."

"Have fun."

"I'll try."

Deidrick left to go see Nisha, and Matthias went inside. Mrs. Harrison sat at the kitchen table, and when she saw him, she kept her eyes on him. Matthias recalled what Allison had told him about their mother being worried about him after the shooting and decided to see for himself if it were true.

"Listen," said Matthias. "The way I acted towards you last time."

"It's alright," said Mrs. Harrison. "Have you eaten?"

"Not yet."

"Do you want something to eat?

"Sure."

Mrs. Harrison got up and began fixing Matthias a plate of food.

"I mixed the corn and mashed potatoes together just how you like it," said Mrs. Harrison, setting the plate before him.

"You remember that about me all these years later?" asked Matthias. It impressed him that she remembered such a small detail about him.

"I'm your mother."

His mother. Last time it angered him to hear those words from her. But Matthias did not feel anger again. Instead, he felt glad because she still wanted to be his mother. She had not discarded him after all.

"My mother," repeated Matthias. "You've been worried about me, and I've been avoiding you for all this time."

"I understand. You were mad at us because we didn't prioritize you. I know that now."

"I figured you saw me as easily discardable. You had two sons left so what was it to get rid of the problem one."

"Matthias, you're my firstborn child. You're the one that made me a mother. You'll never be discardable to me."

"And what about him?"

"At this point, I don't even know myself," sighed Mrs. Harrison. "We all might be discardable to him."

"I don't think you are," said Matthias. "The way I see it, everything he does, he does with you in mind."

"If that's the case, why do I feel like I don't matter to him?"

"Probably the same reason I do. Because he's never made it clear whether we matter to him or not."

"Well, I know someone who matters to me," said Mrs. Harrison. She squeezed Matthias's hand and asked, "Do you think you can give me a second chance to be your mother? Without my reputation involved this time?"

"Eh," said Matthias, pretending to think it over. "I'm in a giving mood. You can have another chance."

"Thank you. I love you."

"I... love you too."

Chapter Thirty-Five:
Deidrick

Deidrick was prepared to tell Nisha whatever was necessary to get her into a relationship. He needed her, especially if he had a child on the way. That child would need a mother that was not incarcerated, and Deidrick knew that Nisha was the perfect choice to fill that role. Therefore, if he finally had to make good on his promise of a relationship, then so be it. After running a hand over his head and exhaling through his mouth, he lifted the flowers in his hand and knocked on the door.

"Hey," said Deidrick when Nisha opened the door. "I need to talk to you."

"What about?"

"Can I come in?"

Nisha stepped to the side and let Deidrick in.

"These are for you," said Deidrick, handing the flowers to Nisha. He had stopped by his Uncle Malcolm's and taken them from the many arrangements that had been gifted to Derek.

"What's all this for?" asked Nisha, setting the flowers to the side.

"I'm ready to commit to you now."

"Deidrick."

"No, let me finish," said Deidrick. "I'm ready to commit to you but first I need to be honest with you."

"Okay."

"I slept with Sharon," admitted Deidrick. "And she's pregnant... and it might be mine."

"I knew it," said Nisha, pursing her lips. "I knew it."

"Nisha, I'm sorry," said Deidrick. "But we can have a fresh start now. We can be together like you've always wanted."

"This is so typical of you," laughed Nisha. "Now you want to be in a relationship after your fun is over?"

"Nisha."

"No!" interrupted Nisha. "I gave you three years – *three* – to figure out what you wanted to do, when I really shouldn't have even given you one. You've flirted with other girls, you slept with Sharon and maybe other girls too for all I know, and now you possibly have a baby on the way. And you did all this while we 'weren't together' as you like to say. So, if you felt comfortable doing all that before we were in a committed relationship, I can't imagine what you would do once we were in one."

"Nisha, don't act like you're innocent in all this."

"That's the problem right there!" cried Nisha. "Instead of taking accountability, you're trying to flip the situation to make it seem like I'm wrong! Yeah, I entertained another guy who flirted with me to make you jealous, but that was after three years of waiting on you to get it together!"

"You didn't just entertain another guy," argued Deidrick. "You entertained a guy who kidnapped my brother and tried to kill me! He showed up to the shop because you told him to!"

"Don't try to turn this around on me, Deidrick. We're talking about you and what you did. And if you want to go there, you slept with and impregnated the girl who *orchestrated* your brother's abduction and recruited Hakeem into it. So, you're guilty too."

"So, that's it?" said Deidrick. "You're throwing three years out the window just like that?"

"Three years of what?" said Nisha. "Of lying to myself about what you were doing and wasting my time believing that you were really going to be with me? You threw it out the window when you decided that your fun was more important to you than a relationship with me. I'm not going to be with you, Deidrick. Not after this."

"Cool," said Deidrick. "Do you."

"I will, just like you've always done," said Nisha. She picked up the flowers and shoved them into Deidrick's chest. "So why don't you take these half-dead flowers that you stole from Derek, and get out?"

Deidrick left. Nisha had abandoned him. But he did not care as much as he thought he would. If Nisha did not want to be with him then he would not force it. There were plenty of other women for Deidrick to choose from who would be more than happy to take her place. And he would be more than happy to take them and their sweet love into his arms.

Chapter Thirty-Six: Derek

Derek was glad the trouble was over. With the kidnappers caught, he could focus on healing his leg. Knowing the kidnappers meant to hit Derik and mistook them for each other made Derek feel that same unfamiliar feeling. He was glad that Derik was safe, but it came at the cost of him almost losing his own life. And it was all because they had once again been mistaken for each other. But Derek did not like the feeling or the thoughts it brought with it, so he kept shoving it down.

"Hey," said Uncle Marlin, entering his room.

"Hey," answered Derek. He was still unsure whether his uncle had told the truth during the standoff.

"I'm leaving at the end of the week," said Uncle Marlin. "Going to stay with your grandparents until my house is rebuilt."

"Do you have to leave?" asked Derek.

"Yeah. It's time."

"I don't want you to go."

"At first, you didn't want me to stay."

"Now, I want you to. I'm going to miss you."

"I'm just moving across town."

"Uncle Marlin?"

"Yeah?"

"What you said to Dee-Three... did you mean it?"

"Seriously? You've been asking me this whole time to say what's on my mind, and when I finally do, you question whether I meant it?"

"Because it was a life-or-death situation."

"I say what I mean, and I mean what I say. It doesn't matter the situation."

"Okay."

"You thought I made it all up?"

"I don't know. I just..."

"Hey," said Uncle Marlin. "I wouldn't give someone false hope like that. It's not my style."

"Okay," said Derek. "I'm proud of you."

"Thanks," said Uncle Marlin. "You hungry?"

"A little."

"I'll go make you something."

"Thanks."

Uncle Marlin left the room, and Malcolm entered.

"Uncle Marlin's leaving," said Derek.

"I know," said Malcolm. "But you'll still get to see him around. Like at church for example."

"How am I going to see him at church when none of us go?"

"Because we're all going to start going to church again."

"We are?"

"Yeah," said Malcolm. "I told The Big Guy if He let you live, I'd go back. And since Marlin was with me when I made the promise, he's responsible for making sure I keep it. Which means we're all going."

"What if I hadn't lived? Would you still have gone?"

"I don't want to think about that," said Malcolm. "You are literally the greatest blessing of my life. You're not allowed to leave the Earth before I do."

"I don't think you can control that."

"I know. But I don't want to imagine life without you in it."

"I don't either."

"You know, you were right to call me out on the whole Monique thing."

"Just like you were right to call me out about Granddad."

"I'm glad I have you. Even if the whole situation left a bad taste in my mouth, I'm glad it at least gave me you."

"Me too. I know if I ever need anyone to set me straight, I can count on you."

"You know I've got you."

"Just like I've got you."

Someone knocked on the front door.

"I'll get it," said Uncle Marlin. He answered the door and said, "Hey Dad."

"Every time I come here, you have a plate in your hand," said Granddad Derrick's voice.

"It's for Derek."

"Oh, it's for me?" joked Granddad Derrick. "Thank you!"

"No, it's not for you."

"It was a joke. Where's your brother?"

"In Derek's room."

"Okay," said Granddad Derrick. They came to Derek's room and said, "Hi!"

"Here," said Uncle Marlin, handing Derek a sandwich.

"Someone's happy today," said Malcolm.

"It's a nice day outside and I didn't want to stay in the house."

"That's good. What are you doing for your birthday next week, Dad?"

"Your mother is throwing me a party."

"That should be fun."

"Yeah," said Granddad Derrick. "Especially since my T n' T will be there."

"Your arms?"

"You and your brother. You're both my T n' T."

"Your trial and tribulation?" asked Malcolm.

"No," said Granddad Derrick. "My tough and tender."

"Your what?"

"My tough and tender," said Granddad Derrick. He looked at Uncle Marlin and said, "Marlin is my tough one. He pushes me to my limits to be the best I can be. I know if I ever need to hear the raw truth, I can go to him."

Uncle Marlin looked away.

"And Malcolm, you're my tender one," said Granddad Derrick, looking at Malcolm. "You encourage me when I'm down. You let me know that it's okay to not always be okay, and that its okay to not be perfect."

"Dad…," said Malcolm.

"Both of you are important to me," said Granddad Derrick, taking hold of his sons' hands. "You're both my boys and I love you."

"I love you too, Dad," said Malcolm.

Uncle Marlin shook his head. But he held onto his father's hand and squeezed it. Granddad Derrick smiled at them both, and Derek smiled too. It made him happy to see his family returning to normal again.

Chapter Thirty-Seven:
Allison

The day of Granddad Derrick's birthday had arrived. The family patriarch was turning sixty-seven, and the whole family would be at his house to celebrate. It was the first time they would all be gathered for a happy occasion, and Allison was excited. Nanna Kiana had tasked everyone with something that got them away from the house while she took Granddad Derrick to visit his friends. Allison and her parents had been tasked with cleaning the house, and she suspected it was to allow her parents an opportunity to talk privately. Her father had moved into the house the day before and had slept on the couch, while Mrs. Harrison slept in their bedroom. Neither one had spoken to the other, and Allison was determined to stay out of it.

"Yo," said Mr. Harrison, coming into the living room. "Can I ask you something?"

"Go ahead," said Allison.

"Uh...," said Mr. Harrison. "Did you... did you... enjoy our chess match?"

"Uh, yeah," said Allison. "Is that... what you wanted to ask me?"

"Uh... no," answered Mr. Harrison. "Um... do you feel like... like I hate you?"

"Uh...," laughed Allison awkwardly. "Uh... that's um... very out of left field."

"Your cousin told me I needed to see where I stood with everyone, so that's why I'm asking."

"I see," said Allison. "Well, it… it doesn't matter. I know you're not an emotional person, so it is what it is to me."

"I'm sorry," said Mr. Harrison, crossing his arms over his chest and looking at the wall.

"Huh?"

"I said I'm sorry," repeated Mr. Harrison, looking at his daughter. "I don't want you walking around thinking I hate you, because I don't."

"You don't?"

"No."

"But you didn't want me."

"That doesn't mean I hate you."

"You never told me you loved me before."

"I never thought it was necessary."

"You didn't think I wanted to hear that?"

"I didn't think it mattered."

"Then you do care about me?"

"Yes."

Allison did not know what to say. She wrapped her arms around him and felt him stiffen. It surprised her to know how much hearing those words affected her. Her father had never shown any kind of affection toward her, and she had never expected him to.

"How long are you going to hug me?" asked Mr. Harrison.

"I'm cherishing the moment."

"Why?"

"I've never been hugged by you before," revealed Allison. "I may never get this opportunity again."

He did not answer. But he did put his arms around her. The way he did it was awkward, but Allison did not care. Her father cared for her, and that was all that mattered.

"Marlin," said Mrs. Harrison. Mr. Harrison let Allison go and looked at his wife. She held up a trash bag and said, "I need you to take this out."

"Alright, I'll do it in a minute."

"I need you to do it now."

"I said I'll do it in a minute."

"Why do you have to be difficult?"

"Because Leya, you've pissed me off."

"Marlin, not today," sighed Mrs. Harrison. "I don't feel like arguing with you."

"We're not going to argue," said Mr. Harrison. "I just want to get one thing straight. Bernard didn't have to pay me to marry you. I married you because that's what you wanted."

"If you don't love me, just say it," said Mrs. Harrison. "Say it and get it over with."

"I'm not going anywhere," said Mr. Harrison. "I don't want to be with anyone else except you, Soleya."

"That doesn't mean you love me," said Mrs. Harrison. "For all I know, you're just keeping me around for pleasure and to maintain your house."

"Do I look like your father or Quincy to you?" said Mr. Harrison. "If that's all I wanted, I could have gotten someone less argumentative."

"But you didn't because you're loyal, right? That doesn't mean you love me."

"What more do you want?" huffed Mr. Harrison. "I'm not cheating on you. I give you everything you want. What else do you want?"

"I want to feel loved," said Mrs. Harrison. "I want to know that you feel the same excitement I do when I see you lying next to me in the morning. I want to know that you don't regret marrying me. I want to know that I'm in your heart, Marlin. But if I'm not, at least tell me now so I know where we stand and can act accordingly."

"Honestly," said Mr. Harrison. "I didn't love you when we first got married."

"I knew it."

"I didn't," repeated Mr. Harrison. "I thought you were cool, and I didn't mind you liking me or wanting to date me, but I didn't love you. You were just a means to get away from my father. But when I got around your family, and I saw how they treated you, something changed. You weren't just a means anymore. You were my wife and I had to protect you and get you out of there. And the more time I spent with you getting to know you, the more I realized all I wanted to do was see you happy. Everything I do and have done for you since we got married is because I want you to be happy. I figured as long as you were happy, what I felt wouldn't matter."

"Why would you think that?"

"Because... I don't know. I just did, okay?"

"Marlin, we're married," said Mrs. Harrison, cupping her husband's face. "Why wouldn't I care about how you feel?"

Mr. Harrison pressed his hand over Mrs. Harrison's. He looked uncomfortable, like he wanted to say more but was scared to. His hand held onto his wife's and squeezed it, and she smiled at him. Her smile brought out his smile, and it seemed they communicated without words.

"Allison, could you give us a moment alone?" said Mr. Harrison.

"Yes sir," said Allison. She left the house and sat on the porch. Eventually, Nanna Kiana returned with Granddad Derrick and they looked at her curiously.

"What are you doing out here?" asked Nanna Kiana.

"Dad told me to leave so he could talk to Mother."

"They must be making up," said Nanna Kiana.

"They're making something alright," mumbled Granddad Derrick. "And on my birthday too!"

"Oh hush!" chastised Nanna Kiana. "Wouldn't be the first time something's happened on your birthday."

"Something else can happen on my birthday too," said Granddad Derrick, wrapping his arms around Nanna Kiana's waist. "Maybe a romantic evening for two after everyone's gone?"

"Gone where?" said Nanna Kiana. "They all live here with us."

"I guess we'll have to go somewhere quiet then," said Granddad Derrick, nibbling on Nanna Kiana's ear. He whispered, "Maybe down by the creek where we had out first kiss. Where we went the night we got married."

"I remember that," sighed Nanna Kiana happily.

"You looked so beautiful in the moonlight that night."

"You did too."

"And now you're even more beautiful."

"And you're even more handsome."

"Handsome enough to put everyone out for the night?"

"Derrick!" cried Nanna Kiana, her cheeks becoming red. "You... you... meathead! You are a meathead!"

"I'm just trying to love on you," said Granddad Derrick. "Besides, it's not safe to go in there right now."

"Meathead. I married a meathead."

"Yes. You, a sophisticated, gorgeous lady, married a cute meathead with good grades."

"You still remember all that?"

"How could I forget? That's the first time we met."

"It was, wasn't it?"

"Yeah. And that night changed my life forever."

"Mine too."

"And now here we are all these years later, still together."

"Oh, you're never getting rid of me. The only way out is death."

"Well then, you're going to have to leave first because there's no way I'm leaving you behind."

"And leave you here by yourself to make a mess? Not happening. You need constant supervision so The Lord is going to have to take you first so I can be sure you're in safe hands."

"I guess we'll have to go together."

"I guess we will."

Granddad Derrick snuggled his head into Nanna Kiana's shoulder. They stood like that, eyes closed, wrapped in each other's love. That was what Allison wanted someday. Someone she could grow old and look back on life pleasantly with after she had explored her share of the world. Not someone who was forced upon her to alleviate some-one else's burdens. While Allison watched her grandparents hold each other, she wished most of all, to one day have the happiness they felt in her own life.

Chapter Thirty-Eight: Matthias

While Allison and her parents were preparing the house for the party, Matthias had been tasked with picking up the cake from Brewer's. He brought Derik with him to get him used to being in public again. Although Derik had gone out with Mayor Perry the weekend before, he was still adjusting to everyday life. And Matthias hoped to make that adjustment as easy as possible for him. As he drove to Brewer's, Matthias leaned back in his seat, letting the music bump from his speaker and vibrate the car just how he liked.

"Matty?" said Derik.

"Yeah?" said Matthias.

"I'm sorry."

"What for?"

"You told me not to take Granddad's gun, but I did anyways. I put everyone in danger."

"Yeah, you did. But it's all over now."

"Not for me it isn't. Even though I know they've all been caught, I still feel like they're just around the corner waiting to grab me."

"Anyone waiting around a corner to grab you will have to go me first."

"Don't joke like that."

"Okay."

Matthias did not know how to tell Derik that he felt similarly to him. Before being shot, guns had never bothered Matthias. But since the gas station incident, he got queasy whenever guns were even mentioned. He knew it was nothing compared to what Derik experienced, but it was similar. They pulled into Brewer's parking lot, and Matthias put the car in park.

"You coming in?" asked Matthias.

"Yeah," said Derik.

They went inside and found Ralph sitting behind the counter.

"Hey!" said Ralph when he saw them. "Look who's out of the house!"

"Hi Ralphie," said Derik.

"How're you doing?"

"I'm fine."

"That's good."

"I'm surprised you're behind the counter, Ralphie," said Matthias.

"Yeah, well Miki's off and Nicki had something with cheer," said Ralph. "So, I'm holding down the fort today."

"Cool."

"What can I help you guys with?"

"Nanna said she reserved a cake for Granddad's birthday."

"Oh yeah. Let me get that for you."

The cake was a chocolate one covered in white frosting. 'Happy Birthday Derrick!' was printed on the top in black letters.

"Here you guys are," said Ralph, handing the cake to Matthias. "Mrs. Kiana's already paid for it, so you're good to go."

"Good, because I wasn't paying for it," said Matthias. "Thanks Ralphie."

"No, thank you," said Ralph. "Especially for protecting Diana that one day I wasn't there. She won't let me here the end of it, but I owe you one."

"Alright," laughed Matthias. "Have a good day."

"You too. And Derik?"

"Yeah?"

"I'm glad to see you're okay."

Matthias and Derik returned home. As they set the cake in the kitchen, Nanna Kiana received a phone call. She answered it, then took the phone to her husband."

"Here Meathead," said Nanna Kiana. "It's for you. It's on speaker."

"Hello?" said Granddad Derrick.

"Happy birthday!" yelled Aunt Nancy, Aunt Paulette, and James.

"Thank you," said Granddad Derrick.

"Hold on," said Aunt Nancy. "There's someone else who wants to wish you a happy birthday. Go ahead."

"Happy birthday, Unc," said Jordan.

"Aw, thanks Jordan," said Granddad Derrick.

"I'm sorry for how I acted at your house."

"Apology accepted. You know I love you, right?"

"I know."

"Alright, I'll come visit you when I get a chance."

"Okay."

While Nanna Kiana and Mrs. Harrison cooked a special birthday dinner for Granddad Derrick, Matthias decided to approach his father. He did not know what he would say or how he would say it, but he knew they needed to talk. Especially because they would be residing under the same roof indefinitely.

"We need to talk," said Matthias.

"Okay," said Mr. Harrison.

"I talked to Mom, and she said you were the who put me out."

"I was."

"Why?"

"What do you mean 'why'?"

"Why did you put me out?"

"Matthias, you're not stupid so don't act like it," said Mr. Harrison. "What am I supposed to do when I come home and find you beating your brother senseless? Or when I take him over there to straighten things out with you and see you pull a knife on him?"

"I was fourteen and angry."

"Like that makes it any better."

"Well, why'd you leave me over there? You never came back for me."

"I did the next week. But you were still angry, so I left you there."

"For seven years?"

"Yeah."

Matthias paused to consider his next words carefully. He thought about how James told him that he could not blame others for his role in things.

"Alright, I get it," said Matthias. "I messed up. But so did you."

"I never said I didn't."

"Bro, you separated me from the family for seven years and you act like you don't care."

"It's not that I don't care. I just don't know what you want me to say."

"I want you to say why you left me over there for seven years. Why didn't you come back for me?"

"Because you're like me," said Mr. Harrison. "You have destructive anger. And I didn't want to deal with it the same way my father dealt with it."

"But you didn't deal with it at all. You threw me away."

"I didn't throw you away. I did what I thought was best for you and your brother by separating you two."

"By giving me to the Campbells?"

"My options were my parents, your mother's parents, my brother, or your mother's sister," said Mr. Harrison. "I know how my father deals with destructive anger. He just gets angry himself and takes it out on the person that's angry. That's why I didn't give you to him. There was no way I was giving you to the Perrys. Your uncle wasn't mature enough to handle you. So, that left your mother's sister. And then, you were still angry. Why would I bring you back when you're still angry and could possibly harm someone else? That's not smart."

Matthias was silent.

"I know now that you guys felt like I wasn't all that great of a father," said Mr. Harrison. "But I did what I thought was best for the family at the time. Now, if you want to be mad at me for that, then okay. But I didn't do it to get rid of you. I did it to keep everyone safe, including you."

Matthias did not know what to say. So, he walked away. It was easy for him to accept his mother's side of events, but it was not easy to accept his father's. He realized he still had a lot of work to do regarding his anger. But even so, he could be glad about the progress he had made. His relationship with his Deidrick was good, his relationship with his mother was improving by the day, and he no longer felt the need to cope with his old coping mechanisms. The road to happiness would be long for Matthias, but he was willing to take the journey.

-

Chapter Thirty-Nine: Deidrick

Deidrick did not know when he would reveal the news about the baby to the family. He was only three when everything with his uncle's pregnancy scandal happened, so he was not sure how the family would react. But with each passing day, he convinced himself more and more that the baby could not be his. It could not be because he was not ready for one.

"Hey," said Uncle Malcolm, coming up to him.

"Hey," said Deidrick.

"So…," began Uncle Malcolm. "When do you plan on telling everyone the big news?"

"Not tonight," said Deidrick. "The only ones that know are you, Matty, and Nisha."

"You told her?"

"Yeah."

"How'd she take it?"

"Not well."

"So, it's over?"

"It never started. Now, it never will."

"Dang Cornbread, I'm sorry."

"It's alright. I'm not stressing over a girl."

"So, do you have a plan in place yet?"

"As soon as it's born, I'm getting a DNA test done."

"That's it?"

"For right now, yeah. I'm not taking care of a baby that's not mine."

"Cornbread, you've got to prepare like it is yours. You don't want the baby to come, and you're not prepared for it."

"Look Unc, I'll figure all that out once I know *if* the baby is mine."

"Alright," said Uncle Malcolm. "I'm trying to tell you."

"I know what I'm doing."

"Okay."

Uncle Malcolm left him alone. As Deidrick sat around, waiting for dinner, he noticed his father sitting alone. He realized he had never thanked his father for saving his life, and figured it was about time he do so.

"I respect what you did," said Deidrick, approaching Mr. Harrison.

"What did I do?" asked Mr. Harrison.

"You told Derik what he wanted to hear to save our lives," answered Deidrick. "You did what you had to do, and I respect it. I've always respected that about you. You've always made sure we were good."

"That's my job."

"You know, this is the second time you saved my life. If I didn't know any better, I'd say I was your favorite."

"I don't have a favorite."

"I know," said Deidrick. "I could care less whether you like me or not. You've done right by me, and I respect you for it."

"You respect me?"

"Yeah, I do."

"Then you don't mind if I tell you what I think of you?"

"Go ahead."

"Alright," said Mr. Harrison. "Out of all my children, Deidrick, I think you're the weakest."

"What?"

"You make tough situations for yourself and then tap out when it's time to face the consequences."

"That's what you think of me?"

"Yeah," affirmed Mr. Harrison. "I'll give you an example. You just said you respected me, but then in the same breath you called me a liar."

"I never called you a liar."

"You did, when you said I told Derik what he wanted to hear."

"That's different," said Deidrick. "Our lives were at stake."

"You're right," said Mr. Harrison. "And I told your brother the truth."

"Then you meant all that stuff you said?"

"I wouldn't have said it if I didn't," said Mr. Harrison. "But you're different from me in that way. You don't always mean what you say."

"I–!"

"Look," said Mr. Harrison, cutting Deidrick off. "You said you respect me, right? If so, then listen to what I'm about to tell you because it's for your own good. Out of all my kids Deidrick, I respect you the least because you don't have any integrity. You'll do whatever it takes to get what you want, and you don't care who you step on to get it. I don't respect men like that. And then on top of that, you don't think before you act. You slept with a girl that tried to seduce me because she wanted something to use to blackmail me into giving her money. Not only did I see through it right away, but I respected your mother enough not to step out on her. But you didn't think about that before you got with her. And that was before you found out that girl helped kidnap your brother to hold him ransom!"

"I know I've made some mistakes."

"And I know she's pregnant."

"I told Uncle Falcon not to tell anyone," grumbled Deidrick.

"Your uncle didn't tell me anything," said Mr. Harrison. "Your little playmate tried to have her cake and eat it too. Right before she got caught, she hit me up for money and said if I didn't pay her, she'd expose you as the father of her baby."

"It's not mine."

"You slept with her unprotected, right?"

"Yeah, but–!"

"Then it's yours until proven otherwise," said Mr. Harrison. "See, I was trying to let you make it, but if you think I'm going to have a son out here with no sense of responsibility, reliability or loyalty embarrassing me than you better think again."

"What do you mean?"

"Look at your brothers, your sister, and your cousin," said Mr. Harrison. "They have goals and things they want to accomplish with their lives. They're doing something with themselves. And they take initiative too. All of them have come to me and truthfully said what they thought of me, and how I fell short in their lives. But you? All you do is your job at the shop and chase girls. That's it. And then you come to me and say you respect me because you thought I lied to your brother? You respect liars and cheaters? I guess so because that's what you do. You have no integrity and its embarrassing."

Deidrick could not respond, because he was too shocked by his father's harsh words.

"But you know what," said Mr. Harrison. "I got just what you need. If you plan to continue operating out of my shop, you're going to have to start paying the booth fees like everyone else."

"You're going to charge me to use my booth?!" cried Deidrick. "I've been using that booth for years!"

"And I've been eating the cost of it, trying to help you out. But it's time for you to man up."

"Bro, come on! You're doing too much!"

"I haven't done enough yet. In fact, I'm just getting started. If you want to continue living in my house when it's rebuilt, you'll need to start paying rent. If you don't like that, then I suggest you start looking for a place for you and your child to stay."

"Seriously?! I'm your son!"

"And?"

"What about Queenie? Are you going to charge her rent too? She's an adult too."

"No, because Allison is a high schooler living with her parents."

"This is so jacked up."

"No, this is life," said Mr. Harrison. "It's time you stop being my son, and start being your own man."

"I am my own man!"

"Yeah, an embarrassing one. And when that child comes, and it turns out to be yours, it will be your responsibility alone. You're not going to try and pawn it off on everyone else."

"Bro!"

"I'll let you decide when you want to tell everyone else the big news," said Mr. Harrison, standing up to walk away. "Enjoy the party."

Deidrick could not believe it. His whole life was turned upside down, all because of a baby that might not be his. He was not ready for such a big change in his life. But he knew sooner or later he would have to embrace it. Five months of freedom remained until that big change would come out of the snake that had ruined his life. And he planned to live those five months to the fullest.

-

Chapter Forty: Derek

Granddad Derrick's birthday dinner was a successful one. Nanna Kiana had made sure that he had all his favorites on the table. The man of the hour sat at the head of the table, beaming to have his family around him, celebrating him.

"I'm so thankful to have you all here with me today," said Granddad Derrick. "And I'm happy to have made it to see another year. These past months have been hard on us, but I'm so glad The Lord saw fit to bring us all together again. I couldn't have asked for a more perfect and joyful day than I've had today. To see you all sitting here with me... it warms my heart. Thank you."

Dinner went well. And afterward, everyone had fun dancing and enjoying themselves. Derek hopped his way on his crutches to use the bathroom. After handling his business, he stood at the mirror and stared at himself.

"How long?" asked his reflection.

"How long until what?" answered Derek.

"How long until you admit the truth?"

"What truth?"

"That you're angry. At Monique, at Dee-Three. Angry at all the people whose actions led to you being unable to dance anymore."

"No, I'm not angry."

"You sure?"

"I'm sure."

"I don't believe you."

"Well, you should because I'm telling the truth."

Derek left the bathroom. As he passed under the family picture in the hallway, he heard his voice again.

"You know you can't escape me, Derek," teased the Derek in the family photo. "Just like you can't escape Granddad Derrick or Cousin Derik. There will always be three of you around. To everyone else, you'll always be Granddad's mini-me or interchangeable with Dee-Three. You'll never be just Derek Harrison."

"So?"

"So?" laughed the other Derek. "That's why you got hit. Because you couldn't just be you. You were mistaken for him."

"That's not his fault."

"Isn't it?"

"Go away," muttered Derek under his breath. He hopped away and came upon the hallway mirror.

"Don't you get it, Derek?" questioned the other Derek. "You can lie to everyone else but not me. I know how you think and feel because I'm you. I'll always know the truth."

"If that's the case then you should know I don't blame Derik for what happened. And you should know I don't care anything about that woman either."

"But you do," taunted Derek. "You care that Monique didn't stay for you. And you're mad that Derik running away led to you getting hit by a car. You're angry."

"Leave me alone!" grunted Derek.

"Fine!" said the other Derek. "Live in denial! Go on believing that you don't blame Derik for you possibly never being able to dance again! Continue telling yourself that you're not affected by Monique rejecting you! Make yourself comfortable in your lies! But when you're finally ready to admit the truth, you'll know where to find me."

Derek stormed out onto the porch. He did not know why he had such terrible thoughts. There was no way that he blamed Derik for what had happened. It was wrong to. And he knew he did not care anything about that woman. But even with the knowledge, he felt that unfamiliar feeling inside him growing stronger, and it was becoming harder to shove it down.

"D-Money?" said someone. Derek turned around and saw Derik sitting on the porch. "Are you alright?"

Derek wanted to say 'no'. He wanted to tell Derik about the terrible thoughts he had, and about the unfamiliar feeling that was slowly overtaking him. And he wanted to tell Derik that he felt that feeling strongest when he looked at him. But he did not. One look in Derik's eyes told him that Derik felt what he felt. That Derik was also pushing it down and battling his own terrible thoughts. So, with even more effort, he swallowed it down and sat beside his cousin.

"I'm fine," said Derek. "I just needed air."

"Me too," said Derik.

"I'm glad your back."

"You told me that."

"I won't stop telling you either. Unless you want me to, of course."

"I don't mind. It makes me glad to know I have people who care."

"You've always had people who care."

"I know now."

Derek looked at the setting sun and how it had painted the sky a myriad of oranges, reds, yellows, and purples.

"Remember last time we sat out here and I thought you had a secret girlfriend, and you said the family was thin?" asked Derek.

"Yeah," said Derik. "And then you chopped me."

"And you chopped me back."

"And we kept chopping each other until Queenie stopped us."

"It seems so long ago but it hasn't even been a year."

"Yeah."

"Did you enjoy your day with Mayor Perry last week?"

"It was alright," said Derik. "All he talks about is himself and cars though."

"Why do you think he asked you to do that?"

"To make himself look like a caring grandfather. I knew the reason then when he asked."

"Well, why'd you do it?"

"Because it's not fair for people to think he was involved when he wasn't."

"Would you do it again?"

"Heck no. I did him this one favor to clear his name and that's it."

"Wow."

"There you guys are," said Granddad Derrick, coming outside. "What are you both doing out here?"

"We needed air," said Derik.

"Ah," said Granddad Derrick, sitting in between them. "I guess we all have something in common other than our names then."

"Are you having a good birthday?" asked Derek.

"Yeah," Granddad Derrick. "Especially because my D n' T are here."

"Your what?"

"My Drumaine and my Tremaine," said Granddad Derrick. "I'm happy that even though life got hard for you both, I'm glad that you both made it through."

"Yeah, but we're not the same as we were before," said Derik.

"I know," said Granddad Derrick. "But even still, I'm thankful. Because it could've been way more devastating, but The Lord saw fit to spare us the grief."

Granddad Derrick put his arms around his grandsons and smiled.

"You know most grandfathers only get maybe one grandson named after them," said Granddad Derrick. "But I got two. That means I'm doubly blessed."

"And we're blessed to have you Granddad," said Derik.

"Yeah," said Derek. "Even if we don't always show it."

"Yes, we're all blessed indeed," said Granddad Derrick.

The three of them sat there, looking out at the sunset. It was beautiful to Derek but also foreboding. It was not just setting to end the day but to end life as he knew it. His whole life and everything he wanted for it had been altered. And as he stared at that sunset, he felt that unfamiliar feeling start to rise again. Derek thought back on what it had been labeled as in his thoughts. Anger. What Derek felt was possibly anger. He was possibly angry that he had lost so much, and he did not know who to blame for it. But Derek refused to be angry, and he refused to blame Derik or Monique. That anger was an unfamiliar feeling to him, and it scared him to feel that way. So, with all his might, he pushed it back down, hoping that one day he would be strong enough to stop it from coming out before it consumed him.

Read more from the *Creeke* series
Creeke
Creeke: Summer Vacation

Other books by Ronald Savage Jr.
The Honor Society
Ten Little Tales